Book Two of the Cairnmor Trilogy

In the dense jungle of Malaya in 1942, Doctor Rachel Curtis stumbles across a mysterious, unidentifiable stranger, badly injured and close to death.

Four years earlier in 1938 in London, Katherine Stewart and her husband Alex come into conflict with their differing needs while Alex's father, Alastair, knows he must keep his deeper feelings hidden from the woman he loves; a woman to whom he must never reveal the full extent of that love.

Covering a broad canvas and meticulously researched, Changing Times, Changing Tides follows the interwoven journey of well-loved characters from The Call of Cairnmor, as well as introducing new personalities, in a unique combination of novel and history that tells a story of love, loss, friendship and heroism; absorbing the reader in the characters' lives as they are shaped and changed by the ebb and flow of events before, during and after the Second World War.

Sally Aviss

Changing Times, Changing Tides

Changing Times, Changing Tides
by Sally Aviss

Published by Ōzaru Books, an imprint of BJ Translations Ltd
Street Acre, Shuart Lane, St Nicholas-at-Wade,
BIRCHINGTON, CT7 0NG, U.K.
www.ozaru.net

First edition published 14 February 2015
Printed by Lightning Source
ISBN: 978-0-9931587-0-4

For my husband Peter
with my love.

Contents

PROLOGUE

Malaya
January, 1942

Doctor Rachel Curtis crept through the dense jungle on her hands and knees, keeping low; protected from view beneath a canopy of palms and ferns. She crawled forward as far as she dared.

In the oppressive tropical heat and high humidity, sweat poured down her face and into her eyes but she dare not move to wipe it away. Deadly scorpions and spiders scuttled over her hands and legs but she dare not shake them off.

Rachel held her breath and lay still.

For days, she and her colleagues had been treating the wounded and exhausted Allied soldiers who had been arriving continuously by rail and road. For days, everyone at the 1st/5th Division (Australia) Casualty Clearing Station at Kuala Tengeh had gone without sleep and proper food. In desperate need of a few moments' respite, Rachel had filled her water container and wandered away from the clearing into the jungle, seeking shelter beside a small pool at the base of a waterfall.

It was this action that saved her life.

Now, from her hiding place, Rachel witnessed an atrocity that would give her recurring nightmares for the rest of her days. Without warning, without time to evacuate the remaining patients and medical personnel, an advance party of enemy commandos arrived. The marauding, battle-high soldiers wreaked havoc on the hospital site and without hesitating, slaughtered patients, orderlies, doctors. They rounded up the nurses, forcing them to line up against the empty ambulances, where they were ruthlessly machine-gunned. The petrol tanks of the vehicles exploded in a sheet of flame and debris.

There were no survivors.

Rachel cowered in the enveloping foliage; sickened by what she had just seen, trembling uncontrollably, her hand covering her mouth in a monumental effort to stop herself crying out in revulsion and fear and anger. Desperately, she tried keep her body still; desperately, she tried not to let any involuntary movements alert the enemy to her presence by making her protective shelter shake in a wind that did not exist elsewhere.

However, the soldiers did not linger. They had their orders to advance and disappeared as quickly as they had come, torching the evidence of the massacre as they left, leaving behind a scene of complete and utter devastation.

Rachel lay still for hours, waiting until it was nearly dark; waiting until she was certain they had gone. Eventually, carefully, she extricated herself from her hiding-place and lifted her head above the level of the ferns.

Nothing moved, no one was there. No sentry, nobody left behind to check for survivors or witnesses.

She was alone.

She stumbled towards the ravaged hospital, her legs stiff and unresponsive after her enforced immobility. Shocked and dazed by what she had seen, she stood in the middle of the still smouldering ashes.

An intense anger replaced numbness; anger on behalf of her murdered colleagues; anger on behalf of the brave lads who had already suffered in battle and who had been forced to endure further horrific agony. But above all, anger at the inhumanity of those who had committed this atrocity with their unjustifiable brutality and cruelty towards the helpless and the weak.

Rachel sank to her knees and wept as she had never wept before or would ever weep again.

Later, much later, she filled her army-issue drinks canister from the tap on the stand-pipe – which miraculously had survived the conflagration, albeit burned and scorched, but still producing clear, refreshing liquid – drinking as much as she could manage and then re-filling the bottle.

She had to get away in case the soldiers returned. There was nothing she could do here; nothing she could have done. She could not help anyone; they were beyond help. It was now a matter of her own survival. Somehow, she had to find her way to safety.

But which way? The railway was out of the question, even though the station was close by. The airfield would already have been overrun. To the east lay high, virtually impregnable jungle-covered mountain ranges; to the west, the coast. Here were the Straits of Malacca and the prospect of a boat, but it was too far to travel on foot and the risk of capture too great. In the north, the invading Japanese army would have set up command posts and supply depots. That left the south and the two main roads.

How far had the enemy advanced by now? She had no idea. What should she do? She could not possibly hope to outrun them. She had to come to a rapid decision.

Cautiously, Rachel set off in what she hoped was a westerly direction, with the intention of intersecting one of the roads that would take her southwards to Singapore. However, there was also extreme danger here. She had learned enough about military tactics during her time with the Australian Imperial Force to realize that sentries and road blocks would be posted everywhere. She had no choice but to attempt a hazardous trek through the rubber plantations and jungle.

She reached the road from Rumah Sayong at about midnight. From her hiding place beside the road, Rachel could see a steady column of armoured personnel carriers and infantry travelling in unbroken formation. Look-outs checked constantly as they walked alongside the vehicles, their rifles poised, ready to repel any Allied attack.

Rachel crouched low, moving backwards, predator-like, away from their vigilant gaze. She stumbled over the exposed root of a tree and rolled precipitously down a steep incline, landing heavily on her shoulder. In agony, she lay still, alert; listening for signs of pursuit, of investigation. But none was forthcoming, the soldiers continued on their way.

She breathed out and tentatively moved her body. Waves of pain shot through her dislocated shoulder and down her arm, which hung useless by her side and she nearly cried out in agony and frustration. There was no chance that she could reverse the damage by herself and there was no one to help her.

Defeated, she sat back and her head touched something that moved. Recoiling in terror and stricken with fear, she jerked herself away, exerting enormous self-control to stop herself from screaming.

Her knee twisted as her ankle buckled under her and she fell heavily against a tree, banging her shoulder against its implacable solidity. There was a popping sound and her shoulder returned to its socket, but now her ankle and knee were burning and throbbing with pain.

Tearing strips of cloth from her shirt, she dipped them into a pool of clear rainwater that had collected in centre of an unfolding fern and created make-shift bandages, strapping both injuries as tightly as she could using only one hand.

Through the darkness, she could just discern the outline of a body propped up against the tree. Carefully, cautiously, mindful of the agonizing pain in her left leg, she crawled towards the motionless human being.

He was filthy and virtually naked; a strip of native cloth covering his private parts. His body and face were caked in mud and his hair matted. There was a mass of congealed blood on the side and back of his head. His face was puffy and heavily bruised, likewise his chest and arms. She thought at first he was dead.

She felt his pulse. It was there – but only just.

Carefully, she lifted his head and put her water canister to his parched lips. After feeling the first refreshing drops, he seemed to revive and soon drank greedily. Rachel had to restrain him and reclaim the container before all the precious liquid disappeared.

He stared at her briefly and then fell back against the tree. She regarded him closely; squinting through the darkness. He was not Japanese, that much was certain. Nor was he Chinese or Malay. Gently, she felt round his neck for any dog tags or other means of identification. There were none. Unexpectedly, he grabbed her wrist and held it tightly in a protective movement, keeping it away from his body. He didn't speak, but looked at her again. Even in the darkness, she could see his eyes were filled with fear and confusion. Quietly, she tried to reassure him and with her other hand released her wrist from his grasp. His arm went limp and he sank back against the tree.

Suddenly, Rachel heard the unmistakable sound of movement coming towards her through the jungle foliage. Gripped by fear, her chest tightening, she knew that escape was impossible. She couldn't move the man, he was too heavy. Besides which, her injured shoulder would not withstand his weight and her knee and ankle precluded her from being able to get very far unaided.

There was no question of her leaving him. She had to stay and offer what protection she could, whatever happened. Her decision was not driven by bravery or courage or even her own lack of mobility, but by a deeply-held conviction that the injured and vulnerable came first.

Rachel made him as comfortable as she could and then sat back, close to him, her heart pounding, her mouth dry, every sense heightened. There was nowhere to run, nowhere to hide; nothing she could do to defend herself.

Stoically, she awaited their fate.

CHAPTER 1

London
January, 1938

"It's a fantastic opportunity!" After his initial disclosure, Alex Stewart was unsure how to proceed, what to say next.

"I know it is," said Katherine. "But..." She sat down on the settee, trying to conceal her disappointment.

Alastair regarded her sympathetically, torn between delight for his son and an instinctive understanding of the emotion his daughter-in-law was experiencing.

"To be offered a tenancy at Lord Cameron's Chambers is such an honour for any barrister!" continued Alex persuasively.

Katherine bit her lip, resisting the temptation to remark that since when had honour and prestige become more important than all the plans they had put together towards their future life on Cairnmor; a future that she had hardly dared hope for?

All through their courtship she had patiently borne the constant meeting and parting with which they had had to contend, knowing that Alex lived and worked in London and she on Cairnmor, a remote island situated off the west coast of Scotland.

It was inevitable from the beginning that one of them would have to make a sacrifice so they could be together. In the end, she had been the one to do so, not only resigning her teaching post because of her marriage, but also leaving behind her friends on the beautiful island she loved so much and which had been her home for most of her life.

It would seem that for the second time, Katherine would be the one to compromise.

"We've been married for seven months, our baby is due in July..." She sighed. "So, I suppose if you added our going to live on Cairnmor, everything would have been too perfect, too good to be true."

Alex was effusive in his reply, sensing that she was about to agree to his accepting the post, just as he had known she would.

"It can be perfect still, my darling. You're happy here, you've come to love London and I know you love the house at Maybury."

All of these things were true; she couldn't deny them, nor did she try. Instead, she observed, "Michael and Mary will be disappointed."

Alex was quick to respond. "Lord Cameron has offered Michael a tenancy as well. He was so impressed with our work at the House of Lords Appeal that he would like both of us."

This was news to Alastair, who pretended to be huffy. "So, I suppose I had nothing to do with the Appeal at all!" He smiled at his son, not really offended. He had enough work to do at present overseeing Katherine's father's inheritance.

"Oh, Dad. No, he did say he was hopeful that you would continue to work with me in exactly the same way that you always have. He would be delighted if your firm of solicitors also worked closely with the barristers at his Chambers."

"I'm flattered!" Alastair looked at Katherine and smiled. "However, your grandfather has left me quite a challenge. It is going to take a considerable time to unravel the complexities of it all."

"I'm so glad Rupert asked you to supervise the whole thing. He was very concerned about the lack of progress negotiating the details of the will. It needed someone of your calibre to coordinate and galvanize the solicitors in London and Glasgow. Especially now that he and Mhairi have gone back to Canada to sort out their affairs."

"You see," Alastair said to his son, "at least someone appreciates my true worth!"

Alex laughed and turned towards Katherine. "So, what shall I do, my love?"

"You have to accept, of course. There's no choice. I couldn't live with my conscience if I asked you to give up an offer like this. Lord Cameron has always recognized your abilities and you are a fantastic advocate. It would be foolish not to accept."

Alex was delighted. "Thank you, my darling." He kissed her hand in a flamboyant gesture. "You won't regret it, I promise."

"Well," said Alastair, "in that case, you'd better thank his Lordship on my behalf and say I shall be delighted to accept his kind offer as soon as I am able."

"But once the paperwork for Rupert's inheritance was completed, you were going to sell your solicitor's practice," said Katherine, knowing that Alastair had planned, and was also looking forward, to making his home on Cairnmor.

"Things change." He smiled at her. "It would seem that our lives are inescapably entwined."

"Whither thou goest…"

"Exactly."

"Well, when you two have finished quoting the Book of Ruth, I'll go and reply formally to his Lordship's letter. I wonder what Michael will decide to do?"

However, before either Katherine or Alastair could respond, he had disappeared out of the sitting room.

Katherine's shoulders sagged and she leaned back into the deep comfort of the sofa. She needed time to come to terms with this latest, unexpected change in their lives. This did not go unnoticed by Alastair who hesitated before speaking, trying to find the right words of consolation. Instead, it was Katherine who spoke first. "Michael won't accept, you know."

"No, I don't think he will."

"If he doesn't, then it will be an enormous wrench for both him and Alex not to be around each other. They've been the closest of friends and colleagues for so many years – at Oxford, of course, then working together and supporting each other at Royal Court Chambers."

"Yes." Gently he upheld her, sensing her effort to contain her own disappointment.

"Mary never has managed to adjust to living in the city."

6

"No."

"And Michael has always wanted to work the land. It's an ideal arrangement for both of them to live on Cairnmor. No, I don't think he will accept." Katherine fell silent.

"And you will miss Mary."

"Oh, yes."

"You've been friends for a very long time."

"All our lives."

"And it will be difficult not to realize the dream."

"Oh, Alastair, so hard." Her eyes filled with tears.

"But, there is the baby to look forward to. I shall be the proverbial proud grandfather and show the little one off to all and sundry when I take him or her out in the pram, strolling leisurely in Kensington Gardens, while you put your feet up and take a well-deserved breather from motherhood!"

Katherine laughed, despite herself, which was exactly what Alastair had intended. Then he added, "As ever, be kind to yourself. Make the adjustment gradually."

She smiled. "But I'll need to get over the shock first."

"It always takes a while to change direction."

"Yes."

"And you've had a great deal of direction changing to do in the past year or so."

"You can say that again!"

"You've had a great deal…"

"Oh, do be quiet." They both laughed. Then she said, "Thank you, Alastair."

He nodded, accepting, knowing that their mutual closeness and friendship was one of the great joys of both their lives. "You're welcome. Now, do you think this clever, disruptive husband of yours has had time to finish his letter? If he has, I suggest that after lunch, the three of us go out for a walk. Then, this evening, how about a trip to the cinema? A bit of escapism wouldn't go amiss, I think. You choose…" He handed her the newspaper.

Katherine scanned the listings page, glad of the distraction. "Well, there's *The Prisoner of Zenda*, *Oh, Mr Porter* or *Lost Horizon*."

"*Lost Horizon*, definitely," said Alex, coming back into the sitting room just as Katherine spoke.

"I suggest *Oh, Mr Porter*," responded Alastair quickly. He felt that the loss of Shangri-La and the struggle to regain it would be just a little too close for comfort for Katherine.

"Actually, I'd prefer to see *The Prisoner of Zenda*. It's a very good story and I quite like Ronald Colman. Although he's in *Lost Horizon* as well," she added, for the moment undecided.

"*The Prisoner of Zenda* it shall be!" said Alex, checking that his father was agreeable to the suggestion by raising both eyebrows in his direction. Then he added, pretending to be jealous, "What do you mean, you've always quite liked Ronald Colman?!"

Katherine smiled. "Yes, he's just one of my many heroes…!"

"Huh!"

And the dulcet tones of the dinner gong coming from the hall precluded any further repartee.

CHAPTER 2

London
March, 1938

By the end of March, Alex had been at Lord Cameron's Chambers for nearly three months and Katherine was feeling restless and lonely. He had thrown himself wholeheartedly into his new job, working very long hours, and consequently, she had seen very little of him.

He seemed to have one heavy case-load after another, often arriving home late in the evening, tired and irritable – unwilling to discuss the day's events if it had not gone well in court or, having won his case, returning home on a high, seemingly possessed by an endless supply of energy.

All this she found difficult. Too much activity was hard to cope with while being pregnant and when Alex worked into the early hours researching his next brief, as he often did, she was fast asleep by the time he came upstairs. There seemed to be very little opportunity to talk properly or simply *be together*.

Michael had decided not to take up Lord Cameron's offer, just as she and Alastair had surmised, and had returned to Cairnmor with his wife Mary. Katherine missed her friends very much and occupied her time as best she could. But, excellent and enjoyable as the abundant cultural opportunities in London were – and she loved the variety they afforded – she would have preferred to be with Alex.

She wondered whether she was asking too much of her married life, of her husband, who meant the world to her and who hitherto had always appeared to be so attentive and loving.

Perhaps she just needed extra patience, she told herself. His job was new; the challenges and responsibilities ones that Alex obviously felt the urge to meet with greater effort and application than ever before. She knew he was putting enormous pressure on himself, far more than was necessary as his work had always been excellent. He did not need to push himself so hard and yet he did. All the time.

Eventually, Katherine bemoaned all these things in a letter to her mother, pouring out her heart to the only person that she was able. Yes, she could have talked to Alastair, they were close enough, but he was very busy himself and she was reluctant to trouble him.

Mhairi replied quickly, full of sympathy for her daughter.

How well I understand, she wrote. *When your father first became Director of the Music Academy, I hardly ever saw him. He was working hard, absorbed and fulfilled by the nature of the job and trying to earn a decent living for us both.*

Like Alex, he can be over-conscientious at times and that isn't easy when you're at home all day on your own looking forward to seeing your husband in the evening. With us, Rupert was so preoccupied that I felt left out, whereas

9

before, I had been the centre of his attention. I'm happy to say that this stage of our married life didn't last very long.

When I could bear it no longer, I decided to do two things. Firstly, to talk to him. I made him sit down and listen to me. I was reasonable and calm – nagging would have been counter-productive, although I certainly felt like it! I said that we had to make time for each other, that I missed him dreadfully.

Rupert, bless him, had been so absorbed that he hadn't noticed my frustration. He was very contrite, loving and apologetic and to his credit, no matter how busy he was, he put aside time each week so that we could do things together or just be together. It worked a treat, I have to say.

The second thing I decided to do, was to take up a useful interest of my own. I decided that if I studied shorthand and typing, then I might be able to work at the Academy with Rupert. This would mean we could really be together.

So that is precisely what I did. I found a course that took place in the afternoons, enrolled on it and gained my qualifications with very fast speeds in both shorthand and typing.

Reflectively, Katherine put down the letter. Yes, her mother had impressed all of them with her abilities while they were gathering evidence on Cairnmor for the Appeal at the House of Lords. They couldn't have achieved so much so quickly without her secretarial skills.

She picked up the letter again.

After a few months, I began to work at the Academy, eventually moving up to run the Administration Department. It meant that I understood exactly what Rupert was doing each day. We always had so much to discuss and talk about that it made our lives very entwined.

I'm not sure that this arrangement would suit every married couple, but it certainly works well for us. I know you can't work with Alex, but do try and talk to him, dearest. I'm sure that he will listen to you and then you can sort something out together.

When your father saw in your letter that you were spending about two hours a day practising the piano, he was delighted and, ever the professional musician, said you should consider giving a recital. I gently pointed out to him that being pregnant was not the right time to embark on that particular venture!

We're so looking forward to seeing you all in the summer and hope to be there before the baby's born. It took such a long time for us to know you, dear Katherine, that it makes a grandchild seem doubly special.

We still haven't found anyone suitable to take over the directorship of the Academy yet. I suspect that Rupert is dragging his heels a little, which is understandable, considering all that he has achieved, and is still achieving, here in Halifax.

I wish you luck in talking to Alex. As a desperate measure, you could always take up shorthand and typing. You never know, it might come in useful one day! You could teach yourself. Pitman's is the best. If you need help, just ask.

Look after yourself, sweetheart, and try not to fret.
All love and thoughts,
Mhairi xxx

Katherine sat on the window-seat with the letter in her lap. Idly, she looked out of the window and then at the clock. It would be at least another two hours before either Alex or Alastair were supposed to be home. She thought about the shorthand and typing. It might be fun. It was certainly something different and it was something she'd always wanted to try.

Acting on impulse, Katherine put on her coat and hat and walked to the shops in South Kensington. She found a stationer-cum-bookseller best suited to her needs and asked for a shorthand instruction manual. The shopkeeper produced the required tome – all three hundred and one pages of it – and wrapped it for her neatly in brown paper, which he tied with a piece of string.

"You'd best have an ink pen, ink and a special nib, as this can help with the strokes, so my wife says, and she should know. Some have to be heavy and some light. We have a really good quality one here, with lovely nibs. I've put in three of those and a bottle of ink as well. Shall I add these to the bill?"

Katherine nodded; it would seem churlish to refuse.

The shopkeeper settled into his stride. "It's a good idea to use a pen when you're learning but a nice soft lead pencil when you actually come to take dictation. We have some over here. Would four suit you?"

"Er, yes, thank you," she replied uncertainly.

"Now, you'll need something to write on. I suggest these – nice thick notepads with the lines spaced out at three-eighths of an inch, the recommended distance. You'll get through at least three."

"How about a rubber?" Katherine's suggestion was tentative; she was reluctant to disturb his flow.

"Oh no, my wife says it's always best to circle any mistakes. It's quicker for one thing and then you know not to include those words later."

"Ah, I see."

Thus suitably kitted out, she paid for her purchases. Thanking the shop-keeper for his help, she walked home in a slightly dazed fashion, somewhat taken aback by having been drawn into making such a flurry of purchases. She had only thought as far as an instruction manual.

Katherine smiled to herself. She would have an amusing little tale to recount that evening at supper – *if* she and Alex or Alastair managed to eat the meal together. That too had become something of a rarity these days.

When she arrived home, she slung her coat over the back of the settee in the downstairs sitting room and asked Mrs Thringle, the housekeeper, for a pot of tea and some cake. Katherine settled down and opened the book.

Fun?! It looked impossible. She was used to deciphering symbols at speed when reading music, but this seemed doubly hard to work out. She wondered how she would be able to learn it in the first place, let alone recall it and write it down quickly. Perhaps it would all make sense once she became familiar with its visual language.

Katherine began to read:

Sir Isaac Pitman (1813-1897) developed a method of shorthand for the English language by using a phonetic system where the symbols record sounds rather than spellings.

Well, that seems clear enough, she thought, before reading on.

Vowels are shown by dots or dashes (which can be light or heavy) or other marks written next to a main (consonant) stroke. If the vowel sound occurs before a consonant, it is written on the left of this main stroke, if it occurs afterwards, it is written on the right.

She paused to consider this before continuing.

Horizontal strokes show a vowel mark above the main (consonant) stroke if the vowel sound occurs before or below the main stroke if...

Katherine found her concentration wandering. This was impossible. She was absorbing nothing from the words she was reading. Even the symbols made things no clearer.

She put the book aside as the ever-cheerful housekeeper brought in her tea. They heard the sound of a key in the lock of the front door and Alastair came into the sitting room, depositing his briefcase beside the desk. Mrs Thringle disappeared to fetch another cup and saucer and Alastair came over to Katherine, curious as to what she was doing. Silently, with a wry expression, she handed him the text book.

He scanned the first few sentences and laughed. "Ah, yes. Rather you than me. It's a bit like Gaelic when the uninitiated first start to learn it! Seems impossible, but all right once you get the hang of it."

"I'd rather learn to write Gaelic all over again. It was far easier!"

"Whose idea was it to start learning shorthand?"

"Mhairi's. Well, sort of. If I do manage to get anywhere with this, can I borrow your typewriter because I thought I might learn to type as well?"

"Of course, you'd be most welcome. But why? Are you thinking of becoming a secretary?!" he asked mischievously.

Katherine replied in kind, feigning an expression of long-suffering. "Yes, I thought I'd join the ranks of the underpaid, overworked women in employment and earn myself a crust."

"Well, you do need the money desperately."

"Absolutely. All I have are poor rags and a hovel in which to live. It's so sad." They both laughed. "No, it's just a bit of fun really. I felt I needed something else to do during the day while Alex is earning the money to keep me in the manner to which I've become accustomed."

Alastair chuckled but beneath the humour, he was concerned for Katherine. "Is everything all right?"

"I'm just a bit bored that's all, waiting for the baby to be born." She shrugged her shoulders in a gesture of resignation.

He regarded her carefully. "Yes, and if pigs could fly...!"

"Am I that transparent?!"

"To me you are."

Katherine sighed. "I was going to talk to Alex this evening. I wrote to Mhairi a couple of weeks ago and poured out my woes." She paused, trying not to sound uncharitable. "You see, I haven't seen much of him recently. And when he does come home he's either too tired or too energetic. He's *so* wrapped up in his work. I'm trying to understand – I mean it's all new and he needs to make a good impression, but I do miss his company. I feel a bit aimless and useless. I'm doing lots of piano practice…"

"So that's productive at least," said Alastair, trying to be positive.

"Oh, it is. And I'm enjoying it." She sighed, again. "However, I also know the layout of every museum and art gallery from memory. I've read just about every book in the house and then some but…"

Katherine looked up at Alastair. He came to sit beside her and she tucked her hand companionably through the crook of his arm.

"But there's a limit to how long one can do these things on one's own, isn't there?"

Katherine was grateful for his understanding. "Yes, there is. That's exactly it. It's much nicer to share it with someone."

"Why didn't you say something to me?"

"Because you've been very busy yourself, with your solicitor's work and the R.N.V.R. exercise you've just been on, as well as that staff course at the Imperial Defence College. You've looked so tired just recently that I didn't like to trouble you."

"I'm afraid I have been rather occupied of late."

They were silent for a moment, contemplative; both of them highly aware of the reasons for Alastair's compulsory, increased involvement as a regular member of the Royal Naval Volunteer Reserve.

"Will there be a war, do you think?" asked Katherine, bravely airing the topic she had been assiduously avoiding.

"The Navy think so."

"And the Government? I mean one can only glean so much from the newspapers."

Alastair considered before replying. "They are trying to avoid conflict with a policy of appeasement. But they are also buying the country time in order to allow us to build up our own armaments, which are sorely under strength at present. Our defensive and offensive capabilities are woefully inadequate. The Nazis are way ahead of us."

"Oh, Alastair, no one wants war. The spectre of it is just too awful to contemplate. I hope it never comes to that."

"So do I. I've been through it once and I never thought to see such a possibility again. But we have to be prepared." Then Alastair lightened the mood by saying, "Now, before we become too downhearted and serious, what did Mhairi say?"

"Oh, she was very sweet." Katherine fetched her mother's letter from the bureau and gave it to him.

"Are you sure she won't mind?"

"Of course not."

When he had finished reading, he said, "So, you decided to have a go at shorthand?"

"Yes, hence all this stuff. You have a look at it. I can't make head nor tail of the actual symbols at the moment."

Alastair read the first page properly this time and laughed. "Neither can I. However, Gaelic in shorthand would be worse!"

"Can you imagine it?" Katherine smiled. "Although phonetic Gaelic is far easier to understand than the correct spelling."

"Perhaps Sir Isaac was a secret Gaelic speaker."

"Aye, and he invented his own brand of shorthand to get his revenge on the English-speaking world for all the wrongs committed by the dreaded Sassenachs against the Scots!"

"I tell you what," said Alastair, "if you help me with Gaelic again, which I've probably forgotten completely as we haven't done much recently, I'll help you with the shorthand. We can make a complete dog's breakfast of it together! If Alex is busy, then I'm free this weekend."

"All right, you're on." They shook hands with mock solemnity. "Although you were making good progress with Gaelic while we were together on Cairnmor and you were recovering from pneumonia."

"*Tapadh leibh*, ma'am."

"*'s ur beatha!* See, you haven't forgotten some of it at least!" And they both laughed.

"Forgotten what?" said Alex, coming into the room with a burst of energy, home early for once.

"Who I am..." quipped Alastair, acquiring a suitably vague and vacant expression.

Alex smiled and kissed Katherine on top of her head. She held out her hand to him, feeling heartened by his relaxed and cheerful expression.

"How was your day?" she asked.

"Well, I have some excellent news." He smiled at his wife. "You and I are going to take a trip to America."

Katherine was surprised. "America?!"

"Yes."

"How? Why?"

"The how is on the *Queen Mary*. We shall sail out in two weeks' time and spend a whole month in New York. Just think of it!"

Katherine was astonished. For a moment, she was not quite sure how to respond.

"The why is because, along with three other barristers from different Chambers, I have been selected to take part in an exchange with a law firm, as they call it, in the States. We'll be shadowing our opposite numbers in court and during briefing sessions. Then, they'll come over here to do the same. The idea is that we have a greater understanding of how each other's legal system works. Isn't it exciting?"

"Well, yes." Katherine was cautious, hesitant. "And did you ask to go on this, or did it just drop into your lap?"

14

Alex was silent. His father regarded him speculatively.

"I asked."

"Oh. Why didn't you discuss it with me first?" she said quietly.

"Because I wasn't sure I'd be chosen."

"That wouldn't have mattered. I'd like to have known, Alex, and been party to the decision."

"But isn't it exciting? We'll stay in a luxury hotel and be able to explore the city."

Katherine was unimpressed. "And how often will you be working with this 'law firm'?"

Again, Alex hesitated. "Every day, all day. Except at weekends, of course," he added quickly.

"Of course." A rare note of sarcasm crept into her voice. "And what do I do during the week?"

"Well, there will be dining out in the evenings, you can explore New York, go shopping with the other wives…"

"Since when has shopping been one of my priorities?"

"Oh, darling, it will be great! Please be happy for me."

"I am. But I'm not sure that *I* want to go."

This time it was Alex who was taken aback. "What do you mean, not sure that you want to go?"

"Exactly what I said."

Alastair sensed that Katherine was not going to give way on this. Discreetly, he left the room. He would not interfere, this was something they had to resolve together, but he would feel the pain of their disagreement, nonetheless.

Katherine and Alex stared at each other, both standing their ground. Once again, Alex tried his best to convince his wife. "You'll be in the lap of luxury for the whole journey. So different from when we go to Cairnmor."

But we never go to Cairnmor, she thought. *We haven't been back there since we got married.* However, she refrained from saying so and instead replied, "That's irrelevant."

"The *Queen Mary* will get us there in about four or five days. She holds the Blue Riband for the fastest crossing of the Atlantic. I've always wanted to travel aboard a ship that can do that sort of speed."

"Have you?"

"Well, I've wondered what it was like."

"Ah. I haven't. Also, you seem to have forgotten that I'm five months pregnant. I have absolutely no desire to cross the Atlantic, even if it is aboard *Queen Mary*, just to trail round New York for a month on my own or in the company of other women whom I don't know and may not get on with. Besides which, the whole thing will be incredibly tiring physically and I'm not willing to risk our baby in order to go." Katherine was adamant. She had to put the health of their child above anything else.

"It's all arranged. You have to come."

"No. I'm sorry, Alex, but this time I'm going to dig my heels in. You go and have a good time. But I am staying here."

"At least think about it."

"No."

Katherine stood up, inner tension causing the growing infant to move into such an awkward position and kick her under the ribs with such strength that she felt as though there was more than one baby inside her. It added an immediate physical discomfort to the emotional upset.

Angry, and on the verge of tears, she walked out of the room.

Ignoring the fact that it was nearly supper time, oblivious to Alastair coming into the hallway from the dining room where he had been pacing the floor waiting for the argument to be resolved, Katherine collected her coat and went out of the house, slamming the door behind her.

CHAPTER 3

London/Glasgow
March-April, 1938

Immediately, Alex came rushing out of the sitting room intending to go after her but Alastair laid a gentle, restraining hand on his arm.

"Let her go," he said quietly. "In this particular instance, she'll get over it more quickly if you allow her to work through her anger in her own way."

Alex was indignant, disappointed by Katherine's refusal to go with him. "She's never reacted like this to anything I've arranged before."

"You've never reached the limit of her patience and forbearance before."

"Oh."

Alex's anger gradually subsided as he became aware of his own self-absorption. "I pushed her too far this time, didn't I?"

"Yes."

"I just wanted us to be together. And it's such a great opportunity to travel abroad."

"Of course, but there's more to being together than physically going places."

Alex was suitably chastened. "Yes."

"You've been very involved in your work these past few months and I think Katherine is feeling neglected. That's also part of her anger. This pre-arranged trip to America was just the final straw." Alastair placed his hand on his son's shoulder and smiled. "Try and make it up to her when she comes home. Now, I shall take myself off upstairs and have supper on a tray in my sitting room. An evening in front of the fire with a good book will be most welcome. Then I shall have an early night. See you in the morning."

"Thanks, Dad. See you."

Alex went back into the downstairs sitting room, leaving the door open so that he would hear Katherine as soon as she came in. He undid his briefcase and began to sort through his papers. Unable to concentrate, he moved over to the window-seat, Katherine's favourite place, and looked out of the window, watching for her.

He was out of the house the moment he saw her coming round the corner into Cornwallis Gardens and took her into his arms. "I'm so sorry."

"It's all right."

"I have been rather selfish."

Katherine took a deep breath. "Yes," she replied honestly.

"How can I make it up to you?"

"By being the man I fell in love with, not the stranger you've become recently." She looked up at him, the pain showing in her eyes.

He kissed her cheek. "I'm afraid I have been a bit caught up in my work of late."

"A bit! Completely obsessed would be more accurate."

"It's difficult not to be, though. There's so much to do."

"I know and I try to be patient, but I am your wife. Please don't push me into the background or take me for granted."

Alex sighed. "I'll do my best."

Only half-convinced, Katherine said, "Thank you."

"So, what would you like to do this evening?" he asked, changing the subject as they turned for home.

"Supper would be good to start with," she responded, forcing a smile, the atmosphere between them still tense. "I'm very hungry."

Alex placed his hand on her stomach and said, with a greater levity than he actually felt, "Well, you'd better eat, otherwise our offspring will wonder why it's not getting any nourishment! Do babies think, I wonder?"

"I have no idea. But this one certainly responds to emotions and to music," she replied, as they went up the steps into the house.

For the rest of the evening, Alex did no work and was dutifully attentive towards her. However, it took Katherine a long time to recover from this particular episode. She was a woman of deep feeling and although slow to anger, once roused, it took time for the after-effects to dissipate.

Until his departure for the States, to his credit, Alex did make the effort to spend as much time as he could with Katherine and she was grateful for this, glad to be once more in the company of her husband for whom she had given up so much and loved so dearly.

It was therefore even harder to say goodbye as she and Alastair went with Alex to Southampton Docks. Katherine stood on the quayside waving to him until *Queen Mary* had drawn away. Downcast, she remained silent for the whole journey home.

She and Alastair ate supper together and after Mrs Thringle had brought them coffee in the downstairs sitting room, Alastair said, "I have nothing to do as far as the R.N.V.R. is concerned for the time being, but I do have to go up to Glasgow this weekend to see Laurence Hart at Mathieson's Shipyard and meet my fellow solicitors to try and resolve one or two problems." He paused and smiled at Katherine, knowing the effect his next words would have on his daughter-in-law. "I was wondering whether you would like to come with me?"

Katherine's expression changed, all at once becoming alive and alert. "Yes?" she said, anticipating his next words.

"And then spend a couple of weeks on Cairnmor."

"Would I like it?! Oh, Alastair, that would be wonderful. Thank you so much for suggesting it!"

Alastair chuckled. "It won't be too much for you? There's a great deal of travelling..."

"Of course it won't be too much. I'm familiar with the train journey and it's usually quite a pleasant crossing on the steamer at this time of year," replied Katherine, quelling a momentary pang of guilt that, for the sake of her unborn child, she had refused to travel to America with her husband aboard a luxury liner. Yet here she was, about to embark on a lengthy trip to Glasgow and Cairnmor.

The difference? She would be going home, the journeys and destinations were known quantities and she felt so very safe with Alastair. No, there was no need to feel guilty, she had made the right decision.

"Good, that's settled then. I'll make the necessary reservations for the journey…"

"…and I'll write to John and book rooms for us at the hotel in Lochaberdale, and let Mary and Michael know that we're coming." She could feel her spirits rise at the mere thought of actually being *there* on the island.

"I have another suggestion." Alastair couldn't resist an impish smile.

"Yes?"

"You've been doing well with the Pitman's recently, haven't you?"

"I'm up to about fifty words per minute. Mrs Thringle and I have been having a lot of fun and I've been writing down everything she says in shorthand. She's been a really good sport and it's been such a help."

"Well, I was wondering if you'd act as my unofficial secretary. You see, as I'm representing your father on this occasion, I should like to keep my own independent record of what has been said at meetings with the solicitors and the Board. It also means that you become involved with what's going on. It's a good idea for the Members to meet you – after all, Mathieson's was founded by your grandfather, now belongs to your father and will become yours one day. You can test your speeds in a real situation. If you'd like to, that is," he added, not wishing to be presumptuous.

"Oh, Alastair, I'd love it! But am I good enough yet?"

"Do the best you can. There's no pressure, I'm just grateful for the help. Now, so that you are fully conversant with what is going to be discussed, I thought it might be a good idea to go through some of the details this evening and tomorrow."

"This is just the sort of thing I need to do."

"I know."

They set to work immediately. Alastair's explanations were clear and concise and Katherine's questions pertinent and relevant. She was quick to absorb details and, using the knowledge she had gained when she and Alex had travelled to Mathieson's in the search for her parents two years previously, she understood fully what was to be discussed.

The following Friday, they took the night sleeper from Euston Station to Glasgow Central, arriving early on Saturday morning. Katherine felt her spirits rise as soon as the train crossed the border into her beloved Scotland and even Glasgow in the rain held a special charm for her.

After booking into their rooms at the Central Hotel, they travelled to Mathieson's Shipbuilding and Engineering Firm in Govan. Laurence Hart, the managing director, greeted them – friendly and welcoming as always.

He was obviously thriving in his work and even the extra hours and demands of weekend working since his appointment had not dampened his spirits or his enthusiasm for the shipyard, which was his pride and joy. He was justifiably proud of its well-deserved reputation for quality and efficiency but was far too modest to claim that its continuing success was due in no small measure to his guidance and vision.

Laurence was keen to show them round before they got down to business. Fortunately, the rain had stopped and as the sun emerged from behind the clouds, the River Clyde and its associated industries took on a completely different aspect after being shrouded in the murky gloom that inevitably accompanied the rain.

"We currently have two destroyers and a cruiser under construction for the Royal Navy, as well as a passenger vessel for the merchant fleet and two smaller ancillary ships," said Laurence, as they walked carefully among the giant cranes, sidestepping chains and industrial equipment that littered the walkways, dwarfed by the huge ships under construction, and deafened by the metallic reverberations of rivet guns and hammers against metal plates.

"What does next year look like?" asked Alastair, raising his voice above the incessant noise and keeping careful watch over Katherine's progress, offering his hand whenever he saw she needed support.

"In addition to a couple of merchant ships, there are another two destroyers and a frigate scheduled, with the promise of more to come in 1940, including an aircraft carrier. The Navy is increasing its expenditure radically. Whether this continues, I suppose, is dependent on whether there's a war or not. Given the current political situation, I personally think war is inevitable."

"Unfortunately, I have to agree," said Alastair.

Katherine reacted with growing concern to this last, almost matter-of-fact exchange between the two men. "What will you do if that should happen?" she asked Laurence, as they moved away from the worst of the racket.

"Shipbuilding is regarded as a reserved occupation. Therefore, unless I specifically request it, I'm exempt from being called up into the one of armed forces, should conscription be introduced."

"Please don't request it. We need you here."

"Don't worry, Katherine. The most useful contribution I could make to any war effort is at Mathieson's. My skills and expertise will be needed to build ships to fight the enemy. I can do no better than that. Each man will have his place in the scheme of things."

These were sound and sensible words but Alastair could see that Katherine was finding this conversation difficult and, as her eyes filled with tears at the reality of what an armed conflict could mean for those whom she loved, he put his arm round her shoulders in a gesture of comfort.

"Try not to worry," he said. "War may yet be averted."

Katherine nodded but given the preparations that were under way nationally, she sensed that this was unlikely.

Along with the rest of the country, she had heard Neville Chamberlain's radio broadcast outlining the 'Government Scheme of Voluntary Service'. Shortly afterwards, the family had received the booklet issued to every household illustrating the tasks for which volunteers were needed – A.R.P. wardens, the Auxiliary Fire Service, the Territorial Army to name but three.

The Prime Minister had tried to reassure his listeners that Voluntary Service was only a scheme to "*make us ready for war*", going on to emphasize the fact that he would continue to do all he could to "*preserve the peace*".

Katherine knew it was a double-edged sword but, on reflection, probably the only sensible option. It was not easy though and she found it all very unsettling.

At the conclusion of the tour, after eating lunch in the staff canteen, they stayed in the quieter surroundings of Laurence's office for the remainder of the afternoon. While he and Alastair were talking facts and figures, Katherine rested in one of the arm chairs in the office, her feet up on a footstool that Laurence had found for her.

Lulled by the comforting sound of their voices, she drifted off to sleep. From time to time, Alastair glanced across to check on her well-being, but she seemed perfectly settled and content.

In the middle of the afternoon, Laurence's secretary brought in a tray with tea and a rather large Dundee cake. Katherine woke up with a start, disturbed by the intrusion.

"Hello," said Alastair, smiling at her.

She returned his smile and stretched. "How long have I been asleep?" Easing herself out of the chair, she straightened her back before walking around the room.

"Days. It's time to go back to London," he teased.

She narrowed her eyes at him. "Well the two of you look remarkably spruce considering you've been here for the same amount of time."

"Oh, we've been home and bathed and changed – several times," replied Alastair.

"Uh-huh. Well, as I obviously won't have eaten for all that time and you have, I shall have *your* share of the cake."

"Ah, well, now that's a different matter." And they both grinned at each other.

"Shall I do the honours?" asked Laurence, pouring out the tea, slicing the cake and handing round the cups and plates.

"Thank you, I'm ready for this." Gratefully, Katherine drank her tea and ate most of her cake before placing her plate on the table beside her. Thinking of their earlier tour of the shipyard, she asked, "Who designs the ships that you build for the Royal Navy? Do you do that here?"

"Not as a rule. It's usually done in-house by their own architects and draughtsmen. However, because of the high quality of the design team at Mathieson's, some of our designers have, in recent years, worked under naval control on frigates and corvettes, which are then constructed here as well as other shipyards," replied Laurence.

"Doesn't the Royal Navy have its own shipyards?" asked Katherine.

"Yes, but not enough, so most naval ships are built by private industry. However, not all yards can handle the requirements of large warships. Mathieson's is one of only fourteen left in this country with that capability. There used to be more, but in peace-time, and with many being hit hard by the Depression, quite a few went out of business."

"Is the reason why more shipyards don't build the larger warships just to do with space?"

"No. Many yards have a similar capacity to ours, but naval shipbuilding requires different techniques and equipment than construction for the merchant fleet."

"Such as?"

"Working with armour plate, the use of D-grade steel rather than the more pliable stuff used in merchant shipping. The greater complexity of warships means that you need specialized skills and know-how. Along with other shipyards engaged in this work, we have a few R.N. chaps who oversee the construction process and make sure it's all done to the correct specifications."

"I see." Katherine was thoughtful, absorbing the information. "Do you know, if we've got time, I really think I'd like to know more about the ships of the Royal Navy."

It was Alastair who took up the theme, delighted to be able to talk about the Service that meant so much to him. "It's probably more straightforward if I describe them in general terms first, as there are different classes and slight variations of design within each type. We can then go into more detail later – if you'd like to, that is."

"I would, very much." She settled herself more comfortably in her chair.

"Well, the battleship is our largest warship, with the greatest number of guns and clad in the heaviest armour."

"Like *H.M.S. Hood*?"

"Yes, that's a very famous example, although technically, she's what's known as a battlecruiser, meaning that she's quite fast over the water for her size as she has slightly less protective armour. There are other types of cruisers as well."

"Which I presume are smaller?"

"Not necessarily. They are just lighter, can therefore go even faster and have marginally smaller guns."

"What's next?" Katherine found her interest deepening, sparked by Alastair's underlying enthusiasm.

He smiled at her. "Destroyers. They're armed with guns, torpedoes and depth charges and are renowned for their high speed and manoeuvrability. After this, there are frigates, often used as headquarters ships, and then corvettes, which are patrol and escort vessels. In addition, there are also aircraft carriers and submarines."

"Which are self-explanatory."

"Yes."

"Which country has the largest navy?"

"Despite all the restrictions and reductions caused by the signing of various treaties since the Great War, I'm happy to say that the Royal Navy is still the largest in the world," replied Alastair, with obvious pride.

Katherine smiled at her father-in-law, understanding his pleasure. "Could I see what these ships look like? I don't suppose you have a book of some sort?" She looked enquiringly at Laurence.

"I can do better than that!" He went to a large sloping table in a small room adjoining his main office and brought with him a whole sheaf of plans, an expression of boyish delight on his face. "Have a look at these…"

"Goodness! That'll keep us going for a while," said Katherine.

And it did. Together at Laurence's desk, they studied the designs – discussing in depth the differences, relative merits and uses of each one. This information enabled Katherine to understand the Royal Navy's capabilities and, although she could not possibly be aware of it, was just one factor among several that in the future was to change the course of her life.

However, for the present, when it came to the Board meeting later that week, Katherine could take her shorthand notes with the benefit of having gained more essential background information, in addition to the groundwork that she and Alastair had already done.

During pauses in the discussion, she viewed the imposing portrait of her irascible grandfather, the late Sir Charles Mathieson – founder, chairman, managing director and for so many years chief designer of the shipyard and engineering firm. She hoped he would be appreciative that his legacy was in such good hands and continuing to thrive, despite the economic ups and downs of the decade.

As the week progressed, Katherine experienced a feeling of great satisfaction in being able to record all that transpired in the meetings. Her confidence and shorthand speeds increased and, if she was unable to transcribe a particular sentence or phrase phonetically, she would write a word or sentence in long hand and employ the short cuts she had developed for herself during her lectures at Edinburgh University. In this way, together with her own memory for conversations, she was able to present a most appreciative Alastair with an accurate account of the business as it occurred.

On their final evening, after a convivial day spent with Laurence, his wife Dorothy and their three young children, Katherine and Alastair bid farewell to their friends and travelled to Oban, where they boarded *R.M.S. Lochfoyle*, embarking on the eight hour crossing to Cairnmor.

The weather was fair and the sea calm, just as Katherine had predicted, but what she had not anticipated was the sheer joy that filled her soul as the steamer approached its destination. There before her, in all its familiarity and beauty, was her beloved island.

"Oh, Alastair," she said, with heartfelt gratitude, putting her arm through his as they stood together leaning against the railings, watching the soaring mountains, rocky inlets and white-gold sands of Cairnmor draw ever closer. "Thank you so much."

"*'s ur beatha*," he replied simply, touched by her transparent delight.

CHAPTER 4

Cairnmor (1)
April, 1938

Michael and Mary were there to meet them at the quayside, and once the steamer had docked alongside the pier and the passengers had disembarked, the four of them greeted each other with affection.

"Welcome home, Katherine," said Michael, giving her a brotherly hug and shaking hands warmly with Alastair. "It's good to see you both."

"It's lovely to be here."

"Look at you!" exclaimed Mary, placing her hand on her dearest friend's stomach. "The baby's really grown since we last saw you."

"Aye, it has."

"But you are well?"

"Touch wood. It's a relief not to feel queasy any more. Oh, it's so good to be home!"

Katherine breathed in deeply, absorbing all the wonderfully familiar sights and sounds of the island – the spectacular scenery, the bustle of activity on the quayside and Gaelic, her native tongue, being spoken all around her.

Alastair shared her delight. He could feel Cairnmor working its magic on him in the way it had always done from the moment he had first arrived in the spring of 1937. Or, he asked himself, was it because of Katherine? He was aware that both things were true.

Michael picked up their suitcases and they made their way along the upward sloping incline towards the hotel.

"Now," he said, taking on the mantle of a tourist guide, "I have a full itinerary lined up for you both. Tomorrow morning at six a.m., we have a fifteen-mile hike across the spectacular glens of Aoibhneach and Cuineas and up the high mountains beyond. Then, there is to be a three mile swim and sandcastle competition on the beach at South Lochaberdale, with the winner having a cup of tea at Katherine's old croft, although I haven't arranged that with the current tenants, so they'll be surprised. Finally, a round of golf on the non-existent golf course on the machair… I seem to remember, Alastair, you telling me that you once played?"

Alastair smiled ruefully. "I did. Very badly, though, I'm afraid. I even had lessons, but I was still hopeless."

"Excellent! Then this will give you some much needed practice. And, of course, an energetic sporting activity like golf after all that trekking will be just the thing for our Katherine in her advanced state of impending motherhood. So," he concluded, "I presume you're up to all of this? We have to show off our lovely island to its owner. Who, I hasten to add, has not visited her new abode since acquiring it." He looked at Katherine sternly. "I hope you're not going to turn into one of these absentee landlords who leaves us independent-minded islanders of

Cairnmor to run things by ourselves, which, of course, is *exactly* what we love to do."

Katherine was laughing so much at Michael's nonsense, she had to stop walking to ease the stitch in her side. "I'm sorry I haven't been back. It's all your best friend's fault," she gasped. "You'll have to take it up with him."

Michael smiled and put down the suitcases as they reached the door of the hotel. "Oh, I fully intend to! Providing Alex answers my letters, that is, which he hasn't to date. I don't know, what on earth does he think he's doing – first of all taking up a prestigious post with one of the top judges in the country and then, worse still, gallivanting off to the good old U.S. of A. on some high-powered lawyer exchange?! He should be here, now, enjoying our meagre hospitality rather than living the high-life, having already caused our new Lairdess to neglect her duty to us poor helpless islanders."

"I shall be helpless with a baby being born at this rate if you don't stop being so ridiculous!" observed Katherine.

"All right, I'll keep mum. Well, not you, that'll be Alex's job in July when the baby's born. How's he doing, anyway?" asked Michael.

"Busy. Far too busy."

"Inevitable, I suppose. Rather him than me. But you can tell us more later. Now, Mary and I will leave you to book in with our fair inn-keeper and when you've had the chance for a wash and a brush-up after your journey, we'll join you for supper, if we may. Tomorrow there's a bit of an evening planned!"

"We'll see you later," replied Alastair, smiling at them both, before picking up Katherine's suitcase as well as his own as they went into the hotel.

John and Marion Fraser welcomed them with more hugs and an exclamation from the hotel manager's wife as to how well Katherine was carrying her baby.

"When's the bairn due?" Marion asked, as Katherine and Alastair signed the register.

"In July."

"July? Och, I was afraid ye were going to say next week, given the size of ye!"

"I know! It would seem that I am quite large. In fact," she added drily, "there have been times when I've wondered if I'm carrying an elephant."

"Aye, ye probably are. But it'll be a handsome one, given its parents!" said John.

Katherine once again experienced a tremendous lift to her spirits at actually being *here* on the island, among the people she knew so well, where humorous exchanges could be made in safety; where there was no pretence, no artifice, just natural conversation based on a secure background of trust and the warmth of long-standing friendship.

Without hesitation, she included Alastair in all of this – he had become such an integral part of her life now. She missed Alex terribly, of course, but Katherine knew that she would still be able to enjoy her stay here, making the most of this rare, wonderful opportunity to visit Cairnmor and be with the people whom she cared about so much.

Supper was fun, full of the lively banter that inevitably occurred when Michael was present. However, the evening finished early, as Katherine was feeling tired after the day's exertions.

The next morning, she slept late and spent most of the time before lunch resting in her room and reading, sitting by the large, floor to ceiling window in a comfortable armchair with her feet up, looking out over Lochaberdale, relishing the magnificent panoramic view of the bay to the headlands beyond.

Cairnmor had been her home for so long and now it actually belonged to her – bought by her father soon after he had learned that he was heir to Mathieson's Shipyard. Since then, she had often considered her responsibilities as landowner, wondering how she could make improvements for the people who lived on the island.

How well she understood what life was like here; how well she understood the struggle for self-sufficiency in a harsh environment; how well she understood the traditions, warmth and vibrancy of this unique community that had nurtured her.

For the first time, the islanders had security of tenure and the independence they treasured, able to have confidence in the future for themselves and their families – this, with Alastair's help, was the one important thing she had been able to achieve so far. She knew there was so much more she wanted to do. But what form should it take?

That afternoon, as she and Alastair went for a walk along the shore of Lochaberdale, passing the line of single storey cottages that comprised the main street of the little township, and out towards the eastern headland, she spoke to him of her thoughts.

"I'm not sure how best to help," she concluded.

"Why don't you ask the islanders?" he replied. "Ask Ross Muir, as Factor and your representative on the island, to do a survey. Find out people's views. See what they would like *you* to do for *them*. It might be that they would like more practical help on their crofts or more modern conveniences: electricity, running water, better housing, a cottage hospital, even a secondary school so that the young people stay on Cairnmor. See what it is *they* want as well. Don't be afraid to ask. Involve Michael. He has excellent knowledge of Scots Land Law and can say what is possible and what isn't."

Katherine tucked her arm through Alastair's, a favourite action of hers when they were together, and considered his words.

"Of course! Why didn't I think of that? You are a very clever, practical man."

"That'll be the day!" he replied self-effacingly.

"Talking about Michael, I wonder if he's ever thought of qualifying as a barrister north of the border? Crofting suits him, but there may come a time when intellectually he will need something more stimulating."

"Then why not suggest it to him? It would keep his intelligent brain active. He could become our resident advocate. It would hardly be an onerous or time-consuming task, but it could be useful should the need arise."

Katherine's subconscious registered the '*our*' in the phrase '*our resident advocate*' but before she could analyse the thought, it disappeared into the ether;

indeed, Alastair was not conscious of his turn of phrase either – not, that is, until they were to recall this conversation much later on.

The evening's entertainment was very much in the Cairnmor tradition. It began with a special supper in the hotel dining room to welcome Katherine and Alastair, to which came Michael and Mary (who had organized the whole occasion), Gordon and Fiona MacKinnon (Mary's parents), Iain (her youngest brother, home from boarding school for the holidays), Robbie MacKenzie (well-respected local fisherman, philosopher and weather expert), Donald and Annie MacCreggan (who delivered the post and ran the post office), Father McPhee (the ever-popular priest), Ross and Eve Muir (the Factor and his wife), and finally, once they finished serving everyone, John and Marion Fraser.

After an excellent meal, they gathered in the comfortable hotel lounge and played charades – a favourite of Katherine's – and once the final phrase had been acted out, the winners had celebrated and they had all re-lived and laughed about the funniest moments, John and Marion served more tea and coffee. Then, as the sun set and the evening shadows lengthened outside, John lit the oil lamps and banked up the fire with fresh peat while Katherine raised the topic that had been on her mind earlier in the day, together with Alastair's suggestion of a survey.

"Och, I can tell ye right away what I'd like," said Robbie. "It's very frustrating that we have to wait a week to get the latest news, especially with the current situation. I want to know what's going on as it happens, not a week later, all in a rush with all the newspapers arriving together at once. A radio would be just the thing."

"We'd need electricity for that," observed John.

"Oh aye, so that's something else to put on yere list," said Robbie, nodding at Katherine who was taking shorthand notes.

"We could use wind power to drive a generator," suggested Michael. "Goodness knows we have enough of it here."

"Aye, and we'll be in the middle of listening to an important broadcast, and the wind will drop and we'd never know what happened next!"

"Perhaps it would be possible to use the generator to charge a battery, then the energy from the wind could be stored for future use. I read all about storing electricity in a periodical when I was on the mainland a while ago," said Ross.

"Aye, that sounds great!" agreed John, enthusiastically. "We could have one here at the hotel and then lots of people would be able to benefit from it at the same time. Might be good for business as well," he added.

"That's most ingenious and certainly worthy of further investigation," replied Alastair approvingly.

"Aye. In these uncertain times, it's essential to keep in touch with what's going on in the wider world," said Father McPhee. "From what I've read, the whole of Europe seems to be heading for disaster."

"I think that's probably true," replied Alastair, glancing at Katherine to check on her reaction, ready to offer reassurance should it be needed, knowing how worried she was by any talk of war.

However, on this occasion, she seemed unperturbed.

"What do ye think, Katherine?" asked Donald. "Ye're our history expert. What do ye make of all of this?"

"It's a difficult situation," she said thoughtfully. "Of course, nobody wants war, that's for certain. And from what I've learned recently, it would seem this country is totally unprepared and we wouldn't stand a chance if war came tomorrow. But, we have to get ourselves ready just in case, and I suppose there comes a time when any country has to support its friends and allies against an aggressor."

"Is Germany an aggressor?" asked Iain.

"Hitler is," responded Alastair, "and as he wields absolute power in his country, then the German people will have to follow him regardless of how they might feel."

"Why? *We* wouldn't here, would we?"

"Fortunately we have too healthy a scepticism for our leaders most of the time," said Michael.

"Also, we have freedom of speech and are not being led astray or coerced, which is what I suspect is happening over there. However, we haven't had to live in the sort of conditions that they have in Germany for the last twenty years," observed Katherine, trying to be fair.

"What do you mean?" asked Mary.

"Well…"

Katherine suddenly became aware of her friends listening intently to her words. Suddenly feeling self-conscious, she was very glad that she had taken the opportunity to read all the newspapers and periodicals that she could find during their stay in Glasgow, allowing the logical, analytical side of her mind to take precedence over the emotional side. History had been her subject at Edinburgh and she recognized that, difficult as it might be to bear, what was happening in the world at that moment was history in the making.

Katherine took a deep breath and began:

"In 1919, the Treaty of Versailles imposed political and military humiliation on Germany as a punishment for causing the Great War. It was decided that reparations should be paid to the Allies as a recompense for all their losses. Many people, myself included, when we studied the text of the Treaty at university, thought it far too harsh and that there could be unforeseen repercussions. I think we are seeing those repercussions now."

"In what way?" Mary wanted to know. "I don't know anything about Germany."

"At the beginning of this decade, the German people blamed the leaders of the Weimar Republic, as the government was known, for accepting such harsh and, what they considered to be, unjust terms. Many didn't believe that their country had lost the war anyway. All industrial nations suffered during the Depression, but in Germany, the combined effects of this, as well as trying to repay the exorbitantly high reparations, were disastrous. There was hunger, rampant inflation and very high unemployment. To cap it all, their best industrial land was under French occupation."

"But surely, that's not a reason to invade your neighbours?" suggested Mary.

"No, it's not," responded Alastair, "but it does enable extreme political thought to flourish and that can give rise to radical forms of government. And the Nazis

28

are a radical right-wing party, there is no doubt about that. There is worse to come from them, I fear."

"But we've had Fascists and Communists rumbling around in Britain for years," observed Michael.

"Ah, but because we have a stable National Government which has steered us through the worst of the Depression, it's highly unlikely that either could gain a foot-hold. However, in Germany, the Nazi party managed to manoeuvre itself into power in the face of a weak and unpopular government." Alastair smiled at Michael, softening the effect of his words, trying to ensure that his reply didn't sound like a lecture.

"At school, our history master told us that under Hitler, the economy has improved and life has been generally much better for the German people," said Iain, joining in the discussion.

"It's improved for most people, and I use the term *most* advisedly, because there is a lot of evidence being collected at the moment about the persecution of the Jews, for example," said Alastair.

"It might not be true."

"Well, son, true or not," responded Gordon, "we've had hundreds of Jewish refugees arriving in this country. I saw some of them with my own eyes arriving in Glasgow at the docks a few weeks back when I was over on the mainland." He nodded his head to emphasize the point.

"And it is an irrefutable fact that Germany has been steadily re-arming itself in defiance of the Treaty of Versailles," said Katherine.

"And we've been caught napping," added Alastair. "Also, the League of Nations has proved to be ineffective in resolving complex international situations. They allowed the Nazis to re-occupy the Rhineland in 1936 and have not questioned Hitler's involvement in the Spanish Civil War. They were very slow to react to the *Anschluss* last month,"

"But many people think that Germany is just reclaiming the territory that is rightfully hers and was taken away unfairly," said Iain, standing his ground valiantly, despite the opposition, prompting his father to observe under his breath, "I'd like to meet this history master of yorn and give him a piece of my mind."

"Och, he's all right, Pa."

"I'm not so sure…" Gordon frowned. "Young is he?"

"Not particularly, Pa. He fought in the trenches in the Great War. Got invalided out. We call him Hopalong Cassidy," added Iain, with youthful callousness. "He really does believe that Germany has lost too much territory, though."

"That might be true of the Rhineland," replied Katherine, "but Austria was not run by Germany before the last war. An ally, certainly, but not governed by her as she will be now and absorbed into the Nazi regime."

"Who will be next, do ye think?" asked Donald.

"Czechoslovakia," said Katherine and Alastair at the same time. They exchanged a brief smile.

"What makes ye both think that?"

"Sudetenland in the north has a predominantly German population," replied Katherine.

"And Hitler will use that as an excuse to go into the rest of the country. It would seem that he is not just interested in building up a prosperous Germany, but has designs on conquering his neighbours as well. That's why he's so dangerous," added Alastair.

"Perhaps a wireless isn't such a good idea after all," said Michael, in a gentle attempt to lighten the mood. "If we don't have one, then we won't know anything and world events can pass us by unheeded."

"I'm afraid," concluded Father McPhee sombrely, "that wireless or no wireless, if there is another war, we none of us will be immune from its effects, remote as we are here on Cairnmor. Unfortunately, war will touch all of our lives and change things forever, no matter where we might live or what we believe."

And with Father McPhee's sobering, prophetic words, the evening came to an end.

When Katherine and Alastair walked up the stairs together to their rooms, she saw an expression of admiration for her in his eyes.

"You've been doing a lot of research recently, haven't you?" he said thoughtfully.

"Yes," she replied, her cheeks warm. "You see, I felt that if I understood what was going on, then I would be better placed to cope with whatever happens. Theoretically, that is."

"And we all need the theory!" He smiled at her. "Goodnight, my dear."

"Goodnight, Alastair. Sleep well."

"And you."

CHAPTER 5

Cairnmor (2)
April, 1938

When Alastair and Katherine raised the question of Michael qualifying as a barrister in Scotland, he said he would look into it. Mary told him he was definitely going to do it and as soon as she had said this, he accepted that he had no choice in the matter.

"Yes, dear," he replied meekly, adding with typical humour, while dramatically placing the back of his hand against his forehead, "Oh no, not more studying!"

From this, they knew it would be a certainty and that he was not averse to the idea. Also, together with Ross and John, they put in place arrangements and plans for the survey to be carried out over the coming months.

Alastair and Katherine went for many walks along the pristine sands of South Lochaberdale, often chatting at length to Robbie as he sat in the warm April sun mending his nets outside his hut next to the dunes; sharing with him hot, sweet tea and fruit cake, one of his home-made specialities.

Alastair remarked that he hadn't tasted cake as good as this since the two men had gone out on Robbie's fishing smack searching for Adam, Mary's first husband, who tragically drowned along with one of his friends.

"Aye, and that was just before you were so ill with the pneumonia. Are ye completely recovered now?"

"Yes, although I still occasionally get tired if I overdo things. I try to be careful."

"So, I suppose going off to sea on R.N.V.R. training exercises in terrible weather is your idea of trying to be careful?!" teased Katherine. "Not to mention working long hours at the office and then all that studying when you get home!"

"Aye, ye've been found out. There'll be no peace now," chuckled Robbie. "They'll think ye can cope with doing everything!"

"That's true. It'll be washing-up and cleaning as well from now on!" remarked Alastair.

"And don't forget the baby's nappy will need changing..." added Katherine for good measure.

"It won't be the first time," he responded.

"Really?" She was impressed.

"Oh yes. All three of them. Edward, Alex and Lily."

She smiled at him. "I shall definitely employ you in that direction then. You can teach me!"

"I think that ye'd better make sure ye book yereself in for some more sea-going exercises, my friend," observed Robbie drily.

Alastair said he would cope and smiled warmly at Katherine, inadvertently causing her to blush. Carefully, he contained his expression, knowing how observant Robbie was but, above all, should she become conscious of her reaction, he was anxious to deflect Katherine from thinking any further than was necessary.

However, for her, the moment passed without heed and it was she, with genuine innocence and much to Alastair's relief, who moved the conversation on by saying, "What about you, Robbie? Were you at sea in the Great War? I was so young at the time, I don't remember much about what everyone did. All I knew was that some people left and some never came back."

"I was in mine-sweepers. Converted fishing boats."

"Dangerous work," observed Alastair.

"Oh, aye."

"Where did you operate?"

"In Scapa Flow and various other places." He seemed reluctant to elaborate further and Alastair did not press him. "How about you?"

"I served aboard a destroyer, a battleship and a sloop. The Navy moved me around quite a bit."

Like Robbie, Alastair didn't go into detail that afternoon but later, when he and Katherine had finished supper and were lingering over their coffee, she asked him to tell her more about his war service. He seemed hesitant at first but after gentle coercion was persuaded to do so.

"Well, I joined the R.N.V.R. in 1913 and after I'd done my initial training and got my commission, at the beginning of the war, I was assigned to a destroyer patrolling the English Channel. I then did a further period of training in 1915, specializing in signals and navigation. After this, I served as a lieutenant aboard *H.M.S. Colossus*, with Dudley Pound as Flag Captain, stationed in Scapa Flow with the Grand Fleet, seeing action at the Battle of Jutland in 1916."

"Robbie was at Scapa Flow as well. I wonder if you saw each other from a distance?!"

Alastair chuckled. "It's perfectly possible of course. He and I should compare notes."

"He seemed reluctant to talk about his war service," observed Katherine.

"Most men are. It's something they would rather keep to themselves. There is a perception that it's very difficult for someone who has not had the same experiences to fully appreciate the fear and suffering, let alone being able to understand the special sort of comradeship that exists in a combat situation. Apart from the latter, war is not a pleasant experience."

"No, I would imagine that it is not." Katherine considered this and then asked, "Do you mind talking about it?"

"It depends on who I'm talking to."

"I can appreciate that. There are people with whom I wouldn't want to share such things." Then she added, "What did you mean when you described Dudley Pound as a 'flag captain'?"

"When a ship is used as the admiral's ship, which *Colossus* was at that time, he hoists his admiral's 'flag', hence the terms 'flagship' and 'flag captain'. The Executive Officer remains responsible for the day-to-day running of the ship itself but where tactics are concerned, the flag captain works closely with the admiral, who has overall command of the fleet."

"What happened to your ship at Jutland?"

"Once Admiral Jellico's battleships in the British Grand Fleet had found and engaged the German High Seas Fleet in the North Sea, *Colossus*, very much at the forefront of events, was hit by heavy shell-fire on her superstructure. But she survived and went on to sink two German cruisers." Alastair shook his head sadly. "So many fine ships sank in that battle – on both sides – and many thousands of men lost their lives. Such a waste. The outcome was indecisive and both countries claimed victory. We lost more ships and men than the Germans did, but their fleet never put to sea again and they didn't achieve their objective of crippling the Grand Fleet and breaking the British blockade of their ports. So who can say? The debate still continues to this day."

Katherine watched the last red-gold glow of a Cairnmor sunset through the window, reflecting on the stupidity of war, its causes and the political decisions that resulted in so much suffering.

"*The pity of war, the pity war distilled...*" she mused.

"From *Strange Meeting.*"

"Yes."

They looked at each other.

"*Now men will go content with what we spoiled, or discontent, boil bloody and be spilled...*" said Alastair quietly.

"*They will be swift with the swiftness of the tigress. None will break ranks, though nations trek from progress,*" continued Katherine.

"How appropriate that is for the world today."

"Isn't it just? The next lines are so profound: '*Courage was mine and I had mystery, wisdom was mine and I had mastery...*'"

"*...to miss the march of this retreating world into vain citadels that are not walled.*"

"Wilfred Owen was such a visionary."

"As well as the greatest of the war poets."

"More so than Sassoon?" asked Katherine.

"I think so," replied Alastair. "Owen's loss was tragic."

"Just a week before the Armistice…"

The sun had dipped below the horizon and John came into the dining room to light the lamps, disturbing them, breaking the spell.

Once he had gone, Katherine asked, "So, what did you do next, after Jutland?"

"Well," replied Alastair, trying to gather his thoughts. "In June 1917, when *Colossus* went for a refit, Dudley was assigned to develop a new department at the Admiralty devoted to forward planning. He requested that I go with him. So, I worked for several months with him in London helping to set up this new venture and remaining with him after his appointment as Assistant Director of Plans.

"We had always worked well together and he was most upset when, having recommended me for promotion to lieutenant-commander, on receiving this, I was sent back to sea in January 1918 instead of going with him when he became Director of Operations. I was put in charge of *H.M.S. Freesia*, an *Azalea* class sloop. After a period of patrolling the Dover Straits and a refit to disguise my ship as a mercantile vessel, we were sent out into the Atlantic in July 1918 operating as a Q-ship, searching for submarines and protecting merchant shipping."

"What's a Q-ship?"

"A wolf in sheep's clothing."

Katherine regarded him quizzically and Alastair chuckled. "A ship used to lure submarines to the surface by pretending to be a severely damaged unarmed merchant vessel. When the submarine closed in for the kill, we'd hoist the white ensign and roll out our guns."

"Did you sink any submarines?"

"Two."

"Any medals?"

"Oh, the usual campaign medals." Alastair seemed evasive.

"And?" asked Katherine, sensing more.

"The Victoria Cross."

For the second time that day she could not help but be impressed. "You've kept this very quiet. How did you...?"

"Oh, for this and that."

"Please tell me."

Alastair took a deep breath and began. "We were in our usual position, lagging behind at the back of the convoy – to make us an easier target – when we came under attack by a submarine. We created an oil slick, made smoke and sent out a 'panic party' of crew members in two rowing boats to make the submarine captain think we were badly damaged and sinking. Then, when the submarine came to the surface for the kill, I ordered *Freesia* to open fire. After disabling the submarine's gun and destroying the conning tower, we took off her crew and sank her. My second-in-command thought I should have just sunk her with all hands, but I didn't agree."

"Yours was the more humane but riskier strategy to carry out, nonetheless."

"Certainly, but I had my conscience to answer to. A few weeks later, we were hit by a torpedo ourselves and *Freesia* really was badly damaged and in danger of sinking. Fires were raging and I kept exhorting the crew to greater efforts, doing as much as I could by going round the ship to find ways of keeping her afloat. Then, as if we didn't have enough to contend with, the submarine surfaced for the kill. It was either him or us and..." he hesitated, "...we got there first. We rescued the survivors, who were brought on board and who, to their credit, helped us put the fires out. By some miracle we survived and with surprisingly few losses, limped home to Portsmouth. Anyway, for all that, they gave me a medal."

Both were silent after he had finished speaking: Alastair, lost in the events of twenty years previously, and Katherine, looking anew at this unassuming man sitting opposite her, seeing the pain of difficult decisions etched on his face; moved by his courage and compassion in the face of adversity.

"I haven't spoken of this to anyone since," he said at length, as they went upstairs to their rooms, "not even Alex."

"It isn't something that one can do lightly."

"No."

"Thank you for sharing it with me."

"'s ur beatha."

Katherine nodded and kissed him lightly on the cheek, an acknowledgement of her affection and their friendship.

After they had said goodnight and he was in his room, Alastair stood for a long time looking out of the window at the gathering twilight, deep in thought, re-living their conversation and her kiss, wanting to be with her still.

This in itself was nothing new but the increasing intensity was, despite having recognized and accepted the depth of his feelings for Katherine a long time ago. He had always tried to keep their full extent hidden from her but in such a way that would neither damage nor change the natural rapport and affection they felt for each other, nor disturb the ease of their companionship.

It was a fine line along which to travel.

A few days before they were due to leave, Donald took them in the post-bus as far as he could along the track leading to old Mrs Gilgarry's cottage, situated at the head of a remote but beautiful glen. They were obliged to travel the rest of the way on foot as the track was only suitable for walking or on horseback. Alastair volunteered to take Mrs Gilgarry's post and bring any letters back with him at the conclusion of their visit.

Donald was suitably grateful. "Aye, that'll be a great help as I've lots to deliver elsewhere. I'll come and collect ye from here in about six hours. Mind yereselves now. The going's quite awkward in places, remember."

"It's only a couple of miles. I used to be able to do it easily," remarked Katherine.

"Aye, but ye were not carrying a wee bairn then," replied Donald.

"That's very true."

"Well, take care now and I'll see ye later." With that, Donald drove away carefully, nursing the only motorized vehicle on Cairnmor along the bumpy track.

They set off at a steady speed; Alastair carrying a knapsack containing water, a Thermos flask and some sandwiches.

It was more difficult than Katherine had anticipated. Notwithstanding her pregnancy, the year in London had considerably reduced her fitness. While living on Cairnmor, she had walked everywhere and would think nothing of covering five or six miles in a day. Now, they had to rest frequently and Alastair could not help but be anxious.

However, it was a lovely day, warm in the sunshine with a gentle refreshing breeze and on their last breather, perched high up on an outcrop of rock, they drank the remainder of the tea from the flask and admired the spectacular scenery – the vibrant green of the sheltered glen with the breath-taking elevation of the mountains behind and the sea spread out before them, the waves sparkling and dancing in the sun.

"I think that Cairnmor is the most beautiful place I have ever been to," remarked Alastair, breathing deeply. "I could come and live here quite easily."

"But not without Alex and me!" responded Katherine quickly. "Whither thou goest... remember?"

Alastair smiled at her. "How could I forget?" he replied. "We'll have to work hard on Alex, though."

"I know."

"Perhaps he will one day," he said over-optimistically.

"Yes, and if pigs could fly…"

"That could be interesting. What would happen if they lost momentum?"

"Then we would no longer say, 'It's raining cats and dogs'. Instead, it would be, 'It's raining pigs' and we'd all be flattened."

"Perhaps someone will invent a special sort of protective umbrella…!"

"We're beginning to sound like Michael."

"It must be catching."

Katherine laughed and Alastair knew that, to him, in that moment, she had never looked so lovely. Taking a deep breath, he packed up the knapsack and helped Katherine to her feet before leading the way carefully along the narrow path.

When they arrived at Mrs Gilgarry's croft, they were greeted with great surprise and delight by the venerable old lady.

"*Ciamar a tha sibh?*" asked Alastair, enquiring after her health, once they had shaken hands.

"*Tha gu math, tapadh leibh,*" Mrs Gilgarry replying that she was well and thanking him. "*Tha i brèagha an-duigh.*"

"It is indeed a lovely day, Mrs Gilgarry. We have enjoyed the sun on our walk," replied Alastair, continuing the conversation in Gaelic.

"Your Gaelic is coming on, young man."

"Thank you. I have been studying it again recently."

"You speak it well."

"I have a good teacher."

"Indeed you do. Now, how is this teacher of yours?" she asked, turning to Katherine. "You look well, girl."

"I feel well."

"But you are quite large."

"Yes."

"May I?"

"Of course."

Mrs Gilgarry felt Katherine's abdomen and stomach, gently probing this way and that. Then the old lady stopped and regarded her, a broad smile on her face. "Katie, Katie. These doctors in England cannot be any good!"

"Why?" Katherine said, slightly alarmed.

"Because, my large little one, you are expecting twins!"

Katherine was so surprised that she had to sit down. "Are you sure?"

"Do you doubt my abilities?"

"Of course not. I'm just taken aback that's all!"

"There is no doubt." The old lady chuckled and gave a shocked but grateful Katherine advice on the best food to eat, how to cope with carrying two babies during her pregnancy and how to keep herself fit and well so that she would be able to deal with whatever difficulties may arise at the birth.

They remained for a few hours with Mrs Gilgarry, enjoying her acerbic comments and wry sense of humour, and sharing her mid-day meal – a nourishing

36

stew, generously laced with home-grown herbs and supplemented with home-made bread, from the pot that was inevitably to be found bubbling away on the lead-blackened range.

Occasionally, Katherine was obliged to interpret for Alastair, but his understanding of Gaelic had increased to the extent that he was now quite good at working out what was being said, even though he could not always find the words to speak the language fluently in response. However, after spending a fortnight on Cairnmor, his Gaelic-speaking abilities had improved in direct proportion to Katherine's shorthand while they had been in Glasgow.

Alastair remarked upon this a few days later as they began the long journey home to London, standing next to each other by the railings of the steamer, watching Lochaberdale and the figures of Michael and Mary gradually disappear into the distance.

When she didn't reply immediately, Alastair glanced at her and his heart went out to her as she looked forlornly at the rapidly receding island that she loved so much.

"We must make sure we come back as soon as we can," he said gently.

Katherine could only nod, not trusting herself to speak, her eyes filling with tears which spilled over and down her cheeks, despite her best efforts to control them. The pain of leaving her home was great and Alastair comforted her, holding her close, giving her his handkerchief with which to wipe away her tears.

"Alex will be home in a few days," he said, in an effort to lift her spirits.

She gave a watery smile and nodded. "It will be good to see him," she managed to say. "Though I have really enjoyed these past few weeks. I thank you for that, so much."

"I'm so glad, so have I, and you're very welcome."

"No Gaelic?"

"Not this time."

He smiled at her with warmth and affection, and she put her arm through his and laid her head on his shoulder until Cairnmor had faded from sight.

CHAPTER 6

Melbourne, Australia
June, 1939

Everyone was saying that war was inevitable. It would happen. Even her mother thought so. And where Great Britain went, Australia would follow.

Rachel Curtis slowed her horse to a walking pace while she considered the matter. She agreed with the general opinion. And she wanted to be involved. She had already made enquiries from the authorities about joining the army as a doctor and serving abroad, but had been met with a blunt refusal.

"You can be a doctor in the army at home, but we don't take women doctors into a war zone. If you want to go, it'll have to be as a nurse. You'll have to re-train as well," they had said.

Nothing she could say had made any difference. It was ridiculous and a bitter pill to swallow. Her professional pride had been hurt.

For as long as she could remember, Rachel had wanted to be a doctor. She had always loved hospitals; she had always loved helping people.

It first began when she was twelve. She fell off her horse and broke a bone in her foot. As the injury was to the growth plate, she had to have an operation because the doctors were concerned that if it didn't set correctly, then she could end up walking with a limp when she was older.

Rachel found the whole experience fascinating. She plagued the doctors and nurses with all sorts of questions. She wanted to know about the bones in her foot, her ankle, her leg. What did they do? What was this one called? Why were the proper names all in Latin? She wanted to know about X-rays and plaster and diagnostics until, in desperation, one of the doctors gave her a medical encyclopaedia to read. This kept her quiet for a while but then it prompted even more questions. The doctors were impressed with her understanding and said if she studied hard, then one day she might be able to become a doctor. This remark made a big impression on her. They gave her the encyclopaedia as a present when she left the hospital.

Apart from the pain, she had thoroughly enjoyed her stay. She loved the atmosphere, the calm orderliness of it and the nurses' shoes that squeaked on the highly-polished floors of the wards. Once she was out of hospital, she didn't mind having crutches and whizzed about on them, making her mother anxious and cross.

After this there was no question about her future profession. She worked hard at school, gaining top marks in her leaving certificate and a place at the prestigious Melbourne University to study medicine.

Her parents were ordinary folk and proud of their clever daughter. They took on extra jobs to help pay for her studies. Her mother made dresses for the rich people in the evening and took in washing during the day. Her father did painting and decorating and washed cars. Rachel took a job as a waitress and between them, they paid her way through Medical School where she worked hard and graduated top of her year.

She became an intern, then a resident at the Royal Melbourne Hospital, singled out as a doctor of great skill and potential. She applied for and was accepted on a training programme to specialize in Tropical Medicine and in her final year, her thesis on malaria gained her moderate fame in learned medical journals. Mentored by one of the hospital's leading surgeons and specialists in the field, Mr Richard Amery, she was invited to give lectures at the University.

It was during a coffee break after one of these that she first met Matthew Harper. He was an equine vet and shared her passion for horses. They quickly got to know each other and became good friends.

It was a rewarding time for Rachel. Having been very single-minded and focused on her studies and her job, she now allowed herself something of a social life. Matt took her to dances and the cinema. Friendship quickly developed into romance; romance into a serious relationship. For two years, they went out with each other.

Then one day, Matt asked Rachel to marry him. With great difficulty, she refused. Although she loved him, she wasn't ready for a husband and family just yet – she was still too much involved with her work. Their relationship cooled somewhat after this but they still continued to see each other fairly regularly.

In her professional life, Rachel gained an enviable reputation for success, both in diagnosis and treatment. There were tough times along the way, all doctors had to contend with that. However, Rachel had always felt great responsibility for her patients and became distraught when she was unable to save the life of one particular patient whom she had been treating for a number of years, professional detachment having turned to friendship over time. Rachel blamed herself but there was no blame attached to her. Everyone said that she had kept this patient alive longer than any other doctor could have done.

Nonetheless, she took it very hard and deemed herself to be a failure. Matt tried to console her, but she pushed him away, putting up protective barriers and blocking out her emotions, not wanting to feel the pain of loss. In the process, she kept distancing herself from him, alienating him, until eventually he could take no more and ended the relationship. It hit her harder than she dared admit, even to herself.

After this, Rachel threw herself into her work with even more determination and drive. Her parents, with whom she got on well, worried about her. She often looked thin and pale. She had never had many friends, even in childhood, preferring to spend time in the library studying rather than playing tag with other youngsters outside. Now, as an adult, she had few people to whom she was close. Her friendships were either work-related or at the livery stables where she kept her horse. There was very little time for socializing, given the long hours she worked.

She began taking long, solitary rides into the hills around Melbourne, carrying her sketch pad, watercolour paints and brushes in the saddle bags. Rachel would sit for hours painting the beautiful scenery around her home. She found it therapeutic. It was her escape from the pressures of the hospital; from the emotional demands of her job.

She saved up her holidays and travelled all over Australia finding spectacular scenery to paint. If she went into the outback, her parents were frantic with worry. What if... crocodiles, dangerous spiders, poisonous plants, snakes, hostile tribes...? But Rachel always came home safely, refreshed and ready to get on with her life.

There were no more serious boyfriends after Matthew. She was not beautiful in the classical sense but her face was full of character and her thick auburn hair glossy and distinctive. She had worn glasses as a child but as she grew into adolescence, she discovered to her great satisfaction that she no longer needed them.

Men found her attractive, certainly, but also too preoccupied with her work and for some, her manner was too forthright. She, for her part, found too many of them obsessed with settling down, searching for a suitable wife to look after home and children. She knew she wasn't that sort of material. Or perhaps she just hadn't met the right man...

In 1938, Rachel celebrated her thirtieth birthday. Well, her parents held a birthday party for her, to which came grandparents, uncles, aunts, cousins. She endured it rather than enjoyed it but went along graciously with the whole thing as it gave pleasure to her mum and dad, who had worked so hard to give her a good education and whom she loved dearly, and to whom she owed a great debt.

Her aunts and cousins wanted to know why she wasn't married yet. She deflected their questions politely but firmly and breathed a sigh of relief when it was all over and she could escape back to her flat and her own company.

Now, Rachel skilfully guided her horse down the wooded slope. There was a stream at the bottom and she dismounted, removed the bridle, and allowed her horse to graze on its grassy bank, while she sat beside the clear bubbling water, staring at it, lost in thought.

What should she do? She knew she wanted to serve her country. She could best do that as a doctor. She was absolutely convinced of that. Perhaps the authorities could be persuaded to change their minds. It wouldn't be the first time she had argued a case strongly on a matter of principle. Nor would it be the last. She had to try.

But if war came, go she would – as a nurse or a doctor. Her specialism would be needed if European War turned to World War. Yes, she would go and if it had to be as a nurse, then she would make sure she was the best one in the service.

Replacing the bridle, she mounted her horse and set off for home, her decision made.

CHAPTER 7

Maybury
June, 1939

Katherine woke up with a start. She had been dreaming. Vividly.

She was here in Mistley House, going into early labour all over again. Even now, a year later, she could recall the pain and difficulties and the long drawn out process of the birth because the second of her precious babies was the wrong way round. It took a great deal of effort on the part of the doctor and mid-wife to deliver the infant safely, not to mention her own part in the process.

She had longed for the skill of Mrs Gilgarry at that moment, instinctively knowing that the elderly lady, with her vast experience of delivering babies on Cairnmor, would have provided the reassurance and encouragement that Katherine had so desperately needed. If only Alex could have been with her – she had needed love and support – but men were excluded by convention from the birth-room and, having been nurtured in a remote community as well as being a lady of independent spirit, she had felt frustrated by this.

Gently, she eased herself out of bed so as not to awaken her sleeping husband, gathered up her dressing-gown and padded silently on bare feet into the nursery, where the twins were fast asleep, both lying on their backs, peaceful and content, a mirror image of each other, their little hands thrown up either side of their heads.

Katherine knelt down between the two cots, marvelling at her children. Today, they were exactly a year old. This afternoon would be the first birthday party for Rupert Alastair Alexander and Mhairi Anna Katherine, named in honour of her own parents, whom she had only come to know so recently and who, along with Alastair, had become the proud grandparents of her beautiful, alert and intelligent babies.

Rupert, or 'Roo' as Alex nicknamed him to distinguish him from his grandfather, had been born first and it had been little Mhairi, known by her second name of Anna to avoid confusion with her grandmother (they hadn't been able to agree on a shortened version of Mhairi) who had been the one to cause all the difficulties. However, the circumstances of her birth had made no difference to her and she was as energetic as her brother, the two of them inseparable, even at this tender age.

Remarkably, it was when Katherine or, rarely, Alex played the piano for them that they would stop whatever they were doing and listen intently, gravitating towards whoever was playing the instrument, holding onto a convenient parental leg (which made pedalling complicated) and gazing up at the performer with rapt attention.

Alastair thought this to be quite remarkable and predicted a musical career for both of them. He was often to be found sitting at the piano with one or both children on his lap allowing them to 'play' the notes with their little fists to their hearts' content.

Mr and Mrs Thringle were delighted with the new arrivals and the housekeeper and her husband were doting yet practical guardians. Nothing was ever too much trouble for them where the twins were concerned yet Mrs Thringle didn't spoil them or tolerate any nonsense. Never over-protective, she allowed the twins to discover things for themselves and to explore both the London and Maybury houses (within reason). Once the children were crawling and therefore mobile, Mr Thringle had made wooden stair gates to keep them safe.

Because of this support, Katherine could enjoy her offspring while having time to rest, the latter being initially important after the exhausting circumstances of the twins' delivery. She knew that they were always surrounded by loving, caring adults whom she could trust absolutely and she felt no need to employ a nanny. This had caused a great deal of bad feeling between herself and Alex as, at first, he had been adamant that they should. However, she had remained firm and eventually, he had let the matter drop and returned to his work.

Katherine was woken from her reverie by the sound of the bedroom door opening and closing quietly. Alex came into the room and knelt down beside his wife, he too admiring their sleeping babies.

"Are they all right? Did you have to come into them?" he whispered.

"No, they're fine. I just had a dream which woke me up, that was all, and I wanted to see them. It doesn't seem possible that a year has gone by already, does it?"

"No, I can't quite believe it. Is everything in hand for this afternoon's festivities?"

"Yes. Lily's train is arriving at about eleven, so she should be here in time for lunch; Mary and Mrs Thringle are organizing the food; Rupert and Alastair are going up to London to collect great-grandmama Emily straight after breakfast and Thomas the Butler is coming back with them as well. Which leaves you and Michael free as you have a great deal of catching up to do with each other." Katherine raised an eyebrow at her husband. "I think he's a bit upset that you haven't answered his letters."

"I've been busy." Alex was defensive. "You know that if I've been preparing a legal document or been in court all day or had consecutive days of research and meetings to do, the last thing I want at the end of a long day is more writing."

"And Michael understands that only too well. But he is your best friend and does need to hear from you from time to time."

Alex had the grace to look embarrassed. "I know. I'll try to make it up to him while he and Mary are staying with us. We'll take Sam out for a walk later this morning. I haven't done that for a long time in any case."

"Poor old dog. The arthritis in his back leg has been causing him one or two problems recently."

"So Dad told me the other day. I hadn't realized it was quite so bad. I gather he's been rubbing it with liniment."

"And that seems to be helping, though he remarked that Sam could do with one of Mrs Gilgarry's herbal remedies!"

Alex was surprised. "I didn't know she treated pets."

"Mrs Gilgarry has a herbal remedy for just about any ailment, whether human or animal. And they work too."

The children began to stir. Anna woke first, treating her parents to one of the gorgeous smiles that came so readily to her features and never failed to melt the heart of even the sternest of souls. Rupert was not far behind, holding out his arms to be picked up, which Katherine did unhesitatingly, while Alex lifted Anna out of her cot.

Breakfast was a convivial affair with the morning unfolding as planned and after lunch, apart from Mrs Thringle (busy in the kitchen), Sam (asleep in his basket), Lady Mathieson (taking an afternoon nap in her room) and Thomas (asleep while pretending to read the newspaper in the sitting room), everyone else went for a walk along the tow-path beside the Thames and out into the countryside.

Little Rupert and Anna sat up in their pram, one at either end, each of them held in place by a safety harness and protected from the warm June sunshine by a sun-shade. They took a lively interest in their surroundings as the pram bounced along the path on its soft suspension, smiling at whoever came over to them and tickled their toes or spoke to them.

The party stopped after a mile or so and spread blankets on the grass, where they all sat, allowing the twins to have a break from the constraints of the pram. Rupert and Anna had a wonderful time, crawling from person to person, being lifted high in the air amid much giggling, or being shown a leaf or a twig or a wild flower.

Enjoying the sun, Alastair lay back on the grass, enabling little Rupert to crawl over him, while Katherine sprinkled her son with flowers left over from a daisy chain that she had been making for Anna. Her father-in-law looked up at her and smiled and she smiled back.

"It's a good job there are no trenches in this field," observed Michael. "Otherwise one or either of the children would most likely disappear into a big, black hole. And," he added, addressing Anna while he tickled her and made her laugh, "it would probably be you, young lady, who would be the one to fall in!"

"Och, don't!" said Mary. "It doesn't bear thinking about. But it was *such* a shock when we first arrived to see trenches being dug in Hyde Park and sandbags round so many of the buildings. I hadn't realized there were so many preparations underway."

"And they're going to take most of the paintings away from the National Gallery," chimed in Lily, Alex's sister, home from boarding school for the weekend especially for the party. "But, I suppose, it's better for the paintings to be safe."

"Since Rupert and I arrived last week, I've found *everything* that's been going on difficult to contend with," added Mhairi, barely able to hold back the deep anxiety she had been feeling throughout this, their latest visit to England. "I was so upset to see so many men walking around in army uniform or wearing T.A. or A.R.P. badges on their lapels. And as for that leaflet that you showed me, Katherine…"

"You mean the one advising householders on the '*choice and preparation of refuge rooms in houses*' and the construction of shelters in gardens?"

"Yes, that's the one. And the precautions to take against fire and how the air-raid warden system will operate. And as for the gas masks... Oh, my dear, I worry for all of you."

Katherine put her arm around her mother's shoulder in a gesture of comfort, although she too was anxious. "The worst thing, though, is that they haven't yet come up with a suitable gas mask for children under four. The authorities seem to be very slow in responding to this particular need. Goodness knows how long it's going to take them."

"Where does the world go from here, I wonder?" asked Rupert senior. "We have much written in the papers and spoken of in the newsreels back home, but it seems remote from the reality you folks have over here, although if Britain goes to war, Canada will follow."

"Who can tell where it will lead?" replied Alex. "All I know is that Germany is now established in Czechoslovakia. If you ask me it was a great mistake to allow Hitler into Sudetenland in the first place. So much for the Munich Agreement, and Neville Chamberlain and his shuttle diplomacy, not to mention David Lloyd George's futile efforts..."

"None of the things either of them did was futile, Alex. You have to give them both credit for trying so hard to keep '*peace in our time*', as Mr Chamberlain so aptly put it," interjected Katherine.

"I do, but it wasn't a particularly honourable peace, was it? The Czechs weren't party to the negotiations when the fate of their country was being decided by the French, Germans, Italians and us. Once the Sudeten Germans had been given self-determination within the boundaries of the Third Reich, the rest of the country was vulnerable to attack. The Munich Agreement amounted to nothing more than an invitation for Hitler to invade, which he did in March, of course," declared Alex.

"But at the time, it appeared that Mr Chamberlain had persuaded Hitler to accept negotiation and consultation as a means of solving problems in the future." Katherine had admired the British Prime Minister's efforts for peace the previous September.

"And subsequent events have proved that the document they both signed was not worth the paper it was written on. Hitler is not a man who keeps his word."

"Well, the whole of *this* country, including you, was *very* relieved that war had been averted and very grateful to Mr Chamberlain back then. And it did buy us more time to improve Britain's defences," Katherine reminded him.

"But we're still behind in producing the armaments necessary to fight a major war. Chamberlain keeps dragging his heels. Surely, the fact that the Germans have now occupied that Baltic seaport – what's it called?"

"Memel," said Alastair. He raised himself up into a sitting position, placing little Rupert on his lap, whereupon Anna crawled over to join her brother. "Part of Lithuania."

"Yes, that's it. Surely that, and the fact that they are demanding the return of Danzig from Poland so that Hitler has further access to the Baltic Sea for his warships; surely that should say to our government that they need to get a move on and get the production lines moving. Goodness knows, there's no shortage of labour with all the unemployment that still exists."

"Provided the unions allow non-union unskilled labour to be used," observed Alastair.

"The unions will see sense eventually, I would think. They're daft if they don't," said Michael.

"Well, the Prime Minister has guaranteed Polish independence, so he must have some faith in this country's ability to stand up to Hitler should the need arise," said Katherine.

"And what will we fight with? Words?" Alex had settled into his stride. "Hitler won't allow a flimsy guarantee to stand in the way of his imperial ambitions. No, the only way to stop this megalomaniac is to defeat him militarily. And we've been caught napping."

"I'm afraid all that is so," agreed Alastair sadly. "However, to be fair, Neville Chamberlain has increased the defence budget radically this year. And, as far as the navy is concerned, an accelerated ship-building programme has been in place since 1936, which is just as well, as Hitler has now declared that he's no longer going to be bound by the Anglo-German Naval Agreement."

"Which is?" asked Katherine.

"A treaty signed in 1935 which regulated the size of the *Kriegsmarine* in relation to that of the Royal Navy."

Both babies were silent and still on Alastair's lap, as though they somehow sensed the serious atmosphere. Reflectively, Katherine held out a finger to each of them, which they took in their little hands.

"Which is yet another headache for the government," continued Alex. "Also, now that Italy has occupied Albania, signed the Pact of Steel with Germany – and if you add to that the League of Nations having totally lost any credibility – we have a recipe for disaster. War is inevitable, and sooner rather than later, I should think."

"Then we shall all have to decide what we do whenever that time comes," said Rupert, looking around the assembled family group, fearing for all of them.

"Unless of course, it's decided for us. Then, we won't have any say in the matter," replied his son-in-law.

"Well, for the moment," said Michael, thinking that Alex had said quite enough, "we only have to decide upon the immediate needs of these two adorable children. So, before we all depress ourselves totally with doom and gloom, I suggest that we pop them back in their pram and take them home so that they, and we, can enjoy their first birthday party unaffected by events over which we, unfortunately, have no control."

And with that practical statement, Michael lifted and secured the twins back into their places, whereupon they fell asleep on the journey home, lulled by the gentle motion of the pram.

This, of course, meant that they were lively and into everything for the rest of the day.

The birthday celebration itself was a special family gathering, with presents, party food, much laughter and Alastair filming the whole occasion with his cine camera. The twins were obviously too young to appreciate the significance of all this activity, but the adults enjoyed themselves enormously.

For a while at least, the imminent prospect of war was pushed into the background and the family focused on being together. Great-grandmama Emily sat back observing the proceedings, while her loyal and long-standing butler, Thomas, now accepted as a family friend, watched with joy as the grandchildren of his beloved Rupert took centre-stage.

After Katherine and Mary had bathed the children and they were settled and asleep, the two friends came downstairs to the sitting room, where tea and coffee had been served.

"Have you managed to find a replacement for yourself at the Academy?" asked Alex of Rupert, as Katherine handed round the chosen beverages to each of their guests, Mrs Thringle having retired for the evening.

Rupert shook his head. "Not yet. Mhairi tells me I'm way too fussy and she doubts whether I'll find anyone who comes up to the ridiculously high expectations that I apparently have." Rupert smiled at his wife.

Mhairi nodded. "We shall be old and decrepit before Rupert is ready to relinquish the Academy," she said, patting his hand. "And that's the truth of it. If war really is looming on the horizon, as it would seem to be, he will find it even more difficult to let go," she added.

"Yes, I shall have to stay on, otherwise there is the danger of the whole thing collapsing. We'll lose a great many students to conscription, if that were to be introduced, and I need to be there, at the helm, to preserve what we have for the future."

"What about Mathieson's?" asked Katherine. "You won't be able to come across every few months to board meetings, as you have been doing, if there's a war – it would be far too dangerous."

"Mathieson's is in good hands with Laurence Hart to look after it. I have no worries for the future there," replied her father. "Besides, I imagine we'll still be able to communicate by cable and letter. And Alastair will be on hand to resolve any legal problems.

"Well, you will be much safer in Canada," observed Katherine.

"Yes," said Mhairi, "although we shall miss the twins growing up if war should come and last any length of time." She hesitated and then added, "You and the children could always come and join us."

"That would be a very good idea actually," said Alex, mindful of potential plans to evacuate mothers and children from London in the event of all-out war. "I think you should go."

Katherine experienced a moment of panic which was echoed in Alastair's quickly concealed expression. She shook her head. "No. Much as I'd love to be with you," she said, taking her mother's hands in hers, "my place is here." She regarded Alex's impassive expression for a moment before seeking the reassurance she needed from her father-in-law, which he gave, easing her anxiety.

"And Michael, what will you do?" asked Rupert.

"He's a farmer. That's a reserved occupation," interjected Mary firmly. "He's not going anywhere!"

"Yes, dear," said her husband, wishing with all his heart that it could be so.

"Alex?"

"I don't know." He and Katherine had not yet discussed this, both preferring to avoid the subject.

She spoke quickly, anxiously, to her husband. "Please don't do anything hasty or rash. You're thirty, you're too old to be called up…"

"At the moment…"

"And long may it stay that way. Just as Mary wants for Michael, if you don't have to, *please* don't volunteer for one of the Services. Be an A.R.P. warden or something instead." The whole conversation was making Katherine nervous.

"I'll see," was all he would promise.

"Alastair?" asked Rupert, moving on quickly.

It took a few seconds for him to reply as he overcame a sudden, deep-seated fear for his son, but when he did so, his voice was steady: "Well, I shall definitely be called up as I'm a regular member of the R.N.V.R. But with my age…"

"Fifty isn't that old, Daddy," interrupted Lily, who had been silent but listening intently up to this point.

"Even though you have said very kindly that fifty isn't that old, for which observation I thank you," continued Alastair, regarding his daughter affectionately, "with my age, and the type of courses I've been selected for over the past few years, I think it's likely to be a staff posting of some kind. I certainly hope so."

"So do we all," said Rupert, echoing everyone's feelings.

"I'd like to come to Canada and study at your Music Academy," announced Lily, unexpectedly.

"You would?" Rupert was taken by surprise and looked at Alastair enquiringly.

"This is the first I've heard of it…" He regarded Lily quizzically.

"Hearing all of you talk about war and what you might do, the idea just came to me. Think about it, Daddy! I'd be safe, you wouldn't have to be anxious about me – you'll have enough to worry about if Alex should join up, as well as with what you'll be doing. I'll be eighteen in October." She paused and then added, "That is, if Rupert thinks I'm good enough."

"Good enough!" exclaimed Katherine's father. "You'd be one of the top students at any conservatoire!"

"Oh! Thank you, Rupert," she replied happily, without recourse to false modesty. "I'd love to go anyway. It's always sounded just the sort of place where I know I'd enjoy studying even if there isn't a war. I can't imagine why I never considered it before," she added.

She looked pleadingly at her father, who turned inquiringly to Rupert and Mhairi.

"She could stay with us," said Mhairi, who had always felt that Lily needed mothering, as Roberta, Lily's own mother and Alastair's wife, had walked out on the family a few years previously.

Rupert nodded in agreement. "That would be just fine. We have a flat at the top of the house where you could live and be totally independent, if you wished. But what about school?" he asked.

"I'm a year ahead of my age, so I'm taking my final exams this month. I have a place at the Royal College of Music for September, but I'm sure that could be deferred for a year or so. And who knows what might happen? If there's a war, they might close it for the duration anyway. Please think about it, Daddy," she added persuasively. "It's perfect. Rupert gets an extra student, you don't have to worry about me and I get to study at a highly prestigious music academy that has one of the top flautists in Canada on the staff."

"Rupert and I will discuss it," said her father firmly.

"Of course. But if it's a 'yes'," replied his incorrigible daughter, "I could go to Halifax with Rupert and Mhairi when they go home at the end of August. Please, Daddy." She was good at wheedling.

He narrowed his eyes at her. "There's a lot to talk about – visas, for example."

"Oh, I'm used to giving advice and handling all that kind of thing for overseas students," said Mhairi. "It's not a huge problem, especially if they come from Britain. With your consent, I can set things in motion before we leave."

"Well," said Alex. "I personally think you should go." He turned to Mhairi and Rupert. "Are you sure you want to put up with this unholy terror for a year or so?"

"We can cope," said Rupert, smiling, knowing how fond Mhairi was of Lily, and delighted to have someone of Lily's exceptional musical abilities at his institution. "We'll look after her."

"I know that." Alastair took a deep breath. "Looks like it's settled then," he conceded.

"Thank you, Daddy, thank you so much." She hugged and kissed her father. "It is the right decision."

He smiled with love at his precious daughter. "Yes, I do believe it is," he said, experiencing a huge sense of relief, knowing that he had been worried about what would happen to Lily in the event of a serious armed conflict in Europe.

And so it was, that when Rupert and Mhairi returned to Canada towards the end of July, a month earlier than planned because of the worsening international situation, Lily went with them to begin a new chapter of her life in Halifax, Nova Scotia: a sojourn that was to bring her great fulfilment professionally, and an unexpected joy in her personal circumstances that would last a lifetime.

However, she left behind a country on the brink of war, where life would never be the same again.

CHAPTER 8

London/Maybury
August-September, 1939

At the beginning of August the newspapers were full of reports of German troops massing on the Polish border, and planning continued at home in Britain for a war that no one wanted and even at this late stage, everyone hoped could be avoided.

The Reserve Fleet was mobilized and inspected by King George VI on 9th August and Lieutenant-Commander Alastair Stewart V.C., R.N.V.R. found himself once more on active service. He had no idea where he would be sent or what he would be doing; all he knew was that he was required to report to the Admiralty building in Whitehall that morning for an interview.

Alex had already wished his father the best of luck before he left for Lord Cameron's Chambers and when Alastair came down the stairs, Katherine was there to say good-bye to him.

She had seen him in uniform many times but, on this particular occasion, she thought how distinguished he looked with the slightly squared 'Nelson's loop' and three gold stripes – two wavy with a straight narrow one in between – on the sleeves of his jacket, together with the line of colourful campaign ribbons above his left breast pocket.

Katherine wondered why someone as attractive as Alastair had not been snapped up by some female admirer a long time ago. The merest thought of this possibility caused her a moment of jealousy but before she had time to dwell on its existence, it was replaced almost immediately with anxiety for his welfare and what might befall him.

For this was not just a regular weekend exercise, but active service under wartime conditions. Bravely, she smiled at him as he reached the bottom of the stairs.

"Don't worry," he said, seeking to allay her fears as well as his own. "I'm sure everything will be fine." He turned to the mirror in the hallway and adjusted the knot of his tie, smoothing the collar of his starched white shirt and putting on his Royal Navy officer's peaked cap with its distinctive badge of golden laurel leaves surrounding an anchor with a king's crown above.

He turned back to her and gave her a hug, each needing the reassurance of the other. Alastair smiled and released her gently. "Now, I must go, otherwise I shall be late and that would never do. It will be all right – you'll see."

He regarded her for a moment and after that, he was gone.

Katherine spent the day restlessly. The twins were fractious with both of them teething again. In the afternoon, when she saw that their mother had had enough, Mrs Thringle, a veritable saint, offered to take them out for a walk in the pram, a suggestion that was accepted by Katherine with great relief.

In the event, Mrs Thringle thoroughly enjoyed her excursion in the warm sunshine, pacifying her little charges in the process, and found socializing with the nannies and children in Kensington Gardens a refreshing change. She resolved to do this more often.

Left to her own devices, Katherine considered going to meet Alex at his Chambers, should he be there, but was reluctant to disturb him if he was busy. She knew there would be no point in going to the Royal Courts of Justice, as she had often done before the children were born, because his robes were still hanging up in his wardrobe.

The day was too sunny to stay indoors and Katherine began to walk in the direction of South Kensington. On an impulse, as she reached the underground station, she took the District and Circle Line as far as St James' Park and followed one of the paths that led her onto Horse Guards Parade. There before her, in all its imposing grandeur, was the Admiralty building, drawing her in with its wonderful architecture and symmetry.

Katherine stood for a while, wondering how Alastair was faring, and was about to continue with her walk, when she saw him coming out of a doorway off to the left, looking very pleased with himself. He stopped in total surprise when he saw her and immediately came over to her, a broad smile lighting his face.

"What on earth are you doing here?" he exclaimed, delighted to see her.

She explained about the twins and Mrs Thringle. "But what about you?" she said. "You look like the cat that's got the cream!"

Alastair laughed. "Sorry. I can't help it. Look, let's find somewhere for a cup of tea."

"Sounds good. But please tell me what happened. Don't keep me in suspense!"

They set off into the park with the intention of going on to Piccadilly but as it was such a beautiful day, they lingered under the cool green of the trees.

"To start with, I have a staff posting."

"Oh, I'm so glad, that is *such* a relief." Katherine tucked her hand into his arm as they continued companionably along the path.

"But it gets better. Do you remember my talking about the captain I served under on *H.M.S. Colossus*?"

Katherine thought for a moment. "You mean Dudley Pound?"

"The very same."

"Go on."

"Well, he's now an admiral and a couple of months ago was made First Sea Lord."

"First Sea Lord?"

"The professional head of the Royal Navy and chief naval advisor to the government. The post is also known as the C.N.S., the Chief of Naval Staff."

"He's done well, then!"

"Yes, and deservedly so. He's an excellent staff officer. Now, as soon as he found out when I was to be recalled for active service, he requested that I work with him at the Admiralty."

"I would imagine that an admiral's request is rather on a par with an order?"

"Absolutely. My interview with him today was to outline my role. My particular brief is a roving one and will cover all departments at the Admiralty, getting to grips with each of their functions and advising Dudley on how things are going. His 'ear to the ground' you might say."

Katherine laughed. "More like spying on your colleagues."

"I'm not like that." Alastair pretended to be huffy.

"I know. You're far too nice."

"Ha, that's what you think!"

"It's what I know."

They grinned at each other.

"Mm. Well. Anyway, it's similar to what he and I did in the last war; not exactly setting up something new as we did then, but more finding out, in a helpful sort of way, where there could be improvements and greater efficiency."

"You'll have to tread a very fine line in diplomacy."

"Yes, especially as there will be career naval officers of higher rank with whom I shall be dealing."

"Aye, but you're canny; they won't even know they're being assessed," observed Katherine astutely.

Alastair was not slow to pick this up. "Perhaps you ought to work with me. We'd make a great team!"

"If only! Bit difficult with two young children. And I'd have to join the Royal Navy first."

"Yes, not to do so would present a bit of an obstacle!"

There was an ice-cream seller at the intersection of two paths, so Alastair bought a couple of cornets, both he and Katherine agreeing that something cold in the shade of the trees was preferable to a cup of hot tea in a stuffy tea-shop. They sat down on a nearby bench opposite the lake to enjoy their ices.

"So, is there anything else?" asked Katherine knowingly.

"Am I that obvious?"

"To me you are."

"That's my line."

"And now I've borrowed it. You can have it back whenever you like."

"Thank you." They smiled at each other again. "Well, once everything is sorted out to Dudley's satisfaction, his intention is that I should be made assistant director of a department, such as Operations or Plans or Logistics." With boyish pride, he added, "That will also mean a promotion to Commander."

"That's wonderful. I'm really pleased for you."

"I still can't believe it somehow. It's current Royal Navy policy that a staff job lasts for about two years and then the officer concerned is sent back to sea. The reasoning behind this is that each post will have fresh ideas and a fresh approach when the new appointment is made, and the latest combat experience can be brought to bear in administration. Which is eminently sensible. But, Dudley is determined to keep me on land and so, after two years in one particular post, his intention is that I'll be sent to various naval dockyards such as Rosyth, Portsmouth or Chatham and be able to keep him up to date by experiencing what's going on first-hand round the country. And then I shall return for staff duties at the Admiralty."

"He's really given this some thought, hasn't he?" said Katherine, impressed by the fact that Alastair was held in such high regard.

"Yes."

"Clever man. You must be relieved."

"I must admit that I am. Should there actually be a war, I was not looking forward to being out at sea again in actual combat, though I would have gone if I'd had to, of course."

"And bravely too."

Alastair smiled, not quite knowing how to respond to this praise. *"Tapadh leibh,"* was all he could think of.

"'s ur beatha."

They reached home to find that Alex had not yet arrived, so Alastair changed out of his uniform and until tea they amused the twins, both of whom seemed to have recovered their good spirits.

Alex returned just before supper was served and was delighted when Alastair recounted his news. The evening took on something of a celebration but behind the laughter, the three of them knew that the serious issues were just beginning.

How right they were.

On 25th August, the German Foreign Minister, Ribbentrop, signed a non-aggression pact with Stalin, delivering a 'bombshell' to the British Prime Minister and Government, who had felt the talks that *they* had been having in Moscow were nearing a satisfactory agreement. In the papers, it was reported that Anthony Eden, the former Foreign Secretary, had spoken of the situation *'being as grave and perilous as any this country has faced at any time in her history'*.

That same day, Britain and Poland signed the Treaty of Mutual Assistance and the British Ambassador in Berlin reminded Hitler that the British and French guarantees to Poland remained in place.

For the Bank Holiday, the public were advised to take their gas masks with them, and notices were pasted up on billboards and other highly visible places giving details of air-raid warnings and signals of gas attacks.

There were also rehearsals for the evacuation of children from the capital. However, Katherine was adamant that she would only leave London and go to live in Maybury if the situation became extremely dangerous or intolerable. She would not risk the children's lives, nor her own, but neither did she want to leave behind either Alex or Alastair.

Katherine and Mrs Thringle bought black-out material and made curtains for the windows in both Cornwallis Gardens and Mistley House. Alex and Alastair criss-crossed tape over the windows, as every householder had been advised to do, in order to minimize flying glass if the panes should be blown out by bomb blast or shell fire. They kitted out the deep, protective cellar of the London house as an air-raid shelter while in the garden at Mistley House, Mr Thringle constructed an Anderson shelter, which Alex had managed to procure with some difficulty as not many were yet available to buy. Being on a higher income, the family did not qualify for a free one (which were plentiful) and therefore had to purchase one of their own.

On 1st September, millions of children were evacuated all over the country from cities deemed vulnerable to air attack and, without any declaration of war, German troops marched into Poland.

On 2nd September, Parliament voted that five million pounds would be made immediately available for the '*defence of the realm*' and that the Military Training Act would be extended, so that all men aged eighteen to forty-one would be liable for military service.

Alexander Stewart, barrister, holder of a first-class honours degree in Jurisprudence (Law) from Oxford University, did not wish to wait for his call-up papers and, wanting to choose which Service he went into, immediately travelled to the nearest recruitment office, where he volunteered for the Royal Air Force.

When he came home that evening and told Katherine what he had done, she burst into tears, although she understood his reasoning and did her best to support him in his action. Inwardly, however, she was overwhelmed by a deep sense of unease from which she could not escape. She spoke of it to neither Alex nor Alastair, knowing that both were going through enough emotional stress as it was: Alex, as he began to comprehend the reality of what he had just done and Alastair, filled with anxiety that his beloved son might be placed in mortal danger.

Sunday, 3rd September was another lovely summer's day, sunny and warm. The family were at Mistley House, as was their custom, for the weekend. The twins were having a late morning nap, having been awake since before dawn.

All was quiet and peaceful. A gentle breeze ruffled the curtains at the open French doors of the sitting room. The comforting drone of bees and the dulcet sounds of birdsong could be heard in the garden. In the distance, someone was mowing a lawn.

At fifteen minutes after eleven o'clock, the reassuring sound of mowing ceased and the whole nation stopped whatever they were doing to listen to a broadcast by the Prime Minister, speaking from the Cabinet Room at Number Ten, Downing Street.

They gathered in sombre mood – Alex and Katherine, Alastair, Mr and Mrs Thringle – all seated around the wireless.

'*This morning the British Ambassador in Berlin handed the German Government a final note stating that unless we hear from them by eleven o'clock that they were prepared at once to withdraw their troops from Poland, a state of war would exist between us. I have to tell you now that no such undertaking has been received and that consequently, this country is at war with Germany.*'

Perched on the arm of the sofa, next to the easy chair where her father-in-law was sitting, her eyes full of tears, Katherine put her arm around Alex and he leaned his head against her shoulder. She gave her hand to Alastair, who took it in his.

They listened, still and silent, to the quiet, halting voice of Neville Chamberlain reaching out to the nation on whose behalf he had tried for so long and so hard to win peace by diplomacy and thus avoid conflict.

'You can imagine what a bitter blow it is to me that all my long struggle to win peace has failed. Yet I cannot believe that there is anything more or anything different that I could have done and that would have been more successful.'

However, even the Prime Minister finally had to admit that the only way of stopping Hitler – a man, he said, who would never give up his practice of using force to gain his will, whose word could not be trusted and from whom no people or country could feel safe – was by the use of force. Britain had to come to Poland's aid.

'We have a clear conscience – we have done all that any country could do to establish peace... And now that we have resolved to finish it, I know that you will play your part with calmness and courage.

'At such a moment as this, the assurances of support which we have received from the Empire are a source of profound encouragement to us.

'When I have finished speaking, certain detailed announcements will be made on behalf of the government. Give these your closest attention. The government have made plans under which it will be possible to carry on the work of the nation in the days of stress and strain that may be ahead...

'Now may God bless you all. May He defend the right. For it is evil things that we shall be fighting against – brute force, bad faith, injustice, oppression and persecution – and against them I am certain that right will prevail.'

Suddenly, the world had become a very different place.

CHAPTER 9

The Phoney War (1)
October, 1939

After his initial assessment, Alex was sent to R.A.F. Cranwell in Lincolnshire for officer training. Originally, he wanted to be a pilot but the selection board, at this early stage in the war, considered that at thirty years old his age was against him, even though his eyesight was perfect and his physical response times fell easily within the required parameters. Instead, with his qualifications and experience as a barrister, he was earmarked for the legal department after graduation.

The newly selected recruits were divided into 'flights' and, in common with the rest of the intake, Alex underwent a vigorous physical fitness regime, leadership training, rifle and machine gun practice. He learned about the R.A.F. and its traditions, aeroplane recognition, how an Air Station functioned and the distinct roles of the three arms of the Service: Fighter Command (responsible for the aerial defence of Great Britain), Bomber Command (with its wide-ranging, offensive capability) and finally, Coastal Command (which operated flying boats, sea-planes and shore-based aircraft, often working in conjunction with the Royal Navy).

The recruits spent hours marching up and down the parade ground, drilled by a no-nonsense, mind-numbingly loud flight-sergeant, as well as having their kit and rooms frequently inspected for neatness and cleanliness. They also had to prove themselves capable of using their initiative, of being able to make decisions under pressure and most importantly, leading by example. They were taught that the Service, fellow officers, and the men for whom an officer has responsibility came first above all else. Leadership potential and the knowledge required by junior officers were scrutinized and assessed and the training was, by necessity, of a very high standard.

It took time to become used to the drills, discipline and general rough and tumble of Service life, but for Alex and many of his fellow recruits, it was familiar territory, almost as though they were back at boarding school or university again. There was the same camaraderie, although on a more intense level because of the circumstances of their training.

In addition, there were formal dinners to attend with serving officers, from whom much could be learned, in the splendid setting of the dining room at Cranwell. Alex was accustomed to this setup, having throughout his professional life been part of the dining tradition at Middle Temple, one of the four ancient Inns of Court to which all barristers had to belong.

Despite his earlier preference, Alex was relieved that he would be returning to the law, albeit from a different perspective. It was a profession he loved and he felt it would make the best use of his civilian skills as a member of the armed forces.

His letters home were relatively cheerful and full of all that he was doing. With his appreciation of architecture, he much admired the main building and its surroundings:

It is a relatively modern design, he wrote to Katherine. *Completed in 1933 and opened in 1934, reminiscent in style of a Wren building, with the same elegance. In front of the college is the parade ground (where it feels like we spend most of our life) and a large circle of grass known as the Orange (presumably because it's round) which is flanked on each side by an avenue of lime trees.*

Because of the national emergency, the course length has been shortened and at its conclusion, we shall sit our final exams. If I pass these and all the other things we've been doing, then I'll graduate as a flight-lieutenant. You'll be able to come and see me as there is to be a graduation parade, even in wartime. Traditions remain important and I think this is right. After all, isn't this part of what we shall be fighting for? When I've graduated from here, it'll be off to law school (again!).

Once more, you and I are apart, my darling. We have spent so much of the time we have known each other in different places – before we were married, always waiting for the next letter or meeting, and then afterwards, not seeing much of each other with my working such long hours.

I know we've been pulling in different directions recently and I'm sorry for that. Maybe it takes something like this to make me realize that it has become all too easy for me to take you and the children for granted without truly appreciating what I have.

Kiss the children for me and say that Daddy misses them very much; but not as much as he misses their Mummy...

All my love and more,

Alex xx

P.S. Tell Dad I'll be writing soon – oh and by the way, I've actually written to Michael. I haven't received a reply yet. I wonder what he's up to? Have you heard anything?

Eventually, Alex did hear from Michael. He discovered that his friend had joined the Royal Army Medical Corps and was in very deep trouble with Mary:

I'm afraid I am persona non grata at the moment with my lady wife, he wrote. *I don't think I've ever experienced such a severe scolding and almost wish I hadn't done the deed if I'd thought it was going to cause this much upset.*

I understand her point of view, though. She's lost one husband and is terrified she'll lose me as well. And I can't reassure her on that one because none of us knows what lies ahead. But what's a fellow to do? I would have got my call-up papers eventually because, whether Mary likes it or not, our croft is regarded as a smallholding. I am not classed as a farmer in a reserved occupation and therefore able to be exempt from military service.

56

I joined up on the spur of the moment. I was in Edinburgh to sit my final Scottish Bar exams, and there they were: a Territorial Army unit doing their recruiting bit. So, I signed up and now I'm in the R.A.M.C. Just as you did, I wanted to choose what I did. I don't want to carry arms, but I do want to help people. And this seemed the best way of going about it.

Mary is calming down a bit now, and she's beginning to accept my point of view and forgive me. But I've never seen anyone so angry and I'm sorry to have been the cause of it. Under normal circumstances, I wouldn't have intentionally caused her any distress for the world. We share everything together; we're with each other all day and every day working on the croft. We are so happy and close in our married life. It will be an impossibly hard thing to be apart.

Michael's final sentences caused Alex to reflect on his own marriage. Could he honestly say the same thing? Were he and Katherine as close as they used to be? Did they share everything in the same way as Michael and Mary? Indeed, had they ever really done so?

He thought about the increasing number of arguments and subsequent strained silences, the many times during their short married life when he had, by necessity, been totally involved with his work and she with the children (especially as she had refused to employ a nanny) so that they never seemed to be in the same place at the same time – mentally or physically.

However, given his present situation, there was nothing he could do to rectify this for the moment, so he dismissed the thought, finished reading Michael's letter and resumed his studying.

Meanwhile in London, Katherine was also contemplating the state of her relationship with Alex, having just received Mary's letter – a combination of love, anger and anguish concerning Michael, with a very real fear for his safety.

Did she and Alex still share the same companionship that they had done before they were married or during the heady early days when they were all working on the Appeal at the House of Lords? Did the fact that even before he joined the R.A.F., she had hardly ever seen him, and that he had rarely spent time with the children, mean anything? Because if she objected to his preoccupation or lack of attention to Rupert and Anna, it had inevitably caused a row, something she found deeply upsetting.

Sensibly, though, acknowledging that she couldn't do anything at the moment to try to change the situation, Katherine came to the conclusion that every marriage was different and that even after two years, she was still learning to adjust the balance in her own. Inevitably, the war would mean yet another adaptation for her and Alex to make, the same as many thousands of other couples.

She surmised that they had experienced nothing of what might be to come.

Once war had been declared, it was expected that air raids would begin immediately, with all the accompanying terror that had been predicted. However, as soon as it became apparent that this was not going to be the case, there was a collective sense of relief among the general population and a certain feeling of anti-climax.

The first few months of the war were dubbed the 'phoney war' and 'bore war' by the newspapers and on the surface at least, it appeared as though nothing was happening; even many thousands of evacuated children were allowed to return home.

However, there was one theatre of war where a great deal had been happening from the outset, where a continuous battle of attrition was being fought that would have serious repercussions for those at home: the Atlantic.

Just six hours after war was declared, the *S.S. Athenia*, a passenger liner carrying mainly women and children being evacuated to Canada, was torpedoed and sunk. After the horror and outrage at this barbaric act had subsided, it became obvious that Germany was pursuing a policy of unrestricted submarine warfare on vital British maritime trade, just as they had done in the last war.

Because of this, Alastair's role at the Admiralty changed from that originally envisaged, and owing to his Q-ship experience in 1918, he was assigned to the Operations Department, becoming deeply involved in the re-establishment of the convoy system to protect the vulnerable unarmed merchantmen from the submarines.

In the evenings, whenever he was home early enough, Alastair would spend time with Katherine, talking to her about the situation in the Atlantic, finding release in her sympathy and understanding. He enjoyed playing with the children (who called him 'Daddad', being unable to pronounce 'Granddad' properly as yet) seeking solace in their company and an escape in their childish needs from the deplorable pressures of the day.

His work was demanding and stressful and he found the terrible losses suffered by the British merchant fleet particularly hard to bear, for the enemy was enjoying supremacy in the Atlantic at this, the very beginning of the war.

"But surely that will change?" said Katherine, appalled at the nightmarish scenario Alastair presented.

"One would hope so. We can't continue to sustain shipping losses on this scale for too long. We rely on the supplies from America to keep the country going. Organizing and protecting the convoys is uppermost in everyone's minds."

"Have we had any successes?"

"Yes, we've sunk one or two U-boats, but they've sunk more of our ships. Someone came up with the bright idea of sending escort destroyers to hunt for the submarines. I pointed out that this wouldn't work as submarines tend to be elusive and to send off the escort ships on what amounts to a fool's errand would leave the convoys at greater risk of attack. This is exactly what has happened. Then someone else decided to form hunting groups based around an aircraft carrier. Again, I said that any submarine spotted from the air will have dived by the time the warships arrive. Also, once the aircraft carriers have lost their protective screen, they'll be more vulnerable to attack. Unfortunately, I've been proved right. *H.M.S. Ark Royal* only escaped destruction by a U-boat because the torpedoes detonated too soon. And the enemy actually sank *H.M.S. Courageous*, another aircraft carrier, last week. The ideas are ridiculous and the consequences are disastrous."

"Why don't they listen to you? I mean, you've so much knowledge of tactics." It seemed obvious to Katherine. "Why can't anyone else see it?"

"Well, I've asked for a meeting with Dudley tomorrow to see what can be done. Unfortunately, there are some highly prejudiced R.N. types who see me, a mere R.N.V.R., as an interloper. It's terribly frustrating because we should all be doing what's best for the Service and the country. I tell you, I'm none too popular at the moment because I keep plugging away at it, trying to make them see sense."

Alastair looked down at Rupert who had fallen asleep on his lap while he and Katherine had been talking, with Anna nodding off to sleep on the carpet, her head comically propped up on her doll.

So, they carried both children upstairs and as they tucked them in bed for the night, Alastair said, "I'm sorry to bore you with all of this."

"You're not," responded Katherine quickly. "*Please* don't apologize. And don't stop talking to me about it. You need to share all this with someone and I'd rather it was me. Besides which, I do want to know what you're doing."

"Thank you. It's good to be able to discuss it freely and openly with you." Alastair trusted her implicitly and in Alex's absence, without contravening the Secret Service Act, she had become his confidante, his closest companion.

Unwittingly, she smiled at him in such a way that made him want to take her in his arms – his need of comfort and consolation after the vicissitudes of the day was unbearably strong. However, with a gentle, genuinely warm smile that revealed nothing of his desire, he bid her goodnight, went upstairs to his bedroom and closed the door.

As Alastair undressed, hanging up his uniform with reflective care before climbing into bed, the thought crossed his mind that it was his misfortune to fall in love with unobtainable women – first Roberta, who had never returned his feelings, despite thirty years of marriage – and now Katherine, his daughter-in-law.

With the latter, there was no place for guilt in the direction of his thoughts, as their realization was an impossibility and his acceptance of this unquestioning. His feelings were an unfortunate occurrence and one that he could do nothing about other than ensure that his behaviour towards Katherine was beyond reproach.

Nonetheless, he chastised himself for his folly and fell asleep dreaming of both women – one dream being infinitely more pleasant than the other.

Alex graduated at the end of November and Katherine and Alastair travelled to R.A.F. Cranwell for the parade.

For both of them, there was a strange mixture of pride in his achievement and anxiety for what the future might hold as they watched Alex marching with the other cadets. He looked very handsome in his uniform but for Katherine, on a personal level, it was yet another adjustment she had to make with regard to her husband. On a national level, although it wasn't easy, she had enough belief in the cause for which the country was fighting to realize it was vital that every man fulfilled his duty. Yet she wondered what the extent of that 'duty' might be in Alex's case.

There were sandwiches and tea after the presentation ceremony and Katherine and Alastair were introduced to the man who would be Alex's new senior officer, Wing Commander Guy Beaumont.

"I'm delighted to meet you both," he said, shaking hands with them. "I shall be working closely with Flight-Lieutenant Stewart during the next stage of his training."

"What will that entail?" asked Katherine, stirring her tea and deftly balancing cake, plate and napkin while she did so.

"The study of discipline and criminal law, operations law and administrative law."

"And then?" This was what she really wanted to know.

"Once fully qualified in all of these, your husband, Mrs Stewart, will become a member of the Air Force Department of the Judge Advocate General undertaking a wide variety of Service work – such as, among other things, giving legal advice to R.A.F. Commands and Formations, Station Commanders and R.A.F. Police. If he is posted overseas…" (Katherine's heart missed several beats) "…he could also advise and assist Service personnel and their families in connection with any civil legal problems, though that will become increasingly unlikely given the current situation when all dependents are being advised to come home. Again, if overseas, he may well be asked to take on a liaison role with the army and the navy, depending upon where he is stationed, of course. This role becomes especially relevant in wartime and your husband would be particularly suited to the task."

Katherine was silent, a shiver of fear going down her spine.

To hide his own concern, Alastair said, "It sounds like an enormous amount of work."

"Yes, it is and it's a fascinating mixture. But we're very lucky to have someone of Flight-Lieutenant Stewart's calibre in the R.A.F. As a 'legal eagle', he will also give lectures and presentations to Service personnel on Air Force Law, the Law of Armed Conflict and other specialist legal topics."

Katherine smiled, despite her concerns. "He'll enjoy that," she said, and Alex grinned at her.

"Now, if you'll excuse me, there are other people that I must see. It was very nice to meet you both." They shook hands once again and Wing Commander Beaumont moved across to the other side of the room to speak to a group of officers assembled by the doorway.

"How are the children?" asked Alex after a slightly awkward silence.

"Into everything!" replied Katherine brightly. "But wonderful."

"Teething again…" added Alastair.

"And keeping us up at night…"

"Mrs Thringle can't get over the fact that Rupert keeps producing teeth in pairs. But it seems perfectly natural for him to do so."

"While Anna's just come along singly. But she makes more fuss about it."

"What about things at home generally? How are you managing?" said Alex.

"Aye, we're all fine," replied Katherine, intentionally trying to sound positive.

"But there's talk of introducing food rationing if we carry on losing ships at the rate we are in the Atlantic," added Alastair. "Bob has been digging up the back garden in London so that he can grow vegetables there in the spring, as well as extending the vegetable patch at Mistley House."

Katherine smiled. "Mrs Thringle wants to keep a cow and some chickens."

"I said that would be a good idea, but maybe not in London!"

And Alastair recounted that he had had great difficulty in dissuading their housekeeper from that particular venture and had suggested that the house in Maybury would be a more appropriate alternative. But he had appreciated and praised her resourcefulness.

Their exchange of news was intentionally light; conversation that concealed deeper anxiety. Even though he understood this, Alex felt out of touch with his former life, as so much had changed for him. He sensed that their worlds were diverging but, for the moment, there was little he could do to prevent that happening. He could offer nothing more than a small glimmer of reassurance by saying: "Well, when I've completed my legal training, I'll be given some leave after it's been decided where to send me. So we'll be together for a while at least."

"We've missed you. *I've* missed you, and so have the children. It'll be good to have you at home," said Katherine.

"I know."

He smiled and put his arm around her and they kissed goodbye. Alastair put his hand on his son's shoulder and then gave him a hug as they turned to leave, the affection between them very strong.

With great reluctance, Alastair and Katherine left R.A.F. Cranwell, returning to London to resume their life: he to the Admiralty during the day and she at home, with both of them caring for the children in the evening whenever he was free.

But overshadowing their mutual pleasure in Rupert and Anna and each other's company, the spectre of Alex's unknown posting was never far away.

CHAPTER 10

The Phoney War (2)
December, 1939 - April, 1940

The winter of 1939-1940 was recognized as the worst for forty-five years. Deep snow, burst pipes and a shortage of coal added to the trials and tribulations of the blackout, during which more people were injured than in the war itself up to that point. The railway networks ground to a halt and in many places, the army were required to dig out the frozen trains as not even snow ploughs attached to powerful steam locomotives could cut through some of the drifts.

Snow began to fall in London just before Christmas and one afternoon, Katherine took the twins out to see the winter spectacle in Trafalgar Square, a rare and beautiful sight. Even the lions at the base of Nelson's column were covered in white.

"Snow lions," she told the twins solemnly.

"Blub, blub," replied Anna, pointing to the pigeons.

Katherine laughed and watched Rupert catching snowflakes with his little mittened hands, patting them until they melted, then holding them out again so that more could settle.

"'no!" he exclaimed excitedly, "'no!"

They stayed until Katherine began to feel chilled. Ever watchful as to whether the children were warm enough, she tucked the blanket closer around them as they sat in the large collapsible double pushchair, an ingenious device constructed by Bob Thringle to accommodate the twins who were now too big for the pram.

She crossed the road towards Admiralty Arch, intending to walk through St James' Park and catch a taxi near Buckingham Palace to take them home.

On the way, she passed several news-stands – some with banner headlines proclaiming the disquiet among the general population that Britain had gone to war to help Poland, but seemed to be making no effort to assist the unfortunate Poles in their distress and hour of need.

Others were full of the Royal Navy's first tangible success with the attack on the German pocket battleship *Graf Spee*, which had been harassing and sinking merchant shipping in the South Atlantic since the start of hostilities. Katherine stopped to buy one of the newspapers so that she and Alastair could talk about the Battle of the River Plate when he came home from the Admiralty.

Discussing his work in depth was something they did now as a matter of course, and Katherine looked forward to it, finding herself increasingly drawn into Royal Navy events and matters. She valued their conversations, and it would be refreshing to be able to talk about something positive that evening. It was exciting to see a much needed British success after a strange three months of anticipation and nothingness at home, and bad news from the Atlantic.

Katherine tucked the newspaper into the bag slung over the back of the pushchair and made her way to the park. The snow was still falling, but the sun emerged briefly to create a magical white and gold wonderland.

This the children greeted at first with silent appreciation, their eyes wide with amazement as their mother pointed out things to look at, then with giggles as the snowflakes landed on their eyelashes and noses, and finally with shouts of pleasure, as Katherine released them from the pushchair and they jumped around in the snow, making footprints and throwing it at each other.

Rupert opened his mouth and tried to eat the snow as it fell and Anna mischievously pushed him over so that he landed face first on the grass. After Rupert had got over the shock, he retaliated by pushing her over, which she didn't like at all. So, before their fun was spoiled by an escalating argument and, not allowing them to become too wet so they got cold on the way home, Katherine, amid howls of protest, put her red-cheeked and sparkly-eyed children back into the pushchair and eventually found a taxi to take them home.

Once there, Mrs Thringle took Anna and Rupert off for a warm bath before supper and Katherine sat down with a cup of tea to read the newspaper. The *Graf Spee* had been a prime target for a very long time and the ship had been found by three Royal Navy cruisers who engaged her just off the mouth of the River Plate, causing enough damage to warrant her taking shelter in Montevideo Harbour in neutral Uruguay for repairs.

"Yes," said Alastair, as they drank coffee in the sitting room after supper later that evening. "It's incredibly good news. Everyone at the Admiralty is just buzzing with it. It's caused quite a sensation all over the world. Apparently, some clever subterfuge and diplomatic manoeuvring went on by the British to persuade the Germans that a large fleet of warships was waiting for the *Graf Spee* to leave and that she would certainly be destroyed once she got outside the harbour. So, her captain took, what must have been for him, the painful decision to scuttle her. The explosion could be heard several miles away, apparently, and the battleship took three days to sink."

"In front of the world's press too!" Katherine was amazed.

"I know." Alastair chuckled. "The crews of the *Exeter*, *Ajax* and *Achilles* will be national heroes now. You realize Edward was on board the *Exeter*?"

"Of course! I'd forgotten." They had little contact with Alastair's adopted eldest son and seldom mentioned him. "Roberta will be very proud," she observed, thinking of Alastair's estranged wife, now living with Edward's real father, with whom she had had a love affair when she was a young woman.

Alastair took a deep breath. "Hm, I have no doubt of that. And if she'd been here," he added, unable to conceal a certain degree of bitterness, "I've no doubt also that she would be rubbing my nose in the fact that it is *his* son who is the hero and that *my* son is sitting at some desk supposedly doing nothing."

"I can imagine!" agreed Katherine, having encountered Roberta when she first met Alex's family. She regarded Alastair thoughtfully for a moment and then said, "Would you rather Alex *were* out there in the front line?"

"Of course not. Long may he continue to do what he is doing. Modern warfare requires planners, logistical supporters and lawyers as well as fighting men. It's a complicated business in this day and age, but everyone is essential in the broad scheme of things, every contribution is necessary, no matter how small. It's the pulling together that's the most important thing and that is ultimately what will see this country through. When the chips are down, as a nation, we're quite good at that." He paused then added, "How about you? Would you rather see Alex in a combat situation?"

"No. I have no delusions about heroism, nor do I have any of the patriotic fervour that women had in the last war. I just want him to be safe. And you. I couldn't bear to lose either of you."

"You won't."

"You sound very sure?"

"I am."

"How so?"

"I don't know. Just a feeling, I suppose. But unfortunately, there are no guarantees in this business. I could be wrong."

"I do hope that you're not." Before they became too maudlin by dwelling on gloomy speculation, Katherine changed the subject. "I had a letter from Mary today. She's beside herself with worry, feeling completely out of it on Cairnmor. She's waiting weeks for Michael's letters to arrive now that he's in France with the B.E.F., and frustrated at not knowing what's happening in the outside world until the newspapers arrive each Saturday on *Lochfoyle*."

"I imagine she's not alone in that," said Alastair with feeling, thinking of Robbie and John in particular.

"I wish I could do something to help her."

"Why not invite her to stay with us? It would be company for you, extra help for Mrs Thringle and seems to be the obvious solution. She could come as soon as the weather allows."

"That's a wonderful idea! Thank you so much, Alastair." And Katherine hugged him in a moment of pure effusive gratitude and spontaneous affection. "I'll go and write to her now. Oh, and I'll make sure she brings her ration books and identity card with her. We'll need the extra coupons with an extra mouth to feed."

She went out of the room, leaving Alastair smiling at her obvious pleasure and taking a few deeps breaths of his own to still his rapidly beating heart after her embrace.

Almost immediately after he had finished training, Michael found himself in France with the Territorial Army, who had been sent across as reinforcement for the British Expeditionary Force. Together with the French Army, they dug themselves in along the Franco-Belgian border, expecting and preparing for the static trench warfare experienced in 1914-1918 – a policy that many commentators thought outmoded and short-sighted. However, it was the French military hierarchy who had been given overall control of the Allied troops and the British, for the moment at least, had to adhere to this strategy, even if their senior officers could not see the sense of it.

Along with his compatriots, Michael endured appalling conditions. It was a terrible winter on the continent as well as at home, with blizzards, ice and freezing temperatures. On the military front, apart from a few minor skirmishes, nothing happened. The Allies were waiting for the enemy to make the first move and the Germans, well, the Germans were just… waiting… having missed an early opportunity to attack soon after the outbreak of war.

Morale in many of the French troops was not very high but, on the whole, among the British it was. They showed their fortitude by making the most of difficult circumstances and creating their own diversions and amusements to take their minds away from the obvious discomforts.

Football matches were the favourite. These kept everyone occupied and over the months became highly competitive, with a league table being formed and teams vying with each other for supremacy. However, most of them remained, in the best British tradition, fairly *ad hoc*.

We played yet another match today, Michael wrote home to Mary, one day in the middle of January. *I found myself in goal this time – me! Can you imagine it? You know how hopeless my coordination can be. Dancing, yes. Catching round objects? No. I'm a complete butterfingers!*

Anyway, the match started well – I didn't see the ball at all. All the action was going on up the other end of the pitch. So I just leaned nonchalantly against the goalpost and watched them all going hell-for-leather up the other end. Getting into a right old mess they were. My team's forwards were obviously doing a great job, as the ball kept coming back to the centre line (well, the dirty brown smudge in the snow) and going back up the other end.

Eventually, I got a bit cold, so I walked up and down in front of my goal, flapping my arms and stamping my feet (or rather what had become blocks of ice with boots on). I was so absorbed in this that I failed to notice that the players were all coming towards me in a rush (there's no finesse in some of these games). Taken completely by surprise, at the last minute, I managed to catch the ball by diving into the snow and was proclaimed a hero for my one save. I never saw the ball again after that. At the end of the match, everyone else came off the pitch soaking wet, freezing cold and covered in mud. I was pristine, apart from soggy gloves and a swath of mud down one side of my greatcoat.

The chaps are great out here. We Brits keep ourselves going with humour and endless drills. Fortunately, there's not much for us medics to do apart from a twisted ankle or two and looking out for incipient frostbite.

If the enemy attacked tomorrow, they wouldn't get far as we're highly trained to the peak of efficiency and ready for anything (I'm serious). Still, it's better that they don't attack, I can hear you saying, and I have to agree.

But, my darling, I miss you more than I can say. I look out for your wonderful letters and your dear handwriting and read each one endlessly. If your dad is willing to look after our croft, then do by all means go and stay with Katherine and Alastair in London as they have suggested. I'll feel closer to you as well – and we won't have to wait forever for our letters. I know you don't like the city, but I'd feel happier if you were there.

Write soon, my darling. All my love,
Your very own, Michael.

With Michael's encouragement and the wholehearted support of her parents, Mary arrived towards the end of February, when the extreme weather had begun to ease, pleased to have her time occupied and to be with Katherine again. She did feel closer to her beloved husband and appreciated living in a place where she knew exactly what was going on, almost as soon as it happened – not that there was very much occurring in France, the theatre of war that concerned her most.

It was not easy to make the adjustment to living in London, though. Food rationing had been introduced at the beginning of January and prices of foodstuffs went up as they became scarcer. Queuing for daily or weekly shopping became the norm – a miserable experience in the severe weather which returned for a while and which prompted Mary to remark, with wry humour, that for once, life was easier on Cairnmor and that perhaps she should have stayed where she was!

However, Mrs Thringle was grateful for the extra pair of hands at home and extra 'queuing feet', as she christened them, and Katherine was very glad of her company. The children revelled in the extra attention and Mary knew that she had made the right decision.

Once Alex had passed all his exams at R.A.F. Wittershall and was fully qualified as a legal eagle, he was attached to the Colonial Office in London for a further period of training with the Colonial Legal Service, thus adding to his expertise and further expanding his portfolio of civil, criminal and R.A.F. law, before being seconded to them as an R.A.F. liaison officer.

The family breathed a collective sigh of relief and Katherine was overjoyed to have her husband, and likewise for Alastair to have his son, back home with them. She couldn't quite believe her luck that he was in London and although he was busy, she treasured the times when they were able to be together.

Yet as time passed, Alex became increasingly restless, preoccupied and distant. Katherine could not pinpoint the reason for this, nor would he say when she asked him. Just glad to have him living at home, she did not question him too closely and tried to accept that this was how things were, doing her best to put aside her growing disappointment and frustration.

One evening towards the end of April, Alex was exceptionally quiet throughout supper; withdrawn almost. Once they were alone in the sitting room, he took Katherine aside and held her close. When they drew apart, he did not speak immediately but just looked at her with pain in his eyes, filling her with a terrible sense of dread. Eventually, he began to speak.

"There's no easy way to say this…" he began falteringly, losing his words.

"Then you had better just say it." This was unbearable. She wished Alastair were there with them.

"I've been given my posting."

"Where?" she said quietly.

"Singapore."

"Dear God." Katherine sat down, her eyes filling with tears. "So far away. When do you go?"

"At the end of this month. But it's all right," he added, lifting the tone of his voice.

"Is it?" How could he possibly say that it was all right?

"Yes. It's regarded as a safe posting."

"How?" She failed to understand.

"There's nothing going on in the Far East…"

"At the moment…"

"And they do call it 'Fortress Singapore'."

"Do they?"

"Yes."

Something in his manner prompted her to ask, "Did you have any choice in this?"

Alex was silent. Katherine looked at him, fear and sudden anger making her tremble. He went to comfort her, but she stopped him.

She repeated her question. "Did you?"

"I was offered this posting to begin with," he replied hesitantly. "However, the possibility of visiting R.A.F. stations in this country in an advisory legal capacity was also mentioned but…"

"So there was a choice?"

"Sort of… in a manner of speaking…" His reply was evasive.

"Why did you not discuss it with me?"

"I didn't want to cause you unnecessary anxiety. Please understand my position."

"I'm trying to." But it was hard, oh so hard. "How long have you known?"

"Ever since my secondment to the Colonial Office. I've been working with them on all legal matters concerning Singapore and the Straits Settlements."

"In preparation for this posting…"

"Partly, yes."

"So you've known this all the time you've been at home and you never said a word?"

"Yes."

"How could you do that?!" she exclaimed. How could he have made such a momentous decision and then kept it from her? Why did he not share with her the concerns and fears he must have had?

"As I said before, I didn't want to worry you," said Alex. "Besides, it would have hung over us and spoilt our time together before I had to go away. I was only thinking of you."

"Really?"

She was his wife, they loved each other. She was not a child to be cosseted and protected from reality or have decisions made without her. It insulted her intelligence and showed little appreciation of her capacity for understanding. This was not the first time it had happened, nor would it be the last, she supposed. Providing he came back safely, of course.

She shuddered.

"If, as you say, you had my best interests at heart, did you not consider the fact that to go abroad will cause me far greater anxiety? And what about the children? They need their father. You were given an opportunity that will be given to very few in this war – to accept a posting at home. Why could you not see that? Why did you not speak to me?"

"Perhaps it was because I knew you would try to persuade me to stay."

"You're damn right I would." Katherine was angry now.

"You can come with me."

His words stopped her in her tracks. "What do you mean?"

"What I said. Singapore is a place where wives of Service personnel can go."

"Even in war-time?" Katherine was sceptical.

"Yes. As I said, it's regarded as a safe posting. There are no immediate threats and it is well defended."

Both Katherine and Alex were so absorbed in their argument that they failed to notice Alastair standing in the doorway. He chose that moment to speak.

"Singapore itself may be safe at the moment, but the journey there will be fraught with danger. From submarines and surface warships, not to mention mines and attacks from the air. I do not see how you could ask anyone to go with you. Any ship is vulnerable. So are you in undertaking that journey."

Alex swung round in surprise. "How long have you been there, Dad?"

"Long enough. You left the door open. It was impossible not to hear what was being said."

Katherine's anger subsided as he spoke and she experienced a sense of relief in his presence. "Did you know?" she asked him.

"No. Though I'm sure Alex had his reasons for keeping it to himself." Alastair looked directly at his son. "But, like Katherine, what I fail to understand is, if you really did have the choice, why did you not accept the posting at home? You can serve the war effort just as efficiently as a staff member here if, as in your case, there is no requirement of direct involvement in combat."

"I was needed," replied Alex, with heartfelt simplicity. "It is my duty to serve where I am needed. There are many legal problems out there, civilian and military, and the Colonial Office and the R.A.F. felt *I* was best suited to the task. It means immediate promotion to Squadron Leader on taking up the post."

The atmosphere hung heavily with the weight of the argument, with fear of the unknown, with fear of what was to come. However, the decision had been made and could not be rescinded. They could only prepare themselves for the inevitable parting, something which happened all too soon.

They travelled to Southampton, where Alex was to embark, along with other R.A.F. personnel, aboard a troop ship, part of a convoy headed for India and the Far East.

Alastair hugged his son, both of them struggling to contain their feelings. Katherine and Alex clung to each other, a parting more painful than either of them had ever experienced before; neither of them knowing when they would meet again; not daring to think that they might never do so.

As Alex turned to go, he said to his father, "Look after my family for me."

"Yes," replied Alastair, his voice hoarse with emotion. "Look after yourself, my son."

Alex nodded, not trusting himself to speak again.

Then he was gone, striding up the gangplank, his kitbag on his shoulder; his blue uniform distinctive.

They waved until the ship had left the dock and they could no longer see him. As they moved away from the quayside, Alastair put his arms round Katherine and she rested her forehead on his shoulder as though by this small act of comfort they could ward off the terrible feeling of uncertainty that Alex's departure had created in both of them.

The sense of foreboding that Katherine had experienced months before returned and for a long time, she was unable to overcome its powerful presence.

CHAPTER 11

Dover/Boulogne
May, 1940

Alastair was uneasy. Things were not going well for the Allies on the continent.

The German army had made its move at last. They circumvented the Maginot Line, the great (expensive and incomplete) hope of the French for the defence of their country, and invaded neutral Belgium, Holland and Luxembourg. After a mere four days, the Dutch Army was shattered and the enemy were at Sedan, breaking through the supposedly impenetrable Ardennes forest. However, the majority of the B.E.F., having been hastily moved into Belgium from their defensive positions on the border with France, had yet to come into serious contact with the enemy.

When the signals started to arrive in the Admiralty's Operations Department showing the astonishing speed of the German advance, Alastair sensed that disaster could lie ahead for the British troops. He could see there would be no repeat of the tactics of the last war; the B.E.F. would not find itself bogged down for years in the mud of Flanders. This was a totally different kind of warfare: mechanized, rapid.

As an intelligent naval staff officer, he reasoned that precautionary plans would have to be put in place for evacuation if things went badly. Every available ship that could be found would be needed to bring the men home safely to England. But where would the army be most likely to congregate?

Reflectively, Alastair walked back down the corridor to his office, his pace slow, the sheaf of papers in his hands concerning the U-boats in the Atlantic unread.

He foresaw that the harbours themselves could come under air attack and thus make embarkation difficult. The beaches of the Channel ports, which he knew well, would not be suitable for large, deep-draught ships to get close to the shore, with its many miles of sand that sloped gently into the sea. It was also a treacherous coastline – littered with sand-banks and centuries of wrecks. He well remembered during the last war how this knowledge had been invaluable when he was patrolling the English Channel on *Freesia*, avoiding the hazards upon which many a ship had foundered.

He could do nothing without his commanding officer's approval but in a moment of inspiration, Alastair knew exactly what *should* be done as a preliminary measure. Fortunately, the Chief of Naval Staff was back at work that day, having been on a week's sick leave – the general state of his health had been causing everyone some concern – and after the morning staff meeting had finished, Alastair remained behind for his briefing. Dudley Pound looked pale, but seemed cheerful.

"Do sit down, Alastair," he said. "Now, what do you have for me today?"

Alastair outlined the details of the previous week's events and how the work on protecting the convoys was progressing. A more efficient way of combating the

U-boat menace was almost in place, although more could still be done. Dudley seemed pleased with what had occurred during his absence and listened carefully while his invaluable right-hand man made various suggestions for further consideration.

"Absolutely. Go right ahead with all of those. Sounds admirable, dear boy. I'm glad that your ideas are being listened to at last."

"Thank you, sir. And thank you for your support in the matter."

The C.N.S. nodded and adjusted his position, taking the weight off his painful hip. He leant back in this chair, trying to relax.

"How's the family?" he enquired. "It's been a while since I asked after them. Your two sons, Edward and Alex. How are they? Edward was aboard the *Exeter* if I remember correctly. And I think you told me that he's recently received a promotion?"

"Yes, he has. He came home with the *Exeter* when she returned to Devonport for full repairs after being patched up in the Falklands. He's since been promoted to lieutenant-commander and is now in charge of the destroyer *H.M.S. Wilberforce*. He's busy escorting mine laying operations in the Channel."

"I presume you still have personal contact with him?"

"Of course, but not as much as I should like. I brought him up, Dudley, and although I now know that he's not my own son, I still care for him."

"Indeed. It must have been a dreadful shock to have made that discovery."

"It was. For both of us, I think."

"Of course. Do you see anything of Roberta these days? My wife asked after her the other day."

"No, thank goodness. She leads her own life."

"Now, what about Alex?"

"I've been tracking the progress of his ship and, touch wood, all seems to be going according to plan. He should arrive in Singapore later this month."

"Good, good. I'm glad you took up my suggestion. Keep doing that, by all means. And Katherine and the grandchildren?"

"Doing fine."

"Delighted to hear it. Now, is there anything else for this morning?" Dudley regarded him kindly. He was fond of Alastair and had great respect for this man's abilities. He ought to find a permanent position for him soon. It was time.

"Well, sir, there is one thing." And he proceeded to say what was in his mind.

"Go to it, dear boy!" said Dudley Pound, once Alastair had finished. "Take all the time you want. The BBC will need to be briefed but I should pay a visit to Bertie Ramsay in Dover first. If evacuation is deemed necessary, the operational planning will become his responsibility as Vice-Admiral Dover. Discuss it with him personally – so much more satisfactory than the telephone – and get his approval."

So Alastair did just that. Without further delay, he asked one of the naval clerks to telephone ahead and request an urgent meeting that morning with Admiral Ramsay, and that a staff car should collect him from Dover Priory Station. This done, he collected his cap and walked to Charing Cross station where he was just in time to catch the fast service, arriving in Dover soon after eleven-thirty.

The staff car was there waiting for him and wound its way up the ever steepening slope until they arrived at the castle itself, set high upon the hillside, with its commanding views over the town, the Port of Dover below and the wide expanse of the English Channel.

After showing his pass to the sentry on duty, Alastair was directed to a narrow spiral staircase which took him down to the subterranean casemate complex that comprised the tunnels of Admiral Ramsay's operational headquarters, concealed within the famous chalk cliffs.

After a long, slightly confusing walk, Alastair was shown into the Admiral's Cabin situated at the seaward end of the partitioned offices in the Admiralty Casemate. In this room, a window with a balcony beyond afforded a clear view out over the sea towards France. He was informed that Admiral Ramsay would be available to see him shortly and was invited to wait.

Taking a deep breath, he sat patiently while the man himself was fully occupied dealing with a constantly ringing telephone and numerous signals as well as documents to be read and signed, brought to him by the Wren and Royal Navy officers on his staff. The admiral looked up and smiled briefly in acknowledgement of Alastair's presence and then continued to deal with the urgent tasks before him.

Observing him discreetly, Alastair saw a dapper, courteous and intelligent man who gave clear verbal responses to the matters presented to him and who was adept at speed-reading the documents placed before him for signing. Idly, Alastair wondered what it would be like to work for him, reaching the conclusion that Admiral Ramsay would make an excellent superior officer but would not suffer fools or inefficiency gladly.

Feeling at ease, Alastair sat back in his chair, taking a professional interest in the proceedings.

After about a quarter of an hour, there was a momentary lull in the business and the admiral telephoned for tea to be brought in.

He glanced at Alastair, his regard both genial and penetrating, before picking up a signal lying on the far side of his desk, which he read, put down again, and said, "Lieutenant-Commander Stewart. Good morning. I'm sorry to have kept you waiting. I gather from Dudley Pound that you would like my approval of something?"

"Yes, sir." He waited to speak while the tea tray was brought in.

Admiral Ramsay poured tea into two cups, one for himself and one for Alastair. "Sugar?"

"No, thank you, sir." Sensing that the admiral was waiting for him to begin without further prompting and, as briefly as he could, appreciating that this man's time was precious, Alastair outlined what he had in mind. "The current situation on the continent set me thinking. Things may not go well for our troops over there and it may prove necessary to…"

"Mount a full-scale evacuation."

"Exactly."

"Go on."

"During the last war, I was in command of a sloop patrolling the Straits of Dover and the English Channel. It's an area I know well."

"Likewise. I commanded a Monitor there in 1915." The two men regarded each other with an immediate understanding.

"I also have a pleasure boat, a motor cruiser, so I've spent many summer holidays on the south and east coasts as well as sailing over to the Channel Ports in France. The sandbanks and wrecks make navigation difficult and the gently sloping beaches are not suitable for large vessels or troop carriers to get close in to the shore. This is where a fleet of small boats would be essential to ferry men to the warships out at sea. It is most likely the soldiers would have assembled on the beaches, given that the ports themselves will probably be under attack from the air or even captured."

Admiral Ramsay smiled and took a sip of his tea. He showed Alastair the last of several sheets of foolscap upon which he had written an extensive preliminary list of plans and requirements for evacuation of the B.E.F.

At the bottom of the page, with a question mark after them, were the words: *Small boats of various kinds needed for ferrying from the shore?*

"We are of one mind. What else?"

"Pleasure cruisers like mine would be eminently suitable. They are motorized and would be faster than rowing boats, although the latter will be essential too," replied Alastair.

"Yes. As you can see," Admiral Ramsay indicated the papers in front of him, "this has been my thinking also. It is the logical course of action. However, we would need to know how many we could have at our disposal and of what specifications…" He smiled and looked directly at Alastair. "It's from this that your idea stems, isn't it?"

"Yes, sir." *Goodness, this man is astute*, thought Alastair. "My idea is that if we broadcast something on the BBC, requiring the owners to let us know details – name, length, draft, engine size and so on – then that information would be readily available should it prove necessary and the owners could then be contacted."

"An excellent idea. It will save a lot of time. Go ahead with that. I'm all for forward planning. I'll leave it with you to arrange from the Admiralty. But keep me posted."

"Of course, sir."

The telephone rang again. Admiral Ramsay let it ring for the moment and stood up. "I appreciate your coming here in person, Lieutenant-Commander Stewart."

"Thank you, sir, and thank you for seeing me at such short notice."

Admiral Ramsay nodded and went to pick up the telephone. "I hope we meet again one day. Now if you'll excuse me…"

"Of course, sir."

The two men shook hands and Alastair saluted, a gesture which the Admiral returned.

The meeting was at an end, but Alastair left Dover with a lightness in his step, his mind clear and his spirits lifted. He knew he had just encountered an exceptional man and he hoped that their paths might cross again one day.

A few days later the family, including Mr and Mrs Thringle, gathered round the wireless to listen to the nine o'clock news, just as they did every evening, but at the conclusion of this particular bulletin they, and everyone else in the country who was following the broadcast, heard these words: '*The Admiralty have made an order requiring all owners of self-propelled pleasure craft between thirty and one hundred feet in length to send any further particulars of them to the Admiralty within fourteen days from today, if they have not already been offered or requisitioned.*'

Alastair grinned at Katherine and she smiled back, sharing his pleasure. Naturally, there was no public mention of how this information might be used but Alastair had the satisfaction of hearing his idea broadcast by the BBC and the knowledge that in helping to set up the Small Craft Registration Order, he may have contributed to something of real value, should future events deem evacuation necessary.

The response was immediate and overwhelming. People wrote in from all over the country with details of their boats. Under Alastair's supervision – he had been charged with overseeing this task – an enormous register was compiled by naval clerks at the Admiralty of almost every small craft that lay in the creeks, rivers, ports and estuaries of Great Britain: a potential armada of small ships that could be called upon should the need arise.

Five days later, the prospect of having to rescue troops from France on a massive scale became an unfortunate reality and on that day, Vice-Admiral Bertram Ramsay was charged with the momentous task of planning for and carrying out the possible evacuation of the B.E.F. and her Allies. Alastair knew that if and when that should happen, the naval responsibility for the soldiers' welfare would be in a very safe pair of hands.

Meanwhile, Mary was beside herself with anxiety. She had not heard from Michael in over a fortnight and Alastair was unable to furnish her with any facts that might allay her fears. She listened to every news bulletin but it revealed nothing that could help her. She had no idea where Michael was and her tired and overwrought imagination created all kinds of terrible scenarios.

It did not help her state of mind when the May Bank Holiday was cancelled and the general population were advised to remain working as usual, and not travel unless it was absolutely necessary.

Unknown to the public, the government was aware that every train would be needed to transport the troops away from the ports on the English side of the Channel as quickly as possible should evacuation become necessary. Emergency timetables were organized and the railways had a practice run when the so-called 'useless mouths' – the wounded, non-combatant and some medical personnel – were brought across to England during that week.

However, Michael was not among these; he should have been, but fate had taken him in a different direction.

He was in Belgium when the German army broke through. The B.E.F., sent there by the panicked French generals instead of being allowed to remain in their defensive positions on the border, thus fell into the trap set by the enemy.

The British fully engaged the Germans on 14th May but were unable to stop their advance (despite putting up fierce resistance and holding onto their positions) because of the military difficulties encountered by their French and Belgian allies either side of them. They were then hampered in trying to set up new defensive lines, and in the subsequent rapid fighting retreat, by the many thousands of refugees who had taken to the roads.

The R.A.M.C. could do no more than offer immediate assistance to the wounded. There was no opportunity to establish field hospitals, only field dressing stations, and even these had to be quickly dismantled and the wounded dispersed as the enemy advanced.

Michael was assigned to transport duties and found himself in a field ambulance – treating and collecting the wounded from the battle front, accompanying them across the border into France and transferring them to waiting ambulances (that then took the soldiers onto Dunkirk and home) before returning to collect more injured men.

By 19th May, the situation was looking grim. German armoured brigades had made rapid progress along the Somme valley towards Abbéville, as well as the roads leading to Boulogne and Calais. They had successfully isolated some of the French forces from the main body of their army to the south and pushed the British further and further back into France, eventually hemming them in on three sides.

Because of this, Michael was ordered to take as many of the wounded as he could away from the battle front because of a planned British counter-attack at Arras and then, together with three other ambulances, make for Dunkirk, from where they would be taken back to England. He was reluctant to leave in view of the coming counter-offensive, where it was inevitable that casualties would be high, but knew he had to obey orders.

Therefore, his small convoy of four ambulances set off, accompanied by a bren-gun carrier as their only means of armoured support. Each vehicle had a driver and an R.A.M.C. private, along with equipment, some supplies and water.

Progress was slow; the roads choked with refugees fleeing ahead of the German advance. Michael was in the last vehicle, which became separated from the others by the crowds of people with their belongings piled onto anything that had wheels – carts, prams, bicycles.

The lead ambulance had the map. Anxiously, Michael hoped that he would be able to catch up. They could hear the sound of guns and shells in the distance, but for the moment they were untroubled by attack.

However, at a crossroads near Thérouanne, they encountered a motorized column of the *Waffen-SS* heading for the coast. Enemy tanks and machine gunners opened fire, mowing down the civilians and hitting the leading ambulance, which exploded in a ball of flame.

Michael's driver swung their vehicle off onto a narrow side road with such force that Michael was thrown onto the floor. This action saved his life as a few moments later, the driver was caught in a hail of bullets and killed instantly. Michael could do nothing for him.

But a more serious problem presented itself. The dead man's foot was caught under the brake pedal, jamming the accelerator down at full throttle, the ambulance careering dangerously from side to side.

Without thinking, Michael grabbed the steering wheel with one hand, opened the door with the other, kicked the driver's foot clear of the pedals and using the full weight of his body, shoved him out of the ambulance. That action made him physically sick when he later recalled what he had done, but it saved his life and the lives of the wounded in his care, allowing him to throw himself into the driver's seat and bring the vehicle under control.

Immediately, Michael put his foot back down on the accelerator and headed as fast as he could along the narrow road. He had no map, and no idea where he was going. Shell fire exploded around him. Great clods of earth and stones rained down onto the roof but, being a moving target, the ambulance was a difficult target for the lumbering tanks to pinpoint.

Eventually, he had driven out of range, was not pursued and realized he was safe for the moment. He slowed down, shaking with fright and adrenaline.

Darkness was falling and in the shelter of a wooded copse, he stopped the ambulance, turned off the engine and listened. Nothing. Not a sound. He went round to the back of the vehicle to check on the welfare of his patients. He wondered if any of them were still alive after the rough treatment of the past couple of hours.

Michael checked over each man carefully; replacing bandages and dressings, administering morphine where necessary, giving each man a drink of water from their meagre supplies and recounting to them what had happened. Miraculously, they had all survived.

Only after he had seen to their needs did Michael go over to a nearby stream and wash the blood off his hands and face. It was then he was sick as images of their escape came back to him.

One of the wounded men clambered out of the ambulance and with great difficulty, hobbled over to him. He put his arm on Michael's shoulder.

"You did well, mate, back there. You couldn't have done anything else. The driver was dead. He didn't know no different."

Michael smiled a wry smile. "Thanks."

"Just thought you ought to know that," he said, as he struggled back towards the ambulance.

Some minutes later, Michael found him slumped against one of the wheels. He could see he was bleeding heavily and went over to him to dress his wounds again. But it was too late – his erstwhile friend was dead. His action of comfort had cost him his life. Or had it? Michael would never know.

Having removed the man's identifying dog tags, he pulled the body across to the nearest tree and covered him with the autumn leaves that still littered the floor, pausing momentarily to say a small prayer.

"It's all I can do for you," he muttered apologetically.

Wearily, he climbed back into the driver's seat and started the engine. He had to press on, no matter how tired he felt. But which way? He stopped the ambulance again and looked up at the sky. Mary had taught him about the stars and their positions but were they the same here in France as on Cairnmor? Who could tell? He began to drive again.

The road took him over the brow of a hill, and he could see the last vestiges of the setting sun. From this, he deduced that he was travelling in a roughly north-westerly direction.

At Desvres was a crossroads. Which way? He stopped again. There was a signpost: Baincthun, Saint-Martin-Boulogne, Boulogne. The coast. Relief. He turned left onto the Boulogne road and trundled along this for some hours. He stopped only to refill the petrol tank, throwing away the last empty can.

At dawn, he reached his destination and emerged from his wooded country road only to find himself in the middle of a furious battle for the port.

Without stopping to think, Michael rammed the accelerator down to the floor, driving as fast as he could down the hill, looking neither right nor left but focusing completely on his objective – the harbour, where he could see a couple of destroyers loading troops and wounded.

He drove straight through a battery of German artillery in the process of bringing forward their guns and who were so dumbfounded by his sudden appearance that they failed to react. He drove straight through a whole platoon of enemy infantry, scattering them in all directions, past the British rear-guard, who saw him coming and gave him covering fire until, miraculously unharmed, Michael screeched to a halt by the docks, much to the surprise of the Royal Navy personnel laying demolition charges.

He sat there for a moment gripping the steering wheel in a complete state of shock, his knuckles white and his heart hammering in his chest, before being directed by a remarkably smart Welsh Guardsman to a safer place in which to transfer his patients from the ambulance onto the nearest ship, which was about to leave.

Still shaking, Michael did as he was ordered and was about to board the destroyer himself, when a major from the remnants of a Durham Light Infantry Brigade asked him if he would tend to some wounded by the Gare Maritime and assist his men in bringing them onto the ship.

Having completed this task, Michael was just about to leave the quayside once again when one of the Royal Navy demolition party was injured by a burst of machine-gun fire and Michael immediately went to his aid.

Seeing this, a Royal Marine officer then asked if he would volunteer to stay behind and treat any further wounded until the next destroyer arrived. His heart thumping once again, Michael remembered his promise to Mary not to put himself deliberately into a dangerous situation but he knew that, as the only medical person there, he was needed. Despite strong misgivings, he agreed.

"Good man," said the officer.

Briefly, regretfully, Michael watched as the destroyer edged its way out of the harbour. Turning to follow his companion away from the quayside, he put any additional thoughts regarding his own safety out of his mind and got on with what he had to do.

Michael went back to his ambulance and replenished his medical bag with as many supplies as it would hold. He slung that across one shoulder, adding another one over his other shoulder, and swung a knapsack that contained all of Mary's precious letters (his talisman against harm) onto his back. Then he took up his place with the other men and together they carried out the tasks to which they had been assigned, with Michael full of admiration for the courage and calmness of the soldiers operating under withering fire from the enemy, gaining inspiration from their demeanour.

On the perimeter of the embattled town, the Welsh and Irish Guards put up a brave and stiff resistance, holding the Germans back for several more hours. Eventually, however, they were overwhelmed by sheer weight of numbers and, running low on ammunition, were forced to withdraw to protect the harbour and the evacuation of the wounded and other members of the B.E.F.

By nightfall, Boulogne had been completely cut off by the enemy. It would only be a matter of time before the German soldiers reached the docks themselves.

CHAPTER 12

Dunkirk (1)
May/June, 1940

On Sunday, 26th May, Bertram Ramsay was ordered by the Admiralty to commence the evacuation of the B.E.F. from Dunkirk in an operation to be known as 'Dynamo', a code name thought up by a member of his staff as their operations room in Dover had previously housed an electric generator.

Once the signal had been given, Alastair travelled to Maybury, where the family had gathered as usual at Mistley House for the weekend. After supper that evening, he went down to *Spirit of Adventure* and brought the motorboat alongside his private jetty on the River Thames at the bottom of the garden. He moored the boat fore and aft, before beginning preparations for the long voyage to Dunkirk. Every available craft would be needed to evacuate the beleaguered army and he knew that his was particularly suited to the task.

Some days earlier, Alastair had handed over the information that he and his naval clerks had so painstakingly compiled and catalogued to the Small Vessels Pool at the Admiralty, whose responsibility it would now become. He had been thanked for his efforts but told that they would take things from there and that his services would not be required.

Feeling somewhat miffed at this attitude, Alastair then asked the C.N.S. if he could travel to Dover and offer his assistance to Admiral Ramsay and his staff, whom he realized were becoming severely overburdened with the mountain of work that was increasingly being loaded on to them. Dudley Pound vetoed this suggestion and said he was needed here in London. Alastair had consoled himself by ensuring that the urgent messages coming from Dover were given top priority by the people to whom they were directed.

However, he still felt thwarted. He wanted to do something *more*.

Once it became apparent that Operation Dynamo would become a reality, Alastair seized the opportunity to pressure the C.N.S. into releasing him temporarily from his duties at the Admiralty in order to take *Spirit of Adventure* over to Dunkirk.

"An admirable idea, old man," agreed his commanding officer, having finally realized that his assistant was frustrated by being in London, no matter how useful his present work.

Having thus been given permission, Alastair made the necessary arrangements for his departure, leaving a trusted R.N. colleague (who would be unafraid to get things moving if some superior officer showed reluctance) to deal with the important task of relaying any signals from Dover to the right department.

So, here he was now at Mistley House on this auspicious Sunday, about to face the unknown once again but this time with his own 'little ship', rather than one of the Royal Navy's somewhat larger vessels.

After she had finished the washing up and settled Rupert and Anna, Katherine walked down the garden to speak to him.

"You're really going aren't you?" Anxiety made her tone sharper than she had intended.

Alastair looked up at her. "Yes," he said quietly. "There's no choice is there?"

"No," conceded Katherine. "There isn't."

His calm determination mollified her and silently, she helped him remove the items that would be surplus to requirements: cushions, books, sleeping bags; remnants of holiday necessities.

"Would sandwiches and flasks of tea be helpful?"

Alastair was grateful. "That would be wonderful, thank you." He smiled, and Katherine did her best to respond.

Once inside the house, she prepared as much food as she could, adding tins of corned beef, spam, potatoes, carrots and peas from their precious pre-war larder, filling two flasks with tea and several bottles with water. Mary and Mrs Thringle came to help, both of them sharing Katherine's dismay that yet another member of the family was about to be placed in a perilous situation.

After gathering the provisions, they carried them to the boat, handing everything down to Katherine as she stowed things away in the cabin lockers. Once this was done, she returned to her room and sat on the window seat for a while, watching Alastair as he quietly went about his preparations. He had become her mainstay, her security. Without him, she would be lost.

Suddenly, she was filled with a deep conviction that she was powerless to resist. She knew she had to go with him.

After telling Mary and Mrs Thringle what she intended to do, she went upstairs to the twins' bedroom and stood for a few moments, studying their innocent sleeping faces. Tenderly, she pushed a lock of curly hair back from Rupert's forehead and stroked Anna's cheek with her finger. She had no worries for the children's immediate welfare, for they would be safe and content with Mary and Mrs Thringle.

However, she could not deny that what she was about to do was madness. Why was she going to do it? But the answer to that question would have to wait; this was not the time for inner philosophical debate. Right now, there was no time to delay.

Immediately, she took a pair of trousers out of her wardrobe and ran down the stairs to the laundry room, locating Alastair's spare uniform polo-neck jumper – she noticed that he had already taken his other Royal Navy sea-going clothes – and her Wellington boots. Quickly, she dressed in these and tied up her hair with a head scarf, Cairnmor style, knotting it securely at the back. But it wasn't right. She looked too much like a woman. She took it off again.

Katherine went to the kitchen and removed a pair of scissors from the drawer. Back in her bedroom, after taking a deep breath, she cut her hair until it was short. It looked somewhat unkempt, so she tried to shape it a little more but only succeeded in making it worse. Briefly, she studied her reflection in the mirror. It would have to do.

She had now run out of time, so she covered up her unruly style with a woollen hat. Trying not to grieve for her hair, which now lay in long, red-gold hanks on the dressing table, she put on Alastair's duffel coat and looked at herself in the mirror once again. At least her figure was well hidden.

Finally, she carefully laid her engagement and wedding rings in a drawer, picked up her bag of spare clothes and put on a pair of gloves before going downstairs to face Alastair.

As casually as she could, she strolled down the garden to join him.

"And where do you think you're going?" he said, amusement showing on his face as he regarded her outfit.

"With you," she said, a note of defiance in her voice.

Alastair laughed. "No," he said.

"Yes."

"No!"

"Yes!"

"Katherine…!"

"I'm coming with you."

"You can't."

"Why not?"

"Because you're a woman and I wouldn't be allowed to take you."

"At least take me as far as Sheerness. Then, after you've registered the boat, I'll… get the train home."

Alastair looked at her suspiciously but made no further protest. He took a deep breath. "All right, then. We'll do that. What about the children?"

"They're asleep. They'll be fine with Mary and Mrs Thringle. It's all arranged."

Alastair could not argue with this and knew when to concede temporary defeat.

Soon all was ready and the housekeeper and Mary came to see them off on their "escapade" as the former had christened it. Mr Thringle appeared at the last moment, very out of breath, but with an expression on triumph on his face. He produced eight double cans of petrol from his wheelbarrow.

"How on earth did you manage to acquire those?!" exclaimed an amazed but grateful Alastair. "I could only buy two cans from the garage. He wouldn't sell me any more, and of course I couldn't tell him why I wanted them, as what's happening is very hush-hush."

"Bob, you didn't tell old Skinflint anything, did you?" asked Mrs Thringle, suddenly anxious.

"Don't be daft, woman, of course I didn't! No, I just made him an offer he couldn't refuse." He smiled.

"What was that, then?"

"I threatened to expose his black-market dealings if he didn't cough up what I wanted, and with no questions asked either." Bob looked very pleased with himself.

"You didn't!"

"I did. After that, he couldn't wait to give me what I asked for from the secret stash he has behind the garage. I told him I knew all about that as well."

Mr Thringle's smile became more pronounced as he recalled the man's worried expression and his rush to collect the required amount of fuel.

Mrs Thringle said she was proud of him and this caused him to smile even more.

Alastair stowed the petrol in the cockpit lockers, and they prepared to say their farewells.

"The engines are running sweetly, Mr Alastair," said Bob. "I spent all day yesterday giving them the once-over and checking the batteries. There's spare oil in that other locker there and the water tanks are all filled up. She'll give you no trouble, I reckon."

He couldn't say any more, feeling somewhat emotional and wishing he could go, but knowing that his wife had refused to let him on account of his weak chest – a legacy from when he was gassed in the trenches during the last war – he busied himself instead by preparing the mooring ropes for release.

Katherine gave Mary and then Mrs Thringle a hug. "Thank you," she said quietly to the loyal housekeeper. "Thank you for not trying to dissuade me."

"I'll expect you back with Mr Alastair then," she whispered in reply, giving Katherine a knowing wink.

"Take care, both of you," said Mary, a furrow of anxiety on her forehead and tears forming in her eyes.

"We'll be fine!" replied Alastair reassuringly.

Katherine took the ropes from Mr Thringle, Alastair increased the engine revs, gently pushing both throttles forward, and the motorboat moved smoothly away from the jetty as he turned the wheel.

It was both exciting and frightening at the same time. Katherine did not know what might happen but kept her fear to herself and presumed (incorrectly) that Alastair had not realized what she intended to do.

Her father-in-law, for his part, was all too aware of what probably lay in store for the armada of small boats as they chugged their way across the Channel to Dunkirk. He also knew exactly what was in her mind, of course. The question was, how would he manage to dissuade her from carrying out that intention when they reached the Isle of Sheppey? He glanced at Katherine every so often.

She had removed her duffel coat and jumper in the mild evening air and was sitting next to him, her shirt-sleeves rolled up, looking relaxed and to Alastair, particularly attractive. Slightly furtively, she removed her hat.

"Your hair!" he exclaimed, genuinely shocked. "Your lovely hair! What have you done to it?"

She blushed and rifled her fingers across her spiky head. "What I had to do, I suppose."

He covered up his dismay with humour. "You didn't need to go to such lengths, or should I say shortness, just to go to Sheerness!"

She smiled at the tease but said nothing.

It was a beautiful evening, warm and fine, but Alastair was not treating it as a gentle cruise down the Thames. He kept the revs high but without over-taxing the engines and was business-like in his approach when they reached the first lock. The lock-keeper's wife came out to greet them as they moored alongside.

"Why, it's Mr Stewart!" she exclaimed, swinging round the lever. "We 'asn't seen you in a long while. What with the war on and everything. Nice evening for a cruise, though, innit? Ain't seen none of you for months and lo and behold there's lots of you about this evening. Something's going on, ain't it?" She was fishing, trying to find out whatever it was so she could have a good gossip about it.

"Not that I know of," replied Alastair politely but evasively, checking the sides of the boat as the amount of water decreased, lowering them slowly down to the next level.

"How many more locks do we have to go through?" asked Katherine as they continued on their way, leaving the disappointed woman standing by the lock gate watching their departure.

"Seventeen."

"Seventeen?! How long will it take us to reach Sheerness?"

"Two days." He looked her, raising an eyebrow. "And that's even before *I* have crossed the English Channel to Dunkirk."

"Oh." Disregarding the emphasis and avoiding his pointed look, she watched him as he deftly adjusted two levers on the control board. "What are those for?"

"They're the throttles, the accelerators, if you like."

"Why are there two?"

"The boat has twin screw petrol engines."

"Which means what exactly?"

"Two engines and two propellers."

"Running at the same time?"

"Yes. It gives extra power and extra manoeuvrability. They can also operate separately."

"Is the boat easy to steer?"

"Very."

"Can I try?"

Alastair hesitated; not because he had little faith in her abilities, but because to teach her meant that she would produce this as further evidence as to why she should accompany him to Dunkirk, thus making it more difficult for him to dissuade her. However, it was a long journey to Sheerness and he would need to rest at some stage.

Reluctantly, he agreed.

He moved aside while she took the wheel. It only took her a moment to adjust to the feel of the boat and he could see she was in control.

Alastair looked at her quizzically. "You've done this before, haven't you?"

She smiled. "Well, I'm more used to a tiller than a wheel. But the principle is the same."

The penny dropped. "Robbie," he said. He should have known.

Katherine laughed. "He taught me to sail his fishing smack many years ago. Right from when I was a little girl, he used to take me out on fishing trips when the weather was fair and let me hold the tiller while he steered. I grew up knowing the feel of a boat and how they react in different conditions. So helming is no problem."

"You should have said."

"Being able to help you is one of the reasons I wanted to come." (Alastair wondered what her other reasons were.) "But engines are quite new to me."

"It's very simple, once one understands how they work. Here," and he proceeded to explain.

Katherine quickly grasped the idea and after a while, became adept at being able to use one or both engines to adjust the boat's position, reducing or increasing the power according to what was required.

"It's actually easier than sailing. I miss being in the open air though."

"Oh, you'll appreciate the wheelhouse if the weather turns bad." He failed to mention that it might offer some small protection from the conditions that would be encountered at Dunkirk.

Katherine, sensing the slight downward turn in his mood, remarked brightly, "I can steer using a compass."

Alastair was surprised. "You can?!"

"Yes."

"And read a chart?"

"Yes."

"Robbie taught you well."

"He did."

"Bit of a dark horse, is Robbie."

Katherine laughed. "And very learned. Completely self-taught."

"Very much like my father."

"Of course. I'd like to meet him one day."

"And you shall. He loves the fact that he's a great-grandfather. I send him lots of photographs of the children."

They chatted away, interspersed with periods of companionable silence. About midnight, Katherine grew sleepy and Alastair suggested she go below and try to get some rest, which she did, lulled by the gentle motion of the boat and the throb of the engines. She awoke some hours later to silence apart from the tranquil lapping of water on the wooden sides of the boat.

Alastair was deeply asleep on the saloon berth opposite hers, the only other place to rest, the bunk cushions fore and aft having been removed to create more space.

She found that he had placed a blanket over her to keep her warm and Katherine looked across at him, grateful for his thoughtfulness. It was strange yet, at the same time, perfectly natural to see him there, lying close to her. He looked so vulnerable that she wanted to reach out to him…

Quickly, she withdrew her hand and pushed the impulse aside. What on earth was she thinking of?

Fully awake now, she quietly went up onto a deck bathed in early morning light, where tree-lined river banks resonated with the dawn chorus. Absorbed within the beauty and tranquillity of the scene, Katherine jumped when Alastair joined her, while he, as she turned towards him, was all too aware of being next to her; all too aware of the fact that they were completely alone.

Mentally, he reprimanded himself. This would not do. "It's time we were on the move again," he said, trying to make his voice sound as matter-of-fact as he could.

"Is it? Would you like breakfast?" she asked. "It's not too early?"

"No. Breakfast would be good, thank you."

She went back down below and cooked bacon and eggs in the tiny galley, serving it with bread and margarine and hot tea, which they consumed with relish, both of them hungry and thirsty despite the early hour.

Throughout that day and night, Katherine took her turn at the wheel while Alastair rested and vice versa; she now making sure that they were never sleeping at the same time.

They traversed the locks and the miles, eventually reaching the tidal part of the River Thames at Teddington. Catching the fast-flowing ebb tide, they made good progress and sailed under Westminster Bridge, passing Big Ben and the Houses of Parliament on the morning of 28th May. London was a city waking up and from the water, familiar landmarks took on a completely new dimension.

Katherine loved it. There was something incredibly special about being on the river in the heart of the capital. "It's wonderful, isn't it?" she said.

"Oh yes. I love seeing London this way. I'm not sure what it is. It's something to do with the juxtaposition of history and industry, yet it's more, so much more than that. We're passing the historical side now, of course, but once we reach Tower Bridge and the Pool of London, you'll understand what I mean about the industry. And just beyond Tower Bridge is a place called St Katherine's Dock." He smiled at her. "It's where they unload all the spices and perfumes and other exotic imports; at least they did before the war."

"What do they handle now?"

"I don't know. Probably war goods of some description. "

"I like the idea of one of London's docks having the same name as me."

"I thought you might."

They motored under Tower Bridge, with its bascules lowered, and just as they passed the open lock gates of St Katherine's, the sun broke through the misty gloom.

"A gift for you," observed Alastair quietly and Katherine smiled.

However, there was no time to stand and stare as they had to keep their wits about them. Early morning or not, the Thames in London was a busy working river and they were obliged to avoid lighters and ferries crossing to and fro, and large ships, guided by tugs, docking or leaving the wharves, their cargoes unloaded by swinging cranes. They kept a sharp look-out for the debris that littered the water – planks of wood, rope, half submerged wooden crates: the detritus of industry on the water.

In time, as the Thames grew wider and straighter, they were joined by more and more boats of varying size and type. Alastair recognized many of the names from his registry and pointed them out to Katherine, waving back as the owners waved to them.

There was a feeling of excitement; a sense of anticipation.

When they arrived at Sheerness on the Isle of Sheppey that evening, the harbour was crowded inside and out, with boats jostling for position. But the organization was good and they were given clear instructions as to where they should moor *Spirit of Adventure*. Alastair had to give all credit to the Admiralty's Small Vessel Pool for this and Admiral Taylor, who had been placed in charge.

Once they had left the boat and were walking along the quayside to the building where they were to register, Alastair stopped and looked at Katherine.

"This is as far as you go," he said firmly.

"Is it?" she replied, knowing exactly what he meant, but not letting him see that.

"Yes." He was determined not to give in.

"Why?"

"You know why."

"Do I?" She was being deliberately obtuse.

Alastair took a deep breath and taking her by the arm, he steered her behind some oil drums. If they were going to argue, then it should be in private.

"You are not going."

"I am."

"They won't let a woman into a war zone."

"They will if they don't know."

"They won't know because you are not going."

"Oh but I am. This is a national emergency. And you need me."

"If you were discovered, we would both be in serious trouble."

"Surely not."

"You don't know the Navy," said Alastair with feeling. "Besides, what would Alex say?"

"He's not here." There was defiance in her voice and manner.

"True, and you therefore become my responsibility in his absence."

"I am my *own* responsibility," she declared, her anger flaring momentarily. "You are not my keeper. Neither is Alex. Am I not capable of making my own decisions?"

Alastair was taken aback. In all the time they had known each other, she had never before been angry with him.

"Of course you are and I have always respected that, but…"

"But what?"

"I don't want you to be in any danger."

"What about you?"

"That's different."

"How so?"

"It's my duty."

"And why shouldn't it be mine?"

Alastair hesitated for a moment. Then he said, "Because I care for you too much."

Katherine regarded him earnestly, her eyes filling with tears, all anger gone. "And how do you think I feel about you?"

They looked at each other, the argument forgotten.

After a while she said, "Please don't let's argue. It hurts too much."

"Yes." He paused. "Look, I'll make a deal with you. If there's no one else to help me crew the boat, then we'll somehow find an honest way for you to come with me."

"So now you're trying to make an honest woman out of me," said Katherine pertly.

"I've always taken you to be so," replied Alastair calmly.

"Thank you." They smiled at each other. "All right, I'll settle for your 'deal', as you call it. But if it doesn't work out… I could always go with someone else…" She was teasing him now.

Alastair eyed her disparagingly.

"Sorry," she replied.

"I should think so. I wouldn't let you go with anyone else."

"I wouldn't want to."

"I should hope not!"

"I didn't mean it."

"I know."

Friends again, the argument over, they walked towards the harbour building where Alastair was to register *Spirit of Adventure*. The room was crowded and the R.N.V.R. lieutenant responsible for the registration process was under enormous pressure to push everyone through as quickly as possible. Despite this, however, he completed the identification of each vessel and owner efficiently and with the minimum of fuss.

When it was Alastair's turn, the lieutenant said to him, "I'm afraid there are no more naval personnel left to accompany you at the moment, sir. There are some cadets on their way from Chatham, but they haven't got here yet. We've been absolutely inundated. It's quite remarkable." He looked across at Katherine, her woolly hat pulled low over her eyes. "What about the lad you came in with? Couldn't he go with you? If he does, he'll have to sign a T124 first though, sir."

The lieutenant called Katherine over and she waited while he went to fetch the form. Against his better judgement, Alastair remained silent, his heart beating rapidly.

Without saying anything, once the T124 had been produced, Katherine did as she was instructed, giving Kit MacDonald as her name and 'Lochaberdale, Cairnmor, Scotland' as her address, knowing that any correspondence would still reach her there. She deliberately smudged her date of birth but the other details she could fill in fairly honestly. After signing the form and keeping her head down, she handed it back to the lieutenant, who glanced briefly at the completed document and put it away in the folder without comment.

Her heart was pounding. This was harder than she had thought it would be. She had never done anything deceitful in her life but she consoled herself with the fact that she had only stretched the truth and after all, 'Kit' had been her nickname when she was at boarding school.

They returned to the boat in silence. Once they were back on board, when Katherine told him what she had written and that she had been almost truthful, Alastair laughed and said philosophically, "Well, the deed is done now and if we survive the ordeal that is to come, I'll look that form out and keep it as a souvenir. I don't think anyone will read it too closely while we're away, so we needn't worry too much. However," he said looking at her sternly with a raised eyebrow and laughter in his eyes, "I should point out that you're in the Royal Navy for the next month, that you've been paid five pounds and as I am now your commanding officer, you'll have to do exactly as I say, otherwise I'll have you court martialled! That is, if they don't get to me first!" he added wryly.

"Aye, aye, sir," she replied demurely.

Serious once more, they regarded each other.

"Well, this is it," said Alastair, taking a deep breath as he started the engines. "Next stop Ramsgate for the flotilla and then Dunkirk. I wonder if you realize exactly what it is you're letting yourself in for."

Katherine was silent. She was beginning to wonder exactly the same thing.

CHAPTER 13

Dunkirk (2)
May/June, 1940

When they arrived, they found Ramsgate Harbour awash with sea-going craft of every description: motor cruisers, fishing smacks, cockle boats, ferries, lifeboats (brought from the great ocean-going liners berthed in the Pool of London), trawlers, drifters, R.N.L.I. lifeboats and Thames sailing barges. Tugs had been sent by the towage companies and these were to prove invaluable throughout the evacuation, with their huge strength and versatility, undertaking an enormously varied workload and providing an indispensable service to shipping of all kinds.

The atmosphere was infused with anticipation and nervousness. All of them, Royal Navy and amateur yachtsmen together, were about to sail into the unknown; part of an armada the like of which had never been seen before. Many owners of the little ships, volunteer crews, had never been beyond coastal waters or ventured away from the Thames.

Anxiously, these intrepid sailors studied the charts they had been given, trying to decipher and understand the route they were to take, while the naval personnel assigned to take the majority of these boats across, calmly awaited orders and the signal to be off, familiarizing themselves with the vessel beneath them, searching out the quirks of engines coaxed back to life after months of being laid up in a boatyard.

There was no such need on *Spirit of Adventure*. While Katherine steadied the boat, Alastair made final checks, stowing the cork life jackets and additional rations with which they had been issued at Sheerness. He made sure that the dozen or so extra two gallon fuel cans were secure on deck, there being no more room in the cockpit lockers. Watching him, she thought how Robbie would have wanted to share in this and said as much to Alastair.

"Not if he's got any sense!" he replied, putting the large first aid kit they had been given next to the cotton wool and bandages, torn up out of old clean sheets by Mrs Thringle before they had left home.

"It's just that it reminds me of the search and rescue mission on Cairnmor when everyone gathered before going out to look for Adam and his friends," observed Katherine. "It was nothing on this scale, though," she added reflectively.

"No," agreed Alastair, having been an important part of that adventure. "But the principle is the same," he said as he came into the wheelhouse, having completed his tasks. "There, that should do us. The water tanks are completely full and we have those extra containers." He rubbed his hands together and blew out his cheeks. "*Once more unto the breach, dear friends, once more...*" he quoted, looking seaward.

He turned to Katherine, and she discreetly tucked her hand into the crook of his arm as they waited for their next set of instructions.

The vessels were organized into convoys, with the smaller ships (and at thirty-eight foot six inches, *Spirit of Adventure* was included in this category) given a tow across the Channel by tug or Dutch *schuyte*. Their particular tug was called *Enterprise* and once all its boats had been made secure behind, Alastair switched off the engines and he and Katherine were invited to climb aboard, where they remained until they reached Dunkirk.

The captain was a tough, weather-beaten but hospitable old salt, with a pipe clamped firmly between his teeth and which stayed there for the whole journey – on occasions making his words difficult to discern. Katherine remained silent, protecting her disguise, quickly doing up her duffel coat which she discovered, to her dismay, she had inadvertently left open, listening to his discourse about his family in Woolwich and his sister who ran a boarding house in Dover.

That first convoy of little ships sailed from Ramsgate late that evening, Wednesday, 29th May, having been treated to the final remains of a glorious sunset out at sea.

A red sky of a different kind greeted and shocked them as they arrived at Dunkirk: a funeral pyre of burning buildings in the town, with the rows of great oil storage tanks beyond the harbour sending a huge pall of acrid smoke billowing up into the sky; its blackness thrown into sharp relief by the crimson glare of reflected flames; its opacity obscuring the beaches in silent choking oiliness.

Immediately, Alastair exchanged his officer's cap for a tin hat and Katherine removed her woolly hat, following suit, her expression tense and anxious. He took her hand and squeezed it, as though to say, "This is it."

He started the engines and she cast off the tow rope, throwing it back to the deck hand on the tug. Captain Goodsell touched his old battered cap and Alastair gave a half-salute in return. Then they were on their own, negotiating half-submerged wrecks still blazing furiously, feeling their way towards the beaches where patient lines of soldiers stood neck-deep in the water, awaiting their salvation.

Spirit of Adventure motored gently eastwards away from the harbour, in the direction of St Malo and the Bray Dunes, with Alastair calling out as he and Katherine peered through the smoke and darkness, searching for the men they had come to rescue, coughing and spluttering if they breathed in the pungent air too deeply.

At first, they heard nothing. Alastair called out again.

No reply. Once more.

Then an answer.

"'Allo!"

"Hello!"

"Over 'ere, mate." Guided by their voices, Alastair edged the boat in the direction of the sound. A sergeant at the head of the line greeted them. "'Allo. Good to see you. 'Ow d'you want to do this, mate?"

"As slowly as possible. If we capsize that'll be it."

"'Ow many can you take?" asked the sergeant.

"About twenty I should think."

90

Alastair fastened rope ladders over both sides, turning the boat with her bows facing the soldiers. Katherine took over the controls, station-keeping, adjusting rudder and engines as the boat rocked and yawed as the men clambered aboard on either side.

"That's it then," said the sergeant, having counted.

"Aren't you coming?" asked Alastair.

"No, sir. See the lads on first."

"We'll come back."

"We'd appreciate it. Cheerio, then."

Alastair took the helm once again, using both engines, and manoeuvred the boat away from the troops.

Where to? They couldn't see anything through the smoke-filled gloom. Shapes loomed up at them and disappeared, shadowy and ghost-ridden. All the while, he took note of his course from the compass so as to return to the same place.

After nearly ten minutes of cautious progress, they came across a different kind of shape: solid, huge, stationary. A large vessel taking troops on board. Relief.

"Ahoy there," called out Alastair. "Room for any more?"

"Yes, plenty. Bring your boat alongside."

The low beam of a torch was shone briefly in their direction and *Spirit of Adventure*'s precious cargo scrambled up the nets on the side of the ship.

"What are you?" called out Alastair, unable to be sure in the darkness and poor visibility as he could only see the indistinct shape of a vessel.

"A destroyer," came the reply.

It was now slack water. He turned the boat around, adjusted the heading and set off for what he hoped was the same place. He called out as before.

"Over 'ere, mate," came the reply. When he saw it was Alastair again, the sergeant said, "Well, stone the crows! You found us. I didn't think we'd see you again, sir! Come on then lads, first twenty. Up you go."

"I reckon we could try another five."

"You 'eard the man. Look sharpish now."

Once they were full, they headed once again towards the destroyer, discharging the men and nosing their way back carefully towards their adopted area of the beach. By now, grey dawn was breaking and the tide was coming in. The line of men in the water decreased, not advancing as they had been, for to do so now would risk being engulfed by the incoming waves. The brave sergeant was still at the head of the column; all the soldiers wet and shivering with cold.

As the light increased and they were able to work faster, Alastair upped the number of men he could transport to thirty, and the numbers they and everyone else took to the destroyer increased exponentially. Eventually, the warship was full to over-capacity and on the next return journey, they found she had set off back to England.

It was full daylight now and through the obscuring murkiness – the beach and coastline up to about a mile out to sea were still shrouded in smoke – they located another large vessel, a ferry this time, taking on soldiers. As the tide was high, Alastair edged *Spirit of Adventure* closer to the shore, taking care not to go aground. The men continued to wade out and progress was somewhat faster.

Then he saw some lorries being sabotaged ashore. To Alastair, this seemed a terrible waste of resources, although he understood that it was being carried out to prevent them from being used by the enemy. In a flash of inspiration, he realized that once put together in a line nose to tail, they could be used as a make-shift jetty, which meant that more men could be loaded faster onto the boats at any state of the tide.

Quickly, he explained this to Katherine and that he was going ashore to see what could be done. Could she manage to take the troops to the larger vessels? Yes, she said she could. But she would need someone else on the boat with her. He spoke to the sergeant, who volunteered, and put his corporal in charge of the line.

Then Alastair took off his duffel coat, replacing it with his Royal Navy jacket so that his rank would carry authority and, after donning his tin hat once again, he regarded Katherine for a brief moment and lowered himself cautiously over the side and into the water.

"Be careful," she mouthed to him.

"And you," he replied.

Katherine and the sergeant organized the troops onto the boat. Through the choking mist, she could make out the dim outline of a paddle steamer loading up, so she headed that way, offloading their cargo accordingly. As it grew warmer, she discarded her duffel coat, her figure more or less hidden by her woollen jumper, and headed back.

She saw Alastair in conference at the water's edge with the Royal Navy officer in charge of the beach and together they went over to an army officer and spoke to him. Then the three of them returned and soldiers were dispatched to commandeer any working lorries and drive them into the sea. Meanwhile, Katherine and the sergeant continued to take the men out to the waiting ships.

As the tide receded the beach party added more trucks, until by low tide the double line was complete – Alastair having calculated the rise and fall against the height of the vehicles. Bullets were fired into the tyres, puncturing them, sand was thrown into the backs of the lorries as ballast and finally they were lashed tightly together, ensuring they did not move after the tide had come in. All that was needed now were planks of wood to traverse the length of the vehicles, most of which had had their canvas removed. He looked around for a volunteer to act as a messenger.

A man wearing a kilt caught Alastair's attention. He sat slightly apart from the others, muttering to himself.

A nearby soldier said, "Oh, don't mind 'im. Just talks gibberish 'e does. We came across him on the way. 'E sort of tagged along and we can't get no sense out of him. He's just sat there the whole time. Won't give his name nor nothing. Scared out of 'is wits, I reckon."

There was something very familiar about some of the words the man was using. It was certainly not gibberish. Listening for a few moments more and recognizing the language, Alastair immediately went over to him and said, "*Halò. Is mise Lieutenant-Commander Stewart.*"

The soldier looked up in amazement and leapt to his feet. Alastair was rewarded by a flood of Gaelic and a vice-like grip as his hand was shaken. In his fear, the man's English had deserted him and no one could understand him.

"Now," continued Alastair in Gaelic, "if you go to that boat – that one out there," and he pointed in the direction of *Spirit of Adventure*, "there is someone who can speak better Gaelic than I can."

The soldier nodded and looked out to sea.

"I want you to ask her to find a ship with planks of wood to put on top of the lorries. We will do the same here. Understood?"

"Oh yes," said the soldier, relief lighting his face. Did this man really mean 'her', he thought, or did he just get it wrong?

"Then you must bring it back and unload it, yes?"

"Yes."

"Off you go then."

Quickly, he waded out into the sea to *Spirit of Adventure*. The sergeant was dumbfounded when the man started to speak in Gaelic, but nearly fell off the boat when Katherine answered him in the same language. She signalled clearly to Alastair with her thumbs raised that she understood and he responded in kind.

"So, wot's that you're speaking then?"

"Gaelic," she said, aware that her identity had been revealed the moment she made her reply.

"Blimey, you really are a woman, ain't you?!" He chuckled. "Well, I'm blowed. Does the navy know?"

"Not exactly, no. But Lieutenant-Commander Stewart does."

"I should 'ope so, ma'am! How d'you get over 'ere then?"

"On *Spirit of Adventure*!" she replied disarmingly, intentionally preserving her privacy. "Anyway, I'm Katherine Stewart."

"I'm Sergeant Ron Smith, Durham Light Infantry. Pleased to meet you, Mrs Stewart. It is missus, ain't it?"

"Yes."

"And 'oo are you, me lad?"

"Private Angus MacKellar, First Battalion Queen's Own Cameron Highlanders," he replied, standing to attention, his regimental pride self-evident.

"At ease, soldier. Where's the rest of your outfit?"

"Gone." His shoulders slumped.

"What d'you mean 'gone'?"

"Like I said. Gone. Dead. Killed."

"Bloody 'ell. Sorry, Mrs Stewart. Where?"

"La Bassée near Fournes. We were ambushed and overrun by the enemy. I managed to get out. Then I caught up with the English soldiers and came here. It was terrible."

"No wonder you've been out of it. Well, you stick with me son, I'll see you right."

The private's relief was palpable.

"Now, ma'am, we need to find these planks."

Transporting twenty-eight more soldiers, they located their ferry again and helped the troops aboard. Then Katherine spotted a Thames Barge further out to sea, just arriving on the scene. Thinking that it might carry the sort of cargo they were looking for, she motored over to it.

Sergeant Smith hailed them and explained the situation.

"We've got some stuff down below you could use," replied the captain. "We keep it on board for emergencies."

"That'll do us fine, mate."

"Where do you want it?"

"On top of that line of lorries by the beach. See?"

"Yep, I see," said the captain. "I'll follow you."

So, with the *Spirit of Adventure* leading the way, they set off. A light south-westerly breeze had begun to blow and to the consternation of everyone on the beaches and on the water, the drifting smoke from the oil tanks was disappearing rapidly, revealing the lines and groups of men waiting on the beach or climbing into the boats, illuminating everything in glorious, bright, clear sunlight.

"Now we're for it," muttered Sergeant Smith darkly.

And, almost on cue, about fifty *Stuka* dive bombers appeared from the direction of Nieuport, to the north of Dunkirk. Gunfire opened up all along the coast at them – from the beaches, the warships, from armed merchant vessels – an incessant cacophony of sound: deafening, shocking. Machine guns, Bofors, Lewis guns, rifles, anti-aircraft guns, whatever was to hand – all of them blazing away at these harbingers of death and destruction.

Yet still they came; threatening, monstrous.

The formation broke overhead and with a banshee wail, the planes screamed down out of the sky, terrifying and relentless in their attack, selecting a boat, a ship, a group of men. There was nowhere to hide, nowhere to run. The many thousands of men who had already endured this torture over and over again, were once more subjected to its onslaught. They threw themselves down onto the sand, covering their heads with their arms or burrowing into the marram-covered dunes.

The young highlander cowered, screaming on the deck of *Spirit of Adventure* as the bombs dropped, sending spray ten, fifteen foot into the air, drenching everyone with oily water. He had seen his mates, his comrades killed and he was at the end of his tether.

"na dèan sin tuilleadh!" he cried out over and over again, begging for it to stop.

The sergeant grabbed hold of him, taking him below into the saloon, out of sight, talking to him, calming him.

Desperately, from her prone position half hidden by the gunwales, Katherine peered across at the beach. Where was Alastair? She couldn't see him. Where was he? Where was he? Panic and fear gripped her chest. *Please keep him safe*, she prayed, *please keep him safe*.

She saw the bombs blasting sand, men and vehicles in their wake. Soldiers threw themselves into the craters that remained in the aftermath of the explosions, desperately trying to make use of the meagre protection they afforded. Medical personnel ran about with stretchers, trying to help the wounded and dying, flattening themselves against the sand when yet another *Stuka* dive-bombed the beach.

But still she couldn't see Alastair.

The raid was horrifying, barbaric; a half-hour of brutal obscenity. Then all at once it was over and the planes disappeared over the blazing town.

And then she saw him; saw Alastair pick himself up off the sand and begin to wade out to the boat. He climbed on board and wordlessly she went to him and clung onto him, not caring about her disguise.

"I'm all right, I'm all right," he said, holding her close, his face pale and drawn after his ordeal. "I'm so sorry I couldn't get back to you." He brushed the spikes of hair off her face; wanting to kiss her, but not able to. He looked around him at the boat, keeping his arm around Katherine, protecting her, not letting her go. "It's a miracle you weren't hit."

"We was lucky," said the sergeant, now able to bring his shaking, trembling charge back up to sit on the deck. "It wasn't much of a miracle for the poor devils who copped it though, was it? Bloody Jerries." He shook his fist and glared murderously in the direction they had just left before saying abruptly, "Let's get this wood organized, shall we?"

With great teamwork and cooperation, the wood was hauled out of the barge, and painstakingly positioned and made secure across the tops of the lorries until a walkway had been constructed.

"Well, we'll see how this works when the tide comes in a bit later," said Alastair, surveying their handiwork.

But the soldiers were already making use of it, the able-bodied who had survived unscathed, the walking wounded, the stretcher cases – all climbing or being carried on board the Thames Barge from the jetty, which, with her lee-boards up, sat easily in the shallow water. Very soon the boat was full and she set sail for England.

An hour later, the *Me110s* arrived: machine guns strafing and harassing, their violence destructive. However, this time, a squadron of *Spitfires* appeared, diving out of the sun into the formation, breaking it up, scattering the planes every which way.

Everyone's eyes focused on the sky, watching the dogfights taking place above them, cheering whenever a German plane, trailing smoke and flame behind, was shot down. After a while, the enemy could take no more and disappeared over the mainland. The *Spitfires*, at the limit of their fuel, turned and headed for home.

Sergeant Smith volunteered to stay and supervise the loading from Stewart's Jetty, as he had christened it, and persuaded Private MacKellar to assist him, coaxing him out from one of the lorry cabs where he had been sitting, staring blankly out to sea, oblivious of the water as it began to lap around his ankles.

Alastair and Katherine continued as before, close to exhaustion, living on adrenaline and pausing only to snatch a bite of food or drink some water. They learned to work through the air raids, aided by the indefatigable Sergeant Smith and the rapidly recovering Private MacKellar, the jetty proving to be a popular and efficient way of embarking the troops. As more ships were directed towards the area, it became an attractive target for the *Stukas* and *Messerschmitts*.

On one trip, Alastair headed for yet another destroyer, too busy to notice the name as they came alongside, finding their place among several other boats of varying size and description all delivering soldiers.

As the troops were climbing up the scrambling net, the lieutenant-commander in charge leaned over the side and called down, "Hurry it up there. I need to get this ship back to Dover." He stopped in his tracks when he saw Alastair on *Spirit of Adventure*. "Dad! I mean Alastair!"

"Good Lord! Edward! Is this *H.M.S. Wilberforce*? I haven't had a chance to look at the name."

"Wait, I'll come down." He clambered awkwardly to the bottom of the net, holding on with one hand and balancing one foot on the bulwark-capping of the motorboat. "Well, fancy seeing you here!" he said.

Alastair went to greet him but Edward made no move to respond. His adoptive father was left with his hand embarrassingly outstretched; hurt by the unexpected coldness in his son's manner.

Edward seemed not to notice his father's discomfiture. "Who's that?" he said, with a nod towards Katherine.

"Someone who is proving to be invaluable on this mission," replied Alastair calmly and deliberately.

Katherine had to stop herself smiling at his praise. She made sure she was half-hidden by the wheelhouse frame and quietly observed Alex's half-brother.

"Mother wants a divorce," said Edward *sotto voce*, without turning a hair.

Completely taken aback, Alastair said, "What?! I think this is neither the time nor the place to discuss such matters."

"Why not? Who knows when we'll meet up again. If ever."

His anger rising, Alastair said, "Then she can have it. But be very clear about this, Edward. *I* shall decide when I divorce her. I will not be pressurized into doing so. Otherwise, the answer is no."

Edward glared at him, then looked disparagingly over *Spirit*. "So, this is the size of boat that they're giving lieutenant-commanders in the R.N.V.R. now, is it? As you can see, us regular chaps do much better." And he carried on in a similar vein all the time the soldiers were climbing on board his ship.

Oh, he's his mother's son all right, thought Katherine. She listened to him for a few more minutes, then she'd had enough.

Seeing that all their soldiers had disembarked, she revved the engines and abruptly manoeuvred the boat away from the destroyer. Caught totally by surprise, Edward was left dangling precariously in mid-air and obliged to make a highly undignified scrabble onto the ropes to stop himself falling into the sea.

Katherine looked up at the destroyer's deck as *Spirit* departed and was rewarded by barely concealed laughter and a discreet thumbs up from the sailors on deck as they saw their commanding officer's struggle to regain the scrambling net. There was no move to help him.

"No love lost there then by his crew," she observed, as they continued on their way.

"No." Alastair smiled. "I'm glad you did that. I might have hit him otherwise."

"You and me both!" She looked at him sympathetically but there was no time to say anything further, because as they neared the jetty, they were subjected to another air raid, ferocious and terrifying in its delivery.

A destroyer blew up with a roar. They looked behind them. It was *H.M.S. Wilberforce*.

CHAPTER 14

Dunkirk (3)
May/June, 1940

All ships in the immediate vicinity rushed to the aid of the stricken destroyer. The bomb had exploded near the stern of the ship, igniting depth charges, leaving a jagged burning wound from which soldiers and sailors poured out, obeying a primeval instinct for survival.

Through his binoculars, Alastair could see Edward up on the sloping foredeck, urging the men on, half hidden by smoke and flames. He and Katherine watched helplessly as men jumped off the sides of the burning ship into the oily flaming water, those that managed to survive the conflagration clinging onto whatever wreckage they could find.

Another destroyer at great risk to herself came alongside and, in a perilous rescue operation aided by one or two smaller boats, managed to take off the rest of the survivors before leaving quickly. It was not a moment too soon for, with a great hiss and a sigh and one final explosion, the ship sank. It was incredible that she had stayed afloat so long.

To his credit, Edward was one of the last to leave, stepping off the destroyer at the last moment into the sea as the ship went down, to be picked up, apparently uninjured, by a lifeboat already full of survivors.

Alastair experienced a profound sense of relief. Edward was still alive, but he had lost his ship. His father felt for him as well as the men who had been on board, so recently rescued, only for so many of them to lose their lives just when they thought they were on their way to safety.

What a bloody awful business war is, he thought, glancing at Katherine's pallor and shocked expression, unable to lessen its impact for her other than by briefly putting a consoling arm round her shoulders.

The bombing and shelling continued – the Pom-Pom guns of the warships opening up in response to the air attacks. The occasional rattle of machine gun fire could be heard from the countryside beyond the town as the enemy grew closer, with the rear-guard putting up a dogged defence as they held the ever-shrinking perimeter.

Spirit of Adventure continued to ply her trade – backwards and forwards, backwards and forwards, collecting troops, but also gathering whalers, ships' lifeboats and stray rowing boats, all abandoned after their occupants had reached the larger ships. They towed these back to the beaches for yet more soldiers and collected another load for themselves from the jetty.

Alastair and Katherine were now operating in the state beyond tiredness.

Low cloud and mist hung over Dunkirk and the beaches during their second day and there was respite from air attacks because of the poor visibility. It proved to be a good day for lifting troops, except for several hours in the afternoon when most of the Royal Navy ships disappeared – an occurrence greatly resented by the men waiting in long patient lines on the beach who were not to know that the Admiralty, afraid of losing their newest capital ships to enemy action, had had them recalled as a precautionary measure.

Taking advantage of the lull, Alastair and Katherine even managed to snatch some sleep and eat some food. Then, almost as quickly as they had gone, the missing ships reappeared (following persistent pleas to the Admiralty from Admiral Ramsay) and normal service was resumed.

On the morning of the third day, a heavy surf caused by a freshening onshore breeze hampered rescue efforts at the shoreline as motorized craft found it impossible to land. However, Stewart's Jetty, and several others which by now had been constructed along the beaches, once again proved their worth for use by the small to medium-sized boats and larger vessels with a shallow draft. Alastair and Katherine, aided by the indefatigable Sergeant Smith and Private MacKellar, who had both decided to stay on, once more worked *Spirit of Adventure* very hard at her task.

However, early in the afternoon, just as the sea calmed again, the air attacks resumed. About one hundred aircraft approached from the direction of Nieuport, raining fire and destruction upon the town and the beaches, to be followed at half-hourly intervals by still more bombers and then by *Me109s* and *He111s*. Everywhere was now also under constant shelling from German artillery, making the situation nightmarish and inescapable.

"Where's the ruddy R.A.F., that's what I'd like to know?" muttered Sergeant Smith as he directed yet more soldiers from the beach onto the makeshift pier. His words were to be echoed many times that day. However, what he and the others couldn't be aware of, was that the air raids would have been considerably worse had not the R.A.F. already been chasing and engaging the *Luftwaffe* before they reached the coast.

In the midst of all this mayhem, Alastair kept checking the fuel levels. By now, they were running low on petrol, having used up everything originally in their tanks and most of the spare cans. They had refuelled from a drifter bringing in supplies the previous day, but only a small amount could be allocated to each boat and Alastair had no idea when another would appear.

After making yet another assessment, to his dismay, he calculated there was only just enough fuel to reach Dover or Ramsgate. It was imperative they set off immediately.

He took on board the last ten soldiers standing on the jetty and was about to call out to tell Sergeant Smith that he should come now, when the fearless sergeant, standing on top of the lorries urging the next batch of troops to come off the beach onto the empty jetty as quickly as they could and "not to 'ang around as tho' you was on a Sunday picnic," was felled by the burst of machine-gun fire from one of a pair of *Me110s*, which had appeared out of nowhere, targeting the lorry pier. The planes were so close they could see the pilots' faces.

"No!" screamed Katherine. "No!"

Without thinking, she leaped off the boat onto the top of the lorries and scrambled her way to the beach end of the jetty, where he lay in agony. She was quickly joined by Private MacKellar, who had followed her, stumbling and falling over the splintered planks of wood and ruptured canvas as he ran.

Carefully, he lifted his friend and carried him back to *Spirit*, running the gauntlet of another spray of bullets which caught him on the back of his left foot just as he reached the boat. He fell to his knees, but intent on rescue, held onto his charge.

"You can't die!" he said frantically, totally disregarding the searing pain that ran up his leg and engulfed his whole body. "You are not to die!" he ordered Ron, who, unable to speak, just stared at him, shocked and trying to hold on to life. With care and surprising gentleness, the soldiers already on board helped both of them onto the boat.

Meanwhile, Katherine had thrown herself into the sea to avoid being hit and, holding her breath, groped her way under one of the vehicles for protection. Alastair, seeing her disappear from sight, thought she had been hurt and leapt over the side into the water, searching for her desperately.

She came up for air, spluttering and choking, and leant back against one of the lorries. With relief permeating every part of him, he waded over to her, shielding her with his body from the continuous strafing. Not for the first time he thought that it was madness to have allowed her to come here; not for the first time, he wanted to hold her close and never let her go.

From above them came the sound of gunfire as the soldiers on board opened up with their rifles, as did the machine gunners on the beach. With apparent disdain for this puny and ineffective attack, the two planes promptly turned tail and headed away; their task executed, their bullets expended.

When Katherine and Alastair climbed back onto the deck, they found that Angus had laid Sergeant Smith on one of the berths in the cabin, trying desperately to stem the bleeding from wounds to his arm, chest and legs. Katherine had never seen so much blood but he was still alive, just.

Together, they pressed wads of cotton wool onto his injuries, but these were soaked in no time, so they pressed on more and more and held them there. She utilized the bandages made from the old clean sheets, blessing the housekeeper for her foresight in providing so many, tying them tightly over the wounds.

It was only then that she became aware of the injury to Angus's foot. There was nothing she could do other than pad and bandage it as tightly as possible. The pain must have been excruciating but throughout it all, Angus made no complaint, beads of sweat being the only indication of the agony he must have been concealing. He really was a courageous man.

Without hesitation and without waiting to take the next batch of troops who had just started to file onto the jetty, Alastair headed *Spirit of Adventure* out to sea. Such was his focus and sense of urgency that he was only dimly aware of shells whistling across the bows, landing in the water, sending up great spumes of spray, or of the accusatory shouts of cowardice and derision from the soldiers left behind, seeing him depart with a virtually empty boat.

There had to be a tug or a Dutch *schuyte* somewhere, he thought desperately. Anything that could give them a fast passage back to England. Neither were there any hospital ships to be seen.

Alastair had to find the quickest way back home with his injured passengers as well as conserve his fuel. Of the officially designated routes, Z was the shortest but too exposed in daylight to the shore batteries at Gravelines; Route Y too far at eighty-seven miles and would take too long. At fifty-five miles, Route X was the most likely candidate, but he would have to negotiate the treacherous sandbanks off Dunkirk and then the Goodwin Sands nearer England. On any route, boats and ships might be subject to attack by E-boat or submarine as well as bombing. A small boat on its own was particularly vulnerable.

He had to take the risk, however. Quickly, he consulted his chart and made some rapid calculations. Then, opening up both engines, Alastair set off for home.

After about an hour or so, they ran into thick fog which, although it afforded a protective cover, slowed their progress and forced him to navigate blind. A large vessel suddenly loomed up out of the murk and almost collided with them. Unbelievably, it was the *Enterprise*, laden with troops.

Alastair could not believe his luck. "Ahoy there!" he called out.

"Ahoy yourself! Need a tow?!" responded Captain Goodsell.

"Now whatever gave you that idea?!"

Alastair caught the ropes that were thrown to him and tied them securely round the Samson post on the deck.

He explained that they were trying to get home as quickly as possible and why.

Captain Goodsell chewed on his pipe for a moment and rubbed his chin thoughtfully. Then he said, "What's your draft?"

"Three-foot nine."

"You'll be all right then." And he took the wheel and the tug continued on its way.

Captain Goodsell's intended route was across a minefield. It was the shortest way home and a calculated risk, but one which the old salt reckoned he could manage safely. Not all mines were on the surface; the most dangerous ones to deep-draft ships were those that lurked beneath the water.

So that's why he needed to know our draft, thought Alastair, shaking his head and smiling to himself after ascertaining their course. Nonetheless, he ordered the soldiers to maintain a careful look-out across the water, while he kept the boat steady in the tug's wake.

Presently, having instructed one of the soldiers how to take the wheel, Alastair went down below. "How's Ron?" he asked.

"Not good, but he's hanging on. He's terribly weak from losing so much blood. He keeps drifting in and out of consciousness and he's so cold. I'm trying to keep him warm, but it's very difficult. I have no idea whether that's the right thing to do. The bleeding seems to have stopped for now on his arms and legs with the pads and bandages, but I have no idea what to do about the wound to his chest. He might have other internal injuries as well. The shoulder doesn't look too good either." She looked up at him. "Oh Alastair, he needs better care than I can give him."

"You're doing fine. He's still alive and at this stage that's the best we can hope for. How's Angus doing?"

"Amazingly well. He won't leave Ron's side and keeps talking to him to bring him round every time he drifts off. He takes no notice of his own injury, which is just awful. I've cleaned it up as best I can but he'll be lucky if he doesn't lose part of that foot."

"The two of them are incredibly brave. They could have gone home two days ago."

"I know, but they wanted to stay and help us."

"That's why I want to get back as quickly as we can. I feel a measure of responsibility, even though it was their decision."

"There really are some heroic, self-sacrificing people in this world."

Understanding her meaning, he didn't reply verbally, but merely nodded, stroking her cheek with the back of his fingers before going back up the companionway steps. Katherine was too preoccupied with her patients to register consciously the tingling on her skin, even though she instinctively placed her own hand on the place where he had touched her.

Alastair had only just stepped back on deck, when they heard a disembodied voice speaking to them through a megaphone: "You are in the middle of a minefield. Follow us and we shall do our best to lead you to safety." From out of the fog came a mine-sweeper, a converted paddle-steamer, the distinctive slap-slap-slap of the paddles reassuring in its continuity and familiarity as they followed behind.

With a sailor's superstition, Alastair just accepted the good fortune they had had so far, but without remarking upon it and thereby tempting fate.

Sometime later, much later, they left the bank of fog behind and emerged into the after-glow of yet another wonderful sunset. But this time, there before them, were the peaceful white cliffs of Dover. Never before had a sight been more welcome.

They were home.

The minesweeper chugged away to the sound of an appreciative blast from the tug's hooter, the tow rope was cast off and *Spirit of Adventure* and her cargo entered Dover's Granville Dock under her own power, after first making themselves known to the Reporting Vessel, which had been placed to monitor all incoming and outgoing shipping.

As soon as he had moored her securely among all the other motorboats, Alastair leapt off onto the quayside and went in search of stretcher bearers, his knees almost buckling under him as his feet touched solid ground after three days at sea. After a struggle, using his rank to overcome objections, he managed to find four R.A.M.C. personnel to come to Sergeant Smith's and Private MacKellar's aid.

Protective as a mother hen, Angus extolled them to be careful as they lifted his friend onto one of the stretchers, insisting that he was going to accompany the sergeant wherever he was taken so that they could be treated together, declaring that no amount of orders or threats of court martial would dissuade him from this. The medics laughed and said it wasn't up to them, but he could stay with them for now.

Katherine had written down hers and Alastair's names, London and Maybury addresses and telephone numbers on a piece of paper, which Angus folded and placed carefully in his sporran. She spoke to him quietly in Gaelic while the men were tending to Ron.

"If we're not still here in Dover, that will be where you can reach us. Please let us know how you both are."

"Yes, ma'am, I will, have no fear of that."

"And it's probably best not to mention to anyone that there's a woman on board *Spirit of Adventure*."

"No, ma'am." He smiled, briefly. "Your secret is safe with me. I'll not mention it to a living soul until the war is over, then I'll dine off it for a very long time!" and, from his prone position on the stretcher, he saluted them both. Then he was away with the stretcher bearers. He would see his sergeant friend right, just as the sergeant had promised he would do the same for him at Dunkirk.

After they had gone, Katherine began to tremble uncontrollably and almost collapsed onto the deck. Alastair put his arm round her and helped her down below.

"I need to get you somewhere to rest other than here," he said. "We'll clean up the boat later."

"I'm so sorry," she said, ashamed, drying her tears.

"Don't be. You have been amazing and it's a very natural reaction to everything. I daresay mine will hit me at some stage. Now, will you be all right if I leave you for a few minutes and go and find Captain Goodsell?"

Katherine nodded.

"Good. I'll be back as soon as I can."

Alastair donned his cap and soiled uniform jacket and set off to the *Enterprise*, working his way through the throngs of soldiers being counted as they disembarked from the ships at the quayside; circumventing the lines of men waiting patiently to be sent onto the special trains and dispersed to various holding destinations around the country. Here, their regiments would be re-formed and there would be yet another train journey to wherever their unit was going to be stationed before they were all given survivor's leave.

It had been decided early on that this would be the quickest and simplest way to bring as many of the soldiers home as was humanly possible. "Get 'em on the ships first; sort 'em out later," had been the practical and logical command from the British senior officers.

After some difficulty and several enquiries, Alastair located Captain Goodsell and went on board the *Enterprise*. The two men shook hands and Alastair thanked him for his help. The tug's captain brushed it aside and then said, "Now if you and your lady wife..." and he laughed at Alastair's shocked expression, "...would like somewhere to kip down, go and see my sister." He produced a slip of paper and an old pencil stub from his pocket and wrote down the name and address and a brief note of explanation. "It's just across the road there and she'll find a room for you, no trouble." He winked at Alastair.

"How did you know Katherine was a woman?"

"Lads don't have a figure like hers! When we first met you, her duffel coat was undone, so I noticed the moment you stepped on board the *Enterprise*, begging your pardon Lieutenant-Commander. I assume she's your missis?" There was a mischievous twinkle in his eye as he said this.

Alastair, rendered speechless by the implications of Captain Goodsell's assumption that Katherine was his wife, let alone anything else, wondered how many other people had spotted that his companion was a woman and thought the same?

Too many, probably.

At that moment exhaustion overtook him. It was all too much effort to offer an explanation as to why he had taken his *daughter-in-law* with him; that she wasn't a wife or a mistress. So he just nodded. It was just easier to leave this man with his assumption. After all, what harm could it do?

The captain took Alastair's silence for acquiescence. "It's all right, your secret is safe with me. I shan't tell a living soul other than my sister that your wife went across to Dunkirk!" He chuckled, adjusting the position of his pipe. "Now you take this and off you go. You've not had much sleep since we first met, I reckon, so get yourself some rest. I hope we meet again one day."

"Likewise, and thank you for everything." Alastair had found his voice again.

"Good luck, Lieutenant-Commander Stewart."

"And you, Captain Goodsell."

They shook hands and Alastair made his way back to *Spirit of Adventure*. He decided not to tell Katherine of this conversation, other than the fact that they had somewhere to stay and that she had been recognized as a woman. Listening, but too exhausted to express concern, she helped him make the boat secure.

Alastair spoke to the R.N.V.R. duty officer on the quayside, giving an order that under no circumstances was anyone to move his boat, as he would be needing it again later.

The young, keen, slightly over-anxious sub-lieutenant said, "Yes, sir, of course, sir, I'll see to it personally, sir." He wrote down the name of the motorboat and where it was berthed. "Sir?"

"Yes?"

"You'll need to make out a report, sir. Admiral Ramsay wants a record kept of each boat or ship and what they have done. I'm trying to get round to everyone, but it's not always possible."

"Who do I give it to?"

"To me, sir. I'll see to it that it's passed on immediately."

"How long are you on duty?"

"I'm off duty in a moment but I'll be back on at 0800 hours tomorrow morning."

"I shall make sure you have it then."

"Thank you, sir." The young man paused, nervous, apologetic, before adding, "I'm sorry sir, but if you are intending to leave the harbour at any time, you and the lad there will need permits to get back in."

Alastair gave Katherine's 'name' as well as his own and was duly furnished with the appropriate documentation. She, for her part, pulled her woolly hat lower down over her forehead to avoid any further possible detection but fortunately, the young officer took no notice of her. With hat, jumper *and* duffel coat, she was sweltering in the hot June sun. She was filthy, didn't smell too good and was in desperate need of a bath. But she was too tired to think; too tired to do anything except *sleep.*

Carrying the bags in which they had packed spare clothes before leaving Maybury, they made their way out of the harbour and crossed the road, finding the boarding house without too much difficulty.

Captain Goodsell's sister, Mrs King, was a hospitable woman but thin and tired-looking. She read the note that her brother had written and said, "Yes, I can give you a room. It's twin beds though. It's all I've got at the moment."

Alastair immediately accepted the offer on their behalf. He and Katherine could debate the morality of this later on. Right now, he felt too worn out to worry about anything.

They were shown to their room and told that the bathroom was just down the corridor. Wrinkling her nose, Mrs King looked at them with slight distaste and said, "I know you must be exhausted after what you've done, but I'd appreciate it if you could both take a bath first. If you leave your clothes outside the door, I'll make sure they're washed."

"Thank you very much," said Katherine, "that's very kind."

Once they were in the room, Alastair said, with some trepidation, "Captain Goodsell and Mrs King are under the impression that we're married."

"Really?" Katherine's manner was distracted and Alastair could not be sure that she had heard him.

"Who's going to bathe first?" she said.

"You can. Did you hear what I said?"

"Yes, but I'm too tired to worry about it at the moment. Besides which, dear Alastair, I trust you implicitly. I've nursed you through pneumonia, you've seen me in my dressing gown many times at home, we've spent several nights together on board the boat and right now all I want to do is wash and go to sleep. We can discuss the implications of our sharing a room if you like when we wake up, but not just now."

And with that, she smiled wearily at him, collected her toilet bag and nightwear and went into the bathroom. She was back quickly, and by the time Alastair had had his bath, Katherine was fast asleep. Overcome with exhaustion, he climbed into his bed and woke up at six the following morning, having slept for nearly eight hours.

Katherine didn't stir as he dressed quietly and returned to the harbour, where he sat on the deck of *Spirit of Adventure*, wrote his report and handed it to the sub-lieutenant. He was just about to go, when the officer said, "Please wait a moment, sir. Admiral Ramsay has issued an order that all personnel vessels should have a lieutenant-commander and ten naval ratings aboard. We've had one or two problems, you see, with a couple of masters refusing to go back over to Dunkirk, so all these ships now have to have Royal Navy supervision. The *S.S. Royal Bluebell* has no master. He's gone home suffering from nervous exhaustion." The young man consulted the clipboard he was holding and said apologetically, "I'm afraid you have been assigned to take her back to Dunkirk."

Alastair, taken by surprise, said, "When does she sail?"

"At 1030 hours, sir." He paused and then added, "I'm sorry you have to go back. It must have been terrible over there yesterday."

Images of the previous day flashed through Alastair's mind. He took a deep breath and nodded. "When am I expected on board?"

"As soon as possible, sir."

He would have very little time to familiarize himself with the ship before she sailed but he also needed to let Katherine know. Thanking the lieutenant, he left the harbour and returned to the boarding house, where he asked the landlady for breakfast for Katherine, which she duly prepared and he took this up to their room.

She had only just woken up and smiled at him sleepily as he came in carrying the tray. To Alastair, she looked so lovely with her hair all spiky and tousled, that it was almost more than he could bear to not take her in his arms.

"Breakfast! And in bed, too. What luxury!" she exclaimed. "Go on, turn round while I make myself decent!" She sat up and covered her nightdress with a cardigan. "It's all right, you can talk to me now without either of us being embarrassed." She smiled up at him and without thinking, he took both her hands in his and kissed them.

"What's all that about?" she asked, taken aback, pulling away from him.

"Nothing," he said, biting his bottom lip.

A shiver of fear went down her spine. "So, what is the bad news you have to tell me?"

He looked at her. "How did you know?"

"I think it's fair to say that we read each other like a pair of books."

Alastair nodded. "That's very true." He took a deep breath. "I've been ordered back to Dunkirk."

"On *Spirit of Adventure*?"

"No, no. Commanding a personnel vessel, a cross-channel ferry called *S.S. Royal Bluebell*." He explained the circumstances.

"When do you have to go?"

"Now, almost immediately."

"Oh, Alastair."

Anxiety made her reach out to him and he took her proffered hands in his, coming to sit beside her on the bed. Neither of them said anything, but they both knew exactly what it was he would have to face when he returned to the other side of the Channel.

"I can't come with you this time, can I?" she said, knowing that to be so, but saying it anyway.

Alastair shook his head, knowing also that she knew the answer. "But I couldn't have done what we did without you. I'd take you anywhere with me if I could."

"And I'd come, too."

"*Whither thou goest...*"

"Yes."

For a few brief moments, he held her in his arms and she clung onto him before he gently disengaged himself, kissed her forehead and left.

Such was her distress, it was only much later that Katherine remembered her breakfast, cold and uneaten on the tray.

CHAPTER 15

Dunkirk (4)
May/June, 1940

Katherine awoke with a start when a door slammed somewhere downstairs in the house. Reaching drowsily for her watch, she found the time to be eleven o'clock. She must have fallen asleep again after Alastair had left.

Awful reality seeped into her consciousness. He would be well on his way across the Channel by now and yet another involuntary shiver of fear and helplessness ran down her spine.

She lay there for a few more moments before getting out of bed and dressing in clean clothes, trying to maintain her disguise as far as she was able. Hungry, despite her anxiety, she ate what could be salvaged of her breakfast and, not wishing to offend their host, she put the remains into a paper bag to dispose of once she had left the boarding house.

Resolutely, after first collecting a front door key from their landlady, she made herself go out and not mope about in their room. She went first to Granville Dock, gaining entry without difficulty by using her pass, and assessed what needed to be done to clean up the mess on board *Spirit of Adventure*.

She made a list of all the things she would need, and was just about to return on deck when she heard voices. She paused at the bottom of the companionway steps, her hands resting on the grab-handles. Two R.N.V.R. officers had stopped by the boat and were deep in discussion.

Standing on tip-toe and discreetly peering up at the quayside, Katherine saw the young sub-lieutenant she and Alastair had encountered on their arrival talking to another officer of the same rank, who was apparently new and being given the 'low-down'. She could not help but overhear their conversation.

"Now," he said, consulting his clip-board, "this is *Spirit of Adventure*. She has to stay where she is, so make sure of that. Belongs to Lieutenant-Commander Stewart. He was over in Dunkirk for three days and survived to tell the tale. He might need the boat again. Admiral Ramsay was most impressed with the report the Commander wrote – not just for all that he did, but the way it was written. Said he wished all reports were as clear and concise as that – and as self-effacing. He's been so inundated with emergency situations from the far shore, it was one of the few he's actually had a chance to look at."

Down below, her heart beating fast, Katherine smiled, experiencing pride at his words.

"Well, from what I know of the Admiral, that's praise indeed. Where's the Lieutenant-Commander at the moment?"

"In charge of the personnel vessel *S.S. Royal Bluebell*. She set off for Dunkirk just after 1030 hours this morning."

"When's she expected back?"

"Who knows? Admiral Ramsay wants an absolute all-out effort today. Wants to try and finish the evacuation if he can. It seems the Germans are closing in on

Dunkirk very fast. We lost an awful lot of ships yesterday and today he's sending over everything possible. The drill is to collect the troops, disembark them here, turn around immediately and go back. Although, having said that, most of the larger, faster vessels like the destroyers and personnel ships have already been doing that for days. Their crews must be exhausted. But everyone will have to manage at least two or three trips today."

"Providing nothing untoward happens between here and there," said his companion. The two men acknowledged the dangers. "Refuelling must be difficult," observed the new officer.

"Oh, it is. There are so many types of ship here – some need coal, some need petrol and some diesel. Then there's the oil. Different grades for different ships. Not to mention repairs – most vessels return home damaged in some way…" (Katherine's heart skipped several beats) "… and what with victualing, replacing ammunition as well as maintenance and operational control, it's a logistical nightmare. But Admiral Ramsay has it all in hand. What he and his senior officers haven't thought of, which is very little from what I've seen and heard, he listens to what other people have to say, comes to a decision and acts accordingly. Delegates too. Knows the right people to place in the job. I take my hat off to him. We couldn't have done this without him at the helm." He hesitated for a moment and then added, "You'll like being on his staff. You'll be exhausted, mind, but you'll work your socks off for him and what we're trying to do here."

"Well, we'd better get on if we're to select suitable motorboats to go over tomorrow."

The two men walked off, still deep in conversation. Katherine emerged from her hiding place, feeling the glow of reflected praise and thinking that she would like to meet this admiral that Alastair and the young officer were so taken with.

When they were far enough away, she climbed up on deck, padlocked the cabin doors and left the quayside, heading up towards the town. On her way, she spotted a chandler's shop and as she went inside, was greeted by the pungent smell of Stockholm tar and the cheerful jingling of a bell over the door. The shop was a veritable Aladdin's cave, selling everything that anyone could possibly need for a journey to sea.

The grizzled old man behind the counter eyed her with curiosity, not sure what to make of her. Katherine smiled at him and he grunted in return. She had shed her duffel coat, carrying it over one arm, and had left her jumper back at the boarding house as it was being washed, so her disguise, wearing a rather feminine blouse, was no longer intact.

She was looking for something that would hide her figure but would not cause her to swelter too much in the hot June sun. She found exactly the right thing in a navy blue, loose-fitting fisherman's smock.

Perfect.

She chose one that was a couple of sizes too large, found a sailor's peaked cap that fitted, which meant she could dispense with the equally hot woolly hat while on land, and completed her purchases with some candles, matches and a container of lamp oil.

She paid for these without saying anything at first, producing the necessary money and required coupons, and received another grunt when she said, "Thank you," as she opened the door to go out. The shopkeeper appeared not to be a great conversationalist, although it was perfectly possible that an unaccompanied woman in a shop that would normally be a male preserve, had rendered him temporarily speechless.

Katherine continued along the path from the harbour up to the town, where she located a hardware shop and bought a pair of overalls, a scrubbing brush, several floor cloths and carbolic soap.

Having completed her shopping and using up her entire month's supply of coupons in the process, she made her way back to *Spirit of Adventure*, where she changed into the overalls, donned her peaked cap and, using many buckets of water, proceeded to swab the decks and clean the cockpit. She then brought the saloon berth cushions up onto the deck and scrubbed them thoroughly with carbolic soap, leaving them to dry on the cabin roof. They looked somewhat ragged, but at least they would be clean. Katherine surmised that *Spirit of Adventure* would need a complete overhaul anyway after this escapade.

She then set to work on the floor of the saloon and cabins and by early afternoon had the boat in a fairly ship-shape condition. At least, it was clean and no longer smelled.

There was nothing more she could do, other than wait for the saloon berth cushions up on the deck and the interior of the boat to dry. Stretching her aching back and tenderly rubbing her sore hands, she realized that she was hungry and that this was a good time to go in search of food. So, changing out of her overalls and putting on her cap and fisherman's smock, she once more made her way towards the town.

Everywhere was full of soldiers. They lined Dover Harbour Station, waiting for one of the hundreds of extra trains that Southern Railway had made available in this time of national crisis; waiting to be transported away from the town as quickly as possible, leaving room for still more incoming soldiers.

They lined the roadside, sitting or leaning against garden fences, lying on the grass verges, sprawled out on benches, waiting for buses or their train. They fell asleep anywhere they could find a space to lie down, knowing they were home and safe, able to give themselves up at last to the utter exhaustion they felt.

Katherine was moved by the immense kindness and care by which these tired and dispirited men were surrounded. They had survived, had stood their ground valiantly, but they had also suffered the ignominy of defeat and endured days of shelling and bombing on the beaches, as well as untold deprivation.

They had expected to be met at home with disapproval and dishonour. But to their amazement, they were greeted with reaction of a very different kind: a warm welcome, cheering, presents from well-wishers, food, desperately needed clothes, shoes and even a postcard with postage already paid to send to their families to let them know they were safe.

Unbelievably, to these weary, dispirited men, they had become national heroes and 'Dunkirk' was rapidly becoming synonymous with strength and fortitude, not a cause for shame. A 'miracle' some people were already calling it.

The Women's Voluntary Service were out in force, distributing sandwiches, hot soup, cakes and masses of hot sweet tea to the tired, hungry soldiers on the trains and in the streets. As she walked, Katherine overheard so many offers of help from local people and so many expressions of grateful thanks and relief from the soldiers, that she felt humbled by the enormity of the achievement and yes, a sense of pride that she had in some small measure made a contribution.

But it was not over yet. There were still many thousands of men over in France needing to join their comrades in England and Katherine's thoughts and prayers went out to them... but most of all to Alastair.

The *S.S. Royal Bluebell* arrived in Dunkirk that afternoon amid a ferocious air attack. As her captain, Alastair was directed to berth alongside the East Pier by the Royal Navy Pier Master.

Everyone was operating under constant air bombardment as well as shelling from the German artillery that was now close enough to have an accurate range. There were air raids every half hour, with hundreds of planes coming over in wave after wave. The destruction was unbelievable.

Destroyers and other armed vessels bombarded the enemy wherever and whenever possible; the noise from the barrage deafening and mind-numbing. But still the troops moved forward on the East Mole; still they kept coming onto the larger ships either side of the pier, the medium-sized ones in the outer harbour and the smaller vessels in the inner harbour area.

Alastair put down three gangplanks to facilitate movement onto the ship and instructed his sub-lieutenant and naval ratings where to direct the men once they were on board.

There were hundreds of stretcher cases and each time a convoy of ambulances drew up on the landward end of the pier, the soldiers had to move aside to make way for them. This slowed the rate of lift considerably, but it had to be done. Alastair had them taken to the stern deck, as this was the quickest and easiest place to reach – to have them going down the companionway into the saloon area below decks would have caused unnecessary delay.

He had hoists rigged to lift on board the seriously injured men lying on wooden platforms. In this way, he could continue to load the able-bodied as well as the walking wounded.

Still more soldiers moved forward onto the pier, waiting their turn with patience and relative good humour before coming onto the ship – their discipline, especially given the pounding they were having to withstand, of the highest standard.

Still the air raids continued. Nobody left their station; there was little panic with everyone working together under constant aerial assault, sharing the same risks and dangers, knowing there was a job to do.

But suddenly, the force of an explosion rocked *Royal Bluebell* in her berth as a trawler across the other side of the pier was sunk by a direct hit, injuring scores of soldiers with shrapnel and debris. As quickly as possible, they were taken on board and treated as best as could be done. The personnel ship herself was hit twice by shore batteries, fortunately with only light damage above the waterline, before the batteries themselves were put out of action by a round of shells from a nearby destroyer, engaging the enemy with accurate and effective shooting.

Rapidly, Alastair directed the operation to extinguish the fires. The damage was patched up, with the sub-lieutenant and young naval ratings showing their mettle, together with the remnants of the ferry's crew working hard alongside them.

For seven hours, the ship lay alongside the East Mole; for seven hours Alastair, his crew and those around them endured an unbelievable onslaught, both mental and physical, until the ship was full and she could at last set sail for England.

He embarked nearly fourteen hundred troops that day and his steadiness and calm direction of the men in his charge while under fire did not go unnoticed by the Pier Master and Senior Naval Officer.

That evening, after eating supper at the boarding house, Katherine returned to Granville Dock and put everything back in its proper place, feeling that the boat was now in reasonable shape.

Destroyers and personnel vessels were coming into the harbour, battered and damaged, to unload their troops but there was no sign of Alastair and *Royal Bluebell*. Katherine sat on deck until it was dark, careless of the need to preserve her anonymity: watching, waiting, until eventually tiredness overtook her and she was obliged to lock up the boat and return to the boarding house. She fell into a dream-filled sleep where she could find no rest, but was always searching for something just out of reach.

When she opened her eyes early the next morning, the first thing she saw was Alastair sitting on the edge of his bed, hunched over with extreme tiredness, watching her. He looked so exhausted and worn out that, filled with love and sympathy, she put her arms out to him and he came to her and lay down beside her, instantly falling asleep as she held him.

In her spontaneous offer of comfort, not once did Katherine consider the morality of her actions or the implications this might have on their relationship, because she saw no possibility for change. He was Alastair, her confidante, her companion and because she was married to his son, the consolation that she gave, having no reason to believe it was any different for Alastair, was innocent, part of the deep, affectionate friendship they shared.

Resolutely, therefore, Katherine suppressed her growing desire for the man beside her, upset by her body's betrayal of her finer feelings. Resolutely, therefore, she refused to acknowledge the complex emotions that dwelt within her heart should she choose to analyse them. Instead, she turned her mind to the most important thing – the fact that Alastair was back with her again; that he had returned safely and needed her consolation.

Eventually, Katherine too fell asleep, but this respite was not to last for long, for Alastair had to return to Dunkirk later that day and within a few hours, would have to prepare his ship for the journey.

There was one more night planned for the evacuation and he was required to be a part of it.

CHAPTER 16

Dunkirk (5)
June, 1940

"Splendid view, isn't it?"

Deep in her own thoughts, Katherine jumped at the unexpected sound.

"I'm sorry. I didn't intend to startle you."

The man was soft-spoken, yet he had the unmistakable air of authority. He looked tired and his skin was pale but he seemed fully alive and cheerful in his demeanour. He sat down at the other end of the bench. His naval uniform sleeves bore the unmistakable rings of a vice admiral.

"Do you mind?"

Surprised, Katherine stuttered, "Of... of course not." Could this be Admiral Ramsay, she wondered?

"Thank you." A moment's silence. "I always think that it's a good thing to be able to escape, even if it is only for a few moments. You see," he said confidentially, "any moment now, my staff officer hovering back there," and he pointed behind him, "will do his best to drag me back to reality."

"And there's nowhere to hide."

The admiral smiled. "Unfortunately not."

"I like to escape too. Walking is excellent in that respect." She had found her voice again.

"I agree. So is sitting here looking out over such a vista as this. One can see almost everything."

"Aye, *almost* everything."

In silence they contemplated the Straits of Dover before them; the sea sparkling in the bright sunlight, the convoy of ships leaving the harbour.

Following her gaze and sensing an inner anxiety, the admiral said, "Do you have someone involved?"

"Yes. Aboard the *S.S. Royal Bluebell*." Katherine chose not to elaborate further. It was enough.

"She has a fine commanding officer now."

Katherine felt herself blush at the praise for Alastair. But still she did not reveal the connection. Instead she merely nodded and asked, "Can it go on much longer?"

The admiral looked at her sharply. "An intelligent question. I hope that tonight will see the end of it. My sailors are tired. What is being asked of them is more than flesh and blood can stand. There has to be a finite time to the evacuation. It cannot continue indefinitely. At least, not without a complete change of personnel operating the ships. And there is no time to arrange for that."

"No."

Deferentially, his staff officer approached and the admiral stood up, his manner cheerful once again. "I have to go, I'm afraid. My brief respite is at an end. I shall leave you to enjoy your solitude."

"Goodbye, Admiral Ramsay. And good luck."

"Thank you." He paused. "How do you know who I am?"

Katherine smiled. "Oh, you're quite famous, you know."

"Really?" He seemed genuinely surprised.

Smiling and with a lightness of step he returned to the staff car parked by the side of the road. Katherine watched until the car had disappeared on the remainder of its short journey up the hill to Dover Castle perched high on the chalk cliffs, beneath which were the casemate tunnels where Admiral Ramsay had his operational headquarters.

Their chance encounter left Katherine feeling glad that she had met him. Now she would be able to picture the man upon whose shoulders rested the ultimate responsibility for the success of the evacuation.

Little did she realize at that moment how closely their paths would be aligned in the future.

She sat for a while longer before resuming her walk, all the while keeping the ships' progress across the Channel in her view.

At 1430 hours that afternoon, along with the destroyers, paddle-minesweepers and other personnel vessels, Alastair received a signal from Admiral Ramsay concerning the arrangements for the evacuation that night from Dunkirk Harbour. The message included the following instructions regarding the berthing arrangements on the East Pier:

Berth A: from lighthouse to trawler wreck
Berth B: from wreck to gap in pier
Berth C: from gap in wall to hut at end of pier
Berths D and E: smaller berths extending to inner end of the pier

The Admiral's orders also made it plain that personnel vessels and destroyers were to have priority in the larger berths as their carrying capacity was the greatest. As on previous nights, the Pier Master would direct the berthing, and traffic control naval motorboats would be used to guide the larger ships around the wrecks and other debris onto their allotted berths. A red Very's light would stop entry to the harbour and a green one would allow entry.

He ordered the use of specially constructed ladders to facilitate embarkation, which were available from Dover Harbour, and advised that all ships should also have boxes available as steps. It was Admiral Ramsay's intention to keep berths A to E constantly filled, and to that end he staggered the departure and arrival times for destroyers and personnel ships on both sides of the Channel, not just from Dover to Dunkirk, but from Ramsgate and Margate as well.

During the course of Operation Dynamo, Admiral Ramsay issued hundreds of signals and it was his attention to even the smallest of details that gave a glimpse into the organizational skills of the man charged with the safe return of the B.E.F. He could also improvise when necessary and allowed others to do the same. This inspired the men under his command and in return, they pushed themselves above and beyond the call of duty, trusting his judgement and exceptional abilities.

So it was that Alastair once more took *Royal Bluebell* across to France, at the same time as Katherine was watching from her vantage point above the town.

The ship travelled without incident across the Straits of Dover, but on reaching Dunkirk they found a strong west-going tide running through the concrete piles of the East Pier, which together with a fresh easterly wind was forcing the ships away from the Mole, as it was known.

They had to be pushed on by one of the motorboats and, with skilful seamanship and gratefully accepted help, Alastair and the ship's coxswain guided *Royal Bluebell* to her berth. Once she was securely moored, he gave orders to begin embarking the soldiers.

The thing that struck Alastair most on this occasion was the complete absence of bombing and shelling. All that could be heard was the sporadic crackle of machine gun fire and explosions from mortars as the rear-guard held the perimeter around the town.

He had psychologically prepared himself for yet another onslaught; indeed, he had expected it. It seemed strange to be here and able to work without interruption or having to steel oneself to cope with the next barrage. He remarked as much to the Pier Master when he came on board to see how things were going.

"I know. I can't believe it either."

"Any idea why?" asked Alastair.

"Well, I expect you know that yesterday afternoon Admiral Ramsay issued orders that there was to be no further evacuation during daylight hours – things were far too hot for ships here yesterday and we were losing too many in comparison with the rate of lift. Just to add to that, all the routes from England are now under pretty accurate shelling during the day, not to mention the E-boats…"

"Yes, I did know that."

"Thought you might. Anyway, the Admiral demanded total air cover from Coastal Command tonight and he's got it too, I might add. He then asked that Bomber Command attack the shore batteries. So, somewhere above us, the R.A.F. is doing its stuff. He anticipates that without interruption, the remainder of the B.E.F. will be evacuated tonight." Then he added, with a smile, "But we reckon that old Jerry has had enough for the moment. He doesn't like coming out when it's dark!"

"If only!" replied Alastair, chuckling. "Well, whatever the reasons, we're all grateful."

"Absolutely. So, everything all right?"

"Fine, thank you, Commander."

"Good. I'll be getting along then. Got to go and visit the other ships on my patch." He paused as he was about to step off the ship onto the gangplank. "Oh, watch out on the way back. Jerry was busy laying parachute mines last night. We think most of them are magnetic. Nasty little blighters! You have been degaussed, haven't you?"

"Yes, someone came on board yesterday and neutralized the magnetic field of the ship. Clever stuff."

"I'll say! Well, go carefully."

Alastair assured him that he would and resumed his stance on the bridge ensuring the embarkation proceeded smoothly. He took on board about a thousand British soldiers together with about the same number of French, all of whom were combatant troops who demonstrated impeccable discipline.

Loaded beyond capacity, *S.S. Royal Bluebell* departed at 2330 on what was intended to be the last night of the evacuation. Despite his tiredness, Alastair experienced a sense of exhilaration as he viewed the now empty pier.

They had done it. The miracle had been achieved.

At that same time, Captain Tennant, R.N., the Senior Naval Officer at Dunkirk, sent the historic signal to Admiral Ramsay in Dover: '*B.E.F. evacuated*', adding, '*Am leaving now*', before he and his gallant Royal Navy officers, most of whom had been there with him since Monday, 27th May, departed Dunkirk for the last time aboard a naval motorboat.

However, following this and much to everyone's annoyance, the French rearguard did not make their expected appearance, and most of the waiting ships assigned to bring them across to England were obliged to return empty or nearly empty to Dover early the next morning.

As soon as they were clear of the harbour, *Royal Bluebell*'s steward brought Alastair a welcome cup of tea on the bridge and said, "Begging your pardon, sir, but there's a deputation of French soldiers who'd like to speak to you. Shall I tell 'em you're busy?"

"No, no, Travers, show them up. They're our guests and it's only right that we should extend them every courtesy. Ask the sub to come and see me as well, but straightaway."

"Righty-ho, sir."

The sub-lieutenant was very quick to respond. "I came as soon as I could, sir."

"Well done, Rutherford. Now, how many look-outs have we got?"

"Ten, sir. All in the positions you specified."

"Good. They're to keep a sharp watch for any object in or floating on the water or any shadows beneath the surface. Is that clear? They'll need to concentrate. I want to take this ship, and us, home in one piece. I'll come and talk to them directly."

"Yes, sir." And Rutherford disappeared out onto the deck.

Almost immediately, there was a knock at the door.

"Come in," called out Alastair, and in walked three French officers, with a major being the most senior rank present.

"*Bonjour*," said Alastair, extending his hand to the major, who returned the greeting.

"*Bonjour, Capitaine. Nous vous sommes très reconnaissants de nous accueillir à bord de votre bateau.*"

"You're welcome."

While Alastair understood enough French to know that the soldiers were grateful to be on board his ship, he wished that Katherine was here and could interpret. Fortunately, though, the French army major could also speak a little English, so between them they managed to communicate fairly well.

116

"Now, how can I help?" said Alastair.

"We have lost our *Général*. We are wondering if you can 'elp us."

Alastair resisted the temptation to say that it was very careless to lose a general, but he thought that this observation might not be appreciated by his guests. So, suppressing a smile of amusement, he asked, "How so?"

"We are wondering if you could make enquiries on our be'alf from the authorities."

"I can try. When did you last see him?"

"Our divisions have been fighting alongside the British rear-guard. When it was the other French soldiers' turn to hold the, 'ow you say...?" He searched for the right word.

"Perimeter?" suggested Alastair.

"Ah yes, the perimeter. When it was the other soldiers' turn, we withdrew through their lines along with the British as arranged and came 'ere to the 'arbour. Our *Général*, 'e stay behind to tell the new *Général* where were the enemy. We do not see 'im again. 'E was supposed to follow us."

One of the soldiers said something in rapid French to his commanding officer, who replied, "*Mais oui.*"

He then turned to Alastair and said, "My comrade says that our countrymen are counter-attacking at this moment. Our *Général*, 'e may be there also."

"So that's why the last French soldiers we were expecting didn't arrive on the pier tonight," observed Alastair.

"*Oui, Capitaine. C'est vrai.*"

"Your General may yet appear."

"'E might. But we would like you to enquire, *tout de même*. You see, we love our *Général*. 'E is a great man, a brave man, and we would follow 'im anywhere."

Alastair found their loyalty touching. "His name?"

The major straightened his shoulders and stood to attention. "*Général* Phillippe d'Artennes du Laurier, the youngest *général* in the French Army, and a great leader of men. His loss is very painful to us." His shoulders sagged.

Alastair was thoughtful. "I can send a signal to see if he's been picked up on Malo Beach. I know that a flight of motorboats was being sent there tonight. It is possible that he has been taken back to England already."

"*Merci, nous vous sommes très reconnaissants.*" Saluting, the three men left the bridge.

After first going up on deck to individually impress upon each naval rating the important responsibility they had for the safety of the ship and everyone aboard, Alastair went down to the communications room and began to draft a signal to Admiral Ramsay in Dover and the Admiralty in London.

At that moment, *Royal Bluebell* was rocked by what sounded like a tremendous explosion followed by a loud graunching sound as she juddered to a halt. Alastair was back on the bridge in a matter of seconds.

"Stop all engines!" His order was obeyed. "Report!" he yelled down the voice tube.

"We've hit something, sir."

"I can tell that."

What had they hit? A mine? There were no fires, no further explosions. He felt relief. It must have been pretty large though, whatever it was. A submerged wreck? A sandbank? He was out on the deck immediately.

"Where?" he shouted at Rutherford, who in the moonlight looked as white as a sheet.

"Mid-ships, starboard side, sir."

Alastair immediately went along the side of the ship, the tightly-packed soldiers making way for him as best they could.

The steward came up to him. "We're taking in water, sir."

"Where?"

"The engine room, sir."

A nasty place. "Man the pumps and stuff the hole with whatever you can find. Mattresses, anything. Improvise. I'll be down in a minute."

A brigadier came up to him. "If any of my men can help, Captain...? We're Royal Engineers."

"Oh yes, please. We need to stem that leak down below. Rutherford will show you where. Use whatever you need. Tear the inside of the ship apart if you have to."

A group of soldiers were ordered below. Alastair's heart beat furiously. With two thousand men on board, the weight of his responsibility was enormous. He had no desire to lose any of them, nor any ship, his own or otherwise.

He hung over the side as far as he could. And there, with the top of its superstructure now protruding at an oblique angle just above the waterline on the falling tide, was a wreck. It looked like a destroyer. With *S.S. Royal Bluebell* being loaded to absolute capacity, there was a lot of weight to bring in contact with the partially submerged ship, which could make any damage potentially disastrous.

But where was the starboard lookout? Why had he not spotted something?

Alastair went down below. They were already up to their thighs in water in the engine room. The second engineer was standing steady, holding the bilge valve open.

"Good man," said Alastair.

He waded over to where the water was pouring in. Sub-Lieutenant Rutherford and some naval ratings arrived with mattresses and with the help of the Royal Engineers, proceeded to pack them into the gash as tightly as they could. After a lengthy, massive physical effort the breach was stopped and made more or less water-tight.

Alastair spoke to the brigadier. "The acid test is whether this stays in place when we start to move."

"Leave it with me, Captain. We'll sort something out."

"Thank you." Alastair then spoke to the chief engineer. "What about the engines?"

"My engines'll do whatever I tell them."

Alastair smiled. "That's the spirit!"

118

There was nothing more that he could do, so he went up on deck and looked again at the wreck. There was no mistaking its distinctive shape and form. It was indeed a destroyer.

In the grey dawn, he could now see some of the hull beneath the surface of the water, a mess of broken and twisted metal. Some of the jagged edges had cut through his heavily-laden ship like a knife and now they were stuck fast, joined together like some grotesque sculpture.

Alastair didn't like the look of it at all. It was going to be a devil of a job to disentangle themselves. To add to his worries, if they were still here once the sky became lighter, they would be a sitting target for patrolling E-boats or the *Luftwaffe*. They had no means of defence and no escort.

Quickly, he went to the communications room and sent a signal to Admiral Ramsay in Dover, as well as to all ships in the vicinity, notifying them of the position of the wreck and asking for assistance if possible.

Then he went back down into the engine room and on his way, prayed for deliverance.

CHAPTER 17

Dunkirk (6)
June, 1940

The fog bank rolled in from the Outer Ruytingen Sands to the south-east of their position, midway along Route X, not far from the Sandettie Bank. Never had the appearance of fog and its protective blanket been more welcome.

Alastair sent a further signal to Admiral Ramsay giving him an update on the weather and their current position. The reply stated that all R.A.F. planes were grounded because of the conditions but if and when the situation changed, then air cover would be provided.

Alastair stood on the starboard side of the ship, deep in conversation with the remaining Royal Engineers and the brigadier on the best way to extricate themselves from the wrecked destroyer. They came to the conclusion that the only way to separate the two vessels was by taking the offending parts from the destroyer with them. He then went back down to the engine room, where the chief engineer was struggling to start the engines.

"They've taken in far too much water, sir," he lamented. "I'm draining them out as best as I can."

"Keep at it, Jackson. We need those engines."

"Aye, aye. And sir?"

"Yes?"

"I'd just like to say that everyone appreciates your efforts. You know what you're about and that gives the crew and the soldiers confidence, sir."

"Thank you, Jackson. We all of us can only do our best."

"Well, we're all glad it was you in command, if you get my drift, rather than the other fella we've always had, the one that went home."

Alastair smiled, gratified. He said, "I understand. We'll get out of here all right, Jackson, just you wait and see. But we do need your engines."

"You'll get them, sir. They've never let me down yet."

"Thank you, Jackson."

Alastair went back up onto the bridge. He asked to see the sub-lieutenant.

"Who was on starboard lookout when we hit?"

"Young Crosby, sir."

"Ask him to come and see me will you, Rutherford? I need to find out what was going on."

The lieutenant hesitated. "He's pretty cut up about it, sir."

"I expect he is. But I'd like to see him just the same."

"Yes, sir. I'll send him along."

Crosby stood with head bowed, fiddling with the cap in his hand, moving it round and round with his fingers.

"Explanation?" said Alastair, trying not to let the anxiety he felt manifest itself in anger with this young man whom he felt had let them all down.

Crosby looked up, close to tears. It was his fault, all his fault, he said. "I'm sorry, sir. I just didn't see it. The wreck was covered by the water, sir."

Alastair could understand that.

"I only took my eyes off the water for a moment, sir…"

"What do you mean, you only took your eyes off the water for a moment?!" There was anger in his voice now. "You were given a job to do, sailor. An important job, a responsible job. As I said to all of you lookouts earlier, the safety of everyone on board depends upon each one of you."

"I was leaning so far over the side so I could see better, sir, that I almost lost my cap in the water. I grabbed hold of it to try to save it and took my eyes off the water, sir. It was only for a moment. And then it happened as quick as that. It's all my fault, sir." He was shaking and trembling now.

Alastair sighed with resignation. It was no one's fault. Just an innocent occurrence with unfortunate consequences. He decided to take no further action and dismissed the rating, instructing Rutherford to take him below and give him a cup of tea. "In fact, tea and sandwiches for everyone would probably go down well," he added.

"Yes, sir. I'll tell the steward. Shall I order a detail of soldiers to help distribute it?"

"A good idea. Thank you, Rutherford."

Alastair glanced at his watch. It was nearly five o'clock. He went back down into the engine room at the same moment as the chief engineer was attempting to restart the engines. They were reluctant at first but, with skilful coaxing, they coughed back into life and kept running.

"Well done, Jackson. Excellent work. Not before time either, because we're rapidly losing the tide and it gets very shallow this close to Sandettie. Nurse them now."

"Oh, I shall, sir."

He then went across to where the detachment of engineers had just finished securing the mattresses and packing anything else they could find into the fissure to make it watertight. "We're there as well, sir."

"Good. Well done, everyone." He took a deep breath. "Now, for the moment of truth." Quickly he went back up on deck and spoke to the brigadier and his men who were busy working on separating the two ships, several of the soldiers risking their lives by standing on the bridge of the wrecked destroyer, sawing and hacking away at the tangle of metal with large, heavy-duty saws and a couple of axes they had found in a store opposite the engine room.

Meanwhile, their comrades on board *Royal Bluebell* had rigged up an ingenious device to help pull away the mangled portion of the superstructure that was holding them hostage. The falling tide meant that more of the destroyer was revealed, making the job slightly easier. However, Alastair impressed upon the sappers that they had very little time before *Royal Bluebell* herself would be stuck fast on the sand bank.

"What we need now, sir," said one of the Royal Engineers, "is for the engines to manoeuvre us away gently and then we can gradually cut the remaining links."

Alastair relayed that request and, with a creak and a groan, the two ships began to separate. "Enough!" called out the soldiers. They continued as before, utilizing the saws and axes. "Again!" and suddenly, the two ships parted.

Immediately, the soldiers were picked up by *Royal Bluebell*'s inflatable boat, which Alastair had previously ensured was standing by in the water, and taken back on board to safety.

When the last man was on the deck, Alastair gave the order to proceed, albeit cautiously given both the state of the ship and the foggy conditions, and as soon as they started to move, a great cheer went up from the soldiers.

He publicly thanked the Royal Engineer contingent and as Alastair made his way down to the communications room to signal Admiral Ramsay that all was well and that they were under way once more, everyone wanted to shake his hand or pat him on the back.

The celebratory singing was loud and raucous from both the British and the French. When the fog lifted as they approached the Downs and the coast of England came into view, and *Royal Bluebell* cautiously increased her speed, the cheer that went up was so loud, Alastair was sure they would have heard it in Dover.

They were met at the harbour with great rejoicing, as the word spread of their escapade. Once all the troops had disembarked, Alastair and the Merchant Navy crew of *Royal Bluebell*, together with the emergency repair team despatched by the Admiral, surveyed the damage. They reached the inevitable conclusion that the ship would not be going anywhere for a while and that repairs would take several days. Work would start immediately.

With nothing more to do, Alastair went back into the W/T Room and sent a signal concerning General Phillippe du Laurier. The reply stated that nothing had been heard of him. However, his absence was regarded as a serious matter and would be taken up with the French authorities in Dunkirk and in England. Admiral Ramsay concluded by thanking Alastair for all his fine work and especially for his success in bringing *Royal Bluebell* back safely. *Will look forward to reading your report*, he added.

Wearily, Alastair smiled at this, and then picked up and re-read an earlier signal that had been received at ten o'clock that morning while they were still at sea – a final appeal sent by Admiral Ramsay to all ships under his command:

'I had hoped and believed that last night would see us through, but the French who were covering the retirement of the British rear-guard had to repel a strong German attack and so were unable to send their troops to the pier in time to be embarked.

'We cannot leave our Allies in the lurch and I must call upon all officers and men detailed for further evacuation tonight to let the world see that we never let down our Ally.

'The approach will be made later and the retirement earlier. The night protection of our fighters which stopped all bombing of the harbour last night will be repeated.''

Tired as he was, Alastair experienced a sense of frustration that if his ship had not been damaged, he too would have been going across that evening and could have finished the job. He sent the signal: '*Unable to take Royal Bluebell to Dunkirk tonight as ship too badly damaged, of course. Can take Spirit of Adventure across if required.*'

'*Thank you. Many motorboats now unfit,*' came the reply. '*Report to the Duty Officer at Granville Dock who will give you instructions as to procedure. I shall therefore expect two reports tomorrow.*'

Alastair chuckled and thought that it served him right for volunteering. However, he replied in the affirmative and, after gathering together his few possessions, he said goodbye to Sub-Lieutenant Rutherford and the other members of the crew, before walking the short distance to Granville Dock.

He wondered where Katherine was.

In fact, she was below deck, reading a book, trying to take her mind off the anxiety she felt when all the other ships had returned and *Royal Bluebell* had not, and then later when she saw the state of the passenger ferry as it arrived.

She also needed to allay her sense of frustration at not being able to go and find Alastair, despite knowing he was back, as well as not being able to stay up on deck too long, nor walk to where the ship was disembarking the soldiers. She was not able to speak to anyone for obvious reasons, although her physical disguise seemed to be successful. She hated not being free to be herself.

Spirit of Adventure rocked. Someone had stepped on board. Katherine looked up in consternation and saw Alastair appear at the companionway steps. She leapt up from her seat, holding onto him tightly with relief and joy once he was inside.

"I've been so worried," she said.

"I've had no means of contacting you."

"I know."

They sat down together on the saloon berth, Alastair remarking that it all looked cleaner than when he had last been on board.

"I should hope so," she replied. "I've worked very hard!"

"I can see."

"Is it over now?"

"Not quite." He explained the circumstances of the evacuation and the condition of *Royal Bluebell*, and that he had volunteered *Spirit* to go across for one more time.

"I'm coming too." Katherine was firm about this.

"I'm counting on it!"

Gratefully, Alastair put his arms around her, holding her close and, too tired to think about what he was doing, ran his fingers through her hair and brushed her cheek with his lips.

He felt his heart-rate quicken and her own respond.

Gently, wisely, he extricated himself and, to hide his need of her, suggested that she make a cup of tea, mentioning that as he had had nothing to eat since the previous day, some kind of food would also be most welcome. Katherine immediately set to work, glad of the distraction… glad to hide her flushed cheeks.

He sat back against the bulkhead wall on one of the berth cushions with his feet up, having first removed his shoes, watching her as she deftly prepared eggs and bacon.

Katherine smiled at him, keeping up a bright flow of innocent conversation. It was so good to see him, to know that he was safe.

"There's so much more to tell you," she said as she brought the food over to him before sitting down, "but I want to hear all about what happened to you first."

Briefly, while he ate, Alastair described his adventures. Katherine was rendered speechless by the realization of how close to disaster he had come. Her whole body suddenly felt weak and she moved closer to him, tucking her arm through his and resting her head on his shoulder. "Oh, Alastair."

"I know." He patted her hand and stood up before he became overwhelmed by what had happened. Or could have happened. Not to mention her proximity to him. Taking his empty plate and mug across to the galley, he said, "So, what have you been up to for the last couple of days?"

"Well, I telephoned home from the boarding house – although it took me several attempts to get through as the lines have been so busy," she replied with something of her usual cheerfulness.

"I can imagine!"

"The children are fine and seem to be coping well without us. Mrs Thringle said they've been very good and no trouble. But it seemed so unreal to be talking to her; like another world, and yet it's our world, the one we know so well."

"I understand exactly what you mean."

"But now, here is the best news. Michael is safe! He turned up a few days ago at Mistley House. He sent a telegram to say he was on his way, and Mary nearly had a fit when she saw the telegram boy as she was convinced it was bad news. Mrs Thringle had to open the envelope for her. Michael had been evacuated safely from Boulogne – isn't that wonderful?! – and has been given survivor's leave. He and Mary have gone to Cairnmor. Mrs Thringle said she had never seen such rejoicing."

"Do we know what happened?"

"Mrs T. was unable to say. It appears that Michael is reluctant to talk about it just yet, but Mary has said she's not letting him out of her sight ever again and that while he's in this country, wherever he's stationed, she's going to find digs nearby so that they can be together as much as possible."

"I can't say I'm surprised. That's a very Mary-ish thing to do. But it's such good news. I'm so pleased."

"Oh, and I met your Admiral Ramsay."

Alastair was surprised. "Really?"

"Yes. I'd gone for a walk up the hill and had stopped for a breather when his staff car pulled up – he was having a short respite from his duties – and we had a brief conversation. He made quite an impression on me, I have to say."

"He does on everyone," observed Alastair. "Do you know, he's even been down on several occasions to speak to the destroyer captains and thank them for their efforts? Not many admirals would take the time to do that."

"Especially in such a crisis as this, given everything he's having to deal with."

"Exactly. Now, dear Katherine, we have to be ready to leave very soon. I'll go and get fuel organized and report to the Duty Officer on the quayside. Do you need to fetch anything from the boarding house?"

"No, everything I need is here. Oh, I've filled up the water tanks."

"You're wonderful." Quickly, he cleared his throat. "Then we're more or less ready."

He took a deep breath and went in search of the Duty Officer. Perhaps he had been over-enthusiastic to volunteer to go over to Dunkirk again. If he was honest, he'd had more than enough.

However, calling upon the last remnants of his emotional and physical reserves, Alastair set about making the final preparations for their departure.

They left early that evening, towed in company with another motorboat, behind a Dutch *schuyte* or 'skoot' as they had become known. It was not a particularly comfortable journey as the wake from the *schuyte* and length of the wire tow-rope caused them to oscillate as though they were on water skis and Alastair had to use all his skill to control *Spirit* and avoid colliding with their neighbour.

From side to side they went, skating over the surface of the water until Alastair could stand it no more. He released the tow rope and they proceeded under their own power to the harbour. This caused them to arrive later than everyone else but it was a more comfortable journey and prevented both of them arriving nervous and completely exhausted.

The wreck-strewn harbour was crowded with French vessels of all shapes and sizes – fishing boats, motorboats – all in the process of being shepherded by Rear Admiral Wake-Walker in a motor torpedo boat into the Inner Harbour to make way for the British destroyers and personnel vessels berthing alongside the East Pier.

Once again, Royal Navy officers were in charge of the organization; once again, they did their work professionally and efficiently.

As the enemy drew ever closer to the town, machine-gun and small-arms fire could be heard and there was a sense of urgency to the task. *Spirit of Adventure* probed into all areas of the harbour, ferrying weary French soldiers from the west pier, the guiding jetty and the inner west pier to the larger ships moored at the Avant Port, the Quai Félix Fauré and of course, the invaluable East Mole. Then they were dispatched to Malo Beach to see if there were any stragglers, calling out as before, this time in French, but they received no replies.

In the pre-dawn light Katherine and Alastair could see that the beaches were empty, but covered with the sad, distressing detritus of a retreating, defeated army – abandoned clothing, machine guns, lorries, cars, Bren-gun carriages, tin hats, rifles and most upsetting of all, dead bodies.

They didn't linger, but headed back carefully towards the harbour through the filthy, oily, debris-strewn water, passing their lorry pier on the way, which by some miracle had survived.

Was it really only three days since they had last been there? To Katherine, it felt like a lifetime ago. Disparate, terrible images flooded into her mind – of the bombing and shelling, and of the men who had lost their lives.

"All right?" asked Alastair, sensing her disquiet.

Katherine nodded. "I'll be okay," she said, taking a deep breath.

As they reached the harbour, they witnessed one of the final moving scenes of Operation Dynamo. The last French soldiers capable of being embarked before daylight had already been taken off by the old destroyer *Shikari*, yet even after she was full, there still remained about a thousand French troops tightly packed on the Mole.

Two generals and their staff stood apart, facing the soldiers, all of whom were standing to attention, their steel helmets reflecting the red glow of the fires that still burnt in the town. In the silence, General de la Laurencie and General Bathélemy clicked their heels, saluted and, together with their staff members, climbed down into the waiting motor torpedo boat and left.

Alastair and Katherine could not help but be moved by the discipline and bearing of the soldiers remaining behind, especially as they must have known they had no hope of being rescued.

Alastair held *Spirit of Adventure* at station-keeping, watching as the *Shikari* drew away from the pier and set sail for England. She was the last large ship to leave and after her departure, two block-ships were sunk at the entrance to the harbour.

With the agreement of the French authorities, Operation Dynamo was completed around 0340 hours on Tuesday, 4th June.

Some British powerboats continued to work inside the harbour, collecting troops until it was no longer safe to do so, and Alastair drew alongside the Mole, preparing to take on board as many as he could.

Suddenly, there was a commotion and shouts of: "*Attendez, attendez ! Écartez-vous, écartez-vous !*"

With some difficulty, the soldiers parted to make way for several of their comrades, who were being bundled towards the forward edge of the jetty.

"*Vite, vite, dépêchez-vous ! Les Boches arrivent ! Vous devez partir. Allez, vite !*"

"*Non, non. Ce n'est pas notre tour !*" protested one of the officers.

"*Mais vous êtes un général important et courageux – et vos officiers aussi. Vous devez partir le premier.*"

"What's all that about?" asked Alastair.

"Apparently, there is a brave, important general among the soldiers and they are telling him in no uncertain terms that he and his officers have got to leave first, and quickly. He's objecting to this, saying that it is not his turn. How unselfish is that?"

The gunfire was becoming louder. It was now or never.

Urgently, Katherine called out to the general, "*Vite, vite, s'il vous plaît, mon Général. La situation devient trop dangereuse. Nous ne pouvons pas rester plus longtemps. Il faut partir maintenant !*"

Thus encouraged by Katherine saying it was not safe and they could not stay any longer, the officers climbed down through the concrete piles supporting the wooden pier onto *Spirit of Adventure*.

"*Nous avons juste la place pour dix autres soldats. Mais dépêchez-vous !*"

Shielded by their comrades, another ten men climbed down through the piles onto the boat. It was not a moment too soon as small arms fire could be heard from the landward end of the pier. But so closely were the troops packed together that, at first, the enemy could make little progress. However, not willing to take any chances, Alastair opened up both engines and headed quickly out of Dunkirk for the last time.

Seeing what had been done, several other French craft waiting near the pier moved in and almost two hundred troops were eventually rescued in this way from the Mole before the Germans finally broke through and the French were forced to surrender.

"*Merci*," said the general, once they had put some distance between themselves and the harbour, "*merci beaucoup, Lieutenant-Commander*." He paused, "*Et... Madame ?*"

"*Oui, Monsieur. Je suis une femme.*"

"*Vous êtes très courageuse.*"

"*Merci. Qui êtes-vous, Monsieur ? Je suis Madame Katherine Stewart. Et voici le Lieutenant-Commander Alastair Stewart.*"

"It is a pleasure to meet you both. Forgive me, Madame, for not introducing myself. *Je suis le Lieutenant-Général Phillippe d'Artennes du Laurier*, at your service," and, with that, he saluted Alastair and with natural charm and unaffected courtesy, bowed and kissed Katherine's hand.

CHAPTER 18

Dunkirk (7)
June, 1940

Once they were out of range of enemy gunfire, Alastair reduced speed a little in order to conserve fuel. The power boats had long since disappeared into the far distance and he correctly surmised that there would be no possibility of a tow across the Straits of Dover this time. They were completely alone and completely reliant upon their own efforts.

Spirit of Adventure's engines kept up a steady, reassuring throb and the twenty French troops on board settled themselves down for a lengthy voyage. Some slept, some stared out to sea, others looked anxiously up at the sky watching for enemy planes. A few scanned the water for mines, but Alastair knew he was in a swept channel and unless the Germans had been mine-laying during the night, which was unlikely given the blanket coverage provided by the R.A.F., then they should be quite safe. Two of the soldiers set up a Bren gun near the prow of the boat as a precautionary measure.

Fast enemy motor torpedo boats were a possible threat, as was the risk of air attack. But Alastair reckoned that the Germans would be more occupied with clearing up the mess in Dunkirk and on the beaches than sending out aircraft to bomb or strafe a lone British motorboat. Besides which, the B.E.F. had long since returned home and there was nothing Jerry could do to change that. They also had many thousands of French prisoners-of-war to deal with and would probably not waste their resources attacking a few isolated soldiers.

Katherine made tea, coffee and sandwiches, taking these round to the tired, unhappy men. They had just witnessed the defeat of their country and left many of their comrades behind in captivity, if not dead. As well, for the time being at least, they were exiled from their homeland. For all of them, the whole thing was an insult, a travesty.

She listened sympathetically, giving comfort where she could, offering encouragement where possible. All the soldiers on board seemed grateful and appreciative of the efforts that had been made by the British on their behalf, both in the military campaign on land and during the evacuation from Dunkirk by the Royal Navy.

They did not have any patience with those who carped about the British or those who accused them of treachery and cowardice. The Battle for France had been lost by the actions of stupid French generals, they said, whose strategy belonged to the dark ages, not the withdrawal of the British soldiers to Dunkirk. In any case, during the campaign, when things were not going well, these same generals refused to contemplate retreat and evacuation, preferring an honourable 'surrender'. It was a policy that cost many thousands of lives which could otherwise have been saved.

Listening to these conversations, General du Laurier agreed and said as much to Alastair. "The men feel let down by our military leaders. They are old men who still live in the last century and who have not the slightest notion of how to fight a modern war. Nor do they understand how to work with an ally. They did not listen; they did not communicate with their own troops, let alone the British. They had their own fantasy of how the war was progressing and this bore no resemblance to what was really taking place."

"From what I've heard as well, I'm inclined to agree," said Alastair. Then he added, unable to resist a small grin, "You realize that your own men were worried as they had not heard anything from you."

"My men! They are safe?" exclaimed Phillippe du Laurier, his face lighting up. Alastair nodded. "Well, a thousand of them, at least."

"But, Lieutenant-Commander Stewart, this is wonderful news! I had hoped they would reach the harbour safely, but I had no way of knowing. We heard stories of cowardly French soldiers who had been hiding in cellars and other places, swarming onto the East Pier when they found out it was going to be the last night of the evacuation. It is shameful that these blackguards took the places of the brave soldiers who had been fighting on the Dunkirk-Furness Canal and then the perimeter of the town. I myself saw many such cowards. It is deeply upsetting to me that tonight we had to leave behind those courageous men on the pier who were the rear-guard. I was afraid that it would be my soldiers who would miss out and be left behind like them. But you say it is not so?"

"No indeed. I took them back to England myself, yesterday."

"*Merci Monsieur.* I thank you from the bottom of my heart." And he put his hand on Alastair's shoulder. "I had hoped that they were safe when I did not see any of my men on the pier earlier, but I could not be sure."

Phillippe du Laurier was genuinely relieved. He had worked hard, he said, to ensure the safety of his men – going against authority, standing his ground, finding ingenious solutions to persuade intransigent colleagues that a planned withdrawal was the only option. It was good to know they were safe.

"Your Major was most concerned for your welfare, as are the authorities in England. It seems you would have made a valuable catch for the Germans," added Alastair.

"About that I cannot say, but I am a young *général* with much experience and fresh ideas and I can bring much to the table to help win back my country, which we will do one day, of that I am certain."

"I share that belief. Things look pretty grim right now, but we shall win through in the end."

"Yes, as long as we all pull together. This is a war that will be won by allied strength."

"How right you are." And the two men regarded each other with mutual respect.

They stood in contemplative silence for some time before Alastair took a deep breath and almost staggered. Suddenly, he felt exhausted.

Seeing this, Phillippe said, "If you would like to take a rest, one of my officers can drive this motorboat. If you are agreeable, he can take over for a while."

"No, it's fine. I'm all right, but I will perch on that stool, if you wouldn't mind passing it to me. There's one there for you if you want it."

"*Merci*, I accept. I too am tired. I 'ave been several days without proper sleep."

"I know the feeling! Where were you fighting?"

"North of Lille. My men, they fight well, putting up a brave resistance. We held out for four days, but were out-gunned and out-numbered. When the military situation was hopeless, getting my men away became my main priority. So I disobey a direct order to surrender and I get my men out under cover of darkness before *les Boches* overwhelm us completely. Then we fight and march 'ere to the coast. *En route*, we find notices erected at the road junction near Dunkirk: '*Français à gauche*; British to the right.' So, I ignore the French sign and march my men to the right!"

Alastair laughed. "Good for you!"

"Straight away, I report to General Gort's headquarters and request that my divisions be deployed with the British, fighting alongside our allies on the perimeter. And so, when the time arrives for the British to come through the other French lines as agreed, leaving that line as the new perimeter, my men go to the harbour with the British soldiers. I stay behind to inform General Barthélemy as to where the German positions are, what their strength is, their armaments but, by the time I have found him and we have discussed the situation, my countrymen are given the order to counterattack and I am obliged to stay. I had missed the boat."

"Literally!" The two men smiled at each other. "But you have made it now, and your men are safe also."

"Oui, Lieutenant-Commander. Je suis très heureux et soulagé."

"Well, I'm glad to hear that someone is happy and relieved," said Katherine, as she came into the wheel-house carrying two mugs of tea and a plate of sandwiches.

"We could just do with those," observed Alastair.

He smiled at her and she smiled back – a brief moment of warmth and understanding – but it held enough for Phillippe to remark, after she continued along the deck with more tea and food, "You are very lucky to have such a wife."

Alastair was silent. He owed it to this man to tell him the truth. "Unfortunately, she is not my wife."

Phillippe looked at him, sideways. "Forgive me, Lieutenant-Commander. But seeing you both just now... I had assumed... also because you have the same surname..."

"A natural mistake. She's my daughter-in-law, actually, and is married to my son, Alex."

"I see." Phillippe du Laurier regarded his companion thoughtfully. "And where is her husband?"

"In the R.A.F., stationed in Singapore."

"I see," said the general, again. Then, he added quietly, "And you and your daughter-in-law, you are very close, *n'est-ce pas* ?"

"We are, yes. Very close. It is just a deep friendship, nothing more."

"But I think you also are in love with her."

Alastair was silent again, not quite knowing how to respond to this man, a virtual stranger.

130

"Forgive me, my friend," said Phillippe quickly, "I am much too forward – I am told it is my worst fault. I should not have been so bold. It was tactless."

"No, no. I understand. It's that part of your character that makes you a good leader." But how to answer him? With honesty, Alastair decided. "Unfortunately, yes, I am in love with her." There, it was said; the words were out. It had now become real, not just part of his inner life. "How did you know?"

"I am a Frenchman, Monsieur." Phillippe smiled and shrugged his shoulders, a very Gallic gesture. "To me, it is obvious." He was silent for a moment and then said, "And she is in love with you."

Alastair was shocked. "Surely not?"

"Without a doubt. But I think she does not know it – yet."

"And that's the way it must stay."

"Of course. You are an honourable man – that is very clear also." He smiled, his expression mischievous. "Perhaps she will just have to be the woman of your dreams."

Alastair smiled back. "Perhaps, although I have never thought of her in that way." He hesitated and then asked, matching du Laurier's frankness, "What about you and love? Or is that a dangerous thing to ask a Frenchman?"

"Ah," replied Phillippe sadly, shaking his head. "I am thirty-eight years old. I have yet to meet the woman of my dreams, but she is out there somewhere, of that I am certain. When I do meet her, then she will have my heart and soul and my utmost fidelity and devotion. At the moment, it is difficult because of the war, but I am a man seeking my one true love. Nothing less will do."

"An unusual Frenchman."

"Perhaps. But that is who I am."

Suddenly, there were shouts from the deck and Phillippe du Laurier was out of the wheelhouse immediately. Alastair could hear a conversation in rapid French. Then, without any warning, one of the engines died.

No, he thought. *No more. I've had enough stress and tension in the past week to last me for the rest of my life.*

He tried to get it started again. It stuttered for a few moments before just fading away.

Phillippe put his head round the door. "My men have seen a German patrol boat in the distance. It is coming towards us quickly. We must go now far away, very fast."

"We cannot go anywhere very fast, not with this number on board. One of the engines has just conked out."

"*Sacré bleu !*" He called out to one of his officers. "This man, he knows about engines – he is the one with the motorboat. He will fix it. We will deal with the patrol boat. Do not worry."

Do not worry?! Alastair switched off the remaining engine and took the officer below where, together, they opened the engine compartment. Katherine came over to look, standing close to Alastair, her heart beating fast with fear, knowing exactly what was going on.

There did not seem to be anything obviously wrong. There were no leaks, the drive belt was intact, nothing else amiss that they could see. Alastair wondered if

131

it could be a blockage in the fuel line or dirt in the carburettor or something in the raw water intake – they had driven through some filthy water in and around the harbour at Dunkirk. The officer did not speak any English, so Katherine was obliged to interpret. He concurred with the prognosis and asked for tools. Alastair produced his toolbox.

They drained the fuel from the float chamber into a container and the man set to work. Alastair could see that he knew what he was doing – calmly removing, cleaning and replacing each relevant engine part in turn.

Suddenly, there was cacophony of shouting and gunfire from the deck: a deafening chorus of Bren gun, rifles, grenades and a series of terrific explosions that almost lifted *Spirit of Adventure* out of the water, followed by the sound of debris raining down on the decks.

Throughout all of this, the officer kept working steadily on the engine as though nothing was happening.

Then Alastair heard a great cheer and was up the companionway stairs instantly. Surrounding them was the wreckage of the patrol boat.

"*Bon*," said Phillippe du Laurier, his face a mixture of strain and triumph. "We have dealt with it just as I said." He smiled at Alastair's shocked expression. "His forward gun jammed and he had not any torpedoes to fire at us. We are very fortunate, my friend. We won the battle. He lost!" Then looking at the wreckage, he added, "There are some men in the water just there. What would you like us to do with them?"

Alastair took in a deep breath. "Let's bring them on board. They can be our prisoners. We'll take them back to England."

"You are the captain of our vessel. That is what we shall do."

At gun point, the German sailors were instructed to swim to the boat and were hauled on board and tied up securely, sitting on the foredeck with three of the French soldiers, who looked as though they would much prefer them to be dead, detailed as their guards.

Alastair went down below again. The officer had taken most of the engine to pieces now and had laid it out on the floor of the saloon. He was methodically cleaning, oiling and greasing each part.

Katherine was sitting on the divan; pale and shocked.

Alastair came to sit beside her and, checking that the man's back was turned and his attention fully occupied with his task, put his arms around her.

Their embrace lasted only for a moment and didn't go beyond the bounds of simple comfort and relief. But Alastair sensed much, much more beneath the surface and for him, it confirmed Phillippe's observation of Katherine's feelings. Not that he needed any confirmation, of course: he had sensed the possibility for some time but had just not admitted it to himself. He hoped she would not start thinking too deeply and realize exactly what it was she felt.

With this acknowledgement, Alastair knew he would have to be even more careful when he was alone with her, but it was becoming harder, much harder to exercise restraint, particularly in the intense situations they had experienced during the past ten days and were still experiencing even now.

With some difficulty, he managed to quell the picture of Alex that sprang into his mind but was powerless to stem the tide of guilt that coursed through him as he and Katherine let go of each other.

Meanwhile, the officer had quietly and efficiently begun to put the engine back together and soon, having checked that the prisoners were secure, Phillippe came down into the saloon and stood watching him while he worked.

Soon, the engine was restored and Alastair went up into the wheelhouse and pressed the starter. The engine leapt into life.

"Ça marche ?" said Phillippe, to the officer. *"C'est du beau travail."*

"Merci, Général."

The man wiped his oily hands on an old cloth and put the tools away neatly. He bundled the replaced parts in the rag and put these with the tool box. He offered to drive the boat and Alastair accepted, confident this time in the officer's abilities.

Katherine made another cup of tea and the three of them sat together in the saloon.

"Your husband," said Phillippe, "does he fly the aeroplanes in the R.A.F.?"

"No, he's in the legal department of the Air Force, and will also be working as liaison officer to the G.O.C. in Singapore and Malaya."

"A very important job," observed Phillippe.

"I suppose it must be. As I haven't had any contact with him since he left, I know very little about what he is or will be doing."

As Katherine spoke the words, she experienced a moment of resentment that she didn't know, to be quickly followed by a pang of guilt that she herself had hardly given Alex a thought during the past ten days. She fell silent, trying to picture her husband in his new work; in a new country about which she as yet knew nothing.

Seeing her preoccupation, Phillippe asked Alastair if he had any other children.

"Yes, a daughter, Lily. She's in Canada, studying at the Music Academy in Halifax, Nova Scotia."

"I have heard of it. It is a most famous establishment."

"Really?" Katherine was roused from her reverie by his words. "My father is the Director and my mother runs the administrative side of things."

"But you are not Canadian…"

"No, I was born in Scotland." She was too tired to explain her background. Perhaps one day. "How is it that you have heard of the Academy?"

"Ah, my father is professor of music history at the Paris Conservatoire and a famous musicologist. Your father and mine may well know each other. My mother is a violinist."

"They do say that music is a small world." Katherine could not quite believe they were having this conversation aboard *Spirit of Adventure* on their way back from Dunkirk during the war.

"This seems incredible to me also," said Phillippe. He turned to Alastair. "What instruments does she play?"

"Flute and piano."

"Ah, my mother started me on the violin when I was very young. Alas, I did not take to it. But I love music with a passion and wish that I could play an instrument. My family is a family of soldiers, diplomats and musicians. *Malheureusement*, I have taken after the military side."

Ever the proud father, on the spur of the moment, Alastair produced his wallet and said, "I have a photo here of Lily, taken just after her seventeenth birthday. It's a particularly good one. You may see it, if you wish."

Out of politeness, General du Laurier accepted, but when he looked at the photo – a studio portrait of Lily, back-lit but very natural – a stillness crept over him. "But she is so beautiful," he said softly. With a tenderness bordering on reverence, he held the image between his fingers, unable to look away.

"The woman of your dreams?" asked Alastair, quietly perceptive.

"*Peut-être.* Perhaps." Phillippe looked up sharply. "But how could you know such a thing?"

Alastair smiled. "I am an Englishman, *Monsieur.* You Frenchmen do not have the prerogative on discernment."

"*Touché.*" Phillippe smiled too. "May I keep this?" he enquired, reluctant to relinquish the photograph. "But not, of course, if it is your only copy."

"Yes, you may keep it," replied Alastair with understanding. "I have another just the same at home."

"*Merci.* You are very kind. I will take the most excellent care of it." He placed it carefully in his wallet and put it in the inside pocket of his uniform jacket.

"Well," said Katherine, becoming her practical, sensible self once more and anticipating future contact between them, "I have written down our names, addresses and telephone numbers in case you would like to visit us one day." She smiled at him, handing him a piece of paper. "And this one is of my parents. Lily is living with them at the moment. Why don't you write to her? Tell her that you have met her father and me and it was our suggestion that you should do so. Then, perhaps one day, you will be able to visit her."

"*Merci, Madame*, I cannot believe such kindness. We are but strangers. *Non, c'est incorrect.* We were strangers. Perhaps now we are friends."

"Yes, Phillippe. Perhaps we are indeed," said Katherine, knowing she was speaking on behalf of Alastair also.

"*Général du Laurier, nous nous approchons de l'Angleterre,*" called down one of the soldiers.

The three of them stood up. The real world had intruded. Once more Alastair took the wheel and brought his valiant boat and her passengers into the harbour.

When all the formalities at Dover had been completed – prisoners dealt with, reports written and submitted, bags packed and bills paid – all that remained was for Alastair and Katherine to bid farewell to Phillippe du Laurier.

"*Au revoir,*" he said. "Until we meet again. *Je suis certain que nous nous reverrons.*"

"Yes, I believe we shall," replied Alastair.

"*Nous nous retrouverons,*" he said, regarding both of them before a staff car whisked him away from the quayside.

Once they were on board, Alastair started up the engines of *Spirit of Adventure*, now refuelled and stocked up with food and fresh water.

"Home?" he said.

"Yes please," said Katherine, hesitating for a moment before tucking her arm through his in the way she had always done, as he took the boat out into open water.

It had been quite an adventure. But it was not over yet.

The Battle for France had been lost but a miracle had been achieved. The threat of invasion loomed and the Battle of Britain was about to begin.

CHAPTER 19

Singapore (1)
September, 1940 - April, 1941

Alex had been in Singapore for six months and he was enjoying every minute. The social life was vibrant – nearly every evening there were any number of dances, bridge parties and cinema visits – a cascade of conviviality of a kind that he had occasionally indulged in before his marriage but never embraced with as much enthusiasm as he did now.

He had always worked hard, for the work ethic was very strong in him, and this had absorbed most of his energy and focus. As a single man, however, Alex had managed to combine his career with evenings out at restaurants or night-clubs, attending concerts, the cinema or theatre with whoever had been his current girlfriend and, afterwards, discreetly spending the night in her flat (if he was lucky) or bringing her home to Cornwallis Gardens if she was particularly attractive and he thought the relationship showed promise.

After his marriage, Alex had naturally put these diversions aside, and when work permitted, it was with Katherine, family or very close friends whom he went out, rather than his wider circle of casual acquaintants – his social life now confined to staid dinners at Middle Temple, invitations from other barristers and their wives, or occasional visits to see a film or play.

However, in Singapore he had resumed the thread of sociability. Here, an evening indoors was unheard of – it was just *not* the done thing. If Alex was found to be off-duty and at home in his bungalow, situated in Orchard Road among the spacious western garden suburbs, then someone would be sure to knock on the door and persuade him to make up a foursome for a rubber of bridge, go to a cocktail party or head along to Raffles Hotel for a drink.

In England, his reluctance to drink alcohol was accepted, but here he was ribbed mercilessly about being teetotal and, to keep everyone off his back, Alex began to drink a glass of wine every now and again. Sherry and spirits flowed freely at the large dinner parties held by fellow senior officers' and diplomats' wives, until eventually he partook of these as well, though he drew the line at smoking cigars.

As an attractive senior officer in the R.A.F. without family in Singapore, he was in great demand to make up an even number of guests at various social functions, dinner or tea parties, escorting many equally attractive single and, indeed, married women, specially selected for him by his hostess. His sensitive nature was once more exposed to the influences he had assiduously avoided since knowing Katherine, and his personality began to expand and alter under the pressure of this seductive affability.

Alex continued to take his work seriously, although it was neither too demanding nor too complex from a legal perspective, and he enjoyed the opportunities given him to prosecute and defend some intriguing cases in the green-domed, recently constructed Supreme Court building.

However, the main thrust of his work seemed to be acting as a diplomatic go-between in the ongoing personal and professional feud between the most senior Army and Air Force officers in charge of their respective Services in Singapore and Malaya – something he found frustrating and futile, failing to understand why two grown men in positions of such high responsibility seemed incapable of putting their rivalry aside and working together.

Alex was often invited to dine at Government House by the Governor and his wife, the latter adopting a special interest in him and taking it upon herself to make sure that he was introduced to all the 'right people' as his "wife and family are in England and the poor man is all alone. We must do what we can for him, ladies," she said to her circle of flower-hatted dowager friends.

At home, Alex would have run a mile from this kind of attention as he despised artifice of any kind, but in Singapore he accepted it as part of the culture, and whenever he was available, he immersed himself in the social whirl.

Very occasionally, he paused long enough to listen to his conscience and knew that if she had been here, Katherine would have loathed what he was doing.

Nonetheless, he was also aware that because *she* was a very attractive woman, should she ever come out to Singapore, Katherine would find herself readily accepted into his social milieu. He made the assumption that she would inevitably become caught up in it, just as he had been. It would expand her horizons, just as it was doing to his.

Alex's letters home gradually reflected the changes being wrought in him. Katherine was not slow to pick this up and worried about her husband.

At first, she had enjoyed reading about the city of Singapore with its many different nationalities: European, Eurasian, Malay, Chinese and Indian, each with their own elites and residential districts in this polyglot city.

The suburbs where Alex lived sounded lovely and she thought he was lucky to have his own bungalow with servants to look after him. She was less than enamoured by his description of the tropical heat, the rainy season, and the ever-present danger of disease from malaria-carrying mosquitoes and dengue fever.

However, as the months went by, she became unhappy when his letters seemed primarily concerned with the parties he had been to and the people he had met. The narrative was suffused with the names of women whom Katherine did not know and where he had taken them – to cocktail parties, tennis parties, bridge parties and parties on the beach.

She felt excluded and anxious. Alex was a member of the armed forces. How could all this be going on, especially during wartime? Surely his duties should take up most of his time and his off-duty hours be spent in the Officers' Mess? But, whatever the circumstances, this was Alex's new life and she was not sharing it, just as he was not sharing hers.

The children were growing and developing rapidly and Alex rarely responded to her descriptions of what they were doing and the things they said. She tried hard to talk to them about 'Daddy', to keep his presence in their consciousness, about how vital his work was, but it was beyond their immediate comprehension and had little lasting effect.

For it was to Alastair that they responded as their father. He was the one who played with them, who helped nurse them if they had a cold, who read to them at night. He was the one who shared their small triumphs and disasters. Indeed, Katherine now felt closer to Alastair than she had ever done to Alex. Apart from the fact that they did not sleep together, he was more like a husband to her than Alex had ever been.

Before long, the change in his ever-dwindling letters became permanent. She began to feel that she did not know her husband any more. Sometimes, when Alastair was working late, she would take out and read through the letters that Alex had sent to her before they were married. Katherine was shocked at the difference between the loving, caring man that she had once known and fallen in love with, and this man who seemed completely caught up in an empty, superficial world.

Katherine presumed he was still faithful to her. Of course he was, she told herself over and over again, trying to convince herself that this was so. However, she was wise enough in the ways of society to know that in his present social setting, temptations would inevitably come his way.

Did he have enough strength of character to withstand these things?

She looked to her own feelings that she had experienced towards Alastair during the time of Dunkirk, feelings that made her blush at the memory but which she had since banished to the back of her mind, dismissing them as being of the moment, merely part of the intense situation in which she and Alastair had found themselves at the time. Maybe Alex would be able to do the same if he did meet someone whom he found attractive.

However, he was mixing with women she did not know, in a situation over which she had no control. Katherine was all too aware of the relationships he had had before they were married and she wept at her own inability to be certain of him.

Alastair also had begun to worry. He and Alex had always been close; had lived and worked together ever since his son had qualified as a barrister. They had caught up on the lost time of Alex's childhood, when there had never been enough contact because of boarding school and then university. Their living together, albeit leading independent lives, had been a bonus, a gift, and Alex had been everything he could have asked for in a son.

True, Alex had always been overly preoccupied with his work. True, he had had many ill-considered relationships along the way, taking his time to find the right woman to be his wife. When finally he did settle on someone, however, he made the perfect choice.

The marriage of the two people (with the exception of Lily and his grandchildren) Alastair loved the most was of enormous importance to him. With a solicitor's objectivity, he had analysed and accepted his own feelings towards Katherine a long time ago, and although he was not always entirely successful in putting these aside, they were not a factor in his present deliberations over his son, nor did he allow them to affect his own and Katherine's natural rapport and friendship.

He was therefore quite anxious when Alex stopped asking Katherine to join him in Singapore, but became seriously worried and suspicious when, at the beginning of February, Alex's letters once again begged and implored her to go out there.

Alastair knew his son well and had every reason to be concerned.

Alex first met Patricia at a tennis party at the beginning of September. She was a tall, willowy blonde, sophisticated and well-educated. She was partnering his opponent and from the moment she stepped onto the court, Alex could not take his eyes away from her. She moved with grace and elegance, serving well and returning his shots with ease. Needless to say, he played badly and he and his partner lost the match.

As soon as it was over, and they had all showered and changed, he asked her out for a drink at Raffles Hotel bar, and very soon after that, they were quickly identified as a couple and invited as such to all the social events.

On the whole, the stratum of Singapore society in which Alex moved was tolerant and there was a ready acceptance that two married people could form a friendship and be seen everywhere together. Patricia's husband was a manager at one of the principal oilfields in Borneo, and she was taking two weeks' holiday on Singapore Island, staying with her aunt and uncle, the latter being an influential businessman in the European community.

Alex persuaded himself that there was no harm in their association: they were just good friends. The fact that he found her very attractive did not set any alarm bells ringing. They were two married people and as such were safe, merely enjoying each other's company.

Much to Alex's delight, at the end of her intended fortnight, Patricia decided to extend her stay and in his off-duty hours, they became virtually inseparable, playing tennis, swimming, driving to remote parts of the island in Alex's roadster that he had purchased.

The first time he kissed her was when they had stopped to admire the scenery, not far from the Causeway that linked Singapore Island to the isthmus of Malaya. The first time they slept together was after a party a few days later, hosted by a friend of Patricia's uncle.

When he collected her for their evening out, Alex had hardly been able to contain himself after seeing her in a low-cut evening gown that left little to the imagination, her hair piled high above her head, her make-up discreet and flattering. He knew they made a dazzling couple and they were indeed the talk of the evening.

They left the party as soon as they were able and he drove back to his bungalow, taking her straight through to the bedroom where he embraced her with barely concealed urgency. He fumbled clumsily at the fastenings of her dress and eventually, with her help, the flimsy garment fell to the ground. As passion overcame him, he lifted her onto the bed and gave himself up to his overwhelming physical desire for her.

In the cold light of morning, Alex was filled with remorse and guilt. Patricia was sympathetic – but only to a certain extent, as this was by no means the first affair that she had had, and she left discreetly so that he could sort himself out.

He was distracted in Court all that day and did not perform well, narrowly avoiding losing what should have been a cut and dried case. He was told by his superior officer to ease off on the socializing. Senior service personnel were allowed a great deal of latitude, much more so than in England, but even here, there was a limit and it was one which he felt that Alex had reached, especially when the social side of things began to affect his work.

Alex agreed and privately resolved to end the affair. But it proved more difficult than he had imagined. He was not in love with Patricia, but he was hooked, addicted and when it came down to it, he could not say the words to finish it.

They became more discreet and were seen less at public events, spending time whenever he could get away in and around a little beach cabin that her uncle owned in Malaya, swimming in the warm and tranquil waters, and making love on idyllic deserted beaches in the shelter of the palm trees or at home in his comfortable bungalow.

Alex deluded himself that this was only temporary, that Katherine would never find out, and that when he went home it would not make any difference to their relationship.

Patricia was everything that Katherine was not and he tried to justify his liaison by finding fault with his marriage. However, he had great difficulty in doing so, as Katherine had always been as near perfect a wife as it was possible to have. Perhaps she was too perfect. But she did love him very deeply, he was aware of that.

He was not yet at the stage to acknowledge that the fault might be his, that perhaps he did not love her enough.

Towards the end of December, Alex was sent across to Malaya to tour the new R.A.F. air stations that had just been completed in the north, east and west of the Peninsular, in order to oversee the legal side of things in each of them. He was away for a month and returned to find that Patricia had been seen out regularly with a handsome diplomat who had arrived in Singapore en route to Java. Rumour had it that she was smitten and was contemplating going with him when he moved on to take up his posting.

Alex was devastated, both by her duplicity and his stupidity. Angrily, he confronted her but she brushed his protests aside, saying that she had never seen their relationship as something "deep and meaningful," just something that was fun while it lasted. But now it was over. She laughed at him cruelly when he said it had meant something to him.

Hurt, embarrassed and guilty, with his emotions in turmoil, he penned a long letter to Katherine, his *one true love*, urging and imploring her to join him in Singapore. It was not too late; he could arrange it via the Colonial Office. The Island was still safe. Contrary to rumours, there was no threat from the Japanese. Also, there was no possibility of extended leave for him just yet, even though he had been out in the Far East for nearly nine months. Some of his fellow officers hadn't been home for two years. It would be a dangerous journey for her, but he was desperate to see her; for her to be with him.

In his mind, he dismissed the possibility that, if she should come, someone might tell her about his relationship with Patricia.

When Katherine showed this latest letter to Alastair, they both knew that something was very wrong. She went for long, solitary walks by the Thames; thinking, deliberating, wondering what she should do. Nowhere was safe, that much was certain.

Alex obviously had no idea of the realities of war, whereas she had seen it first-hand. Dunkirk had changed her, her brief experience of the Blitz had changed her. Then there was the anxiety she felt every day while Alastair was in London, only able to come home to Maybury, where the family now resided permanently for safety, for some of the weekend. This too had changed her.

Could she really go? To do so went against every instinct that she possessed. For days she pondered the dilemma, for days she went over and over it until she was exhausted by her deliberations. In the end, she reluctantly came to the conclusion that, if it was possible, she would have to go to Singapore.

She sent a telegram to Alex to say that she would be coming. His reply was ecstatic – unnaturally so, it seemed to her – and things were set in motion. After weeks of wrangling, negotiation and bureaucracy, Katherine was granted permission to travel. It was impressed upon her that it would be at her own risk and that the authorities in Britain could not be held responsible should anything happen. She was presented with an agreement outlining this, which she duly signed.

Katherine was then given passage aboard the *S.S. Antipodean*, a passenger and supply ship travelling in a convoy to India and then onto Singapore and Java in April, 1941. She would not be the only woman on board: several others were doing the same as her, joining their husbands stationed abroad in the far-flung reaches of the British Empire as yet untouched by war.

Katherine and Alastair travelled together to Southampton, both of them silent with anxiety, she holding his hand tightly as they sat on the train; he making the most of every last second they were together.

He did not approve of her going, she knew that, but he had accepted her arguments and bowed to the inevitable. He understood that her place was with her husband, duty and fidelity being very strong in Alastair's character. He would look after the children and they would be safe with Mrs Thringle to watch over them. They both recalled the tear-stained face of their housekeeper when Katherine had said goodbye.

"Have you got your passport?" he asked, resorting to mundane questions as he could find no other words, trying to hide the depth of his distress.

"Yes, it's in my small travelling case, along with all the other documents, photos, letters, and my other personal, precious stuff. I didn't want to put it in my trunk, in case…" She didn't dare say the words *in case something happens*.

141

Alastair put his arm around her shoulder, seeing her tremble with fear and emotion. He felt a surge of anger, of resentment. This journey was both dangerous and unnecessary. He should never have agreed to let her go. How could Alex have asked it of her?

He came on board with Katherine. Together they found her cabin and saw that her trunk had been delivered. She put her hand luggage on the bed and locked the door as they left. At the entrance to the gangway, Alastair kissed her forehead gently, tenderly, and held her close, and she responded to him, tears streaming down her face. Then it was time for him to go and it took all his self-control to leave the ship.

Katherine watched from the railings with a rising sense of panic as Alastair walked down the gangway; she watched with a sense of dread as preparations were put in place for its removal.

Her heart was pounding and her mouth was dry.

Suddenly, there was a commotion as someone arrived at the last moment and demanded that they be allowed on board as they were part of an important diplomatic mission to Java and could not be refused passage. Their Embassy had booked a cabin on board the ship. The ship must wait.

It did, but there was much arguing and fuss.

While this was going on, Katherine was gripped by such a deep fear, such an overwhelming sense of apprehension that she knew with absolute certainty she could not go. The furore caused by the late arrival of the envoy was the catalyst that galvanized her into action and she seized her chance to escape.

She looked at Alastair below on the quayside and saw his expression mirror her distress. Urgently, she pushed her way along the deck through the crowds of people and ran down to her cabin. Quickly, she unlocked it and grabbed her travelling bag from the bed. She glanced briefly at her trunk. It would have to stay.

Her legs, so leaden when she had come onto the ship, were now full of energy and strength enabling her to speedily regain the companionway and go back up on deck. The gangway was about to be removed when Alastair, seeing her reappear and anticipating her actions, ran along the quayside, arriving just in time to prevent its removal as she reached the exit above him.

"Please let me off the ship," she implored the Purser who was still standing there with his passenger list. "I no longer wish to travel. My cabin is number forty-three and my name is Mrs Alexander Stewart."

"I am sorry, madam, but you are already booked into your cabin. You have to stay on board. This ship must leave immediately. We've already been delayed and we'll miss the convoy if we wait any longer."

Alastair had reached the top of the gangway by now. "Arguing will cost you more time. Let her leave," he ordered.

Seeing someone before him in a commander's uniform, the Merchant Navy man was obliged to obey a senior officer, though he did so begrudgingly.

Quickly, Katherine and Alastair moved down the gangplank to the pier, allowing it to be removed. Together they stood and watched as the ship was towed away from its berth by tugs, then away from the docks.

"Am I very stupid?" she said, burying her face onto his shoulder in embarrassment. "All those weeks of waiting, of form filling, of persuading…"

Alastair smiled, relief permeating his soul. "You won't be too popular, that's for sure!" He stroked her hair and put his arms round her. "Don't worry. We'll sort it out somehow. And no, you're not stupid."

"I couldn't stay on board. I just couldn't stay there and be on board when the ship sailed." She looked at him imploringly.

Alastair understood. "I know." He was curious to know exactly what had precipitated her flight. "Was it fear?"

"Yes, and panic. And something else that I can't define."

He nodded, wondering, recalling his own misgivings. "Now, we must send a telegram to Alex. He's not going to be very happy."

They grimaced at each other.

"That's an understatement," said Katherine, holding on tightly to Alastair as her legs threatened to buckle under her.

In Singapore, when Alex read the telegram, he tore it up angrily. How could she do this, how could she let him down at the last moment? Everything was set, everything was ready for her. He needed her; she was his wife. He'd waited for her, ceased to socialize, become a recluse almost, saving himself for her arrival.

How dare she not keep her word.

However, Katherine's flight was soon justified, for ten days out of Southampton, the convoy came under U-boat attack and the *S.S. Antipodean* was torpedoed off the coast of Africa. She sank in ninety seconds. Had it not been for Katherine's premonition, she too would have been on board.

There were very few survivors left to rescue.

CHAPTER 20

Singapore (2)
November, 1941 - January, 1942

When Rachel Curtis stepped ashore on the quayside at Keppel Harbour towards the end of November, 1941 – part of a contingent of nurses in the Australian Army Nursing Service travelling aboard a liner converted into a troop ship, together with two brigades of the Australian Imperial Forces – she was immediately assailed by the intense heat and noise of the bustling, thriving port.

The soldiers and nurses were ordered to line up on the crowded quayside and then marched along the coast road, turning inland to Alexandra Barracks, where the soldiers remained. The nurses continued on to the new Alexandra Military Hospital situated nearby and were directed to the large accommodation huts where they were to spend that night and the next before setting off for Malaya the following day.

After being shown round the facilities at the hospital, they were given some free time for sightseeing, but were under strict instructions not to go alone and to return before sundown. Rachel and two friends, Sue and Jenny, decided to take advantage of this and set off for Singapore City.

A cacophony of languages and dialects from the cosmopolitan mix of nationalities greeted them as they stepped off the bus in what Rachel assumed to be the Chinese district. The nearby river was jammed with hundreds of barges and boats, the streets festooned with brightly coloured bunting and washing hanging from poles, while carts and rickshaws delivered wares and people to their destinations.

As they explored further, they found it to be a city of contrasts where poverty and overcrowding coexisted with conspicuous wealth and ostentatiousness, especially after they had left the river and discovered the spacious, neatly ordered government and business district that dominated the centre of town.

Rachel and her two younger friends walked past the famous white-painted exterior of Raffles Hotel. Feeling emboldened, they entered its airy, elegant interior and dared to peek inside the door of the Long Bar. There was only one occupant, an R.A.F. officer seated on a bar stool with his back to them, his forehead resting on one of his hands, his shoulders hunched, a glass of whisky untouched beside him on the counter.

"Isn't he the picture of happiness?" observed Sue, one of Rachel's companions. They looked at him again with amusement and quietly stole out of the hotel.

Before them, as they walked along Beach Road, the spire of St Andrew's Cathedral rose invitingly, but they didn't go inside, opting instead to stop and admire the splendid Government House set high on the hillside overlooking the town.

"I didn't expect it to be quite like this," remarked Jenny.

"I don't think any of us did," replied Rachel, her attention fixed on a gracious, green-domed edifice close by. "That is some building," she remarked admiringly.

Walking along from Raffles Hotel, having abandoned his solitary drink, Alex spotted the group of three Australian army nurses standing in front of the Supreme Court. One of them caught his attention, her dark auburn hair glossy in the late afternoon sun, her figure well-proportioned and her demeanour relaxed. She wasn't beautiful in the classical sense but her face was full of character.

Alex stopped where he was, transfixed, his pulse racing.

What an amazingly attractive woman, he thought.

He was tempted to go over to her and ask her out for a drink. He wondered how long she was staying on the island; he wondered what she was like in bed.

Immediately, he chastised himself.

What on earth was he thinking? Hadn't he learned enough lessons? Wasn't it enough that he'd been badly burned already? How long had it taken him to get over the humiliation of Patricia, to make peace with himself, to square his conscience? Two months or was it three? And then, just after Katherine had decided not to come to Singapore, he'd met Miriam. Their affair had been delightful, a wonderful distraction after Katherine's failure to appear and his lingering desire for Patricia. But he'd taken a while to get over Miriam as well when she decided to return to England with her husband.

Alex had resolved that she would be the last one. He had told himself over and over again that he had a wife and children, that he should honour his responsibilities and commitments.

But his old life seemed unreal, a distant dream. Katherine was now merely a picture in a photograph, not a person vivid in his mind, and after working through his loneliness and confusion, he reluctantly acknowledged that his feelings towards her had changed.

In denial that his actions were to blame, he tried to convince himself that this had nothing to do with the other women who had shared his bed, that his unfaithfulness had not weakened his connection to Katherine, that it was merely time and distance that were responsible.

Alex knew that the temptations to be found in Singapore were numerous and strong, and his physical needs very great. The longer he stayed here, the more he doubted his willpower to resist another affair should attraction come his way, especially as he had once again resumed his socializing, albeit more cautiously, after his enforced abstinence following the affairs with Patricia and Miriam.

He needed to go home. He needed to see his family. Why hadn't his leave come through? He'd put in for it ages ago. Why hadn't his request for a transfer been granted?

"Come on, let's find something to drink. I'm thirsty," said Jenny.

"How about Raffles Bar?" suggested Rachel.

"What, the one with Mr Cheerful?" said Sue.

The three of them giggled and moved off, oblivious to Alex's presence as he ran diagonally up the steps behind them, still struggling to resist the urge to approach Rachel, and into the building to collect the documents he had inadvertently left behind in the courtroom where he had been earlier that afternoon.

"He might have left by now," said Jenny.

"True. Come on then, let's go. We haven't got long." And Sue led the way.

They retraced their steps to Raffles Hotel and went into the bar. They found that they were not exactly welcome, but notwithstanding this cool reception, they ordered three ice-cold beers, which they took out onto the terrace to sit and watch the world go by.

"No one seems to be very anxious, do they?" observed Sue. "I mean back home, everyone's getting their knickers in a right old twist about the war. But here, you wouldn't believe there was one going on."

"Apart from all the soldiers," remarked Rachel drily.

"Well, they're not doing a whole load. They're hardly marching off to battle the Japs or whoever it is that's supposed to be the enemy, are they?"

"Before I left home, my dad said that the Americans and Japanese are in the middle of some kind of negotiation. Does anyone know what for?" asked Jenny.

"I think the Americans have frozen all the Japs' assets in the U.S. which means they can't buy any American goods, including oil and rubber," replied Rachel.

"Why?"

"Because the Japanese invaded first China and now Indo-China and they can't let them get away with it."

"How d'you know all this stuff, Rach?"

"I read a *lot* of newspapers and listen to the wireless," she replied.

"It'll be all right though, won't it?" As the youngest member of their trio, Jenny was the most anxious.

Rachel shrugged. "Who knows? If it doesn't work out, then Japan will look for its raw materials elsewhere."

"Such as?"

"Oh, I don't know. Malaya and the Dutch East Indies, perhaps."

"Malaya?! What the same Malaya that we're headed for the day after tomorrow?"

"The very same."

Jenny looked worried. "What's there that the Japs might want?"

"Rubber. There are hundreds of rubber plantations."

"What about the Dutch East Indies?"

"Oil."

"But it's all well defended, isn't it?"

"Don't worry, Jenny," replied Sue cheerfully. "The A.I.F. are here, aren't they? And the British Army as well. What could possibly go wrong? Come on, drink up girls. Let's go back. I don't know about you, but I'm starving! I hope the tucker's better at the nursing sisters' mess than it was on the boat!"

A day later, they travelled up through Malaya in an army lorry, driving through primary and secondary jungle and neat rows of rubber trees. The roads were good and progress was easy. The Chinese and Malay workers on the plantations seemed friendly and many waved to the nurses as they drove by, passing through yet more rubber plantations as well as estates producing palm oil and growing bananas, where the same orderliness prevailed.

"Who owns all of these, Rach?" asked Jenny.

"What makes you think I'd know?!" responded Rachel tetchily.

"All the newspapers you read?!"

"Okay, okay. Well, I like to know about a place if I'm going to go to it." Rachel was only slightly defensive. "Some plantations have been developed by European-owned public companies, some by Chinese or Malay farmers and other enterprising individuals."

"It looks like business as usual everywhere round here as well as on Singapore Island," observed Sue. "D'you reckon they really think they're safe, or are they kidding themselves into believing it and carrying on as though nothing can happen?"

"Probably both," replied Rachel thoughtfully.

After some hours, they reached their destination – a clearing in the jungle where a single, large canvas tent with red crosses on the side and roof had been erected. The surrounding tracks served as parking places for ambulances.

A matron came bustling out to greet them. "Hello, girls. Good of you to come to our little abode in the middle of nowhere."

The three friends looked at each other, uncertain as to how to respond. "Er, thank you?" said Rachel cautiously.

"Don't look so worried. We're quite informal out here. Welcome to the 1st/5th Casualty Clearing Station near Kuala Tengeh."

"I hate to state the obvious," said Sue, puzzled, "but why have casualty clearing stations been created – I assume there's more – even when there's no battle going on?"

"Just in case, Nurse, just in case!"

Jenny looked frightened and Rachel put a reassuring arm around her shoulder. "Presumably they're serving other purposes at present?" she asked their 'host'.

"Yes, dear, they are. We're looking after our Aussie boys by serving as a normal medical facility for them. Let me show you round."

There was something irritating about her manner and Sue made a face behind Matron's back. Rachel and Jenny had to stifle a giggle.

"This is our operating theatre – I use the term theatre loosely, as you can see, girls."

It was a small, austere area set apart under the canvas with several raised boards on trestles. Obviously not willing to linger in its Spartan environment, Matron took them back into the main area of the tent.

"This is the ward. As you can see, just one facility. The soldiers currently here are suffering from a variety of things – malaria, dysentery, the usual tropical ailments. No doubt you've been instructed as to how to deal with these.

"Yes," said Rachel.

She could see that the hospital was well run but was itching to *treat* the patients and not just tend to their needs. It was going to be harder than she thought to be a nurse. Still, that was the only choice she had if she wanted to be here, on active service.

"Let me introduce you to the doctors."

Going outside once more, she led them to a separate tent where two men sat reading at a small table, seated on hard wooden chairs. They looked up when Matron and the three nurses entered.

Rachel gave a gasp of recognition.

"Why, Mr Amery!" she exclaimed. "How good to see you!"

"Dr Curtis!" he stood up with surprise. "How are you?" He came over to her and shook her hand warmly.

Matron stared. *Doctor* Curtis?!

"I'm fine, thank you. How about you?"

"Hot. Sweaty. Had enough. But why are you in a nurse's uniform? Have you been demoted?!"

Rachel smiled. They had always got on well. She couldn't have asked for a better mentor. "It's a long story."

"We have plenty of time."

They sat down and Rachel told him how the authorities had refused to let her come as a doctor, how she had battled with them, pleaded with them, and how in the end, she'd had to accept defeat and undergo a short course to retrain as a nurse in order to be posted abroad.

When she had finished, Mr Amery said, "To be honest, we have greater need of you here as a doctor. You're well experienced in tropical medicine – that thesis of yours on malaria was first rate. We have sufficient nurses here and what the authorities don't know, won't hurt them. If war does come, then I want you working as a doctor. We'll be swamped and hard pressed to cope. How are your surgical skills?"

"Fair."

"Good." He smiled, and raised his eyebrows. "They'll improve with practice." He turned to Matron, who was about to raise objections. "This nurse will be working as a doctor. I take full responsibility for the decision and anyone who questions it will have me to answer to."

"Yes, Doctor," replied Matron meekly.

"Does that mean we have to call you *doctor* now?" said Sue sardonically, as they made their way to the cramped, squalid sleeping quarters they would be sharing with five other nurses.

"Well, if you do, you can empty all the bed-pans for a month."

"You're not going to turn all bossy on us, are you?"

Rachel gave her a disparaging look. "Give me a break, will you? How long have we been friends?"

"Too long!" and they laughed.

Japanese forces landed on the coasts of Malaya and Thailand in the early hours of 8th December, catching the Allies by surprise with the location, speed and efficiency of their invasion, and easily overrunning the ill-equipped and inexperienced Indian divisions that had been hastily despatched to protect the north-east corner of the country.

The Japanese advanced rapidly towards the west and south, sweeping all before them in a relentless drive that took out the hastily-prepared Allied defences, forcing the British soldiers into a fighting retreat. Together with the Australians and Indians, they battled valiantly against the odds, but were unable to stem the inexorable Japanese advance down the Malay Peninsula.

Alex, who had been working solely as liaison officer between the British and the Australians since the end of November, was despatched by his C.O. in Singapore to Malaya with all possible speed to try to solve a series of 'communication' problems between the British high command and the Australian Army and Air Force.

However, Alex could do nothing to resolve the misunderstandings and sheer incompetence that he encountered among some of the officers of both nations. In despair, he realized that if this continued, there was little hope for a successful defence of the country, where the Japanese were rapidly gaining ground.

He could only report these things back to the General Officer Commanding, who dithered around before finally deciding to leave things to sort themselves out, apparently unable to appreciate the gravity of the situation and the need for completely coordinated action.

On the military front, as a result, disaster followed disaster.

Some days later, Alex had just returned to H.Q. in Singapore from yet another futile diplomatic mission when a signal arrived regarding a young Aussie recruit who had deserted his post while under heavy fire. Immediately, Alex was ordered back into Malaya to investigate what appeared to be a definite case for court martial.

His vehement protests that this was an army matter, that there was a battle going on in this particular region, that this journey was unnecessary and stupid, not to mention downright dangerous, received short shrift from his C.O., who stated that the powers-that-be wanted an example made of this recruit to make it clear that such instances would be dealt with swiftly and legally, and that it was his job to make sure it happened.

Alex therefore had no choice but to go with his Aussie driver Dave up country to try to sort it out.

"This is madness," remarked Dave, as they got back into the car.

"You're telling me," replied Alex. "It's a mess, a total shambles. What a bloody ridiculous thing to have to do anyway, let alone now."

They journeyed across the Causeway into Malaya, past the Sultan of Johore's splendid palace and through the as yet untroubled rubber plantations, before eventually reaching their destination.

But there was no one there. The brigade had cleared out. A sudden burst of machine-gun fire nearby made them jump.

"Ruddy 'ell," said Dave. "They can't be that close, surely? What d'you want to do, mate?"

"Back to Singapore with all possible speed. This always was a fool's errand."

"Sounds good to me."

They got back in the car, but on the way back, anxious and hurrying, they lost their way amid the myriad estate roads that criss-crossed the plantations.

Suddenly, on regaining the main road, they came across hundreds of Japanese soldiers advancing on bicycles, their rifles slung nonchalantly across their shoulders.

Alex and Dave couldn't believe their eyes. Surely the enemy hadn't reached this far south already?

Evidently they had.

Rachel was exhausted.

For days they had been treating the wounded yet still they kept coming, more and more as the battlefront grew ever closer. The 1st/5th Casualty Clearing Station should have been evacuated days ago, but no one had come to give the order, so they had stayed put. Just as well, with this lot to look after, she thought.

She wiped her hands yet again and moved onto the next soldier. They were running out of everything – bandages, morphine, quinine, sutures… There was no time to boil the instruments properly before a new intake arrived needing urgent attention. If they didn't get these boys away from here soon, they'd succumb to infection even if they survived their wounds. The tropical heat was a breeding ground for germs and as for the mosquitoes – they had no chance against the little blighters with so few nets to go round.

All too rarely, a small consignment of ambulances would arrive to take away as many wounded as could be carried and, on one such occasion, after Rachel had selected the lucky ones, she had suddenly felt faint. She hadn't eaten or drunk anything in hours or had a break. Mr Amery spotted her sudden pallor and told her to take a breather outside.

"But what about you?" she said.

"I'll have mine when you get back." He smiled wearily and wiped his forehead with the back of his bloodied hand. "Go. Escape for five minutes."

Gratefully, Rachel nodded, washed her hands and left the tent. She filled her drinks canister from the standpipe outside, pouring the precious cooling liquid over her head and face, refilling it once it was empty. She drank copiously as she wandered away from the clearing and into the jungle, sitting down by a small pool at the bottom of a waterfall, completely hidden from view.

It was this action that saved her life, protecting her from the massacre that was to haunt her for the rest of her days.

Dave was about to turn the car round, when they were spotted by armoured vehicles at the head of the motorized column accompanying the soldiers. The vehicles immediately opened fire and with no time to think, Dave swung the car round, put his foot hard down on the accelerator, and headed off into the plantation at break-neck speed. The two enemy vehicles set off in pursuit but were hampered by the cyclists getting in their way, something that caused all kinds of mayhem and allowed Dave and Alex to escape unharmed.

However, Dave was taking no chances and after driving over some difficult rough terrain, he felt they had gone deep enough into the jungle to outrun any possible pursuit. On reaching a small clearing, the car's engine stalled and, needing a breather, Dave switched off the ignition.

"Strewth! That was close!" he remarked.

Alex was shaking. "Not one of life's more pleasant experiences."

"That's an understatement." He lit a cigarette; his hands shaking too as he struck the match. "I have no idea where we are. I lost any sense of direction a while back."

They both got out of the car and spread a map out across the bonnet. "I reckon we're somewhere about here…" and Dave pointed to an intersection between two tracks.

"Behind or in front of enemy lines?"

"Who knows at the rate the Japs are advancing. But I reckon we should go that way."

"Let's try it then. It's too dangerous to sit around here anymore."

But the engine refused to start. Dave looked at the dashboard.

"Ruddy oil light's on. Must've missed that when we were trying to outrun the Japs. Engine must've seized. Shit!" He got out of the car again and put his head under the bonnet, drawing out the dipstick. There was no oil to be seen. "Shit!" he said again.

Pacing around, frustrated at being unable to help, irritation surging through him, Alex felt hot, tired and very afraid. He needed a stiff drink.

The heat was oppressive and inescapable and any sort of motion an effort of will. His shirt was clinging to his body and he could feel rivulets of sweat running down the back of his neck every time he moved. He took off his hat and wiped his forehead with his handkerchief before removing his sodden shirt. Not that that made any difference.

Why on earth had he been sent up here? Why now, when the Japanese were everywhere? The young sapper in question should just have been held under close arrest until his brigade arrived back in Singapore. Now was not the time for legal niceties in the field when a full-blooded battle and retreat were under way.

"Any luck?" he asked.

"Nah, mate. Sorry. *Sir*."

"I prefer the 'mate'." He'd always liked this young R.A.A.F. man's relaxed informality. Such a change from some of the stuffy, regimented, incompetent officers he'd been having to deal with recently.

Of all the Allies, Alex enjoyed working with the Aussies best. The experienced soldiers were realistic and brave, not afraid of a challenge. On the downside, the new recruits were an ill-disciplined lot, having been sent into a very difficult campaign with only a few weeks' basic training. It was the same with the Indian reinforcements, some of whom were so green that they even had to be taught how to hold a rifle. The top brass who made the ridiculous decisions to send untrained youngsters into the fray were culpable. It was like sending lambs to the slaughter.

"What can we do?" sighed Alex, seeing his friend's legs protruding from under the vehicle, where Dave now lay, having given up trying to fix the engine from beneath the bonnet.

"I'm not sure yet. Hang on a mo."

Alex leant against the open-topped staff car and lit another cigarette. The whole campaign to defend the Malay Peninsular was a shambles – a combination of bad

151

decisions and bad luck with insufficient armour and artillery, and not enough experienced soldiers: ill-trained reinforcements hastily sent into action without proper plans, against a disciplined and determined enemy.

The lack of air cover, let alone air superiority, was too embarrassing even to contemplate. And where was the Royal Navy? Alex was no strategist, but it seemed basic common sense to utilize all your resources. No one Service could hope to defend the Malay Peninsula or Singapore Island in isolation. But in the first place, you had to have the right equipment and enough of it, correctly deployed, as well as the political will and military expertise to defend somewhere. All of which was clearly lacking and had been from the outset. Now it was too late.

"Here mate, come and take a look."

Reluctantly, Alex slithered under the car to join the driver. He had always found confined spaces oppressive and avoided them if he could. "I'm not going to be a great deal of help, I'm afraid," he said. "I know very little about engines."

"Not to worry. I just wanted to show you. Look." He pointed to the sump. "Cracked. Completely knackered. It's leaking oil all over the place. Must have hit something when we were avoiding the Japs. We went over some pretty rough stuff back there."

Alex moved so that he could get a better view. His dog-tag cord caught on the wheel axle, almost strangling him. In the suffocating space under the vehicle, he struggled to take it off so, with panic threatening to set in, after squirming his way out, he removed it from round his neck and gave vent to his growing unease by flinging it as far as he could away from the car. He could always pick it up later.

"If I could get this cover off," remarked Dave when Alex re-joined him under the vehicle, having taken several moments to calm himself, "it might be possible to bang it together or stuff it with something and make it serviceable. Then I can see about freeing up the engine. There's a can of oil in the boot which'll help. Can't go anywhere till I fix the sump though. We'd run out of oil in about five seconds flat." Dave looked at his companion. "First of all, we'll need something to hold what little oil we've got left."

"How about a mess tin?"

"Perfect."

"Yours or mine?"

"I'll toss you for it." They both wriggled out from under the car. Dave reached into his pocket and produced a coin. He flipped it up and slapped it onto the back of his hand. "Heads or tails?"

"Oh... I don't know. Heads."

"Ha! Tails. I win! Bad luck, mate."

"Well, I guess at the rate we're going, the Japanese will be here soon and as they probably don't feed their prisoners, it's not going to be too much of a loss. Here..."

Suitably furnished, the driver immediately crawled back underneath the car. He came back out a few moments later. "Nah. Can't get the bloody thing undone. I need a damp cloth to wrap around the spanner so's I can get a grip. It keeps slipping through my hands."

"A shirt?"

"Too big."

"Handkerchief?"

"Too small."

"Fussy blighter, aren't you?!"

"Yep." The two men exchanged a smile.

"How about some bandages from the first aid kit?"

"Perfect. But they'll have to be wet though."

"I suppose you want me to go and find some water?"

"Yep."

"You're enjoying this, aren't you?"

"Too right. It makes a change to give an officer orders. Especially if he's a pommie."

"Enough of that. I'll have you court martialled."

"Nah, you're too nice a guy. It's why everyone in our outfit likes you. You're fair and you know exactly what you're doing. And you can hold your beer. Unlike some I could mention. Well, go on then, don't just stand there!"

"Okay, mate." Alex grinned, adopting an uncannily accurate Australian accent, beginning to feel more like himself again.

"We'll make an Aussie out of you yet!" Dave wriggled under the car again, sliding himself back towards the exhaust pipe in order to obtain a better purchase on the offending sump.

Alex had not gone more than ten yards when a massive explosion rocked the air. The force of the blast propelled him forwards into the undergrowth.

The world went black and Squadron Leader Alexander Stewart knew nothing more.

A platoon of British infantry had just rounded the bend in the track when they ground to a halt and dived for cover as what had been a staff car rose ten feet into the air, disintegrating into a fireball and scattering residual wreckage far and wide as it hit the ground. All that remained of its former position was a large crater in the track.

Cautiously, the soldiers lifted their heads above the level of the vegetation.

"Blimey!" said one of them, "if we'd been a few seconds later, that would have been us!"

"What d'you reckon it was, Sarge? A bomb?"

"Dunno. Could've been a mine. Private Cook and Private Duncan, see if there's any survivors. Tread carefully now, lads."

"What does he mean, survivors? No one could come through a blast like that and live to tell the tale," muttered Private Cook as they moved forward.

"There's nothing left to rescue, Sarge," Private Duncan called back, surveying the devastation.

"Whoever it was, at least they wouldn't have known anything."

The smoke and flames had begun to die down enough for them to inch closer to the scattered debris. "Here, what's this?" Private Cook bent down and picked up an object immediately recognized by every fighting man. He called back, "It's a dog tag, Sarge."

"How did that survive a blast like the one we've just seen? It's a wonder it wasn't burnt to a ruddy crisp! Can you make out the name and number?"

Private Cook rubbed the soot-blackened Bakelite pieces on his shirt. "Just about, Sarge. It's difficult to be sure, though."

"Well bring it with you and we'll hand it in at H.Q., wherever that might be. Let them sort it out. All right, you 'orrible lot, let's carry on."

After Private Cook and Private Duncan had re-joined them, the platoon marched off in what they hoped was the direction of the British lines.

CHAPTER 21

Maybury/London/Cairnmor
February, 1942

It was Monday. Wash day. The weather was bright and sunny with a good breeze blowing and Katherine and Mrs Thringle were busy pegging out the washing on the line. They had been up since first light boiling sheets and pillow cases in the copper, rinsing them and putting them through the mangle. Hard work, but very satisfying. Katherine stood back to admire their efforts.

"There, that will do," she said.

"It certainly will," replied the housekeeper. "Now, how about a cup of tea? There are a few biscuits left from yesterday, providing Master Rupert hasn't eaten them all."

"That sounds like a really good idea."

She squatted down beside the washing basket and suggested to her little daughter, who was playing with the spare pegs, that it was time to go inside.

"Look, Mummy. This is Dolly-peg and this is Danny-peg. They live with their Mummy and Daddad in a big peg-house."

Katherine smiled at Anna as she helped her step out of the washing basket. She looked round for Rupert but he was busy helping Mr Thringle dig over the vegetable patch, his trousers stained from the mud that plastered his little red Wellington boots.

She left them to it. Rupert could have his drink of milk and a biscuit later. He'd come in when his tummy told him it was time.

She and Anna made their way back into the house, her daughter running on ahead with her pegs so that she could show Mrs Thringle.

Then she saw him. The telegram boy wheeling his bicycle up the garden path towards the front door.

Katherine stood rooted to the spot, fear gripping her heart.

The news reached Alastair not long after Katherine received the telegram. He was summoned to Dudley Pound's office just after lunch.

"Come in, Alastair."

The First Sea Lord was welcoming, but his face was pale and his eyes strained. *Either he is unwell again or he has some bad news to impart*, thought Alastair.

"Please do take a seat."

Alastair did as he was asked. Something was very wrong.

"Cigarette?"

He was offered one from a slim silver case, engraved with the Royal Navy crest. He shook his head and declined.

"Sorry, my friend, I'd forgotten that you don't smoke. Do you mind if I do?"

The silence was palpable while he lit his cigarette. Dudley regarded Alastair carefully, sadly. These sort of things were always so difficult and never became any easier no matter how long one was in the Service, but particularly so when it affected someone who was a friend as well as a colleague.

All his previously rehearsed phrases went by the board. They were not needed, for Alastair, perceptive as ever, guessed immediately. Fear and panic hit him in the chest like a sledgehammer. His legs went weak and he began to shake.

"Who is it, Dudley? Edward or Alex?"

"Alex, I'm afraid."

"Oh God, no." His hands went to his face and he struggled to contain his emotions. His mouth could hardly form the words and his voice cracked. "Does Katherine know?"

"A telegram was sent as soon as the R.A.F. knew. Then they contacted me so I could inform you."

"I have to go to her."

"Of course."

"There's no doubt, I suppose?"

"None whatsoever. The car he had been travelling in was blown up by a mine. There was nothing left except his identity tags. There can be no mistake – his name was discernible and the discs had 'R.A.F.' stamped on them. It's the only Service to be so delineated."

"Spare me the details, please. There's time enough for those."

Why? Why Alex? Why anyone?

"Of course. Sorry, old man."

"I must go to Katherine."

"Would you like a staff car?"

"No, thank you. The train journey will distract me."

"Where is she?"

"At Mistley House." How would they get through this? The children would never know their father.

In a daze, Alastair walked out of the Admiralty building, his hand automatically returning the sentry's salute. His eyes kept filling with tears; he couldn't get his arms into the sleeves of his coat. He stumbled, fighting to regain his balance. Somehow he hailed a taxi and instructed the driver to take him to Paddington Station. Somehow he bought a ticket and found the correct platform.

And there, coming through the ticket barrier just as he approached it, was Katherine.

She ran into his outstretched arms and they stood there, holding each other tightly, as though by doing so they could assuage the terrible pain of grief and take away the awful unrelenting reality of their loss. But nothing could do that.

"I needed you." Katherine looked up at him, her eyes full of abject misery.

"That's why I came. I needed you, too."

"I know. Oh, Alastair, why? Why Alex?" She was crying now.

He kissed her forehead and wiped her tears away with his handkerchief. "I know, I know. I've been asking myself the same thing."

"I don't suppose there's a chance he might still be alive?"

"None."

"I don't want to be alone."

"Nor do I."

"What shall we do?"

He shook his head. "I don't know. Work through it together as best we can."

"Alastair?"

"Yes?"

"I want to go home."

He understood. "Yes," he said.

Alastair was given two weeks' compassionate leave and they booked their passage to Cairnmor. The children were too young to comprehend their mother's and Daddad's sadness, although in their baby way, they tried to give comfort: little Anna putting her favourite doll into Katherine's hands, "Because Mummy's eyes have tears all the time", Rupert giving Alastair his best teddy to look after, "To make Daddad smile".

Katherine sobbed when the steamer docked, her relief at being home was so intense. But neither she nor Alastair could escape the raw pain and the numbness in the days that followed, or the unbearable sense of loss.

They stayed at the hotel, her cottage having been let. John and Marion were wonderful, supportive and kind. Likewise Fiona and Gordon, who had seen Mary through the pain of her grief when Adam had been lost at sea and could understand what Katherine was going through.

But there was no Mary for her to turn to – her dearest friend was in Kent where Michael was stationed, together with their new baby, Rose, living as close to him as possible, not wanting to miss any opportunity for them to be together.

Their other friends were discreet and unobtrusively sympathetic – Donald and Annie at the post office; Ross and Eve, the Factor and his wife; Father McPhee, who bided his time until his services were called upon, gently upholding them when they did come to see him.

But, no matter how kind people were, only in each other could Katherine and Alastair find the true comfort and solace that both of them so desperately needed. They each knew, without need of words or explanation, how the other was feeling; they knew when to speak and when to stay silent; they knew when the other needed solitude. There was no need for pretence or false bravery. They wept and grieved and supported each other, finding the strength to carry on through the early, painful days of loss.

When Katherine was alone, it was the Alex she had first met, when he arrived on Cairnmor to begin the search for her parents, that came most vividly to her mind: the romantic, funny, kind man with whom she had fallen in love almost immediately. She wept as she sat in her room, looking down at the harbour where he had walked towards her from the steamer and asked her the way to the hotel.

It was the Alex who had kissed her in the hidden rose garden, and nursed the little cat who blew into their lives so unexpectedly, that she remembered. It was the Alex to whom she had grown so close as they shared their hopes and dreams together in her cottage on the hill, safe and warm while the storm raged outside, the Alex whose eyes were alight with love and desire as she walked down the aisle towards him on their wedding day. It was this Alex that she recalled.

All these images and more sprang into her mind and she wept as though she would never stop. Only occasionally did she think of the Alex that she had not seen for nearly two years: the man who had changed so much in his letters that she no longer knew who he was.

That was not him, that could not possibly be him.

The person she had come to love, here on the island, was the real Alex and nothing that came later in their marriage – the arguments, the awareness that his work always took precedence over their relationship and the children's needs – could take that knowledge away from her.

Hearing her sobs, Alastair came into her room and took her into his arms, upholding her through her grief, sharing her tears, his own soul racked with pain for the clever, talented son he had loved and cherished so much.

Alastair remembered their shared humour, their banter. He remembered the court cases they had worked on together – those they had won, the few they had lost. He remembered Alex in the House of Lords, the pinnacle of his career, standing at the Bar: so calm, so clear-headed, speaking so persuasively among the pomp and splendour of history.

He remembered Alex as a small boy and it was then that Katherine held him in her arms and assuaged his grief. He and Alex had been so close and now he would never see him again, never hear his voice or his laughter.

Alastair railed at the futility of war, its cruelty and its indiscriminate slaughter. But there was nothing he could do to bring back his son.

There was no shortage of friends willing to look after the children when Alastair and Katherine needed time to themselves. The twins were a self-contained unit: happy and adaptable anywhere and with anyone, as long as they were together. They charmed whoever they were with and their winning smiles and rosy cheeks meant they were always the centre of attention.

They enjoyed new experiences: watching cows being milked, feeding hens, collecting eggs, helping to make butter and cheese – all the chores that were a necessity for the islanders, but which held a high level of fascination for their little guests, who had never seen any of these things before and, at three and a half, were inquisitive and interested in everything. Rupert and Anna thought the trip to be a great adventure and loved every moment of it.

On milder days when the weather was kind, they went for walks with Katherine and Alastair, revelling in the freedom afforded by the wide open spaces of the machair. They stopped to look at the distant mountains which were "sooo big and scary," their little faces alive with the wonder of it all. They delighted in the beach and the pristine sands, running backwards and forwards with the waves that washed the shoreline with clear, clean water.

They helped Robbie mend his nets, were fascinated by the myriad objects that he kept in his hut: unusual shells, trinkets and souvenirs from distant shores. Each one had a story, and the twins sat wide-eyed as he recounted how they had come into his possession.

One day, not long before the two weeks were up, Robbie, friends with Alastair, protective of Katherine since childhood, and fond of them both, made them tea and gave them his home-made cake to eat. They sat on the beach, silently looking across to the horizon, while the children made sandcastles with an old bucket and spade that Robbie had managed to unearth.

He was the first to speak. "What will ye do now, Katherine?" he asked, watching her while she picked idly at her cake.

"I have no idea."

Alastair looked up sharply, a reaction that was not lost on Robbie.

"Aye, 'tis early days yet, 'tis early days. There's no hurry. But remember, we're all of us here when ye both need us. Aye." He was contemplative. "I was married once," he added unexpectedly.

"You were?" said Katherine, aroused briefly from the stupor of grief.

"Aye. One day, I'll tell ye all about it. Ye'll get over it lass, ye'll get over it. It might not seem like it now, but it will happen. Ye've a good man here, sitting beside you. Never forget that."

"Oh I shan't," replied Katherine. She looked at Alastair and took his hand, her eyes full of affection as well as the pain that had not left them. "He is the dearest, most wonderful friend I could ever have."

This was not what Robbie had meant and Alastair knew it. However, he also knew that as long as he and Katherine remained together, that was all that mattered and he would try to be content with whatever she was able to give. Keeping hold of her hand, he placed his other on the older man's shoulder.

Robbie smiled. "Give it time, give it time," he said.

Alastair nodded, filled with more gratitude than he could ever express.

They walked for miles through the glens or along the white-gold sands – the island's beauty seeping into their souls, imperceptibly making it theirs once more, just as it had been three years previously when they had last been here. But, as the time passed, Katherine knew she had to arrive at a decision: whether to stay on Cairnmor or go back to England with Alastair.

The day before they were due to leave, she sat silently in the deserted dining room of the hotel, staring out at the view across the harbour as the rain lashed against the window. She had to make that decision, now, immediately, and it was very, very hard.

Alastair came to sit beside her. "What do you want to do?" he asked gently, wanting so much for her to come back with him yet keeping his feelings hidden, not wishing to put any pressure on her; not wanting to pull her in a direction that she did not wish to go.

Katherine was in a quandary. What should she do? Stay here on Cairnmor, or go back to London and Maybury? She had the chance to return to her island for good, to make her home here once again, something of which she had always dreamed, and yet...

Briefly, she regarded Alastair, sitting quietly beside her.

What should she do? Go or stay?

Financially, she was secure with the generous allowance her father had provided for her and personally, she was quite capable of living independently... but... and this was a huge 'but'...

She looked at Alastair again. She was closer to him than any other person, apart from Alex… quickly, she suppressed the sob that rose in her throat at the merest thought of him… even Rupert and Mhairi. She knew Alastair would find it impossibly hard on his own, knew how much they both needed the comfort and support of the other. He was the only father the children had ever known, that they were probably ever likely to know…

Suddenly, she knew what it was she wanted to do. Just as when Alastair was preparing to go to Dunkirk, just as when she could not stay on board the ship to Singapore, Katherine knew she had to be with him.

"I'll come back with you," she said softly. "The children need you. So do I."

Alastair's relief was palpable. "I need you too." He took both her hands in his, a gesture of warm, deep friendship. Yet how much more his heart held for her.

Katherine raised a smile. "But I want to come back here to live after the war is over."

"Then that is what we shall do."

With those words, Katherine and the children became his responsibility and, whatever the future might hold, he would look after them and protect them to the very best of his ability; indeed, just as he, in his unobtrusive way, had always done.

"Thank you, Alastair."

"What for?"

"For everything."

He shook his head. "No. Thank you." Then he said, "Well, if we're going to catch the early steamer tomorrow, we'd better gather the children's things together. They're probably scattered all over the hotel."

"I think Rupert's teddy was sitting on the desk in reception the last time I looked. He'd lent it to John to 'help him do his numbers better'."

Alastair chuckled. "It's a good job we're the only guests staying here."

"Yes, otherwise Teddy would have found the adding up much too hard."

"Indeed he would."

Inasmuch as they were able to, they smiled at each other and together went in search of recalcitrant toys and children.

CHAPTER 22

Maybury/Portsmouth
April, 1942

Mhairi to Katherine

Dearest,

I have no words to express the love that Rupert and I send to you. We only received your letter yesterday. We're so sorry, my darling, so sorry. I wish we were with you. It is a terrible thing that has happened. I cannot imagine what it must be like for you. I'm so thankful you have the children and Alastair. Little Roo and Anna are too young to remember their father and in many ways that is providential. They will always be a source of joy to you and a reminder that you were once married to a wonderful man.

How is Alastair coping? It must be unimaginably difficult for him as well. But you both have each other for support. The two of you are very close and that is such a blessing.

Try to keep strong. One day this terrible war will be over and we can all be together again.

All love and thoughts,
Mhairi and Rupert xxxxx

Phillippe du Laurier to Alastair

Dear Alastair,

I was so sorry to hear your news. The loss of your son must be very painful for you. I cannot begin to imagine. How does Katherine cope? War is hell, n'est ce pas?

I am busy on active service. More than that I cannot say. It is somewhere very far away. I hear from Lily often. You are blessed to have such a wonderful daughter.

I have to go now – duty calls. But I will write again, as always.

Look after yourself, my friend.

My thoughts are with you.

Yours,
Phillippe

Mary to Katherine

Dear Katherine,

I am so sorry to hear about Alex. I don't need to say more, do I? You know that I know what you're going through. Michael is devastated. He really loved Alex. They had always been such good friends.

Sometimes it's better not to dwell too deeply on things, but to allow your body make its own way towards healing. It can be hard, though, when people give you too much sympathy. All you want to do is tell them to go away. But you can't and somewhere underneath you need it desperately.

We may be able to come and see you soon – Michael has some leave due to him. Then we can go for long walks and talk together. And you can see Rose. Can we all come and stay for a while?

Love,

Mary xxxx

When Mary, Michael and baby Rose arrived, Mary noticed how thin Katherine looked. Alex's loss was hitting her very hard and she was often tearful still. She seemed stronger as soon as Alastair came home for the weekend but Mary could see that grief had taken its toll on Alastair as well, who also looked pale and drawn.

Rupert and Anna were fascinated by baby Rose and wouldn't let her out of their sight. Rupert particularly so. When she was asleep, he would quietly steal up to her bedroom and could be found playing quietly with his toys next to her cot, or looking through his cloth books, or drawing her a picture for "when she wakes up".

It was hard to explain to him that, at only three months old, Rose was probably too young to appreciate his efforts on her behalf. Nonetheless, Rupert was not deterred and temporarily, Mr Thringle lost his little helper in the garden and Anna her playmate. At first she felt a bit bereft so she spent more time in the kitchen helping Mrs Thringle or lost in her own little world on the grand piano, playing music that made sense only to her.

Katherine and Mary took themselves off on the Sunday afternoon, leaving Michael in charge of the children, with Alastair asleep in the sitting room after lunch. The household were under strict instructions not to wake him.

Their route took them along the path by the Thames. "It's so peaceful here, it's hard to believe there's a war on," observed Mary.

"I know. I sort of felt guilty when we were living here during the Blitz, but Alastair was quite right to insist that we should be here permanently. Now that the bombing seems to have stopped, I go up to London for a night or two midweek and spend time with him. But it really upsets me to see all the damage that's been done: so many lovely Wren churches, for instance, all reduced to rubble. And the Docks – well."

"Michael and I were there a few weeks back and although I don't have the same feeling for London that you do, I still found it upsetting."

"Alastair and I have been to lunchtime concerts given by Dame Myra Hess at the National Gallery – that's suffered too."

"What about the House of Commons' Chamber? All that wonderful architecture."

"I know. And so many homes destroyed in the East End. I wish I could do something to help."

"Do you ever think about going into one of the Services?" asked Mary.

"Sometimes. But at thirty-three, you and I are too old to be called up, so we would have to volunteer. At the moment, however, I don't feel like doing much at all really. I go through the motions but I've no incentive to do anything apart from be with the children and Alastair. He feels the same. He's finding his work at the Admiralty very tough at the moment."

Mary could see her friend's listlessness. "What about the W.V.S.?"

Katherine looked at her slightly disparagingly. "Would you?"

Mary smiled. "No, probably, not. All those bossy women."

"Quite. But they do a tremendous amount of good work and I've helped out in the village once or twice, but it's not for me." She paused for a moment, thinking. "No, if I were going to do anything, I'd want to be in the Royal Navy, so it would have to be the Wrens for me."

Mary tucked her arm through her friend's, just as they always used to do when they were living on Cairnmor, but on this occasion she felt only a passive response. Katherine was definitely down.

It had been two months now. Where was she at this time after Adam had drowned? In much the same place, she seemed to remember.

She made her voice intentionally bright. "Have you heard anything more from those two soldiers you brought back from Dunkirk? Who were they, Angus and...?"

"Ron."

"Aye, they were the ones."

"We hear regularly from both of them. Ron is still convalescing. Everyone says it was a miracle he survived. He's been invalided out of the army now and his wife is delighted, even though one of his legs has had to be amputated. The doctors are optimistic he'll be able to walk almost normally again one day, though it will take time, given the extent of his other injuries. He's in a wonderful hospital near Edinburgh, with the best possible care and has no idea how much it's costing. He thinks it's free. Alastair and I are not going to disillusion him! Angus lost part of his heel but has recovered well and is back with his regiment. He's also just got married. He and Ron became absolute friends after Dunkirk."

Pleased to see some animation in Katherine's demeanour, Mary asked, "Do the wives get on well?"

"They do actually. It would be a bit of a disaster if they didn't now, wouldn't it?"

Mary smiled. It must be nice to be able to afford to be so altruistic and pay for a friend's care. She also felt vaguely guilty that she hadn't told Michael about Katherine's involvement at Dunkirk but she respected her friend's wish that she should say nothing to anyone. Michael would find out soon enough, no doubt.

Once Alastair had woken up from his afternoon nap, he and Michael went into the study, leaving the children in the care of Mr and Mrs Thringle.

"It seems incredible that it's been nearly two years since the four of us have been together, doesn't it?" said Alastair.

"I know! So much has happened. Now, ever since Katherine wrote about it to Mary, I've been itching to see your letter from the famous Admiral Ramsay, the one he sent you after Dunkirk."

"Really?"

"Yes. If it hadn't been for him and his ships, I'd never have got out of Boulogne."

"You haven't ever told us what happened, how you came to be Mentioned in Despatches."

"Maybe one day," he said evasively. "Now, where's this letter?"

Alastair took it out from one of the drawers of the bureau and removed it from the envelope before giving it to Michael to read. "It's not very long. He came up to the Admiralty for a meeting while I was still on my way back from Dover in *Spirit of Adventure*, so he scribbled me a note."

Dear Alastair,
Sorry to have missed seeing you today. It all worked out right in the end, didn't it?! Congratulations on your D.S.O. You did a splendid job.
Bertie Ramsay

"Did you write back to him?"

"Of course."

"What did you say?"

"I wrote it out in rough first, as I wanted to get it right, although it's very simple. Here," and, slightly embarrassed, Alastair handed Michael the draft:

All in a day's work, but thank you anyway! Congratulations on both your wonderful achievement at Dunkirk and your K.C.B. One of my friends has a personal reason to be grateful to you and the magnificent men in the destroyers under your command."

"Ha! So I'm in there as well!" said Michael, feeling pleased. "But a D.S.O.! How about that! Who recommended you for it?"

"The S.N.O. at Dunkirk."

"The who?"

"Senior Naval Officer."

"What did you do?"

"Made him a cup of tea."

Michael laughed. "Yeah, yeah. So what's been happening at the old Admiralty, then? Katherine said you've had a bit of a promotion."

"She would. Immediately after Dunkirk, I was made an Assistant Director of Operations Division, Home, and promoted to Commander. Caused a right hoo-ha,"

"Why?"

"Because I'm in the R.N.V.R. Some of the recently arrived regular Royal Navy chaps didn't like it one bit. Even the V.C.N.S. didn't like it particularly but he put up with it."

"Is he still there?"

"No. He was the admiral who made such a mess out in Singapore. His misjudgement caused the *Prince of Wales* and *Repulse* to be sunk."

"Surely the Japs did that?"

"Yes, they did, but if he'd organized Force Z, as it was called, more carefully and signalled to the R.A.F. in time to give his small fleet air cover, then they perhaps could have been saved." Alastair sounded bitter. "Everyone was very upset and angry. It was humiliating for the Royal Navy and besides, we can't afford to lose capital ships just like that."

"So, what's next for you?"

Alastair was silent. "Well, I've served more than my two years as a staff officer and the normal Royal Navy practice is two years on staff duties and then a period at sea. Dudley Pound was hoping to keep me on dry land, but that's looking increasingly unlikely given the desperate need for experienced officers on board our ships. I've been a staff officer since 1939, so I'm overdue for a spell at sea."

"Katherine won't like it,"

"I know."

And when the order finally came, she didn't. Not one bit. In fact, in her vulnerable emotional state, she railed against it, something that Alastair found difficult to cope with as his emotional resources were also very low. She didn't blame him, or the Navy, as she had always known that it would only be a matter of time before he was sent to sea. She just couldn't cope with the uncertainty, with the possibility of losing him too.

He did his best to reassure her, and eventually she calmed down, but her reaction shook him and didn't make things any easier for him as he went through the final preparations for leaving the Admiralty and taking up his new duties.

Alastair had been made Executive Officer of the light cruiser *H.M.S. Romney*. As such, he was effectively second-in-command with most of the responsibility for running the ship, leaving the ship's captain free to concentrate on strategy. He had a small staff to help him, with a lieutenant-commander as his chief assistant, who took on most of the paperwork, and a lieutenant as his right-hand man.

He was delighted to discover that on the *Romney* this was to be his old friend Jack Rutherford, now promoted, who had been his sub aboard the *S.S. Royal Bluebell* at Dunkirk. For his part, Jack was relieved: he had begun to think he was going to be the only R.N.V.R. officer on board. For Alastair it was an excellent posting, one of great import and responsibility, and he could not help but feel a sense of excitement, his first positive emotion since receiving the news about Alex.

The *Romney* was berthed at Portsmouth and Katherine came down from Maybury prior to his departure to be given a guided tour of the ship.

For some reason, Alastair failed to introduce her to his shipmates as his daughter-in-law, just giving her name, with a sense of pride and gentle possessiveness, as 'Katherine'. Surprised and touched by the unexpected omission and public gesture of affinity, her heart beat a little faster as she made no attempt to correct him and, with a sudden feeling of freedom, spontaneously added the surname 'Mathieson'.

From that moment, they subtly and subconsciously changed the tenor of their relationship.

When the time came to say farewell, Alastair came with her to the entrance of the dock gates walking, as they always did, with her arm tucked through his.

Curling a stray strand of hair behind her ear as they stood close together before their final farewell, he said, "Everything will be all right, you know."

"Yes."

Then he held her close to him and kissed her as near to her lips as was possible without actually doing so, smiling when she gave an involuntary gasp.

"Write to me," he said.

"Of course." How could she do otherwise?"

Reluctantly, Alastair left her, half-turning as he walked until she was no longer within his view.

CHAPTER 23

Mill Hill/Greenwich
May, 1942 - May, 1943

With Alastair about to go to sea, Katherine, for the first time, began to give serious thought about her own individual contribution to the war effort. She wanted to find something that would be of value to support the work Alastair was doing, even if it was only indirectly and from a distance. In this way, she knew she would feel closer to him in mind and spirit wherever he was.

She also needed to do something *different* for her own sake: something that would help to assuage the agony of Alex's death, that still haunted her with unceasing regularity, where every emotional response, be it joy or sadness, related or unrelated, was accompanied by a searing, crippling pain followed by the inevitable numbness which prevented her from finding her way back into the world of feeling.

On the train journey back from Portsmouth, Katherine mulled over possibilities for the path she should follow, as well as whether or not she had the courage to make such a dramatic change in her life. After considerable inner debate, she realized that there was only one course of action she wanted to take. It was a bold step, a risky step, but by the time the train drew into Waterloo Station, she knew exactly what she was going to do.

Therefore, buoyed up by Alastair's optimism, the memory of their farewell and her own needs, the first thing that Katherine did when she arrived home was apply to join the Women's Royal Naval Service.

Once her application had been accepted, she reported to the recently opened training depot at Mill Hill in North London, a huge establishment with a capacity for training nine hundred 'Wrens', as the Service personnel were known colloquially.

For two weeks, Katherine would be resident at Mill Hill, leaving the children in the care of Mr and Mrs Thringle, who had been remarkably understanding and supportive. She knew that Anna and little Rupert would be perfectly fine for the short time she would be absent from home, but she worried nonetheless and felt guilty that she was going to be away from them. She wondered constantly how they were faring.

On arrival, everything seemed very strange and at first, Katherine began to doubt the wisdom of her decision. After being given the regulation bluet probationer's uniform and having a medical check, she was sent for an interview. After the two women had saluted, Chief Officer Baker shook Katherine's hand and invited her to sit down.

"Now, I have to ask you some questions. Nothing to worry about, my dear, all part of normal procedure. We do give all probationers a form to fill in but I find meeting each of my probationers personally to be more helpful as it means I can get to know each of you and will therefore be able find the best placement for you. Shall we begin?"

Katherine nodded. "Yes, ma'am."

"Name."

"Anna Katherine Stewart."

"Date of birth?"

"27th September, 1909."

"Place of birth?"

"Cathcart, Glasgow."

"Current address."

"17 Cornwallis Gardens, South Kensington or Mistley House, Maybury, Oxfordshire."

"Married?"

"Widowed."

"I'm sorry." The Chief Officer's expression was sympathetic. She could see that Katherine was still grieving. "In the Services?"

"Yes. My husband was a Squadron Leader in the R.A.F., attached to headquarters in Singapore as Liaison Officer to the G.O.C. He also worked in the Legal Department. He was killed in Malaya in January this year."

"Is that why you decided to volunteer?"

"Partly, yes. I felt I needed a distraction, a change, something to help me come to terms with his loss. Also, I wanted to be a part of the Royal Navy."

"Good. Any children?"

"Yes. Twins, a boy and a girl."

"How old?"

"Nearly four."

"A demanding age. Any problems with childcare?"

"Not at the moment."

"Well, with two children, you'll be what's classed as an 'immobile' Wren. I dislike the term, I have to say, but what it means is that at the completion of your training, you'll be found a position that will enable you to live at home. How does that sound?"

Katherine was relieved. "Ideal. Thank you."

"Now, do you hold any qualifications?"

"I studied for an honours degree in history at Edinburgh University."

"Class? Though I do realize, of course, that your degree won't have been officially conferred. However, in our eyes, it definitely counts and we recognize such an achievement. It will only be a matter of time before we women receive the credit we deserve."

Katherine felt grateful to hear the sentiment expressed in such a determined fashion. "I was awarded the equivalent of a First."

"Excellent. What did you do before you were married?"

"I was a teacher."

"Good. Do you speak any other languages apart from English?"

"Yes, Gaelic and French."

"Fluent?"

"Yes, in both."

"Any other skills? Shorthand, for example?"

"Yes. I can manage a hundred and ten words per minute in Pitman's. I type as well."

"Excellent. Speed?"

"About sixty-five words per minute."

"Which shorthand and typing qualifications do you hold?"

"Er, none."

Chief Officer Baker regarded Katherine closely and frowned. "You have none and yet you say you can do speeds like that? Where did you learn?"

"I taught myself and our housekeeper tested me."

"I see." She sat silently for a moment, thinking. This was interesting. She decided to continue with the next question. "Do you have any other relatives in the Services?"

"Yes, my father-in-law."

"Which branch?"

"He's a Commander in the R.N.V.R., currently serving aboard the cruiser *H.M.S. Romney* as Executive Officer. Before that, he was an Assistant Director of Operations Division, Home, at the Admiralty. My brother-in-law is in the Navy also. He's a lieutenant-commander."

"Good. Good. What about your own parents?"

"My father is Sir Rupert Mathieson…"

Chief Officer Baker's head came up. "Mathieson? Any relation to Sir Charles Mathieson, the shipping magnate?"

"Yes, his son."

"You have distinguished relatives." She paused. "Where is your father now?"

"My parents live in Halifax in Nova Scotia. They emigrated there when I was three."

"So, you grew up in Canada?"

"No, I grew up on Cairnmor."

"Cairnmor?"

"Yes, the Isle of Cairnmor, one of the Outer Isles. You see, my parents were very young and very poor…"

"Poor? Surely not?"

"Yes. They had run away from home in order to be together. After I was born, my mother was ill for several months and unable to look after me. At first, they had nowhere to live and my father was without a job, so some kind friends offered to take me home with them to Cairnmor where I would be safe."

"Safe?"

"Yes, Sir Charles was insistent that Rupert's baby was to be given up for adoption as soon as it… I… was born. Someone did try to take me on several occasions, so my parents needed to make some quick decisions and opted to let me go to the island. The intention was to collect me as soon as they were able. It took them three years to save up the money for Canada and the trip to Cairnmor. My mother travelled to Lochaberdale to collect me but by this time, I was happy and settled and she felt that she couldn't disrupt my life by taking me to live with strangers, even though those strangers would be my real parents. This was something they hadn't foreseen."

"It must have been heart-breaking for her."

"It was."

"Did you know about them?"

"No. The people I lived with brought me up as their own child."

"How did you find out about them?"

"Alastair, my father-in-law, was Sir Charles Mathieson's solicitor and when my grandfather died, he left everything to his son or, should Rupert not be found, to his heir or heirs. Alex, my husband, who was a barrister, came to Cairnmor to begin the search at the behest of his father, and that's how we met. We worked on the case together, found out where Rupert and Mhairi had gone and Alex discovered that the missing baby was me."

"And neither of you knew who you really were all the time you were searching?!"

"No."

"What a remarkable story."

"Yes it is."

"Are you in contact with your parents?"

"Oh yes. I'm hopeful they will come to live here once the war is over. That is certainly their intention."

"Are there any questions you would like to ask?"

"Just one request."

"Go ahead."

"I'd like to be known by my maiden name, if that's all right."

"And that is?"

"Mathieson. It's on my birth certificate. "

"May I ask why?"

"A fresh start. Something to help me regain my independence. Also, I've never had the opportunity to use it before, as I grew up with the surname of MacDonald."

The Chief Officer smiled. "I think that can be arranged without too much difficulty."

"Thank you, ma'am."

Mrs Baker was thoughtful. She had enrolled thousands of recruits in her time but this one was something of a catch. "Thank you, Probationer Mathieson. That will be all."

Katherine stood up, saluted and went out of the room.

She found the intensive, two-week basic training at Mill Hill to be both physically and mentally demanding, crammed as it was into just a fortnight. Extensive drills, taken by Petty Officer Wrens and supervised by a qualified P.T. Officer, took up a large proportion of the time and, as a result, having overcome her aching muscles (most of which she had forgotten she possessed) Katherine found herself fitter than she had been at any time since leaving Cairnmor.

Much of what they did on the parade ground was fairly mind-numbing and for this she was grateful, as it prevented her from thinking too much about Alex. All the marching did, however, manage to create a certain *esprit de corps* among the trainees and this, together with the new sights and sounds as well as the many different people she was meeting and surrounded by, helped take Katherine's mind away from her ever-present grief. She was so tired for those two weeks, she literally fell asleep as soon as her head touched the pillow.

She found that the W.R.N.S. recruits came from all walks of life, with varied backgrounds and experience to match. Despite the inevitable moans and groans about having to get up at five-thirty in the morning to scrub the nine floors of stone staircases or polish an already highly-polished floor or clean piles of cutlery, most girls and women settled well into the routine and pulled their weight.

They were shown how to make their beds, henceforth to be known as bunks, in their 'cabins', envelope style, with sheets, blankets and a blue and white bedspread with an anchor on it. This had to be the correct way up otherwise, they were told, "the ship will sink".

Yes, well, thought Katherine.

Yet, despite several more peculiarities of this nature, she allowed herself to be carried along with the others, who seemed terribly keen and anxious to learn and do their best and whose infectious enthusiasm did eventually serve to lift her spirits.

Katherine found that she was the oldest in her particular intake. The younger girls, some of them no more than seventeen, would seek her out for advice on love and other pressing concerns that occupied the minds of young women. But, in her present fragile emotional state, she found this difficult and could only take so much, gently discouraging them after a short while.

Fortunately, there was plenty to keep them distracted from dwelling on personal issues. They attended lectures on Royal Navy terminology and traditions, and learned all about ranks, ratings and badges as well as the importance of security. These lectures were delivered by the Naval Intelligence Department, accompanied by explanatory films.

A woman doctor from the Central Council for Health Education delivered two lectures on the importance of sex hygiene. It was quite revealing how many young trainees were ignorant of the facts of life, let alone some of the subject matter covered in the talks. There were several things spoken about in these that even managed to shock Katherine.

In addition to all of this, the trainees attended concerts, lectures and made visits to the theatre, giving them the opportunity to experience things of a more cultural nature.

This brief period of training was designed to give the recruits an impression of the very special Service into which they were entering and to infuse them with a spirit of duty and responsibility as they went about their work – an aim that was very successful in its execution wherever Wrens were posted.

During the course of this initial fortnight, Katherine and her fellow trainees were issued with a jacket, skirt, navy raincoat and greatcoat, hat, two pairs of shoes, gloves, three white shirts and a black tie.

The first time she put on her uniform and looked at herself in the mirror, Katherine cried. She felt such a mixture of emotions – a sense of pride at being in the Royal Navy, unease at the radical change this had brought to her life and finally, anxiety at having to face an unknown future. There was little privacy in her cabin but the other girls were very kind and she was grateful for their discreet sympathy and understanding.

At the end of the two weeks, the probationers were divided into specialized or non-specialized categories, according to ability and suitability. With her background and following her final Board assessment, Katherine found herself selected for officer training. After a week's leave at home, she was sent to the Royal Naval College in Greenwich for four weeks as a cadet.

She knew that Alastair had been here on the staff officers' course, so in her next letter to him she wrote: *The thing that strikes me most, apart from the grandeur of the buildings, both inside and out, and the spaciousness of the grounds and the view of the Thames, is the beauty of the Painted Hall. As you walk up the steps between the pillars into the central area and see the glorious colours and vast, perfect proportions, isn't it just awe-inspiring? It makes me feel enormously privileged to be here but at the same time I'm humbled by it.*

I'm glad you were here too: it means I can share it with you completely. Every mealtime in the Hall is a wonder – the best Officers' Mess anywhere! There's also such a lovely atmosphere. Was it like that when you were here?

Yes, that was indeed the case, replied Alastair, writing the letter as he tried desperately to keep pen and paper in contact while the ship heaved up and down, labouring under heavy seas out in the Atlantic. *I shall always be able to picture the Painted Hall. It made a great impression on me, too: a wonderful room.*

He stopped for a moment, feeling slightly queasy as he tried to counterbalance the ship's movement and continue writing. He was pleased that Katherine was at last sounding more positive and said so, the effect being completely spoiled by a line of ink from his pen chasing its way across the page. He smiled. He knew she'd understand. He would have to finish the letter when the sea had calmed down a bit.

In her spare moments at Greenwich, Katherine spent much time taking solitary walks through the park and grounds, finding the atmosphere to be one of restoration and healing. Little by little as each day, each week, progressed she found herself able to think more clearly as the barriers of pain and numbness of Alex's death began to dissolve, bravely taking her first tentative steps back into the world of feeling.

Katherine devoted herself to her work, using it both as an escape and a process by which to strengthen her spirits. The officer cadet course consisted of the usual drills and lectures pertinent to having a position of responsibility, as well as containing constant assessments. In addition, there were social occasions with cadets and serving officers to be organized and hosted.

One of the more important tests set during these dinners was to stand up before a group of senior officers, both W.R.N.S. and Royal Navy, and speak on a previously unprepared topic. The cadets were given a slip of paper on entering the room and this was to be their subject.

After she had been given hers, Katherine smiled as she read the words *Ships of the Royal Navy* and knew she would be able to speak with confidence on this

172

particular subject. So, recalling her visit with Alastair to her father's shipyard, together with everything she had learned since joining the Wrens, she was able to talk freely and easily about the ships, their design and construction, their function and their roles within the Royal Navy. Absorbed in her topic, she actually spoke for fifteen minutes and no one made any move to stop her when she went beyond her allotted time.

The Director of the W.R.N.S., making one of her frequent visits to Greenwich to review progress was greatly impressed by Katherine's knowledgeable and informed discourse on her subject. She remarked that this cadet showed enormous potential as a staff officer and they all agreed that her presentation was, without doubt, the best of the evening. The Director made a note of her name. She was certainly someone to look out for in the future.

Towards the end of the month, following a period of revision, Katherine was given testing exams in her shorthand and typing and passed them both with flying colours, producing the fastest speeds in her Section. After this, at the completion of her course and on graduating from the Royal Naval College in Greenwich as a Third Officer, she was fitted out with her new uniform. Katherine adored the tricorn hat and the badge, with its blue laurel leaves and gold and red king's crown and anchor, and felt very proud to be wearing the single blue band and diamond on the cuffs of her jacket.

She had her photograph taken, and sent a copy to Alastair when she next wrote – a photograph that he carried around with him in the inside pocket of his jacket for the rest of the war. It became his talisman against harm and sustained him while he was away at sea, when grief for Alex sometimes overtook him with such intensity that he could hardly breathe, or he missed home and family so much that he wondered how much longer he could endure the separation.

Sometime later, when Alastair's ship docked at the large naval port in Halifax, Nova Scotia and the ship's company was granted two week's leave while *H.M.S. Romney* underwent boiler cleaning and servicing, he was able to show it to Rupert and Mhairi, who were naturally very proud of their daughter.

He also had a joyful reunion with Lily, whom he had not seen since just before the war started and who had grown into a lovely, assured young woman.

Dearest Katherine, he wrote. *Thank you so much for your lovely photo. I keep it with me all the time, close to my heart.* (Was that too much, he wondered; should he have written it? He decided it was fine and left it in.) *I am so proud of you and I love the fact that we are both now officers in the Royal Navy.*

Your parents are well and send their love. And Lily is positively blooming. But you'll never guess who is here... Phillippe! After taking part in the North African campaign, he persuaded his illustrious leader (you know who – awkward chap, has a rather large nose...) that he should be appointed as Free French liaison officer to the French-Canadian Army here. Isn't it just so fine and fortunate that I've arrived when he's here?!

But that's not all, dearest Katherine. You know that after Dunkirk, Phillippe wrote to Lily, that she wrote back, and that they have kept up a steady stream of letters ever since? During the course of this correspondence, they fell deeply in love and apparently (according to Mhairi) when they met, you could feel the sparks flying from across the other side of the room!

Phillippe cannot contain his joy and has asked Lily to marry him. She accepted immediately and has been (again according to your mother who, of course, is never wrong about these things!) on cloud nine ever since. They've brought the date forward so that I can give the bride away. How wonderful is that?! I can't quite believe it myself, that I am here at exactly the right time. The wedding is in three days.

But I wish with all my heart that you were here too to share their happiness. I miss you so very much and hope and pray that we'll see each other again soon.

Next time I write it will be to describe the wedding, which I know that you will want in the minutest of details. No doubt Mhairi will do this too, so you'll have as complete a picture as it's possible to have.

You know how I feel about Phillippe and I couldn't wish for a better son-in-law. I am absolutely certain that he and Lily will be very happy. She will stay on here until Phillippe comes back to England and then her plan is, if it's possible, to return with him, as he is likely to be staying in our country for the immediate future.

Your parents have been wonderful to her and she has become very close to them, particularly to Mhairi. She couldn't have been looked after better nor had better musical training during all the time she's been living here.

Good luck with your new post – I know you'll continue to do splendidly, just as you have been doing. Try to keep cheerful, dearest Katherine, though sometimes it's very hard, isn't it?

I'll write again as soon as I can and hope it won't be forever until you receive this letter.

I miss you more than words can ever express.

My love as always,

Yours, Alastair xxx

After graduation, Katherine's first job was as secretary and personal assistant to Chief Officer Baker at Mill Hill. Here she quickly gained promotion to Second Officer and then, much to her delight, after several months found she had been selected for the prestigious Staff Course at the Royal Naval College, alongside R.N. officers – one of only two Wrens recommended for each new course. She emerged from this with a First-Class Certificate and a promotion to First Officer.

Following this, Katherine continued to work at the Royal Naval College, this time involved in the training of new recruits. Her duties kept her busy, and their challenges and her achievements gave her the impetus to move forward mentally, away from constant thoughts of Alex.

Alastair and Katherine continued to correspond as regularly as wartime conditions would allow and, as time passed and grief for her husband began to lessen and its hold on her diminish, she began to look out for Alastair's letters with a heightened sense of anticipation. She became so minutely absorbed in the warmth and detail of his correspondence that, one day, she began to wonder if there might be something of a transformation happening in the nature of her feelings for him.

From the very beginning and throughout the time they had known each other, she and Alastair had shared their own very distinct relationship, one that was totally independent of hers with Alex – neither impinging on the other, her feelings for both men completely clear and separate: one innocent, the other, inherently not.

It occurred her that this very innocence in her feelings for Alastair was moving into a new dimension – a natural progression, perhaps, of their already deep and affectionate friendship. She felt it in her responsiveness to his letters, and could trace its initial, unrecognized origins to those brief, quickly suppressed moments during the time of Dunkirk and, later, when she went to see Alastair's ship at Portsmouth – the time when, newly widowed and therefore technically free, she had felt the first stirrings of emotional release.

Hope began to spring in her heart; a small feeling of excitement grew within her. She allowed herself to dwell in the wonder of it for a moment, before her next thought shattered the embryonic dream.

Alastair was her father-in-law. Because of this, there could never be a hope of any other kind of relationship.

Katherine sighed. Whatever she might imagine herself to be feeling, whatever direction her thoughts might be taking her, this fact would always be the great difficulty and moral dilemma. Neither was there anyone with whom she could talk over something of this nature, no one who would truly understand. Not even Mary or Mhairi. There was no one. Except Alastair, of course, and he was the one person she could never tell.

However, there was one thing of which Katherine could be absolutely certain. Whatever happened in the future (and she held onto this thought) she would never be without him, as Alastair would never leave her or the children. She knew she could trust and rely on him completely and be absolutely certain that he would always be there for them.

She would have to be content with that.

Reflectively, Katherine left her position sitting between the colonnades outside the Painted Hall and walked down towards the Thames – a river that she loved so much, a river that connected her to the children at Mistley House, a river that flowed out into the sea and connected her to Alastair, now serving aboard his ship in the Mediterranean.

This was to be her last day at the Royal Naval College. Her sojourn at Greenwich had restored and strengthened her, and she looked back on her time here with appreciation and gratitude. It had been a privilege to have studied and served in such a place, but she knew it was time for her to move on, to broaden her horizons. Katherine wanted to be out in the world, working within the Royal Navy itself, making a direct contribution to the war effort.

Through his letters, Alastair, immensely proud of all she had achieved, supported her in this, sensing also that she needed to find her feet, to be on her own, even if that meant, temporarily, leaving the children behind.

So, on the strength of his encouragement, Katherine had requested a posting, and by great good fortune found she was going to be sent to Portsmouth. She was hopeful that as this was *H.M.S. Romney*'s home port, she would be there when Alastair's ship docked, whenever that might be. He had been away at sea for over a year, unable to get to a British port for his periods of leave, and they had not seen each other in all that time.

That last evening, as she sat in the beautiful Painted Hall with tears in her eyes listening to the uplifting phrases delivered by the Director of W.R.N.S. in a memorable Guest Night after-dinner speech, Katherine knew she needed to see Alastair now more than she could possibly have ever imagined before the astounding developments of the last two years.

CHAPTER 24

Fort Southwick (1)
June-August, 1943

Katherine's posting was in one of five forts built during the Victorian era, known as the Palmerston Forts, high above the city of Portsmouth on the Portsdown Hills. The tunnels beneath Fort Southwick had been excavated in 1942 and were not only the bombproof, underground communication headquarters (known as C.H.Q.) of the Navy, Army and Air Force, but also extensively used by the Naval Commander-in-Chief, Portsmouth – the Second Sea Lord – to serve his operational needs.

Katherine had been appointed as a staff officer in the Operations Department, ostensibly working alongside the Assistant Chief of Staff (Royal Navy). However, the A.C.O.S. was not particularly disposed to involving a woman in operational duties, despite her qualifications. He did not discuss with her any aspects of what the department was working on or events as they unfolded. She was given no operational tasks of her own to deal with, nor were her opinions sought.

Once he had discovered her secretarial skills, however, he felt more comfortable and her assigned role became simply that of taking dictation and typing up the notes afterwards. He saw Katherine merely as someone who could translate letters and documents into their correct format for the C.O.S. and C.-in-C.'s approval.

Disappointed with this attitude, Katherine nonetheless tackled the tasks she was set without outward complaint and utilized her time by observing everything, absorbing the day-to-day routine of an operational command, visiting other departments and learning all that she could.

She did not have an office of her own, but shared a smallish room with Babs Moorcroft, secretary to the Deputy Chief of Staff. They got on tolerably well, although the other woman's attitude was somewhat snooty, because her boss was more senior. For good measure, she also threw into the conversation at every available opportunity the fact that her father was something high up in the city and that the war could not be won without the work he was doing.

Katherine took no notice of this and just got on with the job in hand without making any riposte or comment. She had no time or patience with one-upmanship or snobbery, nor with her own background did she feel the need.

However, working underground was the thing that Katherine found hardest to bear. The lack of freedom and natural light, as well as fresh air within the tunnel environment were difficult to contend with for the eight, sometimes twelve hour shifts they were expected to work. For someone like herself who had grown up with the wide open spaces and invigorating fresh air of Cairnmor, the narrow, claustrophobic communication corridors and enclosed working conditions were an anathema to her. There were no lifts and it was the steep spiral staircases, with the painfully slow progress up or down at duty changeover times, that she found tested her self-control the most. To overcome all of these things, she tried to keep herself busy with her work and not dwell on the discomfort it caused her too much. She was not always entirely successful.

The servicemen working at Fort Southwick lived in caravans in the moat, with dormitories in the tunnels that could be utilized during an emergency. Katherine was grateful that the women were billeted in and around the village of Southwick – at least they could go out into the open air each day. From the outset, when the Wrens left the tunnels at the end of their shift, they were issued with strict instructions not to divulge any of the top secret information upon which they were working. They then had to make their way home through the blackout if they finished late.

Dearest Alastair, she wrote after she had been at Fort Southwick for a few days, *I have been busy settling into my new 'situation' and haven't had a moment spare until now. My work is quite interesting, but I hope it becomes more challenging as time goes on. My 'boss' seems efficient, but tends to rely on his staff quite heavily to organize him and sees me as something of a lackey. Not quite what I had envisaged or trained for.*

My digs are in a small village, about a mile north of my job, in a lovely little wattle and daub (so I'm told) thatched-roof cottage. My landlady is called Margaret and likes to be known as Meg. She is a remarkably spry old lady of 88 years, very alert, and has opinions on everything, so there is never a dull moment. She knows everything there is to know about village life and is described by the Vicar as a "thorn in his side"! However, at her age, I think she's entitled to say exactly what she thinks. She is a quintessentially English version of Mrs Gilgarry, but without the herbal remedy skills and acerbic personality.

Meg has four children, ten grandchildren and three great grandchildren! She has amazing energy and stamina and nothing seems to faze her, although she has a tendency to repeat herself if she thinks the story she has just told is worthy of being told again.

My room is about the size of a postage stamp and the window is even tinier, but I have a lovely view across to the hills and the sun streams in through the window from early morning, just like my cottage on the island, so I feel very much at home. I have a door key and can come and go as I please, which is nice.

The thatch is different from that on C. – there is no need for rope and rocks to keep the roof on as (I would imagine) there are no ferocious storms. It is all very neat and tidy and covered over by thin wire netting for protection. The walls of the cottage slope up and down in a wavy line and the thatch follows this line, making for an interesting shape on the outside. There are many similar cottages throughout the village, as well as some lovely Victorian redbrick and flint houses with tiled roofs, not unlike Mistley House, but much smaller, of course. All the dwellings have red front doors – very distinctive! There is a post office and village shop, two pubs and a lovely church. Oh, and a pump on the village green.

178

It's so peaceful here. There is a thriving community and most of the residents seem to live to a ripe old age – someone has just died at the age of 101 and two others are still going strong at 100 and 98 years. It's obviously the place to be if you want to live a very long life.

There are lovely walks along the quiet narrow lanes which all seem to join up with each other, and dilapidated wooden gates that give tantalizing glimpses of overgrown paths through the woods. I'm looking forward to exploring them on my <u>one day</u> (!) off per week.

I hope all this makes sense – it's quite hard giving descriptions and keeping them as oblique as possible.

I do miss the children, yet there is a certain excitement to being here, despite the shortcomings of my position. I feel guilty at leaving them but I know that they will continue to thrive. It's good also that Mary is once more resident at M.H. as Michael has been posted overseas again. I hope Rupert and Anna will be able to manage without their Mummy for a while. It won't be forever.

But for now, for my own sake, I need to do this. I need to be on my own, to rediscover my identity and inner strength and, hopefully, finally come to terms with Alex's loss as well as making a constructive contribution to the war effort. Then I shall come home, more myself again and better able to cope.

Of all the people that I know, only you will be able to sympathize with this; you who know and understand me so well. But it is very hard for us to be apart, and does not become any easier as the months go by. I long for the day when I shall see you again.

All my love and many thoughts,
Your Katherine xxx

Alastair, sitting in his cabin on the *Romney*, put the letter down in his lap and looked out of the porthole at the grey and choppy conditions of the Mediterranean Sea, before rereading the last few sentences: "*Of all the people that I know, only you will sympathize with this; you who know and understand me so well. It is so very hard for us to be apart, and does not become any easier as the months go by. I long for the day when I shall see you again.*"

Oh, so did he, so did he. His enforced absence seemed like an eternity, even though it was proving to be a positive experience for him too, though not without its dangers and moments of extreme anxiety.

He put pen to paper and wrote his reply, ending with the words: *I do understand. With Alex gone, there will always be a void in our lives which can never be filled, and it is inevitable that moments of pain and remembrance will continue to catch us unawares, no matter how much time has passed or how busy we are. But I'm of the opinion that after a certain level of healing has taken place, there has to come a time for acceptance. And, maybe, we have both reached the stage where we each have to find our own way of finally coming to terms with his loss.*

Yes, it is very hard for us to be apart. I feel that just as much as you do. Our affection for each other and our deep friendship have always been one of the sustaining joys of both our lives. I would not be without that. And, in grieving together and supporting each other through all the traumas and difficulties of the past couple of years, we have drawn ever closer, despite present circumstances of physical separation. I treasure this profoundly. You are never far from my thoughts and I miss you too, very much.

Look after yourself and write soon.

Many loves and all my thoughts,

Your Alastair xxx

When eventually she received it, Katherine lay in bed reading Alastair's letter over and over again, finding comfort and warmth in his words, and laughing at the ending, a reversal of hers.

The day's post had also brought a letter from Mrs Thringle, in which she had enclosed something from the children. Their drawings and little notes brought tears to Katherine's eyes. She could see they were beginning to form their letters really well and their sentence construction was remarkably good, especially as they were so young and had yet to start school.

Katherine experienced a pang of guilt. She should be there at home doing all of this with them, she should be the one to enhance and expand the skills they were acquiring. But with Mary at Mistley House, Katherine knew that her friend, as well as Mrs Thringle, would make sure of just that.

Between July and August, the Allies undertook Operation Husky, the invasion of Sicily, following their joint success in North Africa the previous year. Working at Fort Southwick, Katherine and her colleagues were in a privileged position, as all the signals connected with Husky came through to them for dissemination, and everyone was anxious to keep up to date with the progress.

As with Operation Torch in North Africa, it was an undertaking of enormous significance in changing the course of the war, and Katherine quickly discovered that *H.M.S. Romney*, stationed in the Mediterranean, was fully involved.

The British Eastern Task Force Commander aboard the Flagship *H.M.S. Antwerp*, was none other than Admiral, now Sir, Bertram Ramsay, who she discovered was also responsible for planning and executing the Navy's side of the operation, just as he had been for Allied landings in French North Africa, although on that occasion, he was not in overall command.

Each day, excitement mounted as the signals came in quick succession once the operation was under way. Whenever the latest news arrived, everyone gathered round the tiny signals room, eagerly awaiting the latest despatch: *...ships converging on the island from their appointed stations... heavy seas... have almost reached destination... amphibious landings going to plan... troops landing on the island... heavy surf in some places... opposition mostly light... very few casualties.* Then... *Admiral Ramsay very pleased... whole operation an unqualified success.*

Alastair even sent Katherine a signal: *All well. Home soon, with any luck.*

Babs Moorcroft was beside herself. "How do you know the Executive Officer aboard *Romney*?" she demanded to know.

"Ah," replied Katherine enigmatically, "I know lots of people," and then, unable to resist it, "including Admiral Ramsay."

Babs's face was a picture.

After the excitement and success, Katherine felt happier knowing that it couldn't be too long before Alastair came home, although she was all too aware that with their respective duties it would be difficult to arrange to see each other. However, she consoled herself with the thought that at least they would be in the same country.

She had managed to get back to Mistley House herself only once as, with just one day free from her duties, by the time she had made the slow, awkward train journey from Portsmouth to Maybury, there was very little time to spend with the children. They had all found it unsettling and unsatisfactory, and she resolved to wait until she had proper leave and could be at home with them for longer – whenever that might be.

On her rare days off, therefore, she took long solitary walks along the ridge of Portsdown Hill, revelling in the wonderful view spread before her of Portsmouth Harbour and the Solent – a panorama that stretched right across to the Isle of Wight – using physical exercise to work through her emotions, sometimes still grieving for Alex, sometimes trying to come to terms with her altered feelings for Alastair.

Then one day, out of the blue, an army major walked into her office and exclaimed, "My goodness, if it isn't Katherine MacDonald!"

She looked up in amazement at the sound of his voice and her old name. At first she failed to recognize him, then realization dawned. "Freddie! Freddie Harrison! Aye, well, aren't you a sight for sore eyes?!"

"That's no way to greet an old friend! Ha! You didn't recognize me at first did you?! But you, you haven't changed a bit, Katherine. Still as beautiful as ever!"

"And you're still as blind as ever!" she retorted.

"I see you're still just as bad at accepting compliments."

"And you're just as bad at giving them out at the drop of a hat."

"Well, as you can see, my hat is still in my hand! How about a hug?"

"Not while I'm on duty."

"Ah, still prim and proper, I see. What on earth are you doing here? I never expected to see you in England!"

"It's a long story."

"Well, you'd better tell it to me then. What time are they letting you off the leash?"

Before she had time to think, Katherine replied, "About 1800 hours, if I'm a good girl and I've finished all my work."

"Would you like to go out with me this evening? I can pick you up straight from here at six. We can go to Southsea Pier and hear Joe Loss and his Orchestra. How does that sound?"

Katherine hesitated for a moment. Did she really want to go? Well, why not. "Yes, all right, as long as your wife wouldn't mind."

"Ah, Joyce. Yes, well, we're er… not together any more. We separated some time ago."

"I'm sorry to hear that."

"Yes, well."

At that moment Babs came back into the office, forestalling any further conversation, and Freddie walked out of the door, saying "I'll collect you at six. Don't forget, now."

"I'll try not to."

"Who was that? He's quite good-looking, I must say." She was curious and wanted to know more.

"Oh, he's just someone I knew a long time ago."

"Well, he seems quite keen on you."

"Mm, perhaps." Katherine was non-committal. She had no wish to explain to Babs that this man had once been her boyfriend and that he had wanted to marry her, that she had refused politely as she wasn't in love with him, and that after they had split up, he quickly became engaged to a girl called Joyce, whom she later married.

Freddie collected her promptly at six o'clock, sitting in his little sports car, waiting at the exit she used from the tunnels. He got out of the car and held the door open for her. Katherine carefully lowered herself into the passenger seat. There was not a great deal of room inside.

He drove off in a swirl of grit and dust, not as considerate of his passenger as he could be, more intent in showing off his prowess with the car.

Katherine could see that he had changed a great deal from the callow youth he had once been, and despite their banter and immediate rapport earlier in the day, she felt uncomfortable and was beginning to regret accepting his offer of an evening out. She hoped he would not believe it to be a date.

When they arrived at Southsea Pier and had parked the car, they found their way to the ballroom and went over to the bar to order a drink. She felt out of place in its crowded, smoky atmosphere and very much out of synchronization with this man whom she had known all those years ago.

She wondered where Alastair was and what he was doing at that moment. She wished he were here, with her. Now. Like this. But on a date. Her heart began to beat faster at the thought.

"Katherine…" Freddie's voice pierced her reverie. "You were miles away."

"Was I? Sorry."

"Now, what will you have?"

"Oh, a glass of tonic water. If they haven't any, then just water."

"Can I not interest you in a gin and tonic? Martini? Champagne?"

"Goodness me! No, thank you. I don't drink."

"Still Miss Prim and Proper, then! Tonic water it shall be." And he proceeded to order the drinks.

Katherine observed him quietly. He looked smart in his uniform. Khaki suited him and the red British army badge with the crossed swords, lion and crown above made it distinctive, as was the R.E.M.E. badge on his cap, which he had placed on the counter beside her. His moustache hid his over-wide top lip.

They made their way through the crowded room across to the only available table, which was situated in one corner.

"Now tell me, what have you been doing with your life since Edinburgh?"

"Oh, this and that. I became a teacher."

"What, on that remote island you always wanted to get back to?"

"The same."

"Then what?"

"I met a wonderful man and we got married a couple of years before the war. We had two children, twins. He was killed in Malaya in January, 1942."

"Nasty business, Malaya and Singapore. Fortunately, I wasn't sent there. No, I've been lucky. I've been in the army since before the war. I decided to choose a corps that best suited my abilities and was relatively safe. Well, it has been so far, touch wood. The army hasn't always been the most efficient at placing their recruits in an area that suits their skills, you know. So I applied for the Royal Electrical and Mechanical Engineers after university and got the job, you might say."

"Ah," said Katherine.

"You see, after my training was finished, I was given various postings and became something of an electronics whizz. I was sent to Liverpool soon after Joyce and I got married."

And so he talked and talked, all about himself, his work, elaborating on a variety of subjects, pausing for breath only rarely to see if Katherine was keeping up with him. Most of the time she just nodded and said 'yes' in what she hoped were the right places.

Did I really go out with you once? Did I really count you as a close friend? thought Katherine, as she toyed with her glass, watching and hearing him speak as though it was from a great distance, picturing Alastair sitting across the table from her; both of them able to spend the evening together in complete freedom, unfettered by convention or circumstance.

"Another drink? The same? Something to eat? I'll get it."

"Yes, please." It wasn't worth stating her preference – he'd never taken much notice anyway. Alex had been a bit like that. She remembered how she'd always had to compromise with him, how often in the latter stages of their marriage, if it hadn't been for Alastair and the children, she would have felt restricted and miserable...

Shutting Alex out of her mind, she let her thoughts run on...

With Alastair, everything has always been so easy, so natural. We talk about anything and everything. Isn't that what real love should be? Instinctively knowing who someone is – understanding them, caring for them and upholding them?

And wanting them.

A picture of Alastair in this new context produced a vibrant, inescapable physical reaction in her, its guilt-inducing power jerking her mind back to the present.

Once again, Katherine became aware of the buzz of conversation, loud music and people getting up to dance. Freddie held out his hand to her and smiled. He had obviously not noticed her preoccupation.

"Come on, let's join in," and he led her onto the dance floor. He held her close; too close and subtly, she pulled away from him, keeping her distance without causing offence.

The room was crowded and after several dances, as it was getting late and she had an early start in the morning, Katherine suggested that perhaps it was time to go. Reluctantly, Freddie agreed and went to collect her coat from the cloakroom. They walked to the car and he drove carefully this time along the darkened, deserted streets before ascending Portsdown Hill and travelling down the other side into Southwick village and Katherine's lodgings.

He switched the engine off, and they sat for a moment in silence before Katherine said, as evenly as she could, "Well, thank you, Freddie. It was such a surprise to see you again."

"Yes, it was for me too. But I've enjoyed this evening enormously. It would be good to do it again. How about tomorrow?"

"I'm not sure. I work eight or twelve hour shifts, so I tend not to go out when I'm working. Tonight was an exception. How long are you here for?"

"About two weeks. I'm supervising the chaps while they put in some new electronic wizardry for the communications system. It'll benefit the navy and the air force as well."

Katherine glanced out of the window. Should she go out with Freddie again? Would it give him false encouragement?

"I may have next Tuesday free," she said, keeping her voice neutral.

"I'll still be here then. Just. So, until Tuesday?"

"Perhaps. I may have to work."

She hoped he wouldn't try to kiss her. In the event, he gave her a brotherly pat on her hand and for this she was grateful.

"Goodbye, Freddie." She smiled, opened the door, got out of the car, and quietly let herself inside the cottage without a backwards glance.

That night, she tossed and turned, finding it impossible to sleep, kept awake by thoughts of Alastair – memories of their closeness during the time of Dunkirk, her desperate need to be with *him* rather than travel to Singapore, her desire to return to London rather than remain on Cairnmor, and their fond farewell at Portsmouth. She relived their shared concern for the children, and the times they had laughed together and instinctively sought each other's company – recollections that were vivid and real.

This time, Katherine allowed herself to dwell in her thoughts and to go further – overriding any residual guilt, mentally dissolving the barriers thrown up by their former relationship to each other, and even daring to contemplate a different future for herself and Alastair other than the one convention and accepted morality dictated.

CHAPTER 25

Fort Southwick (2)
August, 1943

In the event, Katherine did see Freddie the following Tuesday. He proved to be slightly better company than before and they drove into Winchester, looking round the Cathedral and the many little shops in the city. The weather was fine and it was a very pleasant excursion.

In the warm summer's evening, after managing to find a secluded restaurant that served a fine meal, despite the strictures of rationing, they walked beside the river and reminisced about their time at Edinburgh and the people they used to know.

Freddie had kept in touch with several of his friends from his course and, before the war, they had even arranged reunions at various places around the country. Now they were scattered everywhere, serving with their various regiments at home and overseas.

How much the war is altering people's lives, thought Katherine. *Like the tides – irresistible and inevitable. Like my feelings for Alastair.*

"You're miles away again," observed Freddie.

"Sorry." After a momentary silence, while she searched for something to talk about, Katherine asked, "What happened with you and Joyce?"

"I'm not sure really. We grew apart, so she tells me, rather than growing together."

"Will you get back together?"

"I have absolutely no idea."

"Do you want to?"

"It's difficult to say."

"Is there anyone else?"

Freddie was quiet. Then he said, "There could be you."

This was what Katherine had feared might happen. "Oh, Freddie. I'm afraid not."

"Why, do you have someone else?" he asked.

It was Katherine's turn to hesitate. Could she allow herself to describe Alastair as 'someone else'? There could be no doubting her feelings for him. But she also knew how hopeless the situation was. He could never count as 'someone else'.

Or could he?

"Katherine?"

She paused but only for the briefest of moments. "Yes, there is," she said, her heart hammering in her chest. "He's called Alastair."

There, the words were finally out, spoken; her innermost thoughts made real.

"I wish it weren't so."

She tried to make her voice and manner kind. "I'm so sorry, Freddie."

He was philosophical. "Well, never mind. It's just one of those things."

"But I'm glad we've met up again."

He turned to her. "So am I." He took her hand in his and they walked back along the river bank to the car.

They drove to Southwick in silence, each of them lost in their own thoughts, but it wasn't an uncomfortable silence and on arrival, he brought the car quietly to a halt outside her cottage.

"Thank you, Freddie."

"No trouble, and I hope it works out with whatshisname."

Katherine nodded and smiled in reply. "And I hope you find a way to get back together with Joyce. It might be worth suggesting to her that you try again. I suspect that you're still in love with her."

"I am."

"Then try."

"You know, I do believe I shall."

"Good man."

"And Katherine?"

"Yes?"

"Let's keep in touch."

She regarded him for a moment, and then said, "I'd like that, even if it's just a Christmas card."

They exchanged addresses and by way of farewell, Freddie quipped, "Till next Christmas then."

"Until next Christmas. Look after yourself."

"And you." With that, he drove away.

Katherine stood on the pavement for a while and wondered if she would ever see him again.

The weather was very hot all through August, with Katherine's work continuing much as before. However, it was cool working underground – a small blessing in an unnatural environment.

She began to make friends with several of the other Wrens stationed at Fort Southwick. On their day off, they would hitch a ride in one of the army lorries, called 'liberty boats', teaming up with their male colleagues and travelling a few miles to the narrow sandy beach on Hayling Island, which had been taken over by Service personnel for the duration.

They would spend the day sunbathing or sitting under whatever shade they could find, swimming, playing cricket (a new experience for Katherine, who found she wasn't particularly good at it but enjoyed herself anyway), or just watching the ships coming in and out of Langstone Harbour. They went to dances and the cinema, and over time, Katherine felt her spirits lift as the inner wounds of Alex's death finally healed.

When this burden of grief, her companion for so long, finally disappeared forever, she felt an absolute sense of freedom, a soaring of life and energy. She was free now to follow her own path, to do whatever she wanted. And in the very moment of this life-enhancing emotional release, there came an intensifying of her desire for Alastair and the knowledge that she wanted to spend the rest of her life with him.

However, during sobering, more reflective moments, Katherine remained much exercised by the fact that he had once been her father-in-law. Her conscience told her it was wrong that she should be in love with him, that she should not think of him in this way and allow her fantasies to gain the upper hand. Logic told her there could be no future for her with Alastair. But, despite her deliberations, she was unable to dispel her feelings – they were too powerful, too absorbing, and she now found herself unable to conceive of him in any other context.

But what of Alastair? How did he feel about her? Instinctively, Katherine sensed that his feelings went way beyond those of affectionate friendship. But, over the years, he had kept the full extent of these to himself and had never, by word or gesture, revealed their depth to her, keeping the fine line of propriety intact.

So, what should she do? Write and tell him how she felt or stay silent? To say nothing would cause her further anguish, yet to reveal everything in her mind might run the risk of her being rebuffed.

One evening, during the course of a long, solitary walk, thinking deeply of her dilemma, Katherine rested for a while on the grass of Portsdown Hill, surveying the panorama spread before her, golden and beautiful at the end of yet another glorious late-summer's day. She came to no conclusion, but eventually stood up and walked slowly home, arriving back in Southwick just before it was completely dark.

Sitting at her desk in her tiny bedroom, she put pen to paper:

Dearest Alastair,

I met up with an old friend just recently, someone I haven't seen in many years; someone of whom I was once very fond. He asked me to marry him all that time ago, but I wasn't in love with him, so I refused as graciously as I could and he found someone else, for which I was glad at the time.

I found him much changed, yet not; underneath he is still the same Freddie I always knew when he was a young man. I valued his friendship then, but cannot see now what I saw in him.

Time changes much.

I have been thinking of friendship and love. Of you and I. About being able to speak one's mind without fear. Of knowing that one's thoughts and feelings are in safe hands. Of affection and companionship.

Of being in love.

We need to talk, Alastair. I need to talk to you, but I don't know if I have the courage to say what I want to say; whether it is right to say anything at all. I could write it all down in a letter, but I would prefer to be with you, even if I have to wait for a very long time before that is possible. (Having said this much, you'll be curious now and will speculate upon all sorts of things!) But perhaps you will read between the lines and will know what I'm trying to say anyway.

In Meg's sitting room is a bookcase with many books on its shelves. The range is considerable and I came across one by Goethe, in an English translation by Thomas Carlyle. Contained among the verses, I found this:

'The world is empty if one thinks only of mountains, rivers, and cities but to know someone who thinks and feels with you and, though distant, is close to you in spirit, this makes the earth for us an inhabited garden.'
I send my love to you,
Your very own Katherine xxx

Of course, Alastair did know and rejoiced in the words of her letter. His reply was a document of loving restraint and wisely, he bided his time, waiting for Katherine to disclose what it was she wanted to say, at a time when she felt that she was ready.

Alastair returned home eventually at the beginning of September but was given a mere two days' leave before he was obliged to take up his next posting – working as Naval Liaison Officer between the Admiralty and General Sir Frederick Morgan at Norfolk House in London on the initial stages of planning the Allied invasion of France.

Meanwhile, Katherine had been temporarily seconded to the naval base at Rosyth in Scotland. Frustratingly, they were not able to see each other, even for a couple of hours. However, when she returned to Portsmouth in October, by a sheer stroke of luck, events were to take an unexpected turn for both of them.

CHAPTER 26

Norfolk House (1)
October, 1943

Towards the end of October, after only a couple of months working with Fred Morgan, Alastair was told to report once again to Norfolk House in London. However, it was not to his present post, as he would have assumed, but to Admiral Sir Bertram Ramsay, who that very day, had taken up his appointment as Allied Naval Commander Expeditionary Force, to be known as A.N.C.X.F., for the invasion of France.

The trees in St James's Square, lit up by early morning sunlight, were resplendent with autumnal foliage, and as Alastair walked across the grass in the small park at its centre, circumventing the tented guards' encampment, past the statue of the Duke of Wellington, he perceived their beauty – yet his mood was tinged with great sadness. Four days earlier he had lost an old friend with the death of the First Sea Lord, Sir Dudley Pound.

On arrival at Norfolk House, Alastair was ushered into an oak-panelled room that managed to be both functional and yet retain a certain elegance of design. Admiral Ramsay smiled and stood up as he entered the room and Alastair saluted. After the formalities were returned and the two men had shaken hands, Bertie Ramsay said, "Please do sit down, Commander Stewart. It's good to see you again."

"Thank you, sir," replied Alastair, choosing one of the two chairs that faced the large mahogany desk. "It's good to see you, too."

"It's sad news, isn't it, regarding Dudley? He was an exceptional staff officer and a great friend to many people. You were close to him, I believe?"

"Yes, sir, I was. We always worked well together. We served together in the last war…" For the moment, he could say no more, as to do so would have made it difficult to contain his emotions. Dudley's passing had reopened the wound of Alex's death, still so near the surface.

Admiral Ramsay was sympathetic to the feelings of the man before him. He knew that Alastair had lost his son, and he understood the processes of grief.

Gently, he said, "I think he would have been proud and pleased if he had known that he was going to leave us on Trafalgar Day, don't you agree?"

Alastair smiled gratefully. "He would have been, yes. He had a particular regard for Nelson."

"He did." After a moment or two the admiral said, "Dudley spoke of you in glowing terms on many occasions."

Alastair was not quite sure how to respond. "Really?" was all he could say.

"Indeed. He also told me that he had specifically requested that you should work on his staff once you had returned to active service. He regarded you as invaluable."

"He became a good friend and I owe him an enormous debt. He put so many opportunities my way. I worked with him from just before the beginning of the war until April, 1942 when I was sent to sea. As of course, you know," he added.

The admiral nodded, recalling the recent Allied operations in Sicily and the clear communications from the Executive Officer of the *Romney*. Then he said, "You've been acting as Naval Liaison Officer for the past couple of months between the Admiralty and COSSAC?"

"Yes, sir."

"COSSAC is a most useful abbreviation, don't you think? Otherwise, 'Chief of Staff Supreme Allied Commander' would be such a mouthful, especially when the Supreme Allied Commander has yet to be appointed."

"Do you have any idea who that might be?" asked Alastair.

"It's not certain yet. I think it will probably be Eisenhower, though I personally think that Alan Brooke would be an excellent choice. But Ike, being an American, is the obvious candidate."

"It would certainly be the diplomatic choice," said Alastair.

"I agree. Now onto our immediate needs. The situation regarding personnel will, of necessity, have to change with my appointment. I'm trying to keep together as many as possible of the naval staff already familiar with the COSSAC plan, as this will enable a smooth transition. There will, however, inevitably be an expansion as the work will become increasingly complex with time."

Alastair wondered where this conversation was going. "Yes, sir." But he had to wait a little longer to find out.

Admiral Ramsay looked down at the file in front of him and said, with no little respect, "You were awarded the V.C.?"

Alastair nodded.

"Perhaps on another occasion I can hear more – citations do not always give the full picture." He paused, and gave Alastair a direct look. "You see, I need someone who can show initiative and who is not afraid to see something through to its proper conclusion. I saw that in you personally during Operation Dynamo." He paused again and smiled. "Now, how would you feel about working for me full-time on Operation Neptune, as the naval side of the Allied invasion of France is to be called, here at Norfolk House?"

Alastair's response was immediate. "It would be a privilege, sir." He already admired this man for his intelligence and extraordinary abilities, so to work with him was almost too good to be true.

"It will mean a lot of hard work and long hours…"

"I'm used to that at the Admiralty. Also, before the war, I was the senior partner in a solicitors' firm. Long hours have always been par for the course."

Admiral Ramsay nodded, appreciating the golfing analogy. He went straight to the point. "I should like you to be my Deputy Chief of Staff. Your main areas of responsibility will be operations, logistics, and plans. You will be working closely with the directors of those departments, reporting to me, as well as to the Chief of Staff. You will also work with the C.O.S. on other matters as required." He smiled broadly. "How does that sound?"

Alastair was taken aback. He had not anticipated a post of such responsibility.

"I wasn't expecting anything like this…"

Admiral Ramsay smiled. "I imagined that would be so."

"It sounds daunting, but an exciting challenge and one which I feel proud to accept. Thank you, sir. But I do have one question…"

"Fire away."

"With a position such as D.C.O.S., will it matter that I'm only R.N.V.R. and not a career naval officer?"

"Not to my mind during wartime. You are a highly qualified staff officer, with recent combat experience and a distinguished Service record. You have held posts of responsibility and between the wars, maintained a regular programme of staff training courses and seagoing exercises. I want the best people for the job on my staff: R.N., R.N.R., or R.N.V.R., it makes no difference to me. Though you may have to take some flak from one or two quarters…"

"I've already had that at the Admiralty. I can deal with it, sir."

"Good. Now, onto what is required. In the planning stage, logistics will be our main focus. To get the necessary forces across the Channel for the invasion is going be an undertaking of enormous magnitude and the plans will have to be detailed and precise. We shall probably have to do several versions if past experience is anything to go by. I need someone like you who has a reputation for meticulous attention to detail, thoroughness, efficiency and who is also able to make constructive suggestions. I have a feeling therefore, that we shall get on splendidly." He smiled at Alastair, who could not help but respond.

"I shall do my very best, sir."

"That's settled then. Now, we need to discuss a personnel matter. With the potential work load that is likely to be put upon you, and indeed all of us, you'll need a good staff officer to assist you and take over your responsibilities when required. I had lunch the other day with the Director of Wrens, Mrs Laughton, and her staff officer, Superintendent Lady Cholmondeley. You must have come across them at the Admiralty?"

"It is hard not to, sir, with their headquarters being in the building. They are a force to be reckoned with!"

Admiral Ramsay laughed. "Indeed. Particularly Sybil, who with her husband, are great friends of mine."

"Particularly Sybil. A lady with, shall we say, an effervescent personality and a silver tongue."

"Which has a tendency to run away with her on social occasions, especially if she's feeling nervous! However, she's very good at her job and I gather that Mrs Laughton would not be without her. Anyway, during the course of luncheon, we were discussing staff appointments and I was outlining my plans for my staff. Mrs Laughton asked if I had or was thinking of giving a W.R.N.S. officer a position of direct responsibility. I said that I had not, but that I was certainly not averse to the idea. 'Well,' she said. 'I know just the officer you need. Her talents are being wasted at the moment by an Assistant Chief of Staff in Fort Southwick who doesn't quite know what to do with her.'" Bertie Ramsay looked at Alastair, a mischievous twinkle in his eyes. "Apparently, the officer in question graduated top of her course at Greenwich, gave a brilliant dissertation on the ships of the

Royal Navy and has phenomenal shorthand and typing speeds. Oh, and she's also fluent in French and… Gaelic."

Alastair was so astonished, he was rendered speechless.

The admiral chuckled and said, "Does she sound familiar?!"

"Katherine," he said, hardly daring to believe that this was really happening.

"First Officer Katherine Mathieson. Yes, your daughter-in-law." Admiral Ramsay enjoyed the moment. "However, it's probably best that we keep the connection between the two of you to ourselves for the time being. Let her prove herself in her work. It's good that she uses her maiden name as this will save awkward questions and circumvent any uncharitable remarks of nepotism. I presume you get on well enough to be able to work together?"

Alastair nodded. "Absolutely. We've worked together before."

"Good. Obviously, I shall have to meet her before I make any appointment official, but having read her file, she sounds ideal."

"She is. I can't think of anyone else I'd rather have as my staff officer."

"In that case, it seems to me that we had better snap her up before someone else does. Can I leave it to you to contact personnel and arrange for her immediate transfer to Norfolk House and A.N.C.X.F., assuming there is to be a satisfactory outcome of her interview?"

"Yes sir, you can."

"Excellent. Therefore, after I have interviewed First Officer Mathieson first thing on Monday morning, if all is well, I'd like to see both of you for a private briefing before throwing you in at the deep end with the full staff meeting at 1000 hours." Admiral Ramsay smiled and stood up. "Thank you, Commander Stewart. Oh, and by the way, do you play golf?"

"Ah, I did some years ago, but not recently. I wasn't very good, I'm afraid. But I'm perfectly willing to try it again."

"Excellent! We must have a round or two together at some time."

"I shall look forward to it," said Alastair, hiding an inner sense of trepidation. He really had been hopeless at the game. He resolved there and then to join the Golf Club in Maybury as soon as possible and have some lessons. He hoped his game wasn't beyond redemption.

The two men shook hands, saluted and Alastair walked out of the room feeling buoyant, unable to believe his and Katherine's good fortune.

Anxious to set things up immediately, as soon as he arrived back at the Admiralty, he put in motion the necessary steps for Katherine's transfer to London. Then, with great effort, he managed to focus on clearing his desk, ensuring all would be ship-shape for his successor, whoever that might be.

His colleagues were pleased for him, but the Vice Chief of Naval Staff was somewhat put out that one of his best subordinates was about to be transferred – and, to cap it all, just before the new First Sea Lord took up his position – even though he had known that Alastair's appointment was about to be made official after Admiral Ramsay had sought his agreement to it during an excellent meal at Claridge's the previous week.

Katherine was called to the Duty Officer's station just before lunch notifying her of the change of posting, effective from the end of that week. The A.C.O.S. was not particularly pleased to lose this very useful secretary, whom he was just beginning to appreciate, but Katherine was delighted. She would not miss the subterranean tunnels at all – it would be a relief to be working in daylight again and she desperately needed more of a challenge, more involvement. True, she had absorbed a great deal during her time at Fort Southwick and latterly in Rosyth, but with her training, she felt frustrated that she was unable to do that for which she was well qualified. Katherine hoped that her new posting would provide such a role for her. But most importantly, she would be seeing Alastair again.

How she longed for that, although her excitement was tempered by concern.

Her rail warrant was not issued until Sunday evening and was only valid for Monday, the day she was due to begin her posting, whatever that was going to be. All during that interminable pre-dawn journey she fidgeted around, impatient for the train to arrive at Waterloo Station. When it finally did, he was there to meet her as she stepped off the train.

Katherine smiled and Alastair smiled back, the expression in their eyes vital and alive.

Without saying a word, he took her suitcase and she tucked her arm into his. Together they walked along the platform as though it were only yesterday that they had last met.

"It's so good to see you," said Alastair, wanting to take her in his arms.

"It's so good to see you," replied Katherine, trying very hard not to tremble. "I've missed you so much."

"I've missed you too."

She tucked her other hand into his arm as well, as though by holding onto him more tightly she could prevent them from ever being apart again.

"I have absolutely no idea why I'm here," she said.

"No?" He smiled at her enigmatically.

"Do you know?"

"Of course. I sent the signal."

"You did? But the signal didn't say why I was being transferred. Oh, Alastair, please tell me. Don't keep me in suspense!"

He chuckled. "I have been appointed Deputy Chief of Staff and you..." (how he wanted to add, "my darling" but dare not) "...you are going to be my staff officer. We shall be working together."

"That's wonderful." She stopped walking and turned to him, wanting him to kiss her, wishing she could kiss him. Instead, she asked, "Who shall we be working for?"

"Admiral Sir Bertram Ramsay!"

"You're kidding!" Katherine could hardly believe it.

"No, I'm not!"

"Oh, Alastair. This is real, isn't it? I'm not going to wake up in a moment and find it's all a dream, am I?"

He regarded her tenderly. "No, you're not. This is very real and very true." Then, against every emotional and physical inclination, he became more business-like. "Now, we haven't got long. You have an interview with the Admiral at 0900 hours, *we* have a briefing immediately afterwards, then a general staff meeting at ten."

"Goodness. Do I look all right?"

He smiled. "You look beautiful," he said and was delighted to see her blush.

"Oh, Alastair, it's so good to be home with you."

"It's so good to have you home with me. It's been such a long time. An age, an eternity."

"Hasn't it just?"

He put his arm round her shoulders and held her close to him while she in turn became aware of a new responsiveness deep within her at his touch – a touch that was both exciting and new, yet at the same time, very dear, safe and familiar.

There was so much she wanted to say, so much she couldn't say.

Alastair, ever sensitive to her emotions, and recalling her enigmatic letter to him, felt the physical change in Katherine as he brought her closer to him. A feeling of delight suffused his heart while a profound sense of relief at having finally come home permeated his soul.

There was so much to say, so much that couldn't be said. Yet.

Together, each keeping their deepest thoughts hidden from the other, they walked towards the underground station and the important new work that awaited them.

CHAPTER 27

Norfolk House (2)
October, 1943

Katherine's interview lasted no more than ten minutes. Admiral Ramsay instantly assessed her capabilities and perceived that, together with her intelligence and social skills, she was indeed the right person for the job he had in mind.

One thing puzzled him, though. When she first walked into the room, he had experienced a moment of familiarity, a moment when he thought they had met before. However, as he was certain they had not, Bertie Ramsay immediately dismissed the thought from his mind and asked that Alastair should join them straightaway.

"Please do sit down," said the admiral to his D.C.O.S. "We have had a very satisfactory meeting and I'm sure that you will be pleased to hear that I shall be making First Officer Mathieson's appointment official."

Alastair smiled at Katherine, unable to conceal his pride. "I'm delighted, sir."

Their C.O. turned to Katherine. "So, welcome to my staff, First Officer Mathieson. I think that I shall call you 'Matty'. Do you mind?"

"Not at all, sir. Alastair has already warned me that I may be given a nickname."

"Yes, it's a particular foible of mine. I tried calling Alastair, 'Stewart' or 'Stewpot', but he said that the latter would detract from his authority and the former sounded like a Christian name and as that was the case, he would prefer his own name. He didn't like 'Al' either. Is he always so troublesome?"

Katherine grinned. "Always!"

"Well, I have no doubt you'll keep him in order!"

"Of course, sir. I shall do my best."

Admiral Ramsay smiled and, moving on to the business in hand, said, "Your duties will be primarily working with Alastair as his staff officer. These will be multifarious and varied and will also involve liaising with and working alongside the departments for which he has primary responsibility. He and I have discussed all this in some detail and he will fill you in during the course of this week.

"Now, I should also like to call upon your services, if I may. No one here possesses the shorthand speeds that you have, excellent and hard-working as the other Wrens are. I shall need you to keep detailed records of our planning meetings, all of which are top secret, and I shall value any suggestions you may have to make during the planning process upon which we are about to embark.

"In addition, I shall use you as a sounding board before presentations and so on, and whenever I may be hard-pressed for time in writing documents myself, I shall utilize your shorthand skills during the thinking process. The notes can then be ordered and typed up afterwards." He gave her an astute look and smiled. "It will be a demanding role for you. All right so far?"

"Absolutely fine, sir."

"Very good. After the morning staff meeting, I'd like both of you to review the COSSAC document. Alastair will take you through it and I'd appreciate any observations you both may have. This applies to all plans and documents that we shall be working on over the coming months."

Katherine couldn't suppress her smile or hide her enthusiasm. "This is just the sort of working environment I've been hoping for. Thank you very much, sir."

Bertie Ramsay smiled. He could see this officer was going to become an asset to his team, and quickly too. "Good. Now, I shall look forward to seeing you both in about half an hour at the staff meeting. Take some time to familiarize yourself with the layout of the building, Matty, where the various departments are located and where the senior staff members are to be found. I'm afraid the two of you will have to share an office for the time being, until we can allocate suitable rooms for you both."

"That's not a problem," said Alastair.

They all stood up, but Admiral Ramsay had not quite finished. "Oh, and congratulations to you both…"

Alastair and Katherine exchanged puzzled looks, wondering what on earth he could mean.

"…on your promotions, *Captain* Stewart and *Chief Officer* Mathieson."

Speechless with surprise, they stared at each other open-mouthed. The admiral enjoyed the moment immensely. "Well, I can't have my D.C.O.S. as anything less than the rank of Captain, can I? And Matty needs the necessary authority for the work she will be required to do. Take some time off this afternoon to go and have yourselves fitted for new uniforms at Gieves."

"Thank you very much, sir, from both of us," said Alastair.

"Now, enjoy your tour." They saluted and left the room, both amazed and pleased, and not a little proud.

A Petty Wren was waiting for them with instructions to give Katherine a guided tour of the facilities at Norfolk House. Alastair accompanied them and they looked at the room in which they would be working. It was spacious, functional and well laid out. They each had a desk and there were filing cabinets and bookshelves waiting to be filled with appropriate documents.

Further down the corridor was a large central space where the typing pool was located, surrounded by offices in a sort of U-shape arrangement with a staircase leading off to the side, one of several in the building that linked the upper and lower floors.

Katherine was introduced *en masse* to the hard-working Wrens who gave her a friendly welcome before the incessant clattering of typewriters resumed as she moved away. Once they were out of earshot and he could be heard above the racket, Alastair remarked discreetly to Katherine, "I'm glad I don't have to work either in or next to that environment all the time."

"So am I. It stops you thinking doesn't it?"

"It certainly does."

Wrens could be chosen from the typing pool by any of the officers to type up documents for them. These were then taken to the Registry Room, where they were collated and filed or circulated for annotating and signing. As they entered this room, one of the Wrens, a Third Officer, approached Alastair without saluting and, in her demeanour, implied a certain familiarity. She seemed to know him well.

"Why, it's Commander Stewart! I'm so glad to see you again. I was so delighted when I heard that you would be at Norfolk House permanently. I do hope it means that we shall be working together again."

Katherine experienced an involuntary moment of panic that disturbed her happy equilibrium.

"I'm not sure how much opportunity there will be, but something might arise." Alastair was courteous but non-committal and Katherine felt relieved.

"I'll look forward to it."

The Wren smiled at him in such a way that made it clear she had set her sights on him. Two of the girls working at the large filing cabinets, exchanged glances.

Katherine felt her mouth go dry. She had never been with Alastair in a situation like this where other women might claim his attention. She was so used to having him to herself that competition, imaginary or otherwise, was a novel experience and not a pleasant one at that.

With Katherine feeling slightly subdued after this encounter, they finished their tour of the various departments and as she identified who was who and where everything was situated, she forgot about the Wren and her spirits lifted again.

The staff meeting was routine but handled by Admiral Ramsay with charm and humour and new staff members were welcomed onto the team. The day's duty rosters and administrative requirements were outlined and, chatting happily as they left the room, everyone began their allotted tasks.

At the end of that first day when Alastair and Katherine reached home, tired but full of enthusiasm, she had a surprise reunion with Rupert and Anna who, with the current cessation of bombing, had come to stay in London at Alastair's suggestion during the half-term holiday, to spend the week with Katherine.

The house was quiet when she and Alastair opened the front door but all at once, the children came rushing out of the sitting room, calling out, "Mummy, Mummy! Surprise!" in a wave of boisterous excitement. It was all too much for Katherine, who, after the exertions of the day, burst into tears.

"Mummy, please don't cry!" said Anna, holding her hand.

"Aren't you pleased to see us?" asked Rupert, afraid that they had done something wrong.

Katherine knelt down on the floor and gathered them to her. "Of *course* I'm pleased to see you both. It's wonderful to see you! It's the best surprise ever. These are tears of joy, not sadness! It's been such a long time and I've missed you so much."

After they had hugged and kissed and Katherine had wiped away her tears, Mrs Thringle came over to her, having waited patiently on the sidelines for the children to claim their mother first. This made for another joyful reunion.

"Thank you for looking after the children. They look so well and happy."

"That's all right, dearie. They're usually as good as gold and I love doing it."

Seeing Katherine smile again, the children's high spirits immediately returned.

"Mummy, Mummy," said Anna. "I've learnt a new piece on the piano. Can I play it to you? *Please*. We've got a proper piano teacher now. He's called Mr Kanski. Is that how you say his name, Daddad?"

Alastair smiled. "Nearly. It's pronounced Mr Kal-in-ow-ski," he said slowly. Anna copied him until she could say it correctly, enjoying the feeling of being able to speak a difficult word.

"I just call him Mr Kal. It's much easier," said Rupert, with a slight shrug of his shoulders.

"So who is he, this Mr Kalinowski?" asked Katherine, intrigued.

"He's a lovely man," replied Mrs Thringle. "Such a kind old gentleman. He's a Polish refugee who's come to live in Maybury and is trying to earn a living teaching the piano. Mr Alastair met him in the village one day and brought him home to lunch. When Mr K. heard Anna playing her own made-up tunes, he offered to teach her and Rupert. Would have done it for nothing too, but Mr Alastair insisted on paying him. Now, because the twins are doing so well, Mr K. has lots of pupils, including some evacuees, who like him because he's in exile from his home, just like they are!"

Mrs Thringle, a great believer in a regular routine, even if their mother had just come home, looked at the clock. "Now children, it's time for your bath and then bed." There were howls of protest. "But after your bath, you may come downstairs and play the piano for your mummy. You'll be impressed," she said to Katherine.

"Then will you read us our bed-time story, *please*?" begged Anna.

"And say goodnight?" said Rupert, clinging tightly onto his mother's hand to make sure she didn't go away again

"Of course I shall," said Katherine.

After they had gone with Mrs Thringle, chattering away happily, Katherine wanted to hear more about Mr Kalinowski. Alastair made them a pot of tea which they took into the sitting room. She took off her shoes and quite naturally and unaffectedly, put her feet up on the sofa, stretching them out luxuriously before her.

"Oh, that feels so good," she said. "I'm sure that my shoes have shrunk a couple of sizes today. Or perhaps it's just that my feet are swollen after going up and down the stairs so many times!"

Alastair resisted a very strong urge to offer to massage them for her. She must have sensed something of his thoughts, because the look she gave him almost made his self-control disappear completely. He took a sip of tea instead, which was too hot and burnt his tongue. Quickly, he put some more milk into the cup and was able to drink it without doing further damage. Alastair thought he had better start talking.

"Stefan Kalinowski was a professor of piano at the Warsaw Conservatoire and a famous concert pianist in his native country. After the Nazis occupied Poland, Jewish people were rounded up and forced to live in what became known as Ghettos. Living conditions were indescribable and their treatment appalling beyond belief. Anyway, one day his wife and two daughters were taken away, along with all the other women and children, and that was the last Stefan ever saw of them. He has no idea where they were taken or whether they are alive or dead.

"He heard all sorts of rumours as to where they were sent but could find out nothing." Alastair paused and drew in a deep breath. "I won't go into any more detail, as it's very upsetting, but knowing about this – not that I needed any further confirmation – has served to reinforce how necessary this war is and how essential it is for the Allies to win.

"Poor, poor man." After a while, she said, "How did he escape?"

"Soon after this, he and some other men and boys were taken to a forced labour camp, first in Germany and then France, in appallingly harsh conditions. One day, a group of them, including Stefan, were taken out into the countryside to mend roads when the accompanying guards were attacked and killed by members of the French Resistance. Stefan was rescued, and taken first across the border to Spain, then by boat to England, where he was claimed as a relative by the Anderson family."

"You don't mean Annette and David who live in Heritage Road?"

"Yes."

"I didn't realize they had any relatives abroad."

"Nor did I, but apparently, Annette's grandmother was Polish and Stefan is her second cousin. The family had always kept in close contact before the war, so on arrival in this country, Stefan knew where to find his relatives and was able to be taken there more or less straightaway."

"How did you meet him?"

"I went for a walk and found him sitting on a bench beside the river. We fell into conversation and I brought him home for lunch. His health is generally poor because what he had to endure was just awful and it's taken a severe physical toll on him."

"So now he's earning a living by teaching the piano."

"Yes. Rupert and Anna adore him. I'd been thinking it was about time they had proper lessons and it seemed too good an opportunity to pass up. Since they've been learning, they've made amazing strides. He's an extraordinarily gifted teacher but, by the same token, I think that we have two precociously talented pianists on our hands." Alastair smiled and she smiled back, her eyes full of love and gratitude for his care of her children and his use of the inclusive 'we'.

Katherine was not disappointed when she heard them play. For the first time in a very long time, she wished that Alex could be here with them all. *He will never know*, she thought. *He will never know his children. How special they are. How talented. Oh, Alex, we did well together.* Pain constricted her chest and her eyes filled with tears.

Then Rupert came rushing over to her full of enthusiasm and said, "Was that good, Mummy, was it good?"

"It was very good," she said, swallowing her grief. "From both of you."

"I 'duct as well. Look! Look!" and while Anna played her pieces again, Rupert conducted her, perfectly in time, with perfect movements.

"How on earth did you learn to do that?!" exclaimed Katherine.

"Daddad took us to a concert and I watched the man stand up and wave his arms about, like this." His little face was alight as he closed his eyes and became lost in the imaginary world of an orchestra.

"Which concert was that?" she asked Alastair.

"The London Philharmonic Orchestra with Malcolm Sargent at the Royal Albert Hall. They both sat through the whole thing and didn't fidget one bit. I'd been quite prepared to take them home after the first half, but they begged me to let them stay. Anna fell asleep on my lap, but Rupert sat and watched the whole thing. He was completely transfixed by it. The couple sitting next to me congratulated me on my extremely well-behaved children."

Comforted by this simple retelling, Katherine was able to add in a matter-of-fact way, "It must have been wonderful to take them out somewhere without fear of an air raid. Thank goodness they've stopped now."

"For the moment, but not for always, I think. There will be more."

"Oh, Alastair, I do hope not."

After the children were in bed and had had their story, Katherine cleared up in the kitchen, washing up their cups and saucers while Alastair dried them. It was a scene of perfect domestic harmony and all she wanted once they had finished, was for him to make love to her.

Alastair felt exactly the same but told himself to be patient. He had waited this long; he could manage to wait another week while the children were here in London.

It will happen soon, he reassured himself. *It has to happen soon.*

CHAPTER 28

Norfolk House (3)
October, 1943

During that first week, Katherine and Alastair settled quickly into their routine. From the outset, it was apparent that they worked extremely well together and they both found in Admiral Ramsay an ideal superior officer. He led by example and was one of those rare beings who could answer any question or query immediately – and, moreover, was willing to do so.

He ran a highly efficient staff and knew exactly what was going on at all times. Any difficulty or problem that arose was dealt with straightaway with consummate skill, and he was not afraid to delegate, trusting the staff he had appointed to carry out his wishes accurately and thoroughly.

Bertie Ramsay was courteous and genial to everyone with whom he came into contact, no matter what their position or rank, from cleaners to senior staff. He knew everybody's name, always said, "Good Morning," and created a friendly and happy environment in which to work. He was admired and respected by his staff and regarded as a 'very great gentleman'. He recognized and praised good work wherever and whenever he saw it and his staff were inspired to achieve that recognition.

However, there was no doubting who was in charge. Admiral Ramsay set very high standards and worked incredibly hard himself, expecting those around him to do the same. He did not tolerate any lack of effort or tardiness and could be very forthright with those he felt were not pulling their weight or whose work fell below the expected standard. Outside of his immediate workplace, he was a master of diplomacy and very good at getting things done in a particular way when he was utterly convinced that he was *right*. He usually was.

There was a buzz to working in Norfolk House that made each day exciting and stimulating. The atmosphere was purposeful, with each person knowing exactly what his or her duties were. Along with everyone else, Katherine and Alastair were required to work long, demanding hours, only returning home when a particular task was completed.

Katherine loved working with Alastair just across the room from her, grateful for their good fortune, yet aware that this state of affairs could not be guaranteed forever in wartime. During the rare moments that they were alone, Katherine would often pause and look up from her papers, watching him writing at his desk. Alastair would catch her and smile at her, his warmth making her blush and her heart beat faster.

However, she was still afraid to speak and kept her feelings very much to herself.

The only fly in this particular ointment of contentment was the Third Officer from the Registry Room who, for the whole of that first week, took every opportunity to speak to Alastair. She would come into their office on the flimsiest of pretexts and corner his attention as often as she could.

Alastair was tolerant and kind but Katherine did not like it one bit. She was jealous. She had to admit it, and yet there was nothing in Alastair's careful demeanour towards this woman that should cause her anxiety. She knew this but even so, she could not help her feelings. If she had any dealings with this particular officer, she was curt and abrupt. By Saturday afternoon, after they had finished their duties at the end of that first week, Katherine knew she could stand it no longer.

On their homeward journey, she and Alastair took the bus as far as the Albert Hall – they liked to vary the way they travelled back to Cornwallis Gardens, sometimes on the underground, sometimes by bus.

However, on this occasion, Katherine was silent and withdrawn, displaying none of her usual cheerfulness. Alastair regarded her carefully, wondering if she was thinking about the children, who had returned to Mistley House that morning so they could be settled and ready for the return to school on Monday. He knew she would miss them, even though he and Katherine had planned to be with them on Sunday, not quite knowing when they would finish work on the Saturday.

As a distraction for her, once the bus had moved off, Alastair suggested that they go for a walk in Kensington Gardens. "It's a lovely day and I'd quite like some fresh air after being indoors for what seems like an eternity today dealing with all sorts of tedious issues."

"Okay."

They crossed the road and walked up the long avenue of tall beech trees, their leaves resplendent in gold and red.

"One of the things I love most about London are the trees. The colours this year are quite wonderful. And trees always have a remarkable power to uplift," said Alastair, hoping to draw her out with one of her favourite topics as it was unusual for her to be so uncommunicative when they were together.

"Hm." Katherine's answer was brief, distracted.

They walked on in silence, Alastair glancing at her every so often, wondering about the cause of her preoccupation.

Eventually she spoke. "Alastair?"

"Yes?"

"Is it possible to transfer that Wren who keeps coming into our office?"

Alastair chuckled. "Why?"

"Because she's a pain in the neck and seems to think you're her personal property."

Alastair stopped walking. "Does she? I can't say I'd noticed."

"She seems to have set her sights on you. The girls in the Registry Room and Typing Pool gossip about it."

"Do they?"

"Yes."

"About me?" Alastair was concerned. "Because I've done nothing."

"I know that and so do they. No, it's just about how much she chases after you. I don't like it."

"Oh?" His heart beat faster.

"She's very attractive."

202

"Is she? Again, I hadn't noticed."

"You do spend an awful lot of time speaking to her."

"You know I don't. That's ridiculous," he replied good-naturedly. Alastair looked at her quizzically. "Katherine, what's the matter?"

She smiled ruefully. "Sorry. I sound like a jealous wife."

Alastair moved closer to her and smiled at her. "Yes, you do, I'm afraid." Then he added, after a pause, "You have nothing to worry about, you know."

"I don't?"

"No, because I think you are the most beautiful woman I've ever known."

"You do?"

"Yes."

"Even more so than Roberta?"

"Definitely."

"Oh, Alastair." She looked up at him, her eyes bright with tears.

They walked on in silence for a while. Then Katherine spoke again, the words tumbling out in a rush. "We've made a good life together since Alex died, haven't we?"

"A very special life."

"There are times when we still grieve for him, times when it catches us unawares."

"Yes." He wondered where this might be leading.

"We've always instinctively understood each other, you and I, right from when we first met. We've always had our own deep and affectionate friendship. We're incredibly close."

"Incredibly," he said, his voice warm.

"And you've become a wonderful father to Rupert and Anna. They're so happy and settled."

"I love them and would do anything for them... and you."

"You would? For me?"

"Yes, you know I would." He smiled at her again and Katherine smiled back. Encouraging her, he said, "But there's more, isn't there? The thing you wanted to say in your enigmatic letter to me."

"Yes."

She fell silent. How could she phrase what was going to be one of the most important, *contentious*, life-changing things she would ever say? She bit her bottom lip, not knowing how to begin; afraid of meeting with concealed disapproval or friendly paternal rejection.

Alastair looked at her, his heart pounding. Was she finally about to speak of all that was in her heart? Was his unobtainable dream about to become a reality? Was it even right that he should allow it to happen? He held his breath.

When Katherine seemed unable to say anything, he prompted her, carefully choosing his words: "Is it... is it that you see the possibility of another... dimension developing in our relationship?"

"Yes." She stopped.

He moved closer to her, almost touching her, but not quite, wanting to be certain of exactly what it was she was trying to say.

"Oh Alastair, I've been so jealous this week. I know there was no cause and it was completely irrational but when that stupid woman made such a… a… play for you, I realized I couldn't stay silent any longer. You see, I wanted it to be me so much."

"But not quite like her, surely?!" Alastair teased her gently.

"No, of course not, she's embarrassing." Katherine managed a rueful smile. "I'm not like that."

"I know, thank goodness! But I understand exactly what you are saying. To have that freedom."

"Yes."

They had stopped walking now and stood facing each other beside the boating lake, a striking couple in their Royal Navy greatcoats and hats. Alastair took her hands in his and listened as she continued.

"I haven't known what to say or do, how to deal with what I've been feeling, whether to tell you or not." Katherine looked at him pleadingly, her manner hesitant, vulnerable.

"Please tell me." His voice was soft, gently encouraging. Wisely, Alastair knew he had to wait for her to say it, had to wait for her to speak the words he longed to hear.

"I'm in love with you, Alastair, and there's nothing I can do to change that," she blurted out.

Joyously, he took her into his arms, letting relief flood through him as she clung to him, allowing his emotional and physical responses to reawaken after so many years of enforced sublimation.

"And I'm in love with you, too, my darling." He held her close, never wanting to let her go; unable to believe this was really happening.

Katherine felt her skin tingle as his lips lingered for a moment on her cheek; the very briefness of his caress tantalizing.

"Oh, Alastair, I've been in such a quandary as to what to do."

"So have I."

He wanted to kiss her properly, but dare not. There were too many people around. It would not do to be seen embracing in public, even though in wartime there was a tolerance and understanding that had not existed before, particularly when it involved members of the armed forces. But it was more than that, much more. They both held positions of responsibility within the Royal Navy and no matter how powerful their immediate needs, they had to be careful and discreet.

Indeed, in their situation, they would always have to be careful and discreet.

So, smiling at her with warmth and tenderness, Alastair tucked her arm into his, a familiar gesture that now held a new, deeper significance for them both. They turned and walked towards home in silence, a silence filled with love and desire, of anticipation, down the steps leading from the Albert Hall, past the Royal College of Music, past the museums in Exhibition Road.

They crossed over Cromwell Road, and once they had gone beyond South Kensington Underground Station, Alastair said in all seriousness, "There will be a great many ramifications for us to contend with now that this particular genie is out of the bottle."

"Yes," replied Katherine. "And it's those ramifications that have troubled me ever since I was at Greenwich."

"As far back as that?" Alastair smiled. So he had been right that she had loved him then.

"Yes. And perhaps even before that. What about you?"

"Ah. This is where my conscience troubleth me seriously."

Katherine chuckled. "Please tell me. I need to know."

"Of course you do. It first began when you ran down the hill into my arms on Cairnmor the night you found out that Mhairi and Rupert were your real parents and after we had read the letter together. So much so, that I couldn't get to sleep afterwards."

"Really?"

Alastair nodded. "And then I almost gave the game away when I said you looked so beautiful as we sat by the seashore during your wedding reception."

"I remember. But I took it to be a lovely compliment made in all innocence."

"It was, and yet it could not be entirely so. But it wasn't until we went to Cairnmor together before the war that I realized I'd fallen in love with you completely. After that, I knew I'd have to be very careful."

"And you've kept your feelings to yourself all this time?"

They were nearly home.

"Well, I had to. There was no choice. What sort of person would that have made me if I had let you see them in any way?"

"Someone that you are not. But it must have been hard, so hard for you."

"It was, sometimes. But I adapted."

"Just as I did. But for you, it was for so many years – oh, Alastair."

They reached the house. Alastair opened the door and once inside, after hanging up their coats and jackets on the coat stand, they looked at each other for a moment in wondrous anticipation. Then, without hesitating, Alastair brought Katherine into his arms and kissed her lips for the very first time: gently, tenderly, yet with an underlying depth and promise that set her pulse racing.

After a while, a long while, he led her into the sitting room where they sat down on the sofa.

"Those ramifications…" he began, putting her hands to his lips.

She raised an eyebrow at him, her heart beating quickly. "Knowing our mutual self-sacrificing natures, despite everything, you're about to put all sorts of obstacles in our way aren't you?"

He smiled. "You know me too well."

"Not yet," she replied, stroking his cheek.

They regarded each other again, a mixture of amusement and desire lighting their expressions as they embraced once more, this time with growing emotional intensity.

Abruptly, Alastair stopped and then said: "Those ramifications…?"

"Much too late for those," she replied joyously.

He chuckled. "It is rather."

She looked up at him. "But we've got to talk about them. So, fire away."

Katherine was confident now. Alastair loved her; was *in* love with her. That was all that mattered; her previous deliberations rendered meaningless by this revelation.

"I'm twenty years older than you."

"So?"

"That means when you're sixty, for example, I shall be eighty."

"Well, if your parents are anything to go by, you'll be a very fit and active eighty-year old. Next?"

"I'm a year older than your father."

"And? I hope that Rupert and Mhairi will just be glad for our happiness. They know you and care for you. We're consenting adults and besides which, it's our life."

"What about our friends?"

"The same. Our real friends will accept us and they will be the only ones worth having."

"There will be some people who will accuse us of all sorts of things."

"Let them. They don't matter. I've been a widow for almost two years, and your divorce will come through eventually."

Alastair had to admire the robustness of Katherine's defence on their behalf. Then he said, teasing her, "I'm not a very good prospect, am I? Old, decrepit, still married…!"

"In that case, tomorrow I shall exchange you for someone else. I'll go and write the advert now…"

She moved to stand up but he pulled her back down onto the sofa and into his arms, loving her response as their intimacy grew.

Eventually, Alastair took her hands in his, becoming serious once more. "This is the difficult one. Technically, I am still your father-in-law. We are and shall be crossing all sorts of socially and morally accepted boundaries."

"But it's not illegal, is it?" It was a statement more than a question.

Alastair smiled. "No. But it's not the 'done thing'."

She sighed, her mood changing imperceptibly. "I know and I've agonized over this one thing for a very long time. But," she added, with more than a touch of defiance, "I love you and want to be with you far too much to care about spurious boundaries that other people have created. No one is being hurt by our *wanting* to be together and our *being* together is so very *right*."

"Oh, my darling, there can be no doubt of that," and Alastair held her close to his heart. "We'll have to be discreet though."

"That goes without saying."

After a moment's silence, he looked at her. "Perhaps we ought to wait until we're married before we… we sleep with each other."

"Do you want to wait?"

He shook his head. "No." He touched her cheek. "What about you?"

"Of course not. Do you think less of me for saying that?"

"How could I possibly do that? I love you too much and I'm very glad that you don't want to wait. Providing, of course, I haven't forgotten how. It's been a while…"

206

"You've been doing quite well so far!"

"Thank you." And they both laughed.

A little later, she asked, "Have there been many women in your life?" Her question was tentative, mindful of Alex's past which had often troubled her. But she had to know, had to find out.

He smiled at her reassuringly, his conscience clear. "No. Only Roberta."

She threw her arms around him with relief. "Oh, I'm so glad!"

Alastair's response to her was immediate and passionate. But there were still things to say, words that had to be spoken.

"However, I do want to marry you and the possibility of us not getting married sometime in the future does bother me. Greatly."

"I would have been very surprised if it hadn't." She smiled, then said, "I would have to change my religion though in order to do so."

He regarded seriously. "I know. And your way of worshipping is very precious to you."

She nodded.

"Then that will be difficult for you, my darling, as I know to my cost. You see, I was raised a Catholic."

"You were? I never knew that."

"And foolishly, in order to marry Roberta, I became an erstwhile member of the Church of England. But I never took communion, nor attended many services after our wedding, apart from christenings and at Christmas. Edward, obviously, was raised C. of E.; Lily too. But I wanted to raise Alex in my faith, so he went to a Catholic boarding school and university college."

"I see." She understood now. This was something that Alex had never explained to her, and strangely enough, she had never asked. "Well, whatever happens, I shall never lose my faith but if I remain a Catholic, we can never marry. So there's no choice. In any case, it will have to be a registry office wedding."

"That's true."

"Perhaps Father McPhee might give us a blessing. He's certainly unconventional enough."

"But this might just be too much, even for him." Alastair could not gauge how the priest might react. They'd certainly have Robbie's blessing though.

"Well, we're not blood-related. Throughout history, there are many examples of widows who have married their *former* brothers-in-law and I dare say there are *former* fathers-in-law somewhere in there too," added Katherine. "With *former* being the operative word."

"What shall we tell the children?" asked Alastair thoughtfully.

"The truth, when they're old enough to understand. But at the moment, you are the only father they've ever known. Their name for you is significant, I think."

He smiled, warmed by her words. "And what happens if *we* have children?"

"Then we do and when it happens it will be wonderful! But we should be careful until we can be married."

"Yes." He looked deeply into her eyes; his own full of gratitude and love for her, as well as the Greek *Eros* he had not been free to express for so long.

They were alone; the family were back in Maybury. There was nothing in their way... and yet...

Katherine perceived a hesitation on his part. "What is it, my love?"

He was silent, wondering how to phrase this delicately, tactfully. "You see, if we are to be together, I have to be certain that you want me for myself and not because you see me as some kind of familial substitute for Alex. I have no wish to be second-best, even to my son."

His words caught her off-guard and Katherine laid her head against his, considering what he had just said. Tenderly, he pushed a stray lock of her hair back into place and gently tilted her chin so he could see her eyes. "Because even now, my darling, if you do feel that way, then I will wait for you."

How could he doubt her? Hadn't he endured enough while married to Roberta, who had never returned his love and ultimately rejected him? Hadn't he waited long enough for her, Katherine?

It was time.

Without further hesitation, taking both Alastair's hands in hers, she smiled and led him upstairs to her bedroom where she opened her arms and her heart to him with such a profound sense of love and joy that Alastair was left in no doubt whatsoever that it was indeed him she wanted and in return, he gave himself to her completely with all the depth of love and desire that he possessed for the woman who meant more to him than anyone he had ever known.

Afterwards, blissfully, they lay close together, their fingers touching; silent, lost in the exquisite beauty of the moment.

Then, unexpectedly, Katherine turned to him and said, "How many sins have we just committed?"

"Too many to count."

"Does that bother you?"

"Not at this moment. No."

"Will it later?"

"Probably not. How about you?"

"The same." Then, after a little while, she said, "What's Mrs Thringle going to say?"

"I've no idea."

"Do you think she'll resign?"

Alastair chuckled. "I doubt it." He turned to smile at her, his eyes full of love. Katherine smiled back and rested her head on his shoulder, safe in his arms, both of them contented, at peace.

In the event, there was no need for concern, because the first thing the redoubtable Mrs T. did when they told her, was to hug them both and say, "Well, I've been waiting for this for a long time. I wish you both all the happiness in the world."

And Katherine cried with joy and relief at her acceptance of them.

CHAPTER 29

Melbourne, Australia
October, 1943

It was four o'clock in the morning: the time when the human body is at its lowest ebb. The hospital was hushed; muffled feet walked by in the corridor outside the room; voices were subdued. Rachel sat quietly, keeping a night-time vigil beside her patient, his breathing laboured and harsh, his skin pale. From time to time, she checked his pulse or wiped away the sweat from his forehead. Absorbed, she jumped as the door opened and a nurse crept in.

"Can I do anything to help, Dr Curtis? You've been here now for twelve hours without a break. You ought to take a rest," she whispered tentatively.

"Go away," snapped Rachel. "I don't need a break."

She could not leave her patient. She was the only one who could save him, who could bring him through this latest crisis.

"Dr Sullivan thinks that you ought to go home."

"Tell Dr Sullivan to take a running jump. It's not up to him what I do. This is my time. I've finished my shift and I'm off-duty until tomorrow. I'll be ready for my rounds when I'm back at work. Now go away."

"Yes, Doctor."

The nurse quietly withdrew, leaving a fresh jug of water on the bedside table. Dr Curtis was the most conscientious resident they had ever had at the hospital but she could also be fearsome at times. The younger nurses were quite scared of her. However, she did take the welfare of every one of her patients very seriously, sometimes too seriously. Especially this one.

For her part, Rachel had always said she would never become close to another patient but this man had caused her to break that resolve. She had saved his life several times and would do so again and again, whatever it took.

After the first crises were over and he was well enough to be discharged from hospital, he had had nowhere to go. So she took him back to her flat and put him in the double bed in her own room while she slept on the couch. Everyone thought she was mad, taking a complete stranger into her home. But she was not mad; he was not a stranger to her.

He spoke little and revealed nothing about himself. He was in and out of hospital, his constitution taking a battering, his mind often confused. He had terrible nightmares and Rachel would go into him and calm his fears.

He became totally dependent upon her and was always pleased to see her when she returned from her shifts. Gradually, as his health improved, he began to do little tasks around the flat – the washing up, a bit of tidying. He read a book or two from her shelf, and one day she took him to the public library just round the corner where he could browse to his heart's content. He made some odd choices, but, she supposed, he was finding his way back after being so ill. Eventually, he was well enough to walk the short distance to the library by himself. Rachel gave him a door key, but worried about him all the time he was away.

The nightmares continued and after a particularly bad spell, Rachel just stayed with him every night and didn't bother with the couch anymore. There was no point, she told herself.

As the weeks went by, he gained a little more strength and one night, he turned to her and cautiously touched her. Gently, she encouraged him until eventually they made love. After this, Rachel knew there was no going back. She had fallen in love with him and frequently chastised herself for being such an idiot. She was taking an awful risk: she still did not know anything about him.

He began to talk a little – they managed to hold short conversations – but he tired easily. Often exhausted herself after her duties, she was happy to be silent until he felt able to speak once more. Then he had become ill yet again.

Now, in the hospital bed, he stirred. She felt his forehead. He seemed much cooler, his breathing quieter. Rachel felt his pulse. His fever had broken. His eyelids flickered and his eyes opened. He looked at her.

"Hello." His voice was faint, but the word was clear.

"Hello," replied Rachel, her eyes filling with tears of relief. Hastily she wiped them away. He had survived another crisis. There would be more, but at least this one was over.

CHAPTER 30

Mistley House (1)
January, 1944

Katherine knocked on the door of Admiral Ramsay's office. He had a letter that he wanted to dictate and had called for her over the intercom. It was late one Saturday morning towards the beginning of January, the end of a particularly trying week where meetings, plans, changes and awkward situations had to be dealt with and resolutions sought.

Just as she went into the room, the telephone rang. The admiral motioned for her to shut the door and sit down. She did as she was asked and waited patiently, pad and pencil in hand, quietly observing him. His capacity for hard work never ceased to amaze her and she was well aware that he expected nothing less than that from those around him. But he also knew how to keep himself mentally balanced and physically well: he had an excellent sense of self-preservation so that professionally he was always alert and ready to give of his best.

Today, however, he looked tired and wan. The telephone call was proving to be a difficult one, during the course of which he had to use the utmost restraint and diplomacy, offering careful explanations of strategy and instructions to be followed.

The person at the other end of the line seemed incapable or unwilling to listen and adhere to what was required of them, and Admiral Ramsay was obliged to find several different ways of expressing the same thing until he could be understood, his wishes that a particular course of action was the most practicable at last made clear.

Eventually, the phone call came to an end and he put the receiver down in a gesture of annoyance, running his hands across his forehead and down his cheeks, his manner one of exasperation.

"Trying to conduct an awkward conversation on a scrambled telephone line is so tiresome. Why are some people so reluctant to take on board the obvious and just accept something that is logical and sensible?" he observed.

"Probably because they can't see it," replied Katherine. "Either they don't have the clarity of vision or the intelligence or they're just too full of what they want to do rather than seeing the broader picture."

"How right you are. But it's frustrating, nonetheless." He paused, a rueful expression on his face. "I'm sorry to be such an old grump."

Katherine laughed. "You're not. It's just been a very difficult week."

"I agree." He sighed. "I need a change of scene. We could *all* do with a change of scene. There's so much work to do regarding Monty's proposal for a five division assault for the invasion, rather than the three originally suggested by COSSAC. And although I support the proposal absolutely, every time there are changes, we have to alter and adapt our plans to suit. It means extra work for the staff, but it has to be done. And until the decision is finally made, we can only expect more changes. What a week!"

"I know. Alastair's been doing his fair share of ranting and raving too."

Admiral Ramsay chuckled. "I expect he has, although I've never seen him out of temper. He just accepts what needs to be done and gets on with it."

"He's a consummate professional and always has been ever since I've known him. But he's allowed to let off steam to me."

"We all need to be able to do that to someone now and again. As I have to you, just now." His smile was tired, but grateful. "But I couldn't ask for a better D.C.O.S. He's an incredible support and knows exactly what's required. It makes my life so much easier and the work gets done in the way that it should. His staff officer's not so bad, either!" He teased her gently, knowing full well that Katherine's work was also outstanding.

"Och, I do me best, sirrr!" said Katherine in broad Scottish accent. "Though it's a terrrrible trial working for you," she added, extending the tease before biting her bottom lip, hoping she hadn't overstepped the mark in Royal Navy discipline of a subordinate addressing a superior officer.

But Bertie Ramsay laughed, taking it all in good spirit. "Well, we'd better get on. This is going to be a complicated top secret document and it will have to be typed up and sent off by despatch today."

"Yes, sir." And they set to work. Once it was completed, Katherine remained seated, thoughtful. Then she said, "Do you have any plans for this afternoon or tomorrow?"

"Not particularly. I thought I might telephone some friends of mine and see if they're available and could accommodate me."

"Well, Alastair and I were wondering if you'd like to come and spend the rest of the weekend with us at our house in Maybury? It's in Oxfordshire, not too far away, just under an hour on the train."

Her heart was beating fast. *Does one usually ask the Commander-in-Chief to spend the weekend?* she thought. *Despite his sociability, does he prefer to keep work and friendship separate?*

"There's a golf course…" she added, "and a Golf Club, which Alastair has joined. He's been practising…" She looked at the admiral meaningfully.

Bertie Ramsay smiled. "I'd like that very much and if there's the possibility of a game of golf anywhere, then lead me to it!"

"Also, if the two of you have any work to discuss, then you could do it over the weekend."

"I think an escape is the order of the day. We'll work better on Monday after a break. But yes, we could, if necessary. It may prove very useful."

"Also, General Eisenhower's new Free French Liaison Officer will be there." Katherine had left the best until last.

"Lieutenant-General Phillippe du Laurier?" Ramsay was surprised.

Katherine grinned at him. "Yes. He's Alastair's son-in-law!"

The revelation had the desired effect. "Then there's no question. I definitely accept. It will be good to get to know him informally in a purely social setting. We're supposed to meet him officially on Monday. I'll be able to have a head start."

"Yes."

He regarded her intently. "I sense a story here."

"There are lots of stories," she replied cautiously.

"Of that, I have no doubt. And I shall enjoy hearing them. Well, get along then. We haven't got all day! I have a game of golf to play this afternoon and some kind people to visit."

Katherine smiled at him, appreciating his words. She paused with her hand on the door handle as she was leaving the room. "The train leaves from Paddington. Shall we meet you by the ticket barrier at... say two-thirty?"

"Yes, that's fine. Can you speak to Flags? And I'll whizz over to Latymer Court and grab my things as soon as I've finished up here. And Matty?"

"Yes?"

"Thank you. This is just what the doctor ordered."

"I'm glad, sir."

After Katherine had recounted her conversation to him, Alastair was delighted yet at the same time expressed a sense of trepidation. "I hope my golf is up to it!" he said. "I gather he's rather good."

"Well, maybe the resident pro will give him a game and you'll be saved. Or perhaps it will rain!"

"I should be so lucky. The social side at home will be fine, though. I'm not worried about that. I'll ring Mrs Thringle and warn her. She'll have a fit at this short notice."

"And be all of a fluster because an admiral as well as a general is coming for the weekend! I am a bit too, only about Bertie Ramsay though, not Phillippe. Did I do the right thing? It's just that he seemed so tired when I was in there just now, and you and I had talked about it... so I decided to seize the moment."

"Of course it was the right thing to do." Alastair lowered his voice and in Gaelic, told her that he loved her. She replied that she loved him too. And then, business-like, they both got on with their work and left Norfolk House just after one o'clock. They travelled directly to Paddington and ate a quick sandwich in the station buffet before meeting Admiral Ramsay as arranged.

Mrs Thringle was indeed a little flustered as she greeted them when they arrived at Mistley House. Her colour was high but she behaved impeccably, much to Alastair's and Katherine's relief, who had been terribly afraid that she would gush and embarrass them all, especially their guest, whom they knew disliked any show of hero-worship.

Lily and Phillippe had gone out for a walk, she said, and would be back later. The twins were playing with their friends in the village and perhaps Katherine could collect them, as: "I'll be busy preparing supper."

After she had disappeared into the kitchen, Alastair said to Admiral Ramsay, "As you can see she rules us completely."

Their guest laughed. "But I would imagine that she's something of a treasure."

"She is indispensable."

Then the admiral forestalled any further conversation for the moment by saying, "While we're here together as friends, I should be so pleased if you would call me Bertie."

"Thank you," replied Katherine. "We'd like that very much. And I'm Katherine."

"Yes, ma'am."

Alastair showed Bertie to his room and they changed into suitable golfing attire. The two men left almost immediately for the golf course and Katherine went to speak to Mrs Thringle, who was making pastry, in the kitchen. She apologized for the short notice.

"That's all right, dearie. The Admiral seems nice," replied the housekeeper.

"He is. He's a lovely man. I'm sorry if this has put you out."

"Not at all, we've got enough food, fortunately. I hope he appreciates plain, ration-based home cooking."

"I'm sure it will be fine, your meals are always delicious. He's a very adaptable sort of person. Lily and I will do the washing-up and clearing away."

"Thank you, dearie." She paused for a moment. "I'm sorry to ask this, but does the Admiral know about you and Mr Alastair?"

The question was unexpected, but a practical one, and Katherine understood why the loyal housekeeper had made it.

"Not yet, although he knows we're close. Alastair was going to tell him this afternoon."

"What do you think his reaction might be?"

"I have no idea. It's a chance we have to take. I'd rather be honest and open and risk the consequences than have to sneak around the whole weekend and any subsequent ones, if this is a success."

"You and Mr Alastair are both too fine as people to do any sneaking. If the Admiral has any character at all, he'll appreciate that fact. If he hasn't managed to guess, having worked with you both for all these months, then knowing about it now won't worry him. You mark my words!"

Katherine was so grateful that she gave the loyal housekeeper a hug, as she had been so anxious as to what Bertie Ramsay might think of them. Having gained his high regard, neither she nor Alastair wanted anything to undermine that.

"Now, now, enough of that. You'll get flour over your nice smart uniform and then I'll have to clean it before you go back to London."

"Well, as you've already got enough to do, I'll go upstairs and change then walk down to Maybury to collect Rupert and Anna." Which is precisely what she did.

Alastair and Bertie had a good game of golf. They played an enjoyable nine holes and Alastair didn't disgrace himself, but lost by two holes. However, he had the sneaking suspicion that the admiral liked to win and was therefore glad that he, Alastair, had not. He was not a competitive soul so it didn't bother him; he just liked to do things to the best of his ability. Besides which, Bertie Ramsay was very good company.

As they walked back to Mistley House, Alastair took the opportunity to talk about his and Katherine's relationship. Bertie listened quietly and remained silent for a while after his companion had finished. At length he smiled.

"Well, the two of you have been incredibly discreet, because neither I nor anyone else have had any inkling."

214

"That was our intention. And that's how it will stay."

"How long have you known each other?"

"Nearly eight years. And because Alex and I lived in the same house, Katherine naturally got to know me too. We gradually developed a very close friendship. She helped me enormously when my wife left me, and then nursed me back to health after I caught pneumonia before she and Alex were married. We lived together in her cottage on Cairnmor for nearly three months."

"And there was no question of anything other than friendship while your son was alive?"

Alastair was horrified. "Absolutely not."

"I knew that would be your answer, but I had to ask."

"In fact, it was only last October, nearly two years after Alex died, that we… initiated the change in our relationship. Although I did have other feelings for her, I kept those very much to myself and waited until Katherine began to realize a change in hers for me. Indeed, I had no idea whether she would ever do so, but was overjoyed when she did." They walked on in silence for some moments. "When I am free, Katherine and I will marry as soon as the war is over."

"Does your ex-wife know of your relationship with Katherine?"

"No. And I would never tell her until I'm once more on civvy-street. She is the kind of person that could do us both serious damage."

"Particularly with your present roles and responsibilities in the Navy."

"Exactly. Fortunately, I have had no personal contact with her since Alex was killed, nor am I likely to, except through our solicitors. She takes no interest in the children and never has."

Admiral Ramsay raised his eyebrows. "In the circumstances, that's probably just as well, although I cannot imagine anyone not wanting contact with their grandchildren."

"If you met Roberta you would," replied Alastair, with feeling.

They had reached the towpath by the lock gates. Alastair hesitated, then said, with no little anxiety in his voice, "All this must sound incredibly sordid to you and you probably think less of us now. I should be very upset if that were the case, because I value your esteem and your friendship, neither of which I want to lose."

Bertie stopped and turned to his companion. "You and Katherine are outstanding members of my team and I couldn't do without either of you. From all that you've told me, I can appreciate the natural progression in the relationship and knowing you both as I do, neither of you would enter into something lightly without a deep sense of commitment. The circumstances are unusual, I must admit, and I shall have to adjust to the idea, but I'm grateful for your honesty and the trust you have placed in me by telling me this. And, rest assured, I don't think any the less of either of you because of this, nor would I wish to disturb a friendship that means a great deal to me also."

"Thank you, sir."

"Bertie."

"Yes." They smiled at each other and Alastair experienced an enormous feeling of relief and gratitude.

It was getting dark, the air becoming foggy and damp. Bertie shivered, despite the warmth afforded by his greatcoat and scarf.

"I think a pot of good, hot tea would be very welcome, don't you?" he said, allowing Alastair to lead the way into Mistley House.

CHAPTER 31

Mistley House (2)
January, 1944

Almost as soon as he had finished drinking his tea, the children claimed Bertie's attention and the first sight that Lieutenant-General Phillippe du Laurier, *Vicomte de l'Artennes – Légion d'Honneur*, hero of the Battle for France and the Free French in North Africa – had of the famous Admiral Sir Bertram Ramsay – K.C.B., M.V.O., Allied Naval Commander Expeditionary Force – was of him on his hands and knees on the floor of the sitting room pretending to be a horse, with Rupert astride his back and Anna imperiously leading them both on an imaginary journey to some far-off land.

Phillippe laughed and immediately lifted Anna high into the air, over his shoulders and upside down behind his back, amid much giggling, thus allowing the noble steed to stand up after carefully depositing his young rider gently onto the floor, who thoroughly enjoyed the experience and naturally wanted a repeat.

Alastair introduced them and Bertie straightened his clothes, came over to the general and Lily and shook hands, while Rupert tugged at his jacket, trying to attract his attention, with Anna pulling on the Frenchman's hand at the same time.

The two distinguished guests looked at each other and, with complete understanding, bowed to the inevitable, knowing they had no option but to be a horse for each of the children. There was much fun and laughter in the ensuing rough and tumble, with Alastair and Lily, having declined to join in, looking on in amusement and amazement.

When he was able to draw breath, Bertie said to Phillippe, with ironic humour, "I trust that you are not going to bring up this little escapade in front of Ike or the other Chiefs of Staff when we meet on Monday."

"*Non.* I will not if you do not! It will be our secret, *n'est-ce pas ?*"

"I'm very glad to hear it."

When Katherine came in to take the children off for their bath, saying it would be bedtime very soon, she was met with childish sulks from Rupert and Anna and great relief from the two men, whose knees were beginning to suffer.

"Ah, *la belle madame*, you have saved us!" exclaimed Phillippe. "These two have enough energy for a whole army and navy put together!"

"Yes, we were in imminent danger of being cast adrift permanently on a deserted island." Out of breath, Bertie sat down with relief onto one of the sofas.

"I'm sorry if they were too much." Katherine was embarrassed and looked at Alastair as if to say, "*Why didn't you stop them?*"

He smiled and said, "I didn't like to spoil the fun!"

She narrowed her eyes at him. "Our guests will be afraid of ever coming here again."

Bertie and Phillippe exchanged a glance. "I think we can put up with it…"

"It will be *très difficile*. But we shall manage…"

"I'm relieved to hear it."

After their bath, the children were allowed to come downstairs and say goodnight. They begged their newly adopted Uncle Bertie to read them a bedtime story, and after ascertaining that he really didn't mind and wasn't just being polite, their mother let them have their way, leaving the three of them together in the sitting room.

Meanwhile, an unusually silent Lily had disappeared upstairs and Katherine went into the kitchen to help Mrs Thringle, while Alastair took Phillippe off to his study, to show him a historic map of France that he had had in his possession for many years.

When the time came to collect the children for bed and announce that it was almost time for supper, Katherine came upon the perfect picture of Anna and Rupert, cuddled up on either side of Bertie with all three of them fast asleep, the book open in his lap. Katherine went to fetch Alastair and they stood for a few moments, enjoying the scene before them.

"I wish we had film for the camera," whispered Katherine.

"Yes, but we'd have to wake him first to ask if he minded."

"And of course, the moment would be lost. But this is a picture that will stay with me for a very long time. Who'd have thought that our C.-in-C. would be fast asleep with the children on our settee?!"

As they gently extracted Rupert and Anna and were preparing to carry them up to their bedrooms, Bertie awoke. The three adults smiled at each other.

"Dinner will be in about ten minutes," said Katherine.

"Formal or informal?"

"Very informal."

"Good. I can therefore relax. I have enough formality during the week."

All the guests were appreciative of Mrs Thringle's culinary skills and, as they lingered over pudding – devised and prepared earlier by Lily – before retiring to the sitting room, Bertie was greatly interested to hear the views of Phillippe on the French Navy. His reply was surprising.

"Our navy is unpopular in France. When the invasion comes, officers will probably be shot unless they are known to belong to the Free French. Therefore, they must be selected very carefully if any are to be sent to France in the early days."

"But why should that be?" asked Lily.

"Because my countrymen have never forgiven *ceux de la Marine Nationale* who went over to the Vichy French instead of surrendering to the Royal Navy. If they had surrendered as they should, then none of the Fleet would have had to be disabled or destroyed by the British to stop it being used by the Nazis. It was a painful thing to see our proud ships so ignominiously treated by an ally. Some people have not even forgiven the British."

"It was a very difficult and painful decision," said Bertie, shaking his head.

"War is always difficult and painful, is it not?" There was unspoken agreement on this. "*Mais oui*, I did not envy your Prime Minister having to give the order or the admiral who had to carry it out. Now, today, if my countrymen only knew how wonderful it is that there are so many Free French Navy ships and sailors ready and waiting to help restore *la liberté*. Then their attitude would be different. *C'est regrettable aussi* that the people of France have never forgiven its army for surrendering to *les Boches* in the Battle of France in 1940."

"Even though there were thousands of French soldiers who fought bravely and so many who, with great courage, went back to continue the fight after they had been rescued from Dunkirk," added Bertie.

"*Mais oui*. But my people only see what they want to see and they have long memories. Like their compatriots in the navy, French army officers going across for the invasion must also be selected very carefully. Once the Allies are established and have advanced into France, there should be acceptance and *les soldats* will be welcomed as heroes."

At that moment, the doorbell rang, interrupting the conversation. When Katherine opened the door, there, in the cold, damp foggy night, holding their sleeping little daughter well wrapped up in blankets, were Michael and Mary.

Katherine was so surprised that she just stood there, her mouth open.

"Well, aren't you going to let this poor, fog-bound group of travellers in then? Or are you just going to stand there doing a very good impersonation of a goldfish?" said Michael, with his irrepressible humour.

Suddenly there were hugs and laughter all round and Alastair came out into the hall to find out what was going on. He was delighted to see the visitors and ushered them into the dining room, to where he brought extra chairs while Katherine introduced them.

"These are two of our dearest friends," she said. "This is Michael and Mary Granger and their daughter Rose. Mary and I grew up together on Cairnmor and Michael was Alex's best friend at Oxford – and for several years a fellow barrister at Royal Court Chambers. Then he married Mary and gave it all up to become a crofter. They live on Cairnmor, or at least they did, until…"

"I foolishly decided to join the R.A.M.C., much to Mary's dismay," interrupted Michael, looking sheepishly at his wife. "So now she follows me around the country. I suppose you could say she's become rather a camp follower."

"Michael!" admonished Mary.

"Sorry, dear."

"I should think so." They smiled affectionately at one another.

"I'll carry on, I think, just going round the table," said Katherine. "So, here's Lily…"

"Haven't we met somewhere before, squirt?" teased Michael, as they hugged each other.

"Yes, horrible beast! But it's still good to see you." He had always been her honorary brother and that role took on an even greater significance now, with Alex gone.

Katherine continued. "But what you don't know, is that she's now married to this gentleman here, Lieutenant-General Phillippe du Laurier." They shook hands.

"Goodness me, Lily. Wherever did you find him?"

"He found me, or rather Daddy and Katherine did," said Lily, not knowing whether to smile at her good fortune at being married to Phillippe or express the concerns she was harbouring concerning her father and… She decided that now was not the time to air the latter and allowed herself to smile at Michael's surprise.

"What?!"

But before he could enquire too closely, Katherine said quickly, "That will have to wait. I haven't finished introducing our guests yet." She was unable to stop herself smiling broadly as she anticipated Michael's reaction to their next guest. "And this, this is Admiral Sir Bertram Ramsay." She was not to be disappointed.

"What, *the* Admiral Ramsay, the Dunkirk and the landings in North Africa and Sicily Admiral Ramsay?!"

"Yes, guilty as charged, I'm afraid," responded Bertie with dry humour.

"Let me shake your hand, sir," and Michael went over to the Admiral, who stood up, "to say thank you. I was at Boulogne and your chaps who evacuated us were absolutely first-rate. I mean everyone talks about Dunkirk, but they forget about Boulogne."

Bertie was privately pleased and gratified but, being a genuinely modest man, merely said, as he sat down again, "All the fighting men involved were very brave."

"You're telling me. It was incredible."

For the first time ever, Michael talked in some detail of all that had happened to him. He told of his drive across country in the ambulance, of his hair-raising charge through the German lines, of his arrival at the quayside.

"We were being fired on by machine guns from the hills overlooking the port, trying to get the wounded, who'd just arrived by train, on board the hospital ship. There were demolition parties working to make the harbour inoperable so the Germans couldn't use it and there were itinerant, non-combatant French, sorry General, who had to be kept off the ships that were moored in the harbour. Then, just when all that was completed, the *Luftwaffe* arrived with impeccable timing, attacked us, did considerable damage and then disappeared as rapidly as they had come. Finally, to cap it all, tanks appeared over the hill towing field guns.

"Suddenly, the destroyers *Vimiera*, I think it was, and *Whitshed* opened fire, with all guns blazing, engaging the enemy almost at point blank range. It was a truly awesome sight. Deafening, but awesome. The Germans were taken so completely by surprise that it stopped them in their tracks. We could see them hopping around, on their field telephones, frantically calling for more air support." Michael paused, allowing full effect for his words. "Anyway, the commander of the *Whitshed* decided it was the right time to get the fighting troops on board, and the brigadier in charge on land agreed. Those two ships alone rescued over a thousand men that day, and that's not including the wounded. Add to that the tally from the other destroyers and one appreciates just what a major achievement it was.

"So I thank you, sir, for all your efforts on the soldiers' behalf. You see, what impressed *Whitshed*'s naval commander the most, when I later overheard him talking to his Number One, was that apart from admiring the steadfastness of all the men under fire, he had the freedom to operate as he saw fit in this kind of situation. He was not bound by irrelevant 'rules of engagement'. He felt empowered by the fact that your orders enabled him, the man 'on the spot', to use his initiative. This he did, bravely and well."

Everyone regarded Admiral Ramsay with a deep, yet unobtrusive, respect. He sat there quietly, arms folded – accepting, moved. Then Michael continued, chuckling as he recalled other events on that day.

"Once we'd cleared the harbour, two other destroyers moved in and engaged the Germans with their guns – destroying, among other things, a field gun hidden in some shrubs, although I have it on good authority that the shrubs put up fearsome resistance. They also got a tank lumbering down the road to the quay and a battery of light guns on the hill. The sailors laughed and cheered when the guns and their mountings all rolled down the slope in a cloud of dust.

"The ships and their crews took a real hammering, though. Brave officers and sailors lost their lives that day, not just the soldiers. The destroyers all got away, including one that went aground in the shallows but which managed to get off again. Your sailors were incredibly courageous."

"Of course, what Michael won't tell you," said Katherine, revealing the only thing she knew, because Mary had told her, "is that he was Mentioned in Despatches for his part in all of this, volunteering to stay behind to help the Welsh Guards with their work and look after any additional wounded, rather than going with the hospital ship that had left earlier."

"Goodness," said Michael, deflecting the praise, "what a room full of ranks and titles we have here – a much decorated Captain in the R.N.V.R. and a Chief Officer in the chirpy Wrens, who also happens to be the daughter of a Baronet; a Lieutenant-General, who is an aristocratic Frenchman, a *Vicomte*, I believe, and last, but not least, a full Admiral – a highly distinguished knight of the realm. I salute all of you," which he did by bowing his head, "while here am I, merely a humble 'pirate,' sorry, private in the R.A.M.C. among this illustrious company. But," and he wagged his finger to make the point, "I'm the only one wearing a uniform who can actually prove who he is."

There was much laughter at this and Katherine thought that it was good to hear Michael's sense of humour again, and to see that he still retained it, despite his experiences.

"Would you like to stay?" she asked Mary.

"Yes, please. Michael's leave is ending and we're on our way to Aldershot and thought to surprise you. We would have been here earlier except, as it's so foggy, the car could only crawl along the road."

Mary adjusted her position, their sleeping daughter still in her arms feeling heavier by the minute.

"Have you eaten?"

"Oh aye, we stopped for a meal on the way and we'd also brought 'emergency rations' with us in the car. But I'd quite like to get Rose into bed."

Katherine and Mary went out of the room, chattering away in Gaelic, very glad to see each other, while Michael went to fetch their things from the car. That done, together with Lily (who remained taciturn and sullen) they washed, dried and put away all the plates, glasses and utensils they had used for the meal. Mrs Thringle had retired for the evening, so Katherine made a pot of coffee and brought this into the sitting room, where Alastair had taken Bertie and Phillippe.

The room was lit by the table-top lamps only and, with the glow from the fire, which Alastair had banked up with fresh logs, it felt cosy and warm. The children were fast asleep upstairs and it was an evening for friends to relax together and enjoy each other's company, recounting stories and telling tales.

Michael opened the conversation by saying to Phillippe, "So, how did you meet Katherine and Alastair?"

"Ah, perhaps they would like to tell the story."

"Thank you very much," said Alastair, knowing full well that Phillippe, with his sense of humour, was aware that Admiral Ramsay would be listening. "You can help me out, though."

"Avec grand plaisir, mon ami."

"That's 'with much pleasure, my friend'," interpreted Katherine, delaying the moment when the story had to be told.

"Get on with it then, stop prevaricating!" said Michael.

"We rescued him from Dunkirk…" began Alastair.

"Dunkirk?!" exclaimed Michael, looking at Mary, as if to say, *'you never told me'*. "And who's *we*?"

Alastair exchanged a glance with Katherine. He took a deep breath. "Katherine and I."

Bertie was immediately alert, his expression a picture of surprise and incredulity. But there was amusement and admiration there too.

"Yes, I'm afraid I did go across to Dunkirk," said Katherine. "Twice."

"What's wrong with that?" asked Lily, not understanding.

"We broke lots of rules and regulations in order for me to do so. Although I did sign a T124 form."

"Ah, but did they know you were a woman?" said Michael mischievously.

"Not exactly. I was sort of in disguise. The officer in charge… mistook me for a lad and we didn't disillusion him. I signed myself as Kit MacDonald, which of course was the surname I grew up with. I gave my address as Lochaberdale on Cairnmor. 'Kit' had been my nickname at school, so the whole thing wasn't so far removed from the truth."

"What happened to the form?" asked Bertie, his lips twitching.

"I believe it was er… mislaid," said Alastair, his eyes wide and innocent.

Bertie Ramsay chuckled. "I imagine it was," he said, viewing his conscientious D.C.O.S. in a completely different light. "You'll have to confess the whole thing now."

"So there I was," continued Katherine, "on my way to France. Alastair was not happy with me. In fact we'd had quite an argument, but I was determined to go."

"Knowing you both, I'm not surprised on either count."

"Katherine proved to be invaluable though," said Alastair. "We couldn't have rescued so many soldiers without her being able to handle *Spirit of Adventure*. She was very brave too."

"It's just as well you failed to mention that you could drive a motorboat when you first went to Mill Hill," said Bertie, a broad grin lighting his face, having taken note of the 'very brave' but choosing not to remark upon it at that moment, "otherwise, you would have been assigned to boat crew. In fact, in the light of this information…!"

"Yes, sir," said Katherine meekly. "Sorry, sir. Please don't put me on boat crew, sir. Won't do it again, sir. " And everyone laughed.

"I don't think any of us want to go through all of that again, but we would if we had to," said Bertie, becoming serious. "The thing I found most difficult was having to conduct a series of heart-breaking operations, each with its own tragedy. But, in the end, we prevailed by dogged perseverance and brave hearts."

"As well as a combination of brilliant improvisation and planning on your part," observed Alastair. Bertie threw him a grateful glance.

"Well," said Michael to Alastair, lightening the mood once more after a suitable silence, "You won't get round your commanding officer by being supportive. It'll still be a court martial for you then a demotion to head cook and bottle washer."

"Not even head cook," said Bertie. "Just bottle washer." He exchanged a smile with Alastair.

"Now don't keep us in suspense. Alastair. Tell Mary and me about Phillippe."

"On the last night of Dynamo, I was ordered…"

"You volunteered. Be accurate now, otherwise it won't even be bottle washer…" interrupted Bertie.

"All right then, if I must. I *volunteered* to take *Spirit* across." Alastair narrowed his eyes at him.

"That's better."

"Anyway, after we had transferred as many French soldiers as we could from the East Mole to the waiting ships, this chap here," Alastair nodded towards Phillippe, "was hustled along by his comrades, so that he could climb down onto our boat. We were the last small motorboat remaining, the Germans were at the other end of the jetty, and Phillippe was reluctant to leave…"

"…as it wasn't his turn in the queue," interjected Katherine, giving the general a pointed look. "And, what's more," she continued, "he'd already stayed behind on the perimeter to give the rear-guard vital information, having sent his men on ahead to be evacuated the previous day. They were very worried about him."

Phillippe smiled a very charming smile. "It is war. Improvisation is essential, *n'est-ce pas ?* Besides, I had absolute faith that I would not be captured by the Bosch, that my Allied friends of the Royal Navy would rescue me and my men whom I had already brought to Dunkirk. So I stayed until I could do no more in the Battle for France."

"Eventually, he was persuaded to board *Spirit of Adventure*," said Katherine, "and, together with his few remaining officers, we set off for home laden right down to the gunwales."

Phillippe then took up the story, recounting it in a lively but matter-of-fact way, as though it was all part of a normal day out. "Halfway across the Channel, the engine, she stops. One of my men, he is an engineer and he tries to fix it. We are… how do you say? Ah! Sitting ducks for any U-boat or E-boat. But a German patrol boat comes close to investigate. He goes to fire but his forward machine gun jams and he has no torpedoes, so my men open fire with everything they have and blow him out of the water. Therefore, we are safe. Quickly, the engine is fixed, we collect a few prisoners-of-war and off we go."

He paused, like Michael, observing the effect of the story upon his audience. They were absorbed and waited for him to continue.

"By this time, it is getting light. One of my men is driving the boat, Alastair and I talk of many things and so begins our friendship. We talk about his daughter, Lily. He shows me her photo. I see the woman of my dreams. *C'est remarquable !* When I get home, I write to her, and she writes back. We fall in love."

"A little later, I am sent by General de Gaulle…"

"He fixed it so he could go," interrupted Katherine, placing the back of her hand at the side of her mouth as though on a stage.

"…as Free French Liaison officer to the Canadian army and navy, to the big navy base in Halifax, Nova Scotia where Lily has been to study music. We meet, we declare our love and I propose. Soon, Alastair arrives with his ship and gives away the bride. So, this is how I am married to my most lovely lady in all the world." He picked up her hand and kissed it. "Many months later, we return to England. Lily will live here perhaps," and he glanced briefly at his wife, seeing her expression change from joy at his kiss to a sudden scowl as he spoke his next words, "with her father and Katherine and be safe, while I take up a new post as Free French Liaison Officer to General Eisenhower. Then, when the war is over, we shall be together for always." He looked at Lily gravely and she lowered her eyes.

Despite this brief interchange, which did not go unnoticed by the assembled company, it was a remarkable story, leaving all of them contemplative of the vagaries of circumstance and life-altering changes that had been thrust upon them… feeling safe, for the moment, in the warm, fire-lit room, from the vicissitudes and uncertainties of war.

"You do realize," said Michael, after a lengthy silence, addressing Bertie, "that you are responsible for transporting all of us in this room, apart from Mary and Lily, wherever we have gone or been sent, travelling in ships under your orders – Katherine, Alastair and Phillippe at Dunkirk, Phillippe in Africa, Alastair and me in Sicily – yes, I was there, a member of the Eastern Task Force that you led! And now, I suppose, it's going to be all your fault, as you're the Allied Naval Commander, for sending the General and me across to France for the invasion, whenever and wherever that is going to be." Michael paused, and the coincidence of this was not lost on those present in the room. Then he added, with customary levity, "You'll just have to stop doing this, you know!"

Bertie chuckled. "I fully intend to once the war is over. But not quite yet."

"No, not quite yet. We need you. But I'll tell you something, I would rather go in one of your ships, under your orders, following your plan, than anyone else's." Michael smiled. "Somehow, when that is so, all the sailors have a confidence, a buoyancy of spirit that was certainly not present on the ship in which I travelled home a couple of months ago after you had returned to England."

"Thank you." Admiral Ramsay was gracious in accepting the younger man's praise. He then asked why Michael was still a 'pirate', much to everyone's amusement.

"Ooh arrgh, me 'earty. Where's me doubloons?!" Then Michael became serious. "I'm still a private, because I have no wish to be an officer. As simple as that. In the same way, I've never wanted to carry arms, although I'd fight if it became a matter of personal survival. But I want to do all that I can to relieve the suffering and agony that war creates. And in doing so, do my bit towards the war effort to break the Nazis. Somehow, I've always felt I could do that better as a private, working 'on the ground', so to speak."

"With your background, if you were an officer in the Royal Navy, I'd ask to have you on my staff," said Bertie, having summed him up, appreciating Michael's qualities and seeing a great deal of untapped potential in this man.

Michael was surprised, yet gratified. "Goodness! You really mean that, don't you?"

"Of course."

He regarded the admiral with an honest open gaze, his outlook undergoing an unexpected and sudden transformation.

"Well," he said at length, his confidence growing, "in that case, perhaps I ought to apply for a promotion pretty quick! Maybe it's not such a bad idea after all!"

"You'd make a very good officer one day whatever Service you are in. If ever you need a personal recommendation…"

"Thank you very much, sir."

The clock on the mantelpiece gently chimed ten o'clock, and with collective consensus, albeit one tinged with reluctance, everyone bid each other a good night and retired to their rooms at the end of an eventful afternoon and evening.

CHAPTER 32

Mistley House (3)
January, 1944

The next morning, Katherine was seated at her desk in the study, ostensibly writing to her mother – trying to answer the numerous letters that Lily had brought with her from Halifax when she and Phillippe had arrived in England the previous week – but, in reality, staring idly out of the window. Thick fog had persisted from the previous day and she couldn't even see halfway down the garden.

A Sunday morning calm pervaded the house. Mary and Mrs Thringle were in the kitchen preparing luncheon. The children were in the nursery with Michael, whose attention they had claimed immediately after breakfast as he had had them all in hysterics while trying to entice Rupert to eat his porridge.

Little Rose and Rupert were always inseparable whenever she came to stay, so Michael, who loved entertaining his captive youthful audience, had taken all three of them upstairs to do just that, thus ensuring that Anna didn't feel left out.

Bertie Ramsay had attended the early morning Communion Service at the Parish Church in the village and after breakfast, he, Alastair and Phillippe had set off for the golf course – the latter wondering what he was letting himself in for. He decided that discretion was the better part of valour and that he would not play on this occasion, but merely observe.

This proved to be difficult as the fog was very thick and visibility less than fifty yards so, "The golf was… interesting!" as Bertie was to remark later during lunch when asked how the game had gone. Nevertheless, they managed eighteen holes, with Alastair and Bertie pairing up to defeat two other club members one up, which was altogether a very satisfactory outcome.

In the meantime, Katherine's reverie was interrupted by a brief knock at the door and Lily walked in, sitting down on the sofa near the desk.

"Do you have a moment?" she asked.

Katherine regarded Lily, thinking that she could still see so much of the vulnerable, yet courageous, young girl whom she had taken under her wing when Roberta had walked out on her family, that first fateful Christmas which Katherine had spent here in this house, a house that had now become hers and Alastair's. How strange it was that things could change so radically and in such unexpected ways.

Katherine put aside her fountain pen after first screwing on the lid. "Of course," she replied carefully, waiting for Lily to speak.

"I'm not quite sure how to say this. You've always been kind to me and we've always been fond of each other, but I'm having a real problem at the moment with… with you and Daddy being together. You see," she continued hastily, seeing Katherine go pale, "when we were in Canada, it wasn't real, if you understand what I mean. It was something far away, distant. I talked to Phillippe about what I feel and he says that in matters of love, the heart knows no boundaries and that Daddy has been in love with you for a very long time, even before Alex… died. Rather than finding that romantic as he does, frankly I find it, well… disgusting."

Katherine was about to respond when Lily continued, her voice full of disapproval and admonishment. "And Daddy's so much older than you. He's your father-in-law, for goodness' sake. Why, it's practically incestuous. "

Shocked, her chest tight and stomach tense, Katherine managed to answer this outburst with a calmness she did not feel, pointing out that Phillippe was in fact fifteen years older than Lily. Did that make a difference to her feelings for him? Did she see Phillippe, the man she loved, or an older man?

Lily's response was immediate: she saw only Phillippe. "But I wasn't once married to his son," she retorted bitterly and promptly burst into tears.

Katherine made no move to comfort her, realizing that any show of affection would be rejected immediately. She surmised that for Lily, this was also about losing Alex, not just about Alastair and herself.

"It must be so hard for you to come home and discover the reality of Alex not being here anymore." She was trying to be reasonable.

"Of course it is," snapped Lily, controlling her tears. "He was my brother. You are his wife."

"I am his widow."

"And I bet you couldn't wait to get my father into bed after you found out that Alex had been killed. You needed a man and my dear, kind parent was conveniently to hand."

Katherine wanted to slap her. "That's a monstrous thing to say and is as far away from the truth as it is possible to be."

Lily was sounding just like her mother and, with a knot of fear in her stomach, Katherine hoped that she wouldn't go crying to Roberta. Potentially, that could be disastrous for Alastair and her in their present positions. Unsure how to handle this, she tried sympathy.

"It must have been very difficult for you being so far away when you first heard the news about your brother."

"He has a name. It's Alex. He's not just my *brother*."

This was becoming ridiculous. "I don't know what to say to you, Lily," said Katherine, in despair. "I am in love with your father, as he is with me. We have chosen our path together and have been honest with our closest friends and family whom we trust and care for. We have entered into our relationship with as much commitment as you and Phillippe."

Lily went to protest, but Katherine continued, not allowing her to interrupt. "Because you've been away, it's perhaps more difficult for you to accept that things have changed. You are making your new life with Phillippe and one day will have your own family to care for. Railing at me is not going to alter anything. It is true that Alastair was once my father-in-law and Alex my husband. But Alex died two years ago. I couldn't mourn him forever. I had to move on."

"Yes, onto my father."

Katherine chose to ignore this cruel, unthinking remark. "You once said that you hoped you would find someone to love you in the way that Alex and I loved each other. I hope that you have found that and more in Phillippe. Seeing the two of you together, I think that is the case. My feelings for Alex have not been debased by my relationship with your father. They have two, very distinct..." she struggled to find the word "...identities."

Lily was subdued at last. "But your relationship with Alex was so wonderful, so perfect."

"No, it wasn't perfect. Perhaps at first, before we were married when you originally saw us together, but once we were married, and remember we had only known each other for a very short time beforehand, reality set in and the relationship only worked as long as I was the one making the compromises. If I dug my heels in, then we would argue. And we did, frequently, and it made me very unhappy. You never saw that side of things because you were away at school and then in Canada."

"It's not like that for me with Phillippe. He is my husband and I would go anywhere and do anything to be with him, just as he would with me."

"And that's exactly how it is with Alastair and me." Then Katherine paused briefly before saying, as gently as she could, "It was not like that with Alex, you see. We rarely talked about things – I mean really talked. We'd skirt round issues and avoid things. And as he was always so preoccupied, there was never any time for real communication. I had no choice but to fit in with him because with Alex, his work always came first, and because I loved him deeply, I had no choice but to accept that's the way it was. But I've had to face the fact that ultimately, I don't think he loved me or the children enough to make the effort and do the same."

Lily's anger flared up again. "Now you're running him down so that you can justify your... your relationship with my father."

"No, my dear, I can assure you I'm not." Katherine sighed. Just as she thought she was getting somewhere, Lily's emotional irrationality took over again. "Alex also changed a great deal after he went to Singapore. His letters were different; he was different. He became someone I didn't know." She regarded the younger woman. "Didn't you see that in his letters to you?"

Lily remained still and a solitary tear slid down her face. Quietly, almost inaudibly, she said, "He never wrote to me at all."

Katherine was appalled. "What?!" *Oh, Alex, what were you thinking of out there? How could you not write to your own sister who loved you so much?*

"No, I never heard from him in all the time he was out in Singapore."

"Did you write to him?"

"Yes, every week without fail."

"Oh, Lily. I don't know what to say, I'm so sorry."

Katherine was about to put her arm round her when, at that moment, Michael came into the room.

"Ah, there you are, Katherine. Just came to tell you that our respective offspring are comfortably ensconced in the kitchen having milk and bickies with Mrs T." He stopped talking and regarded both women, pursing his lips. "Hm. I detect trouble in paradise." He took Lily by the hand. "Well, honorary sis, I think it's high time that you and I went for a walk, despite this pea-souper that seems to have descended permanently upon us." He led her out of the room, pausing only to glance back at Katherine with genuine sympathy, seeing the pain in her eyes and immediately guessing something of the subject matter of the conversation between the two women.

Katherine was still in the study when the golfers returned. Mary and Mrs Thringle needed her help and Alastair was despatched to find her. He discovered her on the window seat, staring out into the murky gloom.

He came to sit beside her and she laid her head against his shoulder. She sighed. "Lily came to see me earlier. She's got herself in quite a state, Alastair."

"What about?"

"Us. Can't cope with it. Doesn't want to cope with it. Won't even try. I don't know how well I handled it. She was almost hysterical and accused us of all sorts of things. She calmed down eventually and shortly afterwards, Michael came and took her off for a walk. But it was most unpleasant."

Alastair was silent. They had been lucky so far with the people they had told. Phillippe, the Thringles, Michael and Mary – all delighted for them – and Bertie, who had been accepting and not judgemental. Katherine had yet to tell her parents. She was not sure how they might react.

"She made me feel as though what we were doing was wrong, something sordid and unsavoury."

"Darling Katherine, it is none of those things. Certainly not to us. And I'm sure you handled it well, far better than you think."

"She seems to blame me though, not you. Fortunately. But my big worry is that she could go running off to Roberta or that it will cause some kind of permanent rift in the family."

"The first is unlikely, the second would appear to be a distinct possibility. I ought to speak to her."

"It might be best. I can't do any more. Phillippe seems to be on our side, but Lily is adamant that she doesn't share his 'romantic view' of our relationship. I'm very fond of her, but this outburst has really shaken me. Part of the problem is Alex. She hasn't yet come to terms with his loss. Coming home has emphasized that for her, I think."

Alastair was thoughtful. He looked at his watch. It was almost lunchtime. There would not be the opportunity to speak to Lily until afterwards, if at all, as they had to return to London. He took a deep breath. "Try not to worry. We'll resolve it somehow." He smiled at her, but Katherine could tell that he was deeply concerned. It was exactly the sort of thing of which they had been afraid.

"It's going to be difficult to say anything with Bertie being here," she observed.

"That's exactly what I was thinking," said Alastair, putting his arm round her and holding her close. "Anyway, my darling, you're needed in the kitchen. I've left our other two guests in my study deep in discussion, so if nothing else, that part of today has been successful."

"How was the golf?"

"I actually played quite well for once. Bertie and I paired up and won."

"No doubt we'll hear more about it at luncheon."

Which, of course, they did.

Throughout the meal, Lily was subdued and didn't join in at all with the general socializing. Michael and Mary helped Katherine clear away the plates and utensils at the end of the meal and when the three of them were in the kitchen, Michael said quickly, "It's a bit of a problem, I'm afraid. She really doesn't like the two of you being together. There was nothing I could say that altered her opinion."

Katherine sighed and nodded. "I was afraid you were going to say that. But thank you for trying, anyway."

"Aye, but she's still very young," said Mary sensibly. "She also hasn't ever truly understood how close you and Alastair have always been. Nor has she seen, as we have, the wonderful inevitability in the progression of your relationship."

Katherine gave her friend a hug, tears pricking her eyes. "Thank you," she said.

"What a lovely turn of phrase," commented Michael. "You should write it down: 'the wonderful inevitability in the progression of your relationship.' I like that."

"But it's true."

"Yes," agreed Michael.

"I must admit, though," continued Mary, "I had a bit of a wobbly moment myself when you first told me, but that's all it was… a moment. Then it was gone. Forever. Knowing both of you as Michael and I do and seeing the two of you together, it's as clear as day…"

"…though perhaps the foggy one we're living through at this moment is not a particularly good example," interjected her husband, his eyes twinkling. He received a good-natured poke in the arm for his witticism. "Ouch!" he said, kissing her cheek.

"As I was saying, before I was so rudely interrupted," continued Mary, looking at Michael sternly, who smiled, "it's very clear that the two of you are so right for each other." She hesitated. "More so than Alex."

"Really?" said Katherine surprised.

"Oh, aye."

"What makes you say that?"

"Och, I don't know. When he first came to Cairnmor, I always thought how lucky you were to find someone as dashing and handsome, as kind and considerate…"

"Steady on, old girl," said Michael.

"Well, he was very kind to me after Adam died," replied Mary amused. "Anyway, he was almost too good to be true. He seemed genuine, and I think he was at the time, but…"

"I'm glad there's a 'but'," said Michael.

"After you and he were married," she continued, pretending to ignore him, "it was almost as though, having found a clever, beautiful wife who obviously adored him, he could then pick up the threads of his old life by giving most of his attention to his work, doing things in the way he had always done, knowing you would be at home waiting for him."

"I think you're right," agreed Katherine. "Do you remember that day when we first met at Royal Court Chambers?" she said to Michael.

230

"How could I forget?"

"Careful," said Mary, getting her own back.

Katherine laughed. "You said to me, as did many other people, Lily included, that you wondered if Alex would ever get married as he was so completely besotted by his work. 'Head down, strong work ethic,' I believe were your exact words."

"Yes, they were. And he was. I had begun to doubt that he would find anyone to settle down with. He'd played the field for a long time with his love affairs and passing infatuations yet..." Michael stopped in mid-sentence, a sudden expression of concern on his face. "I say, you were aware of all that, weren't you? I'd hate it if I'd suddenly dropped some kind of tactless bombshell?" he added hastily, wondering just how much Katherine knew.

She sighed. "Yes, I was aware and no, you haven't been tactless."

"That's a relief. Anyway, no one had come anywhere near to matching his high expectations, enough for him to consider marriage. You came along, were just what he'd been looking for, and in his own way, he loved you for it."

"I know."

The kettle boiled and they prepared tea and coffee, taking it into the sitting room, where Katherine became preoccupied with memories of Alex defending her against his mother during that dreadful Christmas Eve when Roberta had announced that she was leaving the family. Alex must have cared for her then to do that.

Or was it, came the niggling little thought, *that as a barrister, he enjoyed the process of argument and the winning of it? No*, she chastised herself, *that was unkind.* But having once had the thought, the doubt remained. Then she also recalled that her first instinct had been to comfort Alastair – that his sorrow, pain and humiliation had been her initial, overriding concern. She must have loved him even then, but did not know it.

Katherine went over to him and sat down beside him. Yes, just as Alastair had been so with her, she must have been in love with him for a very long time.

He smiled warmly at her, sensing her need to be close to him and, despite Lily's presence in the room, put his arm round her and tenderly kissed her forehead as she leaned back against him, seeking reassurance. Michael smiled at Mary and took her hand and kissed it. Lily got up and walked over to the window.

When Bertie and Phillippe came into the sitting room from the study, where they had been deep in conversation, Katherine poured out the chosen beverages.

"Fruitful discussion?" asked Alastair.

"Indeed," replied Bertie. "I'll go over the details with you and the C.O.S. in the office on Monday before we meet with Ike. Perhaps you can join us, Katherine."

"Of course, sir, I mean Bertie. Goodness, I almost went into work mode then!"

"Not yet," he replied, chuckling. "Let's make the most of what's left of a most enjoyable weekend."

"Do you have family, Admiral Ramsay?" asked Mary.

"Yes, my dear, I do. Two boys. David is ten and Charles, seven." He caught Lily's startled expression and added, by way of explanation, "I married late in life, Madame du Laurier. My wife Margaret is twenty years younger than me, but the age difference is of no significance. She means the world to me and I look forward to the day when I can be home with them all."

"Do they live close by?" said Mary.

"Unfortunately not. We have a house in Berwickshire in the Scottish Borders and my wife stays there with the children. She comes to London as often as she can, though."

"So you are a Scot?"

"My ancestors and family are, although I was born in England."

"It must be very hard to be away from your family. I know I can't bear to be parted from Michael and I couldn't even begin to imagine being separated from Rose."

"War necessitates many things, Mrs Granger."

"Aye, it does."

"Without Mrs Thringle and Mary, who lives with us whenever Michael is stationed within easy reach, I couldn't do the job that I do," said Katherine. "I feel incredibly lucky knowing that Rupert and Anna are in such good hands. Alastair and I see the children as often as we can. But I must confess, I felt very guilty the first time I left them when we went to Dunkirk," she added.

"That's it!" exclaimed Bertie. "That's where we first met, isn't it? I remember now! We sat on a bench high up on the hill overlooking Dover Harbour and discussed the view, and how walking and silent contemplation helps coalesce one's thoughts. I knew I'd seen you before, the moment you walked into my office at Norfolk House for your interview. And you've worked for me all these months and didn't tell me that we'd already met!"

Katherine looked sheepish. "Sorry, Bertie. Well, I didn't want to get Alastair, or me for that matter, into trouble, so I kept quiet."

"Quite right too." He regarded her for a moment. "Your hair was different."

"Er, yes. I'd cut it so that I looked like a lad. It went all spiky."

"Took ages to grow back into some sort of manageable style afterwards as well," said Mary.

"I can imagine."

Suddenly, from across the other side of the room, Lily spoke, her voice ringing out clearly. "How can you all just sit there and accept them? How can you tolerate this liaison between my father and Katherine? She is his *daughter-in-law* for goodness' sake! She was married to my brother! How can *you*, as their commander-in-chief, condone this... this... scandalous relationship going on right under your very nose?! It has to be stopped!"

"Lily!" exclaimed Phillippe, horrified. "*Taisez-vous !*"

Stunned, she instantly obeyed his command and was quiet.

"I apologize for my young wife," he said, looking at her with barely concealed fury. "She has not been herself since we have come here to Mistley House. There are things that she has to acknowledge and work out. She has a great deal to learn. I will help her. But I apologize to my very good and dear friends for her behaviour."

Lily was suddenly frightened, not of Phillippe himself, for she knew him to be a good man, but of the damage she may have done to her standing within their relationship. She had embarrassed him as a high-ranking officer as well as publicly undermining her father who had always been so loving and supportive of her.

She didn't quite know what to do. For a moment she regretted her outburst but it was a very brief moment and determinedly, she pushed the scruple aside. She looked around the room for moral support, but no one made eye contact or any move to give it to her.

She was on her own.

"I think perhaps," said Bertie to Alastair and Katherine with consummate tact, "it is time for us to be returning to London, just as we had previously arranged. I thank you both for your kind hospitality." He smiled. "It has been rather as I described our game of golf in the fog... an interesting experience! I shall look forward to working with you both as usual on Monday morning and trust that you have found my company sufficiently congenial to allow me to stay for the weekend again sometime in the future."

And, with that statement of unequivocal support for Alastair and Katherine, he went upstairs to his room to change into his uniform, ready for their return to London.

Alastair looked at his daughter, framed in diffuse light from the French doors with her face pale and her stance resolutely defiant, before taking Katherine's hand and standing up.

"Understand this," he said to Lily quietly. "Katherine and I are together and wish to be together for the rest of our lives. There is nothing you can say or do that will change that. Learn to come to terms with it. You are my daughter, whom I love dearly. But you are also no longer a child. You belong to the adult world now. Perhaps you should let your behaviour reflect that transition and accept that there are some things that cannot be altered and adjust your ideas accordingly."

Opening the door, allowing Katherine to precede him, Alastair left. Michael and Mary discreetly followed suit, leaving Phillippe and Lily alone.

Still angry, he said to her, "Do not ever in public do anything like that again. *Tu comprends ?*"

"Oui, Phillippe."

Towards her husband, she was contrite, apologetic, full of remorse. But inwardly, she had not changed her opinion one little bit.

CHAPTER 33

Norfolk House/Portsmouth
January, 1944

Katherine was having difficulty in concentrating. Her mind kept returning to Lily's words of the previous day, and consequently, her work at Norfolk House did not absorb her in the same way as it would normally have done.

On the train returning to London with Bertie, none of them had alluded to the awful scene at Mistley House, but deliberately and cheerfully talked of other matters. Bertie's demeanour towards them had not changed in any way and both she and Alastair were grateful for his tacit, unwavering support, though wisely refrained from saying so, as this would have embarrassed their commanding officer. They sensed, quite correctly, that he regarded it as their problem and that they were quite capable of resolving it.

Katherine and Alastair had talked long into the night. Her bright confidence and outward joy in their relationship had taken a knock, and for the first time ever, she found herself consumed by guilt. She didn't say a great deal at first – how could she put it into words? But Alastair, as ever, sensed her disquietude and gently encouraged her to talk about what she was thinking, which she then did, openly and honestly.

Together, they revisited the ground they had covered at the start of their relationship. They were doing nothing illegal as they were not blood-related. True, Alastair was still married, therefore technically, they were committing adultery, words that shocked Katherine when actually expressed, but as his marriage had irretrievably broken down eight years previously and he was in the process of obtaining a divorce, they concluded that it had no bearing on their situation. They understood and were sympathetic to Lily's difficulties, but it was what she might do with the information that had frightened Katherine and prompted her nocturnal anxiety.

Altogether, it was an uncomfortable conversation, but in the end, Katherine realized what she had always known – that the depth of their love and need for each other overrode any other consideration. Lily was an adult now, with her own life to lead, and would have to deal with her feelings as best she could. They concluded that Phillippe would help her in this and ensure that she kept her father's private life to herself. As far as Rupert and Anna were concerned, their absolute commitment to each other and to the children was a stabilizing influence and could only be beneficial. They would cross the bridge of truth only when the children were old enough to understand.

Warmed and reassured, Katherine eventually fell asleep, secure in her lover's arms, but Alastair stayed awake long afterwards, only drifting off to sleep as dawn light filtered through the bedroom curtains.

It was hardly surprising, therefore, that as she put the finishing touches to her comprehensive report, collated from documents that had been handed to her only that morning and upon which she had worked all day, Katherine had found her attention wandering.

Niggles of guilt returned, reactivating her conscience. *She was in a relationship with a married man who had once been her father-in-law.* Expressed in such a bald, crude way, it sounded unsavoury and she felt sullied by the words. At frequent intervals throughout the day, they kept coming back to her; she could not escape them. She had to admit that despite having done her best to put it out of her mind, Lily's outburst had temporarily undermined her self-assurance. With her upbringing and her faith, she understood the extent and consequences of her transgression. It was a salutary thought and one not to be lightly or easily dismissed.

Resolutely, Katherine gathered her thoughts. She had to focus on her work – vital work concerning the complexities of the naval requirements for Operation Overlord, the Allied invasion of France.

She put a new sheet of paper into the typewriter and continued from where she had left off in her conclusion to the report:

The number of ships necessary to transport soldiers and equipment across the Channel (the 'lift') in a five division assault, rather than four with one in reserve, or three, as originally suggested in COSSAC, presents particular problems.

Extra lift will mean stretching Royal Navy resources to the limit. There is also increased cost to consider for which funds will have to be made available by the Admiralty. It may prove impossible in the end, as originally agreed, for the Royal Navy to provide all the ships essential for bombardment, minesweeping and escort without help from our Allies, particularly the United States.

Katherine stopped typing and looked out of the window. Alastair was in a meeting with the heads of departments. She took a deep breath.

The weather is an unknown factor and there is a real threat from U-boats, E-boats and mines. The amount of training of the thousands of craft necessary is, at this present time, uncertain, as is the condition of the beaches designated to receive the landing craft. The artificial harbours may or may not prove to be a practical proposition.

There were so many variables, so many 'ifs' and 'buts'. Katherine knew that all these things concerned Admiral Ramsay greatly, and that he was also becoming impatient with the Combined Chiefs of Staff here at home and in Washington, who seemed to be prevaricating and not making an immediate and final decision. Without that decision, no firm planning for the Royal Navy's role in Operation Overlord could be taken.

If Operation Anvil (the proposal for an Allied landing on the French Mediterranean coast to take place simultaneously with Overlord) were to be

235

postponed, she continued, *then the naval requirements for Overlord could be met. This, perhaps, is the crucial factor in the complex jigsaw of planning for the release and availability of sufficient naval forces to carry out and support an amphibious landing on the continent, while maintaining the transport of matériel necessary to support the armed forces.*

Katherine typed a full stop and took the top sheet of paper and carbon copies out of her typewriter. Quickly, she scanned all the documents she had been working from and then read carefully through her report. She had missed nothing, there were no mistakes and she felt pleased with what she had written. Now, she just needed to take it to the Registry Room for circulating.

Katherine sat for a moment, her mind becoming once more preoccupied with personal matters. She was a grown woman, a free agent. She had already been married and had had two children. She wasn't an innocent girl wishing to preserve her virginity. She was utterly in love with Alastair, and her physical need for him reflected and was part of that love. Their dedication to each other was unquestionable and they shared an unbreakable bond.

Katherine smiled, recalling with deep satisfaction their love-making of the previous night. It would be impossible after all these months to turn back the clock. Returning to a platonic friendship while living under the same roof was inconceivable.

Therefore, she concluded, there was no point in feeling guilty. She had not wanted to wait for them to sleep together until they were married – that would have been pointless and caused them both unnecessary frustration. Alastair's divorce would be finalized in the not too distant future and he was no longer her father-in-law. As long as they were careful in private and publicly discreet, all would be well.

So, having quelled her conscience, feeling a great deal happier, and with her confidence returning, Katherine got up from her desk and went along to the Registry Room.

There was a quiet air of calm efficiency as Katherine entered, with only a low buzz of conversation and the sound of filing cabinets being open and shut. She handed the report to the Wren at the desk who recorded it in a large ledger, where it was assigned a serial number.

"Top copies are to go to Admiral Ramsay, the C.O.S. and D.C.O.S. please, and then to the Directors of Planning, Logistics and Operations for comment and annotating, before being returned to me."

"Yes, ma'am."

"There is some urgency for this report to be seen, as it is a Final Document, so if it could be circulated as soon as possible, I'd be most grateful. Admiral Ramsay needs it as part of his presentation at a meeting on Friday."

"I'll see to it straightaway, ma'am."

"Thank you."

On arriving back in her office, Katherine found a note saying that she should report to the C.-in-C. at once, which she did, and to her delight found Alastair there as well.

236

"Come in, Matty," said the Admiral, "and close the door. Now, I've just come from a meeting with Ike and we discussed where best to conduct Overlord from. He's talking about moving his H.Q. out of London to avoid any bombing. I said that for planning we must be in London, but for operating we should all go out. I also said that for conducting the landing operations we should be best placed at Portsmouth, but it may be difficult to find the large accommodation required for the staff of all the commanders-in-chief – Ike's people, Leigh-Mallory's R.A.F. and Monty's 21st Army Group personnel, as well as Arthur Tedder's lot, seeing as he's Ike's deputy. It would need somewhere as large as Aldershot or Camberley. But these are too far away from Portsmouth, which is where we need to be. My thinking is that Alastair and I will go down there to see what's what and I'd like you to come as well, Matty."

"I'd be glad to, sir."

"Good. Looking at my diary, next Sunday seems to be the only day I have available. Let's hope by then the five division assault will have been finally decided upon. Then we shall know where we are. I dislike all this waffling. Have you managed to complete that report yet? I know I only asked you to do it this morning…" He smiled at Katherine.

"Yes, sir. It's finished and should be on its way to you even as we speak. I took it to the Registry Room a few minutes ago."

"Excellent. I shall need it for Friday."

"I know, sir. I emphasized its urgency."

The admiral nodded. "Thank you, Matty. That will be all."

"Yes, sir." And Katherine went out of the room, leaving him to resume his discussion with Alastair.

At Friday's meeting, with all the commanders-in-chief and their senior staff members present, the COSSAC plan was once more demonstrated. General Montgomery gave his views on it and then outlined his plan for the increased assault forces. Bertie gave the implications of Monty's plan and demonstrated what was necessary to produce the naval forces required, and where they must come from.

Admiral Ramsay seemed pleased when he was congratulated afterwards by two fellow senior officers, who felt it was the "finest analytical survey of a situation that they had ever heard, and that he managed to make what was essentially a damping statement appear not damping". Katherine, still in the room as she had been taking notes of the formal proceedings, overheard this conversation and was delighted for him – and also pleased that she had been able to make a small contribution towards his presentation. Bertie caught her smiling at him and winked at her.

It was finally decided that the five division assault was to be accepted, and at the conclusion of the meeting late that afternoon, it was also decided to draft a telegram to be sent to the Combined Chiefs of Staff in Washington informing them of this.

Alastair and the C.O.S. brought a first version to Admiral Ramsay at seven o'clock that evening and the three of them worked on it for half an hour. Alastair then proposed that the revised draft should be sent to Bertie in the morning, which was done as soon as his commanding officer arrived, and who, after making one small amendment, thought it to be very good. In the end, however, it was not sent as Eisenhower and his C.O.S. were not satisfied with Monty's plan and ordered COSSAC staff to re-draft the telegram.

Alastair was annoyed and went into Katherine's office to bemoan the fact to her. "All that work wasted. More delays. Bertie is completely exasperated. 'Why don't they just get on with it?' he said to me just now."

"Ike is a bit of a prevaricator, isn't he?"

"Yes, and I suppose a further decision will now have to be arrived at during the commanders' meeting on Monday."

"Poor you. I wish I could help, but there's nothing more that I can do. What time are we leaving for Portsmouth tomorrow?"

"About eleven. The car is picking us up from here."

"How nice to be driven."

"Mm. I hope there's no fog."

"It would make the journey… interesting!" said Katherine, recalling Bertie's description of the golf game. She grinned at Alastair, who, having checked that no one was around, blew her a discreet kiss before leaving the room. She responded in kind and then got on with her work – compiling a report from the previous day's meeting.

They left promptly the next morning (no fog) and arrived in Portsmouth in time for lunch with the Second Sea Lord at his house on Portsdown Hill.

Within the inevitable social side that accompanied her posting, Katherine discovered that the facts that her grandfather was Sir Charles Mathieson, and that her father had inherited the baronetcy, proved to be a useful means of introduction in the somewhat exalted company in which she and Alastair often found themselves during the course of their work. She refrained from revealing that she had grown up a poor crofter's daughter on Cairnmor, 'orphaned' at fourteen. In his turn, Alastair failed to mention that his father originally had been a humble shepherd from Skye. They secretly laughed together about this and said, "If only they knew!"

However, within most naval and military circles, with one or two exceptions – for not all senior flag or high-ranking army officers were as egalitarian as Bertie Ramsay – she and Alastair were accepted because of their rank, on the merits of their achievements and because of their personalities. Katherine was much more comfortable with this form of acceptance.

Their first port of call after lunch was the shore-based Royal Navy training establishment *H.M.S. Collingwood*, where they were shown round by Rear-Admiral Sedgwick, its commandant. They found it to be a huge establishment, holding five and a half thousand trainees. It had been built as a hostilities-only training base for ratings of the Seaman Branch and its two hundred acres had been compulsorily purchased in 1939, with the first ten-week course commencing in January, 1940. The basic accommodation was in large wooden huts, and all the buildings surrounded an enormous parade ground which was the focal point of the training.

After spending some time looking closely at the facilities, Bertie considered it to be unsuitable for his purposes but saw that it could be useful for any other establishment that would have to be moved to accommodate him and his staff. They thanked Admiral Sedgwick and continued to their next destination.

This was Southwick House, known as *H.M.S. Dryad*, a moderate-sized Georgian manor house presently occupied by the Navigation School for whom it had been requisitioned by the Navy in 1941. As soon as the three of them walked through the door into the building and stood in the spacious and elegant hallway, with its curving staircase and mottled, reddish-brown pillars, they sensed it would be ideal.

Katherine was delighted and said so to Bertie. "I always loved coming here to deliver messages or for meetings when I worked at Fort Southwick. The grounds are amazing and the house has such a lovely atmosphere. It's so light and airy with all the large windows and gets the sun for most of the day. And the colonnade round the outside is so distinctive. "

Her enthusiasm was infectious and they began their tour by viewing the library off to their right – deciding that it could possibly become the Mess – and two adjoining rooms to the left, both spacious and elegant.

"This first room might be suitable as my office," said Bertie, smiling, "and the drawing room next door could be the operations room. Then I can really keep tabs on what is going on!"

They walked over to the large floor to ceiling windows and admired the view of the gardens and beyond.

"This is just the thing!" he added, rubbing his hands together with satisfaction and turning to study the dimensions of the drawing room once more. Even in January, the sunlight streamed into both rooms and, providing they didn't have to keep the windows permanently shuttered for safety and security reasons, would create a pleasant working environment in the long hard days that lay ahead.

They continued along the ground floor corridor exploring the other rooms, before retracing their steps and ascending the elegant staircase, where light flooded in from a domed window above, to look upstairs, before eventually descending to the basement. At the conclusion of their tour, they knew that they had found the perfect place for their relocation.

"The Navigation School will have to move out though," observed Alastair.

"I'm sure you'll be able to find them somewhere suitable," replied Bertie, his eyes twinkling.

"Thanks," said Alastair.

"You're welcome."

"I suppose you'll want me to help him?" said Katherine.

"Of course."

"Hm. I'll consider it."

"Thank you. That's most kind," said Bertie. "So, onwards to our next venue: the dreaded underground tunnels at Combined H.Q."

"I never thought I'd ever have to go back there. I hope they prove to be most unsuitable," responded Katherine.

"I have to admit to sharing your point of view. I had enough of working underground when I was at Dover."

"Though you did have a wonderful view from your balcony," observed Alastair.

"Indeed. The window in my office and my balcony were a life-saver. My staff christened it 'The Stern Walk' because I spent so much time there pacing up and down during Operation Dynamo! I seem to remember someone taking a photograph of me after it was all over, relaxing in the sun with my feet up on the railings reading through some documents. It was quite a good picture, I seem to recall, though generally I dislike my photograph being taken unless it's something spontaneous like that."

After a short journey, they arrived at Fort Southwick to be greeted by the Station Commander. They descended one of the claustrophobic, steep spiral staircases into the subterranean depths of the tunnel system.

Admiral Ramsay was not impressed by the accommodation. If they moved here, he would have to take over much of the space currently used by C.-in-C. Portsmouth, for whom alternatives would be problematical. Fortunately, it was far from practical for A.N.C.X.F.'s needs anyway; besides, he really did not wish to work underground again.

Once they had returned to the car, Bertie said, "Yes, I think that Southwick House is the place for us. It is most suitable from the point of view of accommodation, and also for its close proximity to the communications centre at Fort Southwick. When we're back in the office tomorrow, I'd like you to start exploring alternatives for the poor old Navigation School and I'll speak to the V.C.N.S. about our need for an H.Q. near Portsmouth, and the possibility of getting Southwick House."

"We'll be popular," remarked Alastair.

"Aye, but it's all in a good cause," added Katherine. "I hope we get it."

"We shall," said Bertie. "You'll see. Especially if the persuasive report you're going to write on our visits today has anything to do with it!"

"I shall do my very best, sir."

"You always do."

And Alastair, quietly proud at Bertie's words, smiled warmly at Katherine who responded in kind. Unseen by them, as he was walking behind them on the way to the car, their C.-in-C. enjoyed the moment, knowing all was well.

They left Portsmouth soon after five o'clock and on arrival back in London, went their separate ways – Bertie to dine with friends, and Alastair and Katherine to have a quiet supper at home. All in all it had been a very good day.

CHAPTER 34

Norfolk House/Southwick House
April-June, 1944

And so the build up to D-Day began.

In February, the original date for Overlord, having been set for early May, was postponed until the 31st of the month, thus giving extra time for landing craft to be built. Mathieson's Shipyard, along with many others all over the country, turned its entire production over to the construction of these essential carriers. Anvil was postponed indefinitely, thus releasing more vital landing craft and ships for the Allied assault.

Bertie eventually secured all the vessels that he had requested, but not without a struggle. Both the First Sea Lord and the Americans thought he was over-estimating, but Admiral Ramsay knew that he had to have enough resources to contend with any eventuality. He was right to be insistent, as future events were to prove.

Finally, after months of anxiety, delays and an inordinate amount of hard work, the complete plans for Operation Overlord were ready to be presented. The date was set for 7th/8th April and an audience consisting of the Combined Chiefs of Staff (senior military figures, both British and American, whose immediate superiors were the Prime Minister and American President), the Secretary of State for War, and all the generals, admirals, air marshals from the higher command of the forces to be employed in Overlord, gathered at St Paul's School in Hammersmith, the London headquarters of General Montgomery's 21st Army Group. Also present were the senior staff officers responsible for compiling the plans as laid down by their Cs.-in-C, including, of course, Alastair and Katherine.

It was an auspicious occasion.

General Montgomery spoke first, for about an hour and a half, outlining the army's plan. After which, Admiral Ramsay spent an hour on the naval problems that would affect the army and how he proposed to overcome them. His presentation was clear and concise, spiced with humour and wit.

Katherine and Alastair were both pleased and relieved for him as they knew how worried Bertie had been about having to speak before such a gathering. However, no one, except those closest to him like themselves, had any inkling from the way that he spoke just how stressed he had been and the detrimental effect it had had on his digestive system...

The chairs were hard and small, this being a boys' school, and after a total of two and a half hours, the audience were feeling the strain. A short break relieved the discomfort for a while, before Leigh-Mallory took centre stage and gave an hour's discourse on the Air Plan.

Many people congratulated Bertie on his talk, which pleased and reassured him. He did feel that it had come off better than he had anticipated, but as he said, it was always difficult to tell about these things. He looked across the room to where his staff were seated and happened to catch Alastair's eye, who gave him a discreet thumbs-up, while Katherine, returning his compliment from January, on this occasion winked at him. Bertie smiled and nodded with understanding.

Following on from this, during March and April came the highly pressured task of translating the plans into operational orders. Where Operation Neptune was concerned, this was enormously complex and everyone at Norfolk House was stretched to the limit of their physical and mental endurance – including Admiral Ramsay.

The C.O.S., having also worked tirelessly, buckled under the strain and Bertie, who had a great affection for him, ordered him to take a few days' leave to stave off a complete collapse. This left Alastair temporarily in charge and, with Katherine by his side, he rose impressively to the occasion.

The Operational Orders for Neptune ran to nearly a thousand pages and each set, when bound, was three inches thick. In addition to this, there were numerous appendices. They were the most detailed orders ever issued by a commander-in-chief, in which every eventuality was covered. Indeed, in the future, Operation Neptune came to be regarded as a '*never surpassed masterpiece of planning*,' and held up as the blueprint to follow in all subsequent amphibious operations.

Its language was simple and clear. In addition to the written orders, there were charts (called 'Mickey Mouse' diagrams) that gave an overall picture, showing the positions of convoys, supporting forces, submarines, minesweepers, minefields and all units expected to be in a particular area at any one time. There were diagrams that indicated the position each ship could expect to find itself in for every hour of the passage, which, when turned over quickly, gave the effect of a moving picture.

The orders covered the vital need to land the maximum number of troops as quickly as possible, the rapid turnaround of ships to keep the army supplied – with each vessel returning to the same designated home port for supplies and equipment – and the administrative arrangements involving every Ministry, port and depot in the country, with the task that each was to carry out. The whole operation was so integrated that the loss of a cargo ship in the Atlantic or the bombing of a factory could upset the timing of the movement of equipment and supplies by rail, land or sea. When any of these occurred, the orders were amended accordingly to compensate.

The complete volume of orders was for senior officers only and those in positions of authority charged with coordinating the necessary transport organization.

Towards the end of April, Southwick House became the headquarters for A.N.C.X.F. In many ways, for Katherine it was a relief to be moving out of London, because substantial night-time German air attacks, nicknamed the 'Little Blitz', had resumed late in January after a lull of nearly two and a half years.

Once more, the general population were obliged to take shelter in the Underground stations as they had done in 1940-41; once more, incendiary bombs were dropped on the capital. The Houses of Parliament, Surrey Commercial Docks, Whitehall, Horse Guards Parade, The Admiralty, St James's Park and Pall Mall, as well as Paddington Station, Hyde Park and Chelsea all suffered damage.

Alastair and Katherine spent the nights sleeping in the cellar of their house in South Kensington, holding each other, kept awake by the roar of the air raids. One morning they were devastated when they arrived at work to find that the area around Norfolk House had suffered badly in the bombing raid that night, and saw many familiar landmarks reduced to piles of rubble.

However, the *Luftwaffe* paid a heavy price for these attacks and lost over three hundred bombers through interception, anti-aircraft fire and aircraft failure. The last night-time raid in the 'Little Blitz' took place towards the middle of April and thereafter, Goering preserved what was left of his bomber force to prepare for the inevitable Allied invasion of Nazi-occupied Europe, whenever that was to be.

Before leaving for Portsmouth, Katherine and Alastair said goodbye to the children, who seemed very sanguine about the comings and goings of 'my parents', as Anna referred to them, feeling very grown up by calling them that.

Leaving them in the care of Mary, who was once more resident at Mistley House, and Mr and Mrs Thringle, Katherine had no worries for their well-being or their emotional stability. But she would miss them... oh, how she would miss them. Alastair shared this feeling absolutely, with neither of them knowing when they would next be able to come home to see them.

The Operational Orders for Neptune were issued on 24th April, and while they were printing, Bertie took a few days' leave at home. Katherine and Alastair travelled to Portsmouth two days later to establish the A.N.C.X.F. headquarters at Southwick Park. They found things had been left in rather a state after the Navigation School had moved out, and began the complicated task of allocating rooms as offices for staff, supervising the moving in and distribution of equipment as well as issuing orders for tidying and cleaning. Everyone did their best to make things ship-shape before the admiral returned from leave.

Sleeping accommodation was cramped, situated in long wooden huts in the grounds. Commanders and below were in dormitories of twelve and sixteen, while Wren officers were in two tier bunks, twelve in a room. Captains and above, including Alastair, shared rooms in the main building, as did Katherine, who by sheer chance found for herself a tiny attic room, which she felt obliged to share with the chief officer in charge of the Wren contingent. They were completely on their own, had total privacy and fortunately got on very well, striking up quite a friendship. Despite the conditions, no one complained, everyone took the discomforts in their stride and a good spirit prevailed.

Bertie returned refreshed and relaxed, and was pleased with all that had been achieved in such a short space of time. However, he knew, as they all did, that it would be at least another week before Southwick House could be considered an operational command.

The time passed quickly. There were meetings to attend, problems to resolve: H-Hour (the actual time of landing the troops) had to be fixed – a decision made more difficult by the differing times of high tides for the five chosen beaches that spanned the wide assault front. They also needed to decide how to overcome beach obstacles, how to meet the need for total air cover and its coordination, and how to tackle the threat of E-boats and U-boats. There were training exercises to observe and report on, ship inspections, and a visit by King George VI. And all the time, the rapid build-up of Allied troops and equipment continued until southern England took on the appearance of an enormous army camp.

Tanks, trucks and jeeps lined the roads of all the coastal towns, and roads and bridges had to be widened and strengthened to accept this extraordinary traffic. Strange craft appeared in creeks and rivers, while existing dock facilities and slipways were improved and new ones built, as ships and boats of all shapes and sizes filled the harbours and ports.

It was an exciting time and yet a nerve-racking one. So much depended upon this. The organization had to be precise. It was going to be the only chance the Allies would have and it had to be right.

On 15th May, the Overlord plans were presented for the final time. Once again, the venue was at St Paul's School in London, but this time it was to be before the greatest gathering of senior military figures in history: the King, the Prime Minister, Field Marshal Jan Smuts – the Premier of South Africa, the British Chiefs of Staff, the Commanders-in-Chief, the Commanders of the expedition, and their principal staff officers were all present.

Eisenhower opened the proceedings, followed by Montgomery, outlining the army's plans and expected progress, ending with a rousing statement of optimism. When it was his turn, Bertie spoke with equal clarity and confidence, describing the part to be played by the navy, adding, with characteristic humour, that the soldiers must not always expect to be landed exactly as shown on the diagram! After this, Leigh-Mallory presented the role of the air force.

Later, Katherine and Alastair were introduced to King George VI, whom they both found very well informed. After His Majesty had moved on, Katherine and Alastair exchanged a brief glance, as though to say "Wow!" before being spotted by Phillippe du Laurier, who came over to both of them, and greeted them warmly.

"*Bonjour, mes amis !*" he exclaimed expansively, such was his strength and confidence, even among the illustrious company they were keeping that day. "I trust you are both well? This is some gathering *n'est-ce pas ?* Bertie was excellent. The best. Very clear and, how do you say it? Ah, yes. No waffling!"

To all of this, Katherine replied that they were well, that it was certainly some gathering, and thanked him for his remarks, saying she would pass them on.

"I have studied his plans for Neptune," continued Phillippe. "They are *exceptionnels, n'est-ce pas ?*" He lowered his voice, speaking in a confidential manner. "The Americans think they are too detailed, but I say they have to be. Nothing must be left to chance. Nothing. If everyone knows what he has to do, then nothing can go wrong. And without the navy to carry the soldiers and the equipment, the Allies could not launch the invasion. And without sufficient planning, it would be a disaster. *Non*, Admiral Ramsay has a brilliant mind. You are lucky to work for such a man."

"We know we are," said Alastair, pleased at the compliment. "However, I hope the admiral in charge of the Western Task Force doesn't decide to disregard the detail in the orders. Bertie's been having one or two problems with him."

"I am not surprised. He is a poor fish, this admiral. *Il est sujet à des crises de nerfs* and behaves with pomp and stupidity. He is always trying to, how you say?

Ah, yes. Save face." Then Phillippe paused. He looked at both of them. "We must talk. But not here. After lunch, perhaps?"

"I'm tied up for the rest of the day," said Alastair, immediately concerned by Phillippe's request. "There is a C-in-C's meeting on H-Hour with the Americans first thing this afternoon, then I imagine that you will have to be back for Eisenhower's gathering later and the closing address."

"*Oui, certainement.* What about you, Katherine? It is important."

"Can you spare me?" she asked Alastair.

"Yes, if you're not too long. I'll jot down the salient points for you. It'll probably be the usual stuff at the beginning. Lots of…"

"Waffling," interjected Phillippe.

"*Exactement !*" replied Alastair.

After lunch, Katherine and Phillippe explored the school and found a deserted classroom tucked away from the main part of the building. Phillippe perched on the edge of the teacher's table, while Katherine sat opposite on one of the front row desks, being careful to avoid the inkwell that was full of dark blue liquid, with her feet resting on a chair.

"Lily?" she said.

"*Oui.* Lily." He took a deep breath. He was very unhappy, despite his earlier bravado. "Things are not good. She shows to me a side to her character that I have not seen before we are married and which I do not care for."

Poor Phillippe. What could she say? "If it's any consolation, if you're talking about her behaviour when we last met, I had not seen that particular side of her either and I've known her a long time. She's always seemed so mature and philosophical about things, with a wonderfully generous nature."

"Like her father."

"Yes. But that day at Mistley House, she sounded so like Roberta, it was uncanny. And made me feel very uncomfortable."

Phillippe was silent. He got up from the desk and went over to the blackboard where he absent-mindedly picked up a piece of chalk and rolled it around between his fingers. "*Oui.*" Then, very quietly, "She has written to her mother."

Katherine went pale. "Oh, no."

"*C'est regrettable*, especially as I forbade her to do so. She is most wilful. However, this morning she has received a reply from Roberta. It is a very cold little note to say that she does not care who Alastair goes out with or what he does, as long as she gets her divorce. Lily tore it up. She was very angry."

"I can imagine."

"I was very angry with Lily."

Katherine looked at Phillippe. "I'm so sorry."

He shrugged. "It is not your fault." He put the chalk back on the ledge in front of the blackboard and came back to sit on the desk. "But that is not all. At the same time, Lily also wrote to your mother, she now tells me."

Katherine, having experienced huge relief at Roberta's response, was once more worried. "I wondered why I hadn't heard from Mhairi recently, even with wartime conditions. I had begun to be a little anxious, as it's most unusual for her. Perhaps this explains why."

She looked out of the window, watching creamy pink petals fall to the ground from the tree outside as it brushed against the window of the classroom in the gentle breeze.

Katherine had not told Rupert and Mhairi about her relationship with Alastair. She had hoped they would read between the lines in her letters, gradually becoming acclimatized to the idea. She wished now that she had been more direct.

"Do you know what Lily wrote in her letter?"

"I made her tell me.

"What did she say?"

Phillippe regarded her carefully before replying. "She has been *très blessante* to you and Alastair."

"Ah," said Katherine, her mouth drawn into a grim line.

"It is not right that Lily should do this to you. It shows a serious flaw in her character and does damage to my friends – her father and you."

"Mais tout cela, c'est très difficile pour vous aussi."

"*Oui.* Perhaps." Phillippe shrugged his shoulders. "But I have written to Rupert this very morning. I do not wish your parents to be upset or… misinformed. They are good people and I am fond of them. Lily is hurting them by her words. She is thoughtless and ungrateful. I do not know how to make her less so."

Katherine saw the sadness and regret in Phillippe's eyes. He was a good man, a brave man; many people knew him as a great man. Lily was a fool not to put her relationship with her husband before her own emotional insecurities or moral judgements.

She chose her words carefully, for Phillippe's sake speaking in French. She touched his arm briefly, thanking him with all her heart for his efforts on their behalf. "Lily may never accept Alastair and me," she said, "but you must not let this come between the two of you. I do not know how you will resolve it, as Lily is less to you now than she was, but I hope for your sake that she works through it soon and is once more fully restored to you."

Katherine paused, trying to find the right way of expressing in French things she would find difficult enough to say in English. "She has had a shock, and is frustrated by the fact that she cannot get her own way and prevent our relationship. Therefore, she lashes out. She no longer has her father to herself. He has put his relationship with me before her feelings, and so she feels rejected, a very sensitive emotion for her, given Roberta's attitude towards her. Perhaps it is this rejection by her mother as she was growing up that comes out now, having been suppressed for all these years. I do not know for certain. I can only guess."

"Perhaps it is so." Phillippe raised his head, hope beginning to filter through him.

"She has seen your anger for a second time and will reflect on that. Perhaps now, let her see your love, because ultimately, it is your love for her that will restore her; your love that will be greater than her resentment and will overcome her sense of rejection, something that lies deep within her." Katherine paused. "But you will need great patience, Phillippe. It may take time and it may take something drastic to make her realize that you are more important to her than anything. She really is in love with you, have no doubt about that. She just has to come to terms with many things in her life that she has not yet done so and has subconsciously avoided. Encourage her with her music. That will help her, especially…"

"When I go across to France on D-Day."

"*Oui.*"

Phillippe nodded. "*Merci, chère Katherine.* I will never forget this conversation. Alastair is a lucky man and I will tell him so."

"Thank you. So is Lily. Now, we had best be getting back."

"Otherwise, we shall face the court martial."

Katherine laughed. "Not good!"

"*Non.*"

The weather was very fine during the rest of May. D-Day, for various practical and logistical reasons was postponed once again – this time until the beginning of June.

For Katherine and Alastair, sometimes together, sometimes separately with Bertie, there were more naval exercises to watch in preparation for D-Day, additional shipboard inspections by King George to attend, numerous presentations, briefings for over three hundred senior naval officers, and a hugely enjoyable evening dining out with the Second Sea Lord and assorted dignitaries aboard *H.M.S. Victory.*

Katherine felt honoured to be included and was quite overwhelmed to be actually aboard Nelson's historic flagship. "I can hardly believe this," she whispered to Alastair as they walked up the gangplank. "He's always been such a hero of mine."

"Mine too," he said, smiling at her, sharing her pleasure.

Towards the end of May, there was a cricket match in the grounds of Southwick House between Admiral Ramsay's Mess and the Wrens, who lost by four wickets with Bertie scoring sixteen runs and then later bowling Katherine out for a disastrous two. It was great fun and just the sort of thing that was needed to escape the pressure of work, but it was exhausting, playing in very long grass and on what was a very hot evening.

Alastair served much sought-after refreshments, wisely declining to participate, and just enjoyed watching Katherine, whom he didn't know played cricket.

"Ah, I got up to all sorts of things while you were at sea!" she teased him when they managed to snatch a few moments alone. He kissed her forehead and held her close, secure in the knowledge that whatever it was, it would have been nothing except innocent.

On 1st June, Admiral Ramsay took over active command of the Neptune forces and general control of all operations in the Channel. But the weather, so settled for most of May, had begun to deteriorate and was forecast to change. For Sunday, 4th June, high winds, thick low cloud and fog were predicted and at the 0415 Commanders' meeting this was confirmed. Later that day the Admiralty issued a gale warning, and Overlord was postponed for the next twenty-four hours.

Bertie spent the day visiting ships in the Solent, reassuring his Assault Force commanders that the weather was going to be all right and they should not worry. The atmosphere at Southwick House was tense.

Then, at the 0415 meeting in the library on Monday, 5th June, the meteorologists predicted a break in the weather – a window of opportunity large enough to launch the invasion. Ike went round the table asking each of his commanders-in-chief what they thought they should do – go or stay…

Bertie and Monty had no hesitation in saying that they should go; Leigh-Mallory, cautiously, said they should take the chance.

So it was, with the wind rattling the window panes and the rain lashing down outside, that it fell to General Eisenhower, the Supreme Commander, to make the most difficult decision any military man would ever have to make. He contemplated for a while and then said, "O.K. We'll go!"

D-Day was therefore set for Tuesday, 6th June and Operation Neptune, to carry the Allied invasion force across the Channel in order to free Europe from Nazi oppression, was launched by Admiral Ramsay within half an hour of Eisenhower's historic decision.

CHAPTER 35

D-Day (1)
5th/6th June, 1944

As darkness fell, the destroyer *H.M.S. Udimore* reached the Isle of Wight, exactly on time after its long voyage down the west coast of Great Britain to join with the great armada that was to be Operation Neptune. Standing on the bridge of his ship, Lieutenant-Commander Edward Stewart R.N. contemplated the task ahead of them. He understood only too well the great significance of what was about to happen and, despite himself, his heart beat rapidly with what he regarded as stupid, infantile excitement at the merest thought of being a part of it.

However, he had found trying to read the top secret operational orders in their entirety an odious task, and after ploughing his way through the first few paragraphs, he had delegated it to his new Number One, Lieutenant Jack Rutherford R.N.V.R., who, it would seem, had served with his erstwhile father aboard the cruiser *H.M.S. Romney*. He thought that being on a destroyer must be a bit of a comedown for the lieutenant but, as Jack never complained and was nauseatingly efficient, Edward shamelessly used and relied upon him to organize and see to most things, including making sense of the enormous amount of material contained in the orders and breaking it down into more digestible chunks.

Strangely, his subordinate had become fascinated by the whole document, until eventually, Edward had had to quell his enthusiasm by giving him the sop that he might be able to hang onto the ridiculously large tome as a souvenir after the war, whenever that might be. Annoyingly, Rutherford hadn't believed him, giving Edward a direct look, but it did subdue him and meant he had been quiet about it ever since. The lieutenant also spent a lot of time looking after the ship's cat, and had made a miniature hammock complete with a tiny pillow for the rather pampered moggie. The cat did keep the rats and mice at bay so the effort wasn't all wasted, Edward supposed.

Jack had told him the precise coordinates the ship was headed for, and had informed him of the individual role *H.M.S. Udimore* was to play – bombarding a specific target of the shore defences, just one of many ships pounding the German batteries continuously with such force that they were either destroyed or unable to operate, thus securing cover for the soldiers landing on the beaches.

But that was yet to come. Edward's thoughts meanwhile, turned to the letter he had received from his mother just before they had left Scotland. He opened the envelope and his eyes scanned the page.

My divorce is proceeding according to plan. That was good, he thought. The sooner she was shot of old Alastair the better. *I have actually heard from Lily, for the first time in years. She last wrote to me to say she was on her way to Canada in 1938. I never bothered to reply. However, this latest was a rather peculiar letter, something along the lines that Alastair has a lover who, it turns out is none other than that no-good widow of Alex. Why she has told me all of this, I have absolutely no idea. I wrote back to say that I couldn't give a tinker's damn who Alastair goes out with or what he does as long as I get my divorce and can marry your father.*

Well, well, mused Edward. *So worthy, sanctimonious old Alastair has got himself a woman. Wonders will never cease. And his daughter-in-law to boot. Ha! I didn't think he had it in him. Well, good luck to him.* Edward wondered what she was like. *Perhaps he'd been a bit slow and should have dived in, so to speak, when she had become available. No, she was probably just as stuffy as Alastair.*

But she was the old man's daughter-in-law… Edward decided to save up that juicy titbit for future reference.

Phillippe du Laurier leant against the railings of the Free French destroyer *La Combattante* looking across the Solent towards the Isle of Wight. Even before darkness had fallen, there was not a great deal of water to see, as the whole expanse was crammed with ships and craft of all shapes and sizes, lying at anchor, moving erratically up and down in the choppy water, waiting for the signal to be off; the sailors and soldiers on board impatient to be on the move and to do the job for which they had been trained.

He was not a happy man. His relationship with Lily had not yet recovered from her irrational behaviour, and their farewell had been strained – his wife tearful, stubbornly refusing to change her attitude, overwhelmed by any number of conflicting emotions. He knew what he was about to face, yet was unable to explain it to her, unable to make her see the dangers that might befall him and thereby bring her round to being his loving wife again.

It was not a good mentality to have on the eve of battle, a battle of such importance that all previous conflicts in which he had taken part paled before it. But there were other reasons for his present state of mind. He was a high-ranking officer, a leader of men. He should be with his valiant XI Corps, to fight alongside them, just as he had done in the Battle for France in 1940 and French North Africa in 1943. But Major Kieffer's special commando unit were the only French soldiers taking part in the D-Day landings – the rest of the Free French having been designated to land later in the month with the follow-up forces, when the lodgement had been established and the Allies were moving inland. Even then, Phillippe would not be able to go with them, as he had relinquished his command when asked by General Eisenhower to join his staff. At that time Phillippe had agreed, weary of conflict after experiencing so much.

However, it was important to him that he should be in France on D-Day, back in his beloved country.

The only way open to him was in the minor role of French Liaison Officer. It was planned that each fighting unit should take such an officer across with them and he had persuaded Eisenhower to release him temporarily from his duties at Supreme Headquarters to fulfil this role, even though his rank was far too senior. Ike had acquiesced reluctantly and assigned Phillippe to the French-Canadian Brigades of Force 'J', to whom he was well-known, destined to land at Courselles, codenamed 'Juno', one of the beaches selected for the five division assault.

Phillippe pondered the enormity of the planned naval and military undertaking that would become a reality in a matter of hours. The designated landing sectors on the Contentin Peninsula in Normandy were places he knew so well. He could not remember how many holidays he had spent there as a child. If he closed his eyes, he could picture the beaches vividly where the soldiers would be landing: the British and French on 'Sword' at Ouistreham in the east, the Canadians on 'Juno' at Courselles – a lovely, picturesque little port – the British on 'Gold' at Asnelles, and the Americans, 'Omaha' at St Laurent and 'Utah' at Varreville to the west.

The Allies would prevail, of that he had no doubt. How wonderful it would then be to take Lily to these delightful seaside towns and villages, to walk along the sands in a land freed from occupation.

Phillippe thought of his countrymen, the years of struggle they had endured, of hardship and oppression, of humiliation and cruelty. He wanted to be there again, once more among the people who spoke his language, who thought as he did. He had been in exile far too long. He needed to feel French soil under his feet.

He needed to go home.

After the order had been given to proceed with Operation Neptune, there was no more they could do for some hours, so Alastair and Katherine drove down to Spithead, finding a quiet place on the high ground overlooking the Isle of Wight in which to be together, to sit and observe.

All the signals had been sent, the orders given, the preparations put in place. Now it was almost time for nearly seven thousand ships from ports and harbours all around the coast, each with its allocated place and designated task, to head across the English Channel to Normandy.

It was the greatest armada the world had ever seen and they wanted to witness its departure.

Flotillas of minesweepers had been busy since the afternoon, clearing the ten channels of the 'Spout' down which the ships would travel to their pre-arranged destinations in Normandy after first congregating in the rendezvous area, codenamed 'Z', which quickly became known as 'Piccadilly Circus'.

The ships of the British Eastern Naval Task Force were heading for Sword, Gold and Juno beaches, while Utah and Omaha were the destinations of the American Western Naval Task Force. Each task force had its own headquarters ship, its own allocated fleet of minesweepers, battleships, cruisers, destroyers, and landing craft – large and small, hundreds of which had left earlier in the day – carrying tanks, motorized vehicles, weapons, equipment and, of course, troops.

All trace of the storm had disappeared and the evening air was calm, although a heavy swell remained on the water. Overhead, Katherine and Alastair could hear the steady roar of planes from the Royal Air Force, some towing gliders, in company with those from the American Air Force. They could picture the close aircraft formations, their fuselages marked with the distinctive three black and white friend-identifying stripes for the invasion. They could imagine the thousands of planes on their way to deliver paratroopers behind enemy lines to capture and hold vital bridges for the troops advancing from the beaches, or to bomb the coast, 'softening up' the German defences, forcing the enemy 'keep its head down' to protect the Allied landings. The whole undertaking was a tremendous feat of inter-service, international cooperation and coordination.

Katherine put her arm through Alastair's, shivering with excitement as the ship's engines of those about to leave started up one by one, until eventually, just as the moon emerged through the clouds lighting up the panorama before them, the vast armada began to move.

It was an awe-inspiring sight, one they would never forget.

They stood silently, close together, moved beyond words by the deep significance of it all, and yet under no illusions as to what would have to be faced on the other side of the Channel.

"Do you wish you were going?" asked Katherine after a while.

Alastair was thoughtful. "Yes and no. Yes, because it would be quite something to see all our plans put into action and to be a part of it, and no, because right now, I'd rather be doing what we're doing."

"I know that Bertie wants to go across as soon as he can. D-Day plus one is what he's anticipating. I'm sure he'll take you with him."

"I certainly hope so."

"I wish I could come as well."

"I know." He put his arm round her shoulders.

"There's been such a tremendous feeling of optimism everywhere, hasn't there?"

"It's been quite remarkable. From the top brass to the lowliest sailor or soldier. While Bertie and I have been out on his tours of inspection, everyone we've spoken to has been so keen and fired up. And confident too."

"They've had a long wait, though. It can't have been easy being cooped up in the ships and landing craft for the past few days."

"No. They'll be glad to be underway at last, in more ways than one."

Katherine was thoughtful. "Do you think it's actually possible that we are going to achieve the complete surprise everyone's been hoping for?"

"With any luck. Everything has been done that can be done. You and I both know how tight security has been. No one's been able to enter or go out of the area without a special pass since 10th April and all leave was cancelled before the final rehearsal."

Katherine chuckled. "Some of the Wrens have been having a good moan about their mail being censored so heavily."

"I'm not surprised. Then there's Operation Fortitude – all those false signals sent out via captured agents, the bombing of railways and supply depots from the Pas de Calais southwards to create confusion, not to mention General Patton's fake encampment. That must have kept the Germans guessing and hopefully, they'll have no idea where the real invasion is going to be launched from. We've done everything that could be done."

Katherine smiled. "I'd love to have seen the cardboard tanks and ships. Apparently they looked quite realistic from air reconnaissance photos. And the idea of dropping dummy parachutists with fireworks near Calais tonight is just brilliant. What with the pretend landings as well – that should keep the enemy confused."

"And scatter their resources, taking them away from Normandy."

They stayed for a very long time, reluctant to leave, glad of this rare opportunity to be alone together, to share a few private moments. Alastair took her in his arms and kissed her.

"I do love you," he said, tenderly stroking her hair.

"I love you too," she murmured.

For a little while longer they remained where they were, seated on the bench, holding each other close. Then, reluctantly, after a last lingering kiss, knowing it was time to return to their duties, they drew apart. Alastair stood up and held out his hand to her, which she took.

"We must be due some leave soon," said Katherine.

He smiled at her ruefully. "I certainly hope so!"

Hand in hand, they walked back to the car and Alastair drove them back to Southwick House.

It was some hours before the last of the ships had gone, and the final engine sounds disappeared into the darkness. The next morning, for the first time in many months, there would not be a vessel to be seen.

It would seem very strange.

"Lieutenant Granger?"

"Yes?" Michael turned round to see who had spoken.

The R.A.M.C. sergeant looked worried. "I'm sorry to trouble you, sir, but we seem to have mislaid the green bags with the spare bandages in."

"That was very careless," he replied good-naturedly. "I'm sure they came on board with the other bags of medical supplies."

"I've searched through those, sir. They don't seem to be there."

"How about the wooden crates with the medical kits in?"

"Looked there too, sir."

"Ah." This was a serious problem. "How about checking to see if they've got mixed up with the equipment for Brigade H.Q. They had some green bags as well, I think."

"Righty-ho, sir."

Michael watched the sergeant move away into the darkness. He knew the bags in question had come on board, because he had countersigned the inventory for the equipment.

The ship's forward movement and the steady throb of the engines were a welcome relief for everyone, having been confined in the former passenger ferry *S.S. Royal Bluebell*, now converted into an infantry assault vessel, for three seasick days, waiting for the weather to improve and the signal to proceed.

Setting off on the ninety-mile route to Gold Beach at Asnelles, Michael knew they were following the destroyers that would be making the initial bombardment, and that he and his R.A.M.C. unit would be in the first wave of troops ashore.

As the ship entered the deep water channel, a huge 'V' for victory sign on the ninety-foot Nab Tower lighthouse shone out in the darkness: a beacon of hope and inspiration for everyone.

"Blimey," said an R.A.M.C. private further down the deck. "I hope old Jerry don't see that! If he does, he'll be down on us like a ton of bricks."

"Funny he 'asn't spotted us before, though, ain't it? We've all been like sitting ducks in the water for the past few days, thousands of us."

"It gives you a thrill though, don't it, to see that?" said someone else, pointing to the 'V' sign.

"Too right. Given me goosebumps, it has," came the reply. "Look..." and his companion pulled up his sleeve and showed his friend.

"Whoever ordered it to be lit up must be feeling confident," said the first man.

"That's because the good old R.A.F. rules the skies."

"About ruddy time too, if you ask me!" replied another.

"But what about the Americans? They must be helping a bit. They've got 'undreds of planes," added someone else.

"Don't talk to me about them ruddy Yanks. My missus thinks they're wonderful. Too bloomin' wonderful, if you ask me," muttered the first man. "They make us Brits feel like the poor relations."

"Still, we need 'em to help us win the war."

"Unfortunately. Cocky bastards though. If we do win the war, they'll probably take all the credit for it."

"Yeah. But we'll pull through in the end. Monty'll make sure of it."

"'E's a good bloke is Monty. Makes you feel you can do anything. It's a ruddy good job 'e'll be in charge of all the fighting forces when we get to France."

Overhearing this conversation, Michael smiled to himself and continued to watch the Nab Tower until it had disappeared into the distance. He felt proud to be a part of it all but nervous at the same time. This would be his first time in charge in a real combat situation.

After the weekend at Mistley House, buoyed up by Admiral Ramsay's confidence in him, Michael had gone straight to his C.O. and said that he would like to be considered for training as an officer. His superior was delighted and, after checking his credentials, immediately sent him on the appropriate course. Now, four months later, Michael found himself on his way to Normandy, responsible for a team of medical personnel.

His orders, after the initial landings, were to set up a temporary military hospital in some suitable building further inland at Creully, one of the towns on the list of objectives for that first day.

"Sir?"

Michael jumped; his reverie disturbed. "Yes, Sergeant?"

"Found them, sir."

"Good. Where were they?"

"Just as you said. The H.Q. wallahs had purloined them."

"Well done, Sergeant. That's a relief."

"It is, sir."

"Thank you, Sergeant."

"Yes, sir." The man walked off, leaving Michael to his thoughts once more.

He had no illusions about combat – his experiences in France in 1940 and Sicily in 1943 had taught him that. He thought of Mary and their precious little daughter Rose, safe and warm at Mistley House.

He had to come back to them. They were his family, his life.

He had to come back.

CHAPTER 36

D-Day (2)
6th June, 1944

"We're halfway across, now, sir." Lieutenant Rutherford approached Edward on the bridge.

"Check our position one more time, will you? Make sure you're right. Go down and see for yourself."

"Yes, sir."

Jack went below to the coxswain, who raised his eyes to the heavens at their commander's doubting attitude. He confirmed their heading as being identical to that of a few moments ago. Jack Rutherford laid an understanding hand on the man's shoulder and went back topsides.

"All correct, sir."

"You're sure?"

"Yes, sir," he replied. How could he give reassurance without sounding condescending? "Look, here's the first of the flashing green dan buoys marking the start of the swept channels. And we're still following that same destroyer." Privately, Jack wondered how this man had been given command. He knew he wasn't unintelligent or incompetent but Lieutenant-Commander Edward Stewart was lazy, definitely lazy.

They watched in silence as their ship glided through the lights, a motor-launch patiently sitting on station to check that each ship entered the channel correctly. Others were on similar duty at the start of each of the channels.

Satisfied at last, Edward went below, leaving Rutherford on deck with the sub. They raised their eyebrows at each other.

"Don't say a word," said Jack.

"Don't need to, sir. Though there's plenty I could say."

"Couldn't we all?!"

They motored on smoothly in the darkness, through the reassuring lights of the channel. Rutherford checked that their anti-aircraft barrage balloon was secure below and above, each individual ship having been issued with this small protection against low-flying enemy planes. In the moonlight, he could just about see those carried by the ships ahead and behind. It was comforting and at the same time exciting to be part of such a vitally important convoy of destroyers. He curbed his impatience to get *there*, to Gold Beach, their destination. He looked at the compass and requested a minor course correction.

This night was going to seem very long.

Jack called to mind the words of the Special Order issued by Admiral Ramsay to all the officers and men of the Allied Naval Expeditionary Force; wonderful words that filled him with pride and determination. He had read them so many times, he knew them from memory. Silently, he mouthed them to himself into the night:

"It is to be our privilege to take part in the greatest amphibious operation in history...

This is the opportunity which we have long awaited and which must be seized and pursued with relentless determination: the hopes and prayers of the free world and of the enslaved peoples of Europe will be with us and we cannot fail them.

Our task in conjunction with the Merchant Navies of the United Nations and supported by the Allied Air Forces is to carry the Allied Expeditionary Force to the Continent, to establish it there in a secure bridgehead and to build it up and maintain it at a rate which will outmatch that of the enemy.

Let no one underestimate this task.

The Germans are desperate and will resist fiercely until we out-manoeuvre and out-fight them, which we can and will do. To every one of you will be given the opportunity to show by his determination and resource that dauntless spirit of resolution which individually strengthens and inspires and is collectively irresistible.

I count on every man to do his utmost to ensure the success of this great enterprise which is the climax of the European war.

Good luck to you all, and God speed."

Jack focused on the photographs of their target, committing them to visual memory. They would fail in their duty unless those two co-ordinates on the chart were shelled accurately. It had to be right: he owed it to Admiral Ramsay and the soldiers who were relying upon the Royal Navy to pave the way for them as they landed on the beaches.

He then reconsidered what Edward had said to him about keeping the entire volume of orders for Operation Neptune – having originally dismissed the suggestion as the lieutenant-commander's patronizing way of trying to dampen his enthusiasm. Jack had enjoyed studying it, felt inspired by the meticulous attention to detail. Everything had been considered, everything anticipated, nothing left to chance.

How he would love to have worked on the document itself, but then again, nothing could take the place of being at sea; to actually *live* the plans. Perhaps he would be able to keep them. He might have a word with his former commander on the *Romney*; they had become good friends and, after all, Alastair was now Admiral Ramsay's D.C.O.S.

Jack smiled. Yes, that would be the thing to do when he got back home, if a mine or a torpedo didn't get them first. Quickly, he shut that thought out of his mind.

"Nearly there now, sir," called the coxswain from below.

Jack felt a surge of excitement. He picked up his binoculars and there it was – land. In the first pale light of dawn lay the coast of France, as yet a shadowy outline, but visible nonetheless. His heart beat very fast. This was it – the real thing, everything they had trained for. He sent the sub-lieutenant below to call their captain, while overhead came the steady roar of Allied bombers on their way to carry out the first phase of the assault by bombing the German fortifications on the coast.

Daylight came quickly after that and with it the magnificent, heart-stirring sight of thousands of ships steaming their way across the English Channel, each with its own pre-appointed task. It was indeed a masterpiece of planning and was now down to all of them, all the fighting forces coming together to make that plan a total success.

The freedom of the Western world depended upon it. It had to go right.

Edward came up on deck just as they reached their position. In keeping with all the other destroyers they turned beam on to the beach, now less than three miles away. It was eerily silent, seeming more like an exercise than actual combat.

"Where's the enemy?" asked Edward, sounding almost disappointed. "I thought we'd be getting it in the neck by now. Just like Dunkirk."

"So did I, sir," replied the sub.

"Either we've caught them napping, or they've been so shocked by the bombing that they're afraid to put their heads up, so to speak," observed Jack. "Half a minute to go, sir," he added, looking at his wristwatch. "The guns are all ready: they've got the targets in their sights."

The tension on board was palpable.

"Stand by, sir," Rutherford said to his commander.

"STAND BY!" called out Edward.

"Now, sir."

"OPEN FIRE!" and for exactly an hour and ten minutes, the ships of the Royal Navy – battleships, cruisers and destroyers – opened fire in one continuous and spine-tingling roar.

Jack stood on the bridge, keeping his attention riveted to the stopwatch in his hand, trying not to think about the poor devils who would be on the receiving end of the barrage: the enemy soldiers who would bear the brunt of this, the heaviest rain of shells ever to be poured on land targets from the sea. However, the Nazis had to be defeated, there was no question of that. But it would be the ordinary fighting men and civilians on both sides who would pay a heavy price so that the liberation of Europe might be secured.

Signals kept arriving at regular intervals until they received one that had been used repeatedly throughout British Naval history, which read: '*Engage The Enemy More Closely*'. Along with the other destroyers, they weighed anchor and moved in closer to the shore, every ship having her own individual minesweeper to clear the way and protect her in her vital task.

The destroyers continued to fire as rapidly as they could, engaging the enemy positions at almost point blank range. Jack kept his eyes on his stopwatch and after their further allotted amount of time, he said, "Cease firing, sir."

The message was duly relayed by his captain and the guns of *H.M.S. Udimore* fell silent, at exactly the same time as the others. As this was done, assault craft full of soldiers passed by on their way to the beaches. Jack Rutherford, shivering with adrenaline and fatigue, found his eyes swimming with tears.

"*Good luck to you all, and God speed,*" he mouthed silently.

His ship's work on D-Day was not over yet by any means. They would be required to bombard enemy positions further inland, assisting the infantry as the battles progressed, but for the moment they were able to stand on the bridge and watch.

Quickly, Jack took out his sketchbook and pencil, committing to paper in swift, bold lines the drama as it unfolded before him.

Michael crouched low in the landing craft, his heart pumping in his chest so violently that he thought it would burst. He checked round to see that his team of medical personnel were all right. Like him, they were wet and cold from the spray and the wind, most of them seasick, looking grim and pale, and clutching their precious medical kits, their knuckles white with tension and discomfort.

In a short, steep sea of three to four foot waves, their Landing Craft Vehicle Personnel carrier – L.C.V.P. for short – went up and down, side to side, up and down, side to side, rolling around relentlessly in a heavy following sea, its blunt nose and flat bottom exacerbating this very unpleasant motion.

For nearly seven miles from their lowering positions, they had endured these debilitating conditions, their cheerful naval coxswain keeping up an unceasing commentary on what was happening around them.

"Oh look, there's Able Seaman Pettifer. He don't look too good, if you ask me. Bit green around the gills." He shouted across to his friend as the boats went up and down, neither of them coinciding. The other's reply was lost in the wind. Then a bit later, "Well I'm blowed. Some idiot's standing up in his L.C.V.P. playing the ruddy bagpipes!"

As he spoke the words, they heard the sound drifting across to them and Michael cautiously peered over the side of their craft to have a look. Sure enough, there was the piper, who had wedged himself against the side of his vessel, playing tune after rousing tune, clearly audible as his L.V.C.P. rode parallel to theirs.

His spirits rising rapidly at the sound, Michael knew he would never forget the feeling of confidence and camaraderie that this brave and foolhardy man inspired in him and, no doubt, countless others. It gave him an uplifting personal connection to Mary and their far distant home on Cairnmor and he blessed the unknown and unknowing piper for this double gift.

A little later on, they heard the sound of a portable gramophone being relayed through a loud-hailer and men singing along to its limited supply of songs. Then a bugler started up, calling the 'Reveille' and any other tune he could manage. The juxtaposition brought smiles to everyone's lips, cheering them, creating a feeling of good heart amidst the tension of anticipation.

"We're surrounded by madmen!" shouted his sergeant into his ear, the only way he could make himself heard.

"You have to admire them though," said Michael, who, having been queasy for a long time, suddenly felt very ill and at that moment was violently sick over the side of the boat.

"Good job you're on the leeward side, sir," remarked their coxswain, with a knowing wink. "Feel any better?"

259

"No," groaned Michael.

"That's the ticket!" came the jaunty reply.

As they approached the shore, the ships' guns ceased firing and for five minutes before they landed, there was a final burst of drenching fire from specially designed craft that launched a continuous salvo of twenty thousand rockets onto the nearby beaches, obstacles and defensive positions. It was the most spectacular thing Michael had ever seen and along with just about everyone else, he forgot about his seasickness as he watched yet another awesome demonstration of British naval firepower.

The German defenders were so stunned by the successive waves of bombardment that they took several minutes to recover. In that vital time, as had been planned, the first wave of assault troops landed – engineers and flail tanks flogging their way through the minefields, armoured bulldozers clearing and demolishing the beach obstacles – all opening the way for the infantry to follow, which they did in their tens, in their hundreds and, as time went on, thousands upon thousands.

In the heavy surf, Michael's L.C.V.P. rushed ashore, expertly controlled by their ever-cheerful coxswain, who threaded his way between the obstacles and deposited them neatly on the beach within a few minutes of H-Hour. The front ramps went down and keeping low, they ran as best they could onto the sands with Michael immediately deploying his men where he could see they were most needed.

The army pushed its way up the beach, its progress slow at first under strafing machine-gun fire and mortars from those enemy troops who had managed to recover sufficiently from the earlier shocking bombardment to mount some sort of resistance.

Working alongside the doctors, Michael and his fellow medical personnel treated the wounded quickly, administering emergency procedures, keeping their bodies as low as possible, hoping they would be lucky and not be hit. As quickly as was possible, the injured soldiers were then carried on stretchers back to the landing craft which, when full, took them to the ferrying vessels anchored off-shore which, in turn, transported them to the waiting hospital ships or barges, and finally, home.

.

Eventually, after fierce fighting from both sides, the British overcame the enemy's forward defensive positions. One Churchill tank flailed its way off the beach and along the main street of Le Hamel, a village close to Asnelles, scattering everything and everyone in its path, thus enabling British infantry to move up in its wake and capture more enemy strongholds from behind.

The British kept coming. Men, equipment, armaments, armoured vehicles, tanks, more men, more equipment, stores, ammunition, more tanks, more equipment, more men.

As the infantry came onto the beach in ever increasing numbers, they finally overcame the resistance of the defenders in the bunkers and on Gold, by noon that morning, little more than five hours after H-hour, the British were in total control of the beach, having cleared several passages through the obstacles and

260

established seven working exits. By nine o'clock that night, Arromanches and the clifftop above the anchorage, so vital for the protection of the artificial harbour to be built there, had been taken, while Royal Marine Commandos fought their way valiantly along nine miles of coast to take Port-en-Bessin.

As Michael and his unit made their way along and up the beach, now free of hostile fire, they continued to treat the wounded, both British and German, as they went, arranging for their safe transport back to the waiting ships.

During brief pauses in his work, as he stood up to stretch his aching back or wipe his hands, he could not help but be impressed by the organization that had been established to keep the continuous stream of vehicles, supplies and troops moving away from the beach as quickly as possible, reducing congestion to a minimum. Any hold-ups could mean a disastrous delay for the advance inland, which needed to be made as rapidly as possible during that first day.

The Royal Navy Beach Master and his men on Gold seemed to be very much in charge, directing traffic, reinforcements and supplies to their correct assembly points. Signs and noticeboards had sprung up all over the beach.

Putting aside the grim reality of what he was having to deal with, Michael allowed himself a moment of reflection. It was an extraordinary feeling to see the British Army return to France almost four years to the day after their ignominious defeat by the Germans, with the subsequent evacuations from Boulogne, Dunkirk and other French ports. What was even more remarkable was that the same man was in charge for both momentous events.

Michael felt proud and honoured to be able to say that he had met and spent time with Admiral Sir Bertram Ramsay, the man who had saved an army and then returned it to France to fight another day.

The Operations Room at Southwick House was a hive of activity – phones constantly ringing, messages being relayed, signals coming in and going out, a lively buzz of purposeful conversation from up to forty people who could be present at any one time.

Bertie and Alastair sat at the senior staff desk a few yards away from the floor to ceiling wall map which completely covered the far end of the former drawing room. It showed the entire south coast of England and the northern coast of France, where the progress of each ship and landing craft could be plotted hour by hour and monitored. In front of this, a travelling step-ladder enabled the Wren plotters to mark quickly the positions of all units at sea.

Together with the C.O.S., both men had spent most of their time there since early morning, analysing the full import of every signal and comparing it to what they could see developing visually in front of them.

Built by the toy firm of Chad Valley on commission from the Royal Navy, the map was an ingenious method of instantly viewing progress. To maintain secrecy, the entire coasts of Britain, France and the Low Countries had been ordered and delivered, but it wasn't until the wooden map was placed *in situ* that it became clear which portions were to be used, showing the exact locations for the D-Day landings. The two carpenters from Chad Valley responsible for its construction were then obliged to spend the following two weeks living and working at Southwick House in order to maintain secrecy.

They had only just been allowed to go home.

Red lines emanated from the ports of embarkation showing the planned courses for all vessels – assault and reserves – which themselves were represented by wooden tags and little Lego-type ships which could be fixed in position or moved according to progress. Three clocks denoted the time at home and on the continent.

"Sir," a Wren telegraphist approached Admiral Ramsay, "signal from Naval Commander Western Task Force, sir."

"Thank you, Timbers." He read it carefully, then remarked to Alastair, "There are further problems at Omaha."

Alastair was quiet. A number of things had gone very wrong in this area of the American sector. Firstly, for some unknown and unfortunate reason, the pre-assault bombing raid by the United States Air Force had failed to materialize. Secondly, the Americans had decided, for whatever reason, to land an hour ahead of the British. This meant that the U.S. naval bombardment lasted an hour less than it should have done, and consequently, fewer of the enemy strongholds and beach defences were destroyed. Thirdly, the admiral in charge of the Western Task Force chose to set his lowering position for the landing craft twelve miles out from the shore instead of the seven recommended in Admiral Ramsay's operational orders – an action which his appointed position of authority entitled him to take if he felt it was warranted by the current combat situation.

However, on this occasion his judgement was unsound, and consequently, many craft foundered in the rough seas with much essential armour and equipment being lost as a result. In addition, the amphibious tanks and lorries were also launched far too early for the conditions – twenty-seven being lost at sea, eight knocked out by gunfire, and at least ten carrying troops completely swamped. Tossed about in the heavy waves, landing craft ended up on the wrong part of the beach and heavy armour in support of the assault troops never materialized.

"What's happened now?" Alastair asked at length. What else could possibly go wrong?

"They've encountered a crack German division on anti-invasion exercises."

"If I were a swearing man…"

"Quite."

"If they'd managed to land even most of their heavy armour, they'd have had more of a chance. This man has always been troublesome and insubordinate towards you and now he's proved it categorically, creating difficulties for the American troops in the process." Alastair was indignant on his C.-in-C.'s behalf.

Bertie nodded and regarded his supportive and understanding D.C.O.S. with gratitude, though he refrained from commenting himself. Privately though, he knew him to be absolutely correct.

"One feels so helpless," observed Alastair.

"Exactly. But the U.S. infantry are brave and resourceful. They'll have a difficult time, but they'll pull through, you'll see."

262

"It doesn't look good though, does it?"

"Not at the moment, I have to admit." Bertie sighed. "Any further news from the other beaches?"

"We're doing very well on Gold and Utah. Sword have overcome their initial problems and are now making good progress. We're still hung up on Juno though."

"What's happening there?"

"Don't know yet, sir. Communications are down at the moment."

Ramsay's expression became sour, as it always did when he was unhappy about something. "Any more losses to shipping?"

"Not as far as I know. Still just the two destroyers sunk by mines that we knew about earlier, and the armed trawler lost while fending off that E-boat attack."

"Well, considering all things, it's gone much better than we dared hope for. Let me know the estimated casualty figures, navy and army, as soon as you have them."

"Yes, sir."

"Now I must go and prepare for this press conference I have to do later this afternoon. Have Matty come into my office, will you?"

"Yes, sir."

"I know I don't need to say it, but keep me posted. Interrupt me if necessary. I want to know every detail, no matter how small, exactly as it unfolds," said Bertie, moving towards the door.

"Of course," replied Alastair as Ramsay went out of the room.

CHAPTER 37

D-Day (3)
6th June, 1944

There was an eerie silence as the landing craft approached the area on Juno codenamed 'Mike Beach, Red Sector'.

Phillippe felt uneasy. His soldier's instinct told him that this was not good. It was too quiet. He held his breath, every muscle tense.

He had good reason to be concerned. As the landing ramps went down and the first men leapt ashore, all hell broke loose. The Germans opened up with everything they had left after the air and naval bombardments: machine guns, field guns hastily brought up from the rear, rifles and heavy mortars.

Their defensive positions were located in pill-boxes and concrete gun emplacements, with many still operational, and the Canadians, seasick and soaked to the skin, were slow to react, suffering heavy casualties as they struggled up the beach, burdened by their waterlogged backpacks. Landing craft hit submerged mines and exploded, and the soldiers who survived this abandoned their equipment and swam for the shore.

L.C.V.P.s piled up on the beach in heavy surf, carried in on the fast flowing tide. Men became tangled up with the vicious barbed wire before it could be removed with wire-cutters, the sappers working bravely to do so amidst a curtain of machine-gun fire.

It was the first time in combat for many of these inexperienced troops and although they had to learn the hard way, they reacted with bravery and resourcefulness, storming pill-boxes with Sten-guns, small arms fire and grenades.

Until these initial openings were created, the majority remained pinned down on the beach. More and more troops started to arrive, thus adding to the confusion, overcrowding and further severe injuries. Medical personnel were ordered to leave behind their wounded colleagues where they fell, but along with Phillippe, they ignored this command, helping as many as they could.

Then, despite suffering high casualties, one Canadian regiment did manage to break through, outrunning their heavy armour in the process and coming face to face with a German defensive strongpoint. They were about to embark on a difficult frontal assault when a Churchill tank, arriving on the scene, blew a huge gap in the sea wall and fired hefty shells into the bunker system, silencing the enemy guns. The cheers that went up gave heart to everyone, including civilians who emerged from their cellars onto the beach to give their French-speaking cousins from across the water a rapturous welcome.

It was a moment of deep significance for these men and women – the local people who knew they were free at last – that the first thing they heard was the French language being spoken by their liberators. But this was nothing compared to their delight when they saw the Free French insignia on Phillippe's uniform. They wept for joy and hugged him ecstatically. In tears himself, it was everything and more than he could have wished for on his return to his homeland, and allayed any doubts he may have had about an unforgiving reception from the French people towards the French armed forces.

Bottles of long-concealed wine were pressed upon him, but he graciously declined as the brigade he was with had to continue their advance. This was met with understanding, and with great regret the local people bid them farewell.

Men and armour, including more tanks, poured through the ever-growing gaps in the sea wall. However, Phillippe did not witness the chaos on the beach that ensued behind him as successive follow-up waves arrived, unaware of the severe delays experienced earlier. Tanks, self-propelled guns and Bren-gun carriers became embroiled in traffic jams. It was a total mess and gave the Royal Navy Beach Masters serious problems, taking hours to bring order out of extreme chaos.

Phillippe had been assigned to the French-Canadians of the Régiment de la Valeur, who, together with companies of Royal Winnipeg Rifles and North Nova Scotia Highlanders, pushed on ahead to the village of Graye-sur-Mer. They engaged the enemy in fierce hand-to-hand fighting, eventually overcoming all resistance and forcing a complete surrender. Anxious to press on and unable to spare any soldiers to act as guards, their commanding officer told the German prisoners-of-war to make their way to the beach, which they did – obediently and without escort, making no attempt whatsoever to escape, glad to be out of the fighting.

After this, the Valeurs took over the lead in the advance southwards out of Graye, their ultimate objective being, at the end of that first day, to make contact with elements of the British 50th Division at Creully, mopping up whatever resistance they encountered on the way.

As they left Graye, they were joined by a stray platoon of the British Queen's Own Cameron Highlanders, whose L.C.V.P.'s steering had broken and who had found themselves on Juno instead of Gold. There, the Beach Master had directed them to form up with the Valeurs as they were on their way to the British lines.

The next village was Banville, but before reaching it, the Brigade encountered stubborn resistance. Casualties were heavy on both sides as casements had to be stormed and destroyed, but the British platoon, ably led by their sergeant and assisted by "C" Company, Royal Winnipeg Rifles, proved to be bravely resourceful in helping to secure the area from the enemy. Many medical personnel, including the doctor, had to remain behind to treat the wounded, both Canadian and German – a time-consuming task as many of the injuries were severe.

The road upon which they then marched after Banville headed south-west. It was flat and straight with wheat fields and a few sparse hedgerows on either side. But here, hidden in the corn, the Germans had placed nests of machine guns. They opened fire as soon as the Canadians reached the first position, mowing down the most forward group of soldiers, including the commanding officer. Phillippe hit the ground and crawled forwards on his stomach to see if anything could be done for the men. But it was not possible: they had all been killed outright.

He crawled back towards and then along one of the drainage ditches which ran either side of the narrow road, and in which the soldiers had taken refuge. After the bitter fighting in Graye-sur-Mer and on the outskirts of Banville, the second-in-command was in a highly nervous state and recognized that he was not fit to take charge. Quite correctly, he therefore asked Phillippe, as the most senior officer present, if he would take over the brigade. This he agreed to do and so, by default, Lieutenant-General Phillippe du Laurier found himself once more in command, on D-Day in his native land.

The first thing that Phillippe did was to speak to each company commander and platoon sergeant. He needed volunteers to crawl through the corn, approach the enemy from behind, marking and then destroying each gun position. It was daring and dangerous, but there was no choice if they were to proceed safely. He found there to be no shortage of men who offered to take it on. He outlined his plan in whispered and written instructions so that each man knew his task, using the Q.C.O.H. sergeant to convey his messages.

Commando-style, flat on their stomachs, out of sight of the Germans, the soldiers quietly and quickly slipped out of the protective ditches and worked their way behind the enemy positions. When they were all in place, they let rip with everything they had, ambushing the machine-gunners from behind with grenades, Sten-guns and rifles. The enemy had no time to react: those who managed to survive the onslaught quickly surrendered and were hastily despatched back to the coast under minimal guard.

It was an audacious attack, carried out with great success and sustaining few Canadian or British casualties. It enabled the Brigade to walk down the road in safety, with confidence and faith in the tactical skill of their new C.O.

On reaching an area of woodland, after first sending in scouts to check that it was all clear, Phillippe, tired out himself, allowed the exhausted men to rest and sleep for an hour or two. He posted sentries on their perimeter to keep a sharp lookout for any hostile approach.

The soldiers had by now endured two days of seasickness, followed by hours of fighting and marching with very little respite. They needed food and drink and a chance to recover. Here they were safe for the moment from any further attacks or ambushes. The *Luftwaffe* were conspicuous by their absence, such was the air superiority of the Allies, which extended for one hundred miles inland from the coast – a fact of which Phillippe could not be aware.

He went round the groups of men as they lay recumbent on the ground, offering encouragement here, congratulations there. They looked up at him with no little surprise: it was rare for such a high-ranking officer to speak personally and spontaneously to the ordinary soldier, let alone a *French* general. However, this man was no ordinary French general: the soldiers realized by now that their new commanding officer was someone special.

Finally, after instructing the radio operator to try to report their position and current status to H.Q., with whom they had lost contact following the fighting near Banville, Phillippe took his tea and mess tin and went over to a big Scotsman from the Cameron Highlanders who was sitting on his own, his eyes closed, leaning back against the trunk of an oak.

"May I join you?" asked Phillippe.

266

"Aye, sir, it'd be an honour," replied the surprised sergeant, who immediately stood up and saluted.

"As you were, Sergeant...?"

"MacKellar, sir, Angus MacKellar." He sat down again.

"You did well back there, Sergeant MacKellar."

"Thank you, sir. I never ask the lads to do what I'm not prepared to do myself."

Phillippe smiled. "*Moi aussi.*" The two men sat in silence for a while, eating their food. "I see you walk with a slight limp. An old injury?"

"Nothing that gets in the way, sir. Got it at Dunkirk. Strafed by an *Me110* while I was rescuing an injured friend. Aye, I lost part of my heel. It was nasty at the time, but it's all right now."

"*Bon.* What about your friend?"

"Oh, he's recovered, just. Got invalided out of the army though. Lost a leg. But he manages well enough. We keep in touch."

"He is alive and that is the most important thing, *n'est-ce pas ?*"

"Aye, it is, sir."

"Whereabouts in Scotland do you come from, Angus?"

"Mallaig, sir. Aye, 'tis a fine little town. There is a good view of the Isle of Skye from the harbour."

"I have a Scottish friend who comes from the Isle of Cairnmor." He was careful not to mention Katherine by name. "I meet er... them when they rescue me from Dunkirk."

"So you were at Dunkirk, too, sir?"

"*Oui.* There are many who were," replied Phillippe quietly.

"Aye, that's true." Angus was thoughtful. "Ron and I were rescued by the kindest, bravest people you could ever hope to meet. We became friends." He was careful to keep Katherine's identity secret, just as he had promised.

"I too have become firm friends with my rescuers. They brought me and some of my men across to England in their motorboat on the last night of the evacuation. She is called *Spirit of Adventure*. I should like to go out in her again one day when all this is over." He looked away into the distance, picturing Katherine and Alastair on the last day he had seen them, at St Paul's School in May. Was it only last month? It seemed an age after today, a different world. But war was like that.

Angus stared at the general. "Lieutenant-Commander Alastair Stewart!" he exclaimed, amazed. "He owns *Spirit of Adventure*. Och, he was the man who rescued Ron and me!"

It was Phillippe's turn to stare. Then he threw back his head and laughed. "*Non !* This cannot be possible! *C'est incroyable ! Quelle coïncidence !* But he is my very good friend. He is a captain now. I marry his daughter! He brought you back home?"

Angus nodded, for the moment overcome, unable to say a word.

"There are forces at work about which we know nothing it would seem, drawing us all together. We will have much to talk about, Sergeant. Perhaps soon it will be possible. However, now we must get back on the road if we are to make Creully before it is dark."

After their brief respite, the brigade made good progress and arrived at their destination at about six o'clock that evening, having encountered no further resistance on the way. They approached the village cautiously, but all seemed quiet, and after making a reconnaissance from a vantage point on higher ground, Phillippe could see the welcome sight of a white star painted on the sides of each vehicle and tank.

"Looks like the British have arrived, sir," said Sergeant MacKellar with a profound sense of relief.

"So have we. Just as planned," replied Phillippe. "And the sun has come out to greet us."

"A good omen, sir?"

"Let us hope so, Angus." There had been enough fighting and killing that day.

"Aye, sir."

War was a distressing and horrific business, thought Phillippe, no matter how just the cause. As a high-ranking officer, he had first-hand experience and had studied its cause and effect, but perhaps one day, should he choose to go into politics, he could bring his knowledge to bear in finding realistic alternatives to conflict between nations. He knew that after this war was over, it was imperative that future governments, working together, should create the right conditions for lasting peace and concord between all nations and avoid the constant cycle of greed and quest for power and domination that had blighted the first half of the twentieth century.

However, despite a growing conviction as to how the future should be shaped, Phillippe knew that he was not yet ready to relinquish his commitment to the military – it would be impractical given present circumstances and also, he would be needed to help bring order in the upheaval and confusion that would inevitably follow the end of the war. But he also was aware that for him, politics, like many in his family before him, would be a serious consideration for his future.

Leaving his men in positions of safety at the edge of the town, with instructions to set up camp for the night, Phillippe, together with a few select officers and the platoon of the Queen's Own Cameron Highlanders, approached the centre of Creully and were greeted by the commanding officer and senior staff of the 4th/7th Dragoon Guards, the latter having been first on the scene to liberate the village earlier that afternoon. They stood in the middle of the Rue de Caen, shaking hands, full of smiles.

From his position in the upper storey of an abandoned house, through his binoculars, the German sniper had a grandstand view as the British and Canadians met in the middle of the street. He also saw... what was that? The uniform of a French officer – *ein Heerführer*, no less.

Heute ist mein Glückstag! It was his lucky day! It would probably also be his last.

The rest of his comrades had cleared out earlier before the surrender to the British, leaving him behind, and with the place now crawling with the enemy, he knew he would have little chance of getting out alive. Well, even though he was alone, he would uphold the honour of the Fatherland and his beloved *Führer* one more time.

Carefully positioning his rifle just out of the open window, his eye glued to the telescopic sight, he trained it onto his prey, his finger poised on the trigger. He waited patiently, choosing his moment carefully.

No, no, not yet. He lifted his head up momentarily. Someone had moved in front, obscuring his view of the general. *Wait… wait…* The man moved away and the Frenchman turned to speak to the officer opposite him. *No, no! That was no good, either. Sideways on. Not clear enough.* The marksman began to get twitchy; the waiting seemed interminable. He was becoming afraid of discovery. *Just a few more moments…* Then he saw the general turn to the man on his right, his back an open target. *Now… now.*

Impatient to complete the deed and be away, the sniper pulled the trigger and fired two shots in rapid succession. The first was too high and grazed the shoulder but after the second, he had the satisfaction of seeing his quarry crumple to the ground and everyone rush towards him.

He now had to move fast. This would be his only chance of escape while attention was turned on the Frenchman. Quickly, he withdrew his rifle but in his haste, he was careless and the barrel caught the window.

He backed away into the shadows of the room and headed for the stairs.

Angus MacKellar instinctively looked up the moment General du Laurier was shot and, out of the corner of his eye, saw a glint of sunlight reflected from an open upstairs window in a building diagonally opposite.

He reacted immediately. Fuelled by blind rage and with a surprising swiftness for someone of his build, he ran along the road into the building and up the stairs, meeting the sniper on his way down. Catching the German by surprise, and with no time to use his rifle, Angus clenched his fist and felled his adversary with one mighty blow. He dragged the unconscious body down the stairs, out of the door and threw him onto the pavement, leaving him for the M.P.s to deal with.

Shaking with residual anger and shock, he then ran back to where Phillippe was lying on the pavement, being tended to by a British medical officer. Unheeding of what anyone might think, Angus threw aside his gun, which clattered onto the cobblestones, and knelt down on the road as close as he could get to his general and prayed that he would survive.

Even before he was called to the scene, Michael knew that something was wrong. He had heard two shots ring out and almost immediately someone ran into the *Hôtel*, now commandeered by the R.A.M.C. and established as a hospital, calling for assistance. Michael shouted for two of his team to bring a stretcher and, after grabbing his medical bag, ran out into the street.

First on the scene, he was stunned to see Phillippe du Laurier lying on the ground in a pool of blood, which gradually began to seep further and further along the cobbles. Michael checked his pulse.

Strong. *Good.* His breathing? Shallow and uneven. *Not so good.* He was unconscious. Shock. *Probably, hopefully.*

Quickly, Michael undid Phillippe's uniform jacket and cut away his shirt. There was a blood coming from the soft tissue just below his neck. It was a clean wound and to Michael, it looked like the bullet had, fortunately, merely grazed the skin. Gently, he checked behind and what he saw confirmed his initial assessment. Deftly, he placed a pad on the wound to stem the bleeding.

He jumped as more shots rang out. Everyone around him dived to the ground, but Michael continued to assess his patient: the cause and direction of the gunfire was not his responsibility.

He could see that the wound to the soft tissue was not the only injury; this was not the place where the heavy bleeding was coming from. Until he knew for certain, he would be unwise to move him at the moment.

"Where was he shot?" he asked an officer nearby.

"From over there," replied the man, indicating the building. "In the back."

Shit, thought Michael, his mouth taut and grim, his suspicion confirmed.

He was reluctant to investigate further out here on the street. With any potential back injury, movement had to be kept to the minimum. There would be time enough when they reached the *Hôtel*. He needed to get Phillippe off these filthy cobbles.

Michael turned to his two colleagues who had arrived with the stretcher. They knew exactly what had to be done. With the additional help of a well-built N.C.O. who had arrived a moment or two earlier and had been kneeling close beside the stricken man praying, the four of them gently and carefully lifted him onto the canvas stretcher, trying to keep his body as straight as possible and avoid any unnecessary, jerky movements. Very slowly, they carried him to the *Hôtel*.

Phillippe's eyes flickered and for a moment, he regained consciousness. Although his lips moved, at first he was unable to speak. His hand briefly touched Michael's arm.

"Don't try to talk, Phillippe," said Michael. "We need to get you inside where I can take a proper look at you."

At the sound of his voice, there was a start of recognition in the wounded man's eyes. "Tell Lily…" Wave upon wave of searing pain coursed through him and he cried out in agony. Then, "Tell Lily…"

"I'm not going to tell Lily anything. You can tell her yourself when you're better," said Michael, trying to instil strength into him. But Phillippe had slipped into unconsciousness again and didn't hear him. Michael's eyes filled with tears.

Hastily, he wiped them away with the back of his hand.

CHAPTER 38

France/England
6th-8th June, 1944

Gently, they lifted Phillippe onto a bed in a room on the ground floor of the *Hôtel*, having first removed his clothing. At least the sheets were clean.

Michael, having stayed with the advancing frontline troops since they had landed that morning, had been charged with the task of setting up a temporary military hospital at Creully once the town had been taken by the British. When this objective had been achieved and the enemy had surrendered, having scoured the deserted streets, he had found the hotel to be the most suitable building. Since then, he had been working hard to organize and establish the *Hôtel* as a hospital.

Cleaning and scrubbing the ground floor had been his first priority, and to that end the medical team, with the willing help of local people who had emerged from their hiding places to greet their liberators with euphoria and joy, had worked ceaselessly. Most of the ground floor was now hygienic, presentable and fit to receive the seriously wounded who were too ill to be sent home immediately.

Carefully, he and his medical sergeant turned Phillippe onto his stomach. Michael washed the wound with boiled, cooled water. Having cleaned up the blood, he could better assess the damage. There was no leakage of spinal fluid around the injury but he knew that Phillippe needed to be operated on immediately. Temporarily, he dressed the wound as well as he could.

He was in a very difficult position. Worryingly, neither of the doctors assigned to him had yet arrived at the hotel. Michael assumed they were still dealing with the injured from the landings that morning. He asked his sergeant to send a despatch rider to the Field Dressing Station at Asnelles with an urgent message. Rapidly, he wrote the details. Time was not on their side.

The Q.O.C.H. platoon sergeant was still there, unwilling, it would seem, to leave Phillippe's side.

"Are there any doctors with your brigade, Sergeant?"

"Aye, there were, sir, but they were left behind at Banville. We had a difficult time there. There were many that needed the doctors' attention. They will follow on eventually."

Michael swore profusely in Gaelic.

The sergeant could not help smiling. "Och, I couldn't agree more, sir."

Michael looked at him.

"I speak Gaelic too, sir."

"Just my luck!" said Michael. "Who's the most senior medical person here with your brigade?"

"A second lieutenant, sir."

"Go and fetch him, will you?"

"Yes, sir."

What was Michael to do? He had never performed an operation of this nature. He might do more harm than good. But without an operation, Phillippe would die.

Standing in the corner of the room, he noticed a young woman, one of the local people who had worked tirelessly to help them clean the hotel. She spoke to him in surprisingly good English.

"*Pardon, Monsieur*," she said. "I could not 'elp but hear what you say. We 'ave a *docteur* in the village. He is very old, some say 'e is stupid, 'as gone in ze 'ead." She tapped her forehead. "But I do not think so. I think 'e is very clever. He pretend when ze Germans were 'ere. So, they leave 'im alone and 'e is now still alive. He may be able to 'elp. Should I fetch 'im?"

"Please." Anything was better than nothing.

However, at first, when the old man was wheeled in some minutes later, Michael's heart sank. He was indeed very old. His hands were gnarled with arthritis and he was unable to get out of the wicker chair. But the blue eyes under his bushy white eyebrows were as alive and alert as those of a very young man.

"*Bonjour*," he said. He motioned to Michael to wheel him over to Phillippe and indicated that he remove the dressing. He pulled down the corners of his mouth.

"How long since he was shot?"

"About fifteen minutes."

"Then it is not too late. You must operate. Show me your hands."

Michael did as he was asked. "Now turn them over." They were scrutinized. "*Bon*. They will do. To operate you need sensitive hands. Now, we shall need..." And he listed all the surgical instruments that would be required for the operation. At that moment, both sergeants arrived at the same time.

"Message delivered, sir," said his own medical sergeant.

"Thank you."

"This is Lieutenant Brady, sir," said Angus.

"Well done, Sergeant...?"

"MacKellar, sir, Angus MacKellar."

"Angus? Surely not?"

"Aye, sir."

"Dunkirk, *Spirit of Adventure* Angus?"

"Aye! The very same." What had the General said about things beyond human understanding bringing people together?

The doctor was impatient. "We must get on." He spoke to Michael and Lieutenant Brady. "Go and scrub up. You will each need a gown and mask. *Allez, vite ! Vite !*" He then said something to the young woman in rapid French. She ran out of the room and a few minutes later returned carrying a bottle of whisky. Michael was not impressed. However, he need not have worried. The old man looked at him with a twinkle in his startlingly blue eyes and said, "Almost eighty per cent proof. I was saving it for a special occasion. To save the life of a famous French general – this is special, *n'est-ce pas ?* Now, we must get to work. What symptoms has he presented?"

"He's unconscious. Shock, of course. But he regained consciousness for a moment. He recognized my voice."

"*Bon.* What does this mean?"

Michael experienced a moment of panic. Didn't this man know? "It means that there is little or no neurological damage."

"*Très bien.* Did he do anything else…?"

"He lifted his arm and touched mine."

"*Bon.* Which means…?"

"He has movement in the upper body."

"*Très bon.* You have knowledge. This is good for me to know. Now the bullet is lodged in the…?"

"Lumbar region."

"Which fortunately means that the level of permanent injury is often much less than other areas of the back. But we must work fast. A sniper's bullet is particularly destructive. You will do as I say and follow my instructions absolutely. Once we have opened him up, I will assess whether or not a laminectomy is necessary."

"And that will depend, of course, on what damage has been done to the vertebrae."

The doctor smiled. "*Oui.* And how much pressure there is on the spinal canal and nerves. But we can tell nothing until we see inside. There may be damage to internal organs as well, hence the bleeding."

And so they began. Placing his faith and Phillippe's life in the elderly doctor's instructions, Michael made the first incision. For several hours in a completely dream-like state, he followed clear and explicit directions and the operation proceeded.

Under anaesthetic, Phillippe remained unconscious. His pulse and breathing were constantly monitored by Lieutenant Brady. Once the bullet had been removed and the pressure on his spine relieved, his breathing improved. Although a laminectomy proved unnecessary, repairing the damage caused by the bullet, took every ounce of Michael's courage. It was a delicate and complicated procedure.

After the operation was over and Phillippe had been made comfortable, Michael began to tremble quite violently. His legs gave way under him and he had to sit down.

"*Très bien.* You have the making of a fine surgeon."

"I don't think I could stand the strain!" Michael removed his gown and mask and threw them to one side. He was curious. "I am not being rude, but how do you know so much?"

The doctor smiled wearily at him. "You mean because I am an old man and live in a small village?" He saw Michael's chagrined expression. "Ah, I am not offended. Before the Great War, I trained as a surgeon. Then I was at Passchendaele. There were many instances of soldiers being shot in the back. I have performed many such operations." He was silent, remembering. "After the Great War, I became *professeur* of medicine at the University of Paris at the Sorbonne. After my experiences in the trenches, my specialism naturally became spinal injuries and rehabilitation. So, you see, I have a small knowledge of what was needed today!"

"I don't know how to thank you," began Michael.

"Thank me when he wakes up," he said, indicating Phillippe with a nod of his head. "Now, I am an old man and must go home to sleep. The young lady will fetch me when I am needed. *Au revoir.*"

"*Au revoir, Monsieur.*"

Michael went out of the hotel and into the street, where he stood for a moment, arching his aching back to relieve the tension. Dawn was lighting the sky in the east; it was the beginning of a new day. Then he went back into the building and in the first room that he came to, lay down on the bed and, totally exhausted, fell deeply asleep.

"How did it go? What was it like?" Katherine was excited and wanted to know all about his trip, so after his return from France, she and Alastair set off for a walk in Southwick Park, even though it was late.

"Amazing! Going across on D-Day plus one, who'd have thought it?! That's all. We can go back now," he teased her.

"Not fair! I want to know the minutest details. Everything."

"Well, we drove down to the harbour and boarded the ship."

"That's not what I meant and you know it, you mean person," she replied good-naturedly.

Once they were out of sight of the main house and surrounding encampment, she tucked her arm through his, happy to have him back safe and sound.

Alastair chuckled. "The weather was not very kind on the journey. Like here, it was showery and overcast. The wind was, oh, I suppose a force four or five. It was blowing a north-westerly so the crossing wasn't terribly pleasant."

"The weather's been horrid since the beginning of the month."

"Yes, which made things difficult over there yesterday and again today. Anyway, *Apollo*, being a minelayer, is a good fast ship and we made good progress, finding the number three-four channel easily."

"Did you see the little dan buoys?"

"You're really taken with those, aren't you?"

Katherine smiled. "I have this picture in my mind of all these rows of little green lights."

Alastair tucked her hand closer into his body. "Well, they were there, marking the channel, all behaving themselves on sentry duty."

Katherine laughed. "Go on."

"On the way, we passed hundreds of craft of all shapes and sizes outward or homeward bound. There were lots of Landing Barge Vehicles, you know, the ones used for transporting bulky stores?"

How could she not know? She'd written about every kind of landing craft or barge hundreds of times. There were at least twenty-three different types – their names ingrained forever in her memory. However, that thought was not without a quiet sense of achievement.

"Unfortunately, many had stopped and were seeking help; many had been abandoned," continued Alastair.

"I imagine Bertie was not pleased."

"No, he wasn't. And you and I have got to sort that out tomorrow and come up with an efficient way of dealing with it."

"Great."

"But this was nothing compared to the chaos at Omaha. We arrived off the beachhead at about 1145 to be met with a scene of utter confusion. To start with, the blockships for Mulberry A had just arrived and were hanging about not knowing where to go."

"It's terribly sad to think of those gallant old warships, that must have seen such action in the past, being sunk and used as breakwaters," observed Katherine.

Alastair smiled. "I suppose you could call it their 'final duty'."

"That's a nice thought." She tucked her other arm over his as well. "I suppose, together with the specially-built concrete caissons, they are a good way of protecting the Mulberry Harbours. Without artificial harbours, the Allies haven't a hope of keeping the army supplied until we capture the ports. So, what did Bertie say when he saw all this? I bet his face was a picture!"

"You're telling me. Grim doesn't even begin to describe it! He said, 'Someone needs to tell them what to do; no one's doing anything. Ships and landing craft are just anchored anywhere and everywhere. It's a mess. There's no organization. Nothing's being unloaded on the beaches, there are stranded craft all over the place, and apart from a few bombarding ships firing over there, there's a complete absence of any activity.' He was furious. And when the W.T.F. commander came on board to discuss the situation, he got a sour reception."

"Quite right too."

"Bertie is very aware of the tragic difficulties encountered by the troops the previous day and is totally sympathetic towards them. You and I both know how well he understands the fighting man – navy or army – and the soldiers love him for it. However, knowing the situation was exacerbated by this admiral's unwillingness to listen to advice, and then today, to discover a total lack of any kind of organization… that really went against the grain. However, apart from a few well-chosen barbs, Bertie remained polite but distant, and I hope their admiral took the hint. But we came away from the discussion with none of his anxieties relieved."

"What about the other beaches?"

"Much better. Bertie was considerably cheered by what was happening on Gold and Juno when we visited them. They were both up and running as they should have been and for Juno that is quite impressive, given the terrible problems they had yesterday. Monty came on board then and he seemed cheerful and optimistic about the land battle. He thought it was going well, and although not all of the first day objectives had been achieved, he said the armies had done very well. I thought he looked tired and strained, but that's hardly surprising given the responsibilities he's shouldering."

"For all his quirkiness, he's a remarkable man, isn't he?"

"Absolutely. But we have three remarkable men in the right place at the right time in Eisenhower, Montgomery and Ramsay."

"Not to mention Churchill and Roosevelt."

"One couldn't ever forget them. You know," said Alastair thoughtfully, slowing their pace as he spoke, "I think that the Allies have three very great strengths that will ultimately win us the war – our ability to plan and work together on every level, the exceptionally high degree of training and preparedness of our troops and a very strong conviction that right is on our side – that we have a just cause."

"This really is history in the making, isn't it?" said Katherine, finding inspiration in his words.

"Yes. And we're here, now, living it."

Her thoughts turned to the soldiers and sailors who would bear the burden of liberating Europe from the Nazis, and the thousands of families who had no idea whether or not their loved ones would be coming home. A sudden pain of grief and remembrance, the first for a long time, tightened her chest.

They stopped walking, and as if sensing her disquiet, in the all-enveloping darkness, Alastair turned to Katherine and held her close, stroking her hair.

"We're very lucky," he said, "you and I."

"We are. Very."

And then he kissed her and for several moments, she was lost in the warmth and tenderness of his embrace.

Much later, when they walked into Southwick House, their happiness was shattered as they were greeted with the devastating news that Phillippe du Laurier had been shot and that he was not expected to survive.

"Does the Supreme Commander know yet?" asked Alastair, hiding the shock he felt.

"No, sir."

"Admiral Ramsay?"

"Not yet, sir. You're the first. We've only just received the signal."

"Please may I see it?"

"Yes, sir."

The text was too brief. It told him nothing. "Thank you, Second Officer Wood."

Alastair looked at his watch. It was past midnight. Katherine had discreetly disappeared, as was their habit on the rare occasions they entered the building together at night. He could only imagine what her thoughts were. It was difficult not to be able to comfort her freely and openly. At this moment, he needed that from her, too.

The light was off in Bertie's office. Knowing he must have retired for the night, Alastair therefore asked that a signal be sent to Creully requesting more details, and that an urgent message be left for Eisenhower when he awoke the next morning. He himself would tell Admiral Ramsay. Ever protective of his daughter, he decided that he would wait to contact Lily until he had received further word on Phillippe's progress, or not, as the case may be.

He thought of his friend, so vital, so alive, always brimming with energy. Somehow, he found it hard to believe that he would not survive. He had grown fond of Phillippe. In many ways he had filled the void left by Alex's death. To lose him as well… Quickly, Alastair turned his mind away from the thought before grief overcame him. Nothing was certain yet.

He went into the shaded light of the Operations Room, finding comfort in its muted, nocturnal atmosphere. Alastair sat down in his customary easy chair in front of the wall map, waiting for the reply to his signal. He knew that for him, sleep was now out of the question, so he occupied his time by reading through all the signals that had been sent and received that day during his absence. However, eventually, he did drift off to sleep, to be awoken just before dawn by someone gently shaking his shoulder. The reply to his signal had come through.

After reading it, without saying a word, Alastair got up from his chair and went outside into the grey morning.

It was not good news.

CHAPTER 39

England/France
June, 1944

A couple of weeks later, towards the middle of June, there was a flurry of activity in Creully but nowhere more so than at the hospital. A royal visit by King George VI was expected that very day.

Accompanied by General 'Pug' Ismay, Churchill's chief military assistant and principal staff officer, the King's private secretary, the King's adjutant and his equerry, together with General Montgomery and various high-ranking army officers, as well as Admiral Ramsay and a few members of his staff, the King would be touring the converted hotel before going on for lunch at Monty's camp, which had been established behind the old *château* on the hill overlooking the town. Bertie was to bring the Royal party across to France aboard *H.M.S. Arethusa* and would be responsible for their safe passage home. It was to be a very distinguished gathering.

Michael wanted the hospital to be at its best. As the resident R.A.M.C. medical officer, he was responsible for the day-to-day running of the establishment. He knew he had it well-organized, but he fussed his staff about the minutest of details until the Territorial Army nurses, who had arrived at the hospital soon after D-Day, told him good-naturedly – for Michael was a favourite with all the staff – that it looked cleaner and tidier than a new pin and that he should stop plaguing them, go and sit down with a cup of tea, and read a newspaper. Smilingly, he ignored them, of course, but somewhat calmer, walked round casting a more objective eye over things.

When shown what had been done, his C.O. (the Chief Medical Officer and Surgeon General) was very pleased with his lieutenant's work and said so, before quickly disappearing back into his little office where he seemed to spend most of his time between performing operations reading medical journals, content to leave the hospital in Michael's and Matron's capable and efficient hands.

And so, the time arrived. The C.M.O. had the staff lined up, ready to greet their distinguished guests as they arrived, with he himself performing the introductions. Michael was first in the line and was presented to the King, who asked him how difficult it had been to set up an establishment such as this under combat conditions.

Michael replied, with a disarming smile, that it was a lot easier than it would have been had the town still been occupied by the enemy.

It took the King only a moment to realize the intended humour of this and he said, smiling also, "I can imagine. But even so..."

"Yes, your Majesty. Even so, it was not easy. The Germans had left the building in quite a mess before they were er... rounded up... and it was getting the place clean that was my biggest initial headache."

"Was it you who first realized that this would make a good hospital?"

"Yes, sir. I was sent ahead to find a suitable location."

"You did well."

"Thank you, sir. It's better than a tent in the middle of a field!"

"Undoubtedly, especially with the weather we've been having!"

"Yes, sir."

"To have achieved what you have done in twelve days is quite remarkable. Keep up the good work, Lieutenant Granger."

"Thank you, sir. I shall continue to try my best."

And the King moved on down the line, shaking hands and pausing for brief conversations.

Almost at the rear of the line of dignitaries came Admiral Ramsay, looking relaxed and preferring to take things in his own time. He recognized Michael immediately.

"*Lieutenant* Granger? I see you've given up piracy, then?!"

"I'm afraid I have, sir. There wasn't much future in it, really. Too many parrots and not enough treasure. Some admiral or other, I forget his name... spent the weekend with him once..." He clicked his fingers, pretending to have difficulty in recalling who he was. "Ah, Ramsay, yes that's the chap, suggested I might try other things."

The accompanying adjutant was dumbstruck. Blustering and red in the face, he was about to intervene and stop this wayward, subordinate junior officer from speaking further to the Admiral in this rude and overly familiar manner when Bertie held up his hand and silenced him.

"So this second-rate imitation of a hospital is all your doing, then?" he continued, his lips twitching, but his expression dead-pan.

"Indeed, sir. I apologize profusely. I throw myself at your feet in complete and abject grovelliness." The two men grinned at each other.

"Well, when your substandard work here is completed, and you have spent the requisite amount of time wearing sackcloth and ashes, the recommendation for a staff posting is still there for you, should you wish to take it."

"Thank 'ee kindly, sir. I knew you wouldn't forget," replied Michael, in a perfect West Country piratical accent.

Out of the corner of his eye, Bertie could see that the adjutant was about to have an apoplectic fit, and as he didn't want to be responsible for the man's demise, he felt it was time to move on. He winked at Michael, who was shaking with silent laughter, and carried on down the line, his eyes twinkling with irrepressible humour.

The tour took them round the wards, where the King had many kind words of sympathy and encouragement to say to each of the wounded soldiers, all of whose injuries were too severe for immediate evacuation.

In a single room on the ground floor just off the main ward, there lay one occupant, supported by many pillows, engrossed in a book, his right arm and shoulder heavily bandaged.

Slipping away quietly from the main group, Admiral Ramsay went in to see the man, who looked up at his approach. He smiled.

"Bertie!"

"Bonjour, Phillippe."

"Forgive me for not getting up to greet you."

"No, no." The two men shook hands. "How are you?"

"I can now move my legs. Look," and Phillippe demonstrated, though not without immense effort and quickly disguised pain. "They tell me it's a miracle after only twelve days."

"The fact that you're alive is a miracle."

"I have Michael to thank for that. And the good doctor who guided him to do so comes to see me every day."

"How long were you unconscious? Three days wasn't it?"

"Yes. And when I came round, who should I see sitting beside my bed, telling me some ridiculous story, but Michael. He had spent hours, so I am told, doing just that in the preceding days."

"Well, I had to make sure your head was so full of my nonsense that you couldn't stand it anymore and had to wake up!" said Michael, coming into the room.

Business-like, he consulted the chart at the foot of the bed before taking Phillippe's temperature and checking his blood pressure. He was taking personal responsibility for the Frenchman's day-to-day progress and recovery, supervising his exercise regime and ensuring that he didn't attempt to overdo things. There was now a close friendship and trust developing between them.

"Alastair wanted to come over immediately after it happened, but I'm afraid he couldn't be spared," said Bertie. "We were very worried about you. The signals we received were not very hopeful."

"It was touch and go for a few days," said Michael, his fingers on Phillippe's wrist as he felt his pulse again. "But this man has the constitution of an ox and, despite my best efforts to carve up his insides, he seems intent on getting better."

Gently, he released Phillippe's wrist and smiled at him. All was well. He wrote the figures down on the chart which he replaced at the end of the bed. "It was our lucky day that the local doctor happened to be a spinal injury specialist. How fortunate and coincidental is that?"

"There were many coincidences that day." Phillippe described meeting Angus and the connection with *Spirit of Adventure* as well as the subsequent events in Creully. "I am more convinced than ever that there are forces in life drawing people together at certain times: things we cannot and should not try to explain."

"Alastair and Katherine seem to be the connecting link between all of us," observed Michael.

"They are indeed," said Bertie thoughtfully. "Like Phillippe and your Sergeant MacKellar, the Dunkirk evacuation was where I first met Alastair, and unknowingly, Katherine as well."

"Talking about connections, yours has to be the most remarkable though," observed Michael. "Evacuating the B.E.F. from France and then being responsible for sending us all back again four years later. The war would have been lost without the army being rescued, and the war can't be won without first transporting the army and supplies back across. Talk about the right man being in the right place at the right time!" Michael was delighted to be able actually to say this to Bertie Ramsay, for whom he carried such a high regard.

"I've hardly done it by myself. But I understand what you are saying." With his deep faith and humility, he could see the guiding hand of Providence in this and in so many things. There was so much for which they all had to be thankful.

After a moment or two, Michael brought them back to the present by saying, good-naturedly, "Well now, that's enough philosophizing for one morning." He turned to his patient. "And you, General, are going to take a nap before lunch."

"Oui, Monsieur," said Phillippe, feigning meekness. "I will comply."

"I'm very glad to hear it." Chuckling, Michael turned to Bertie. "I have to say though, that Phillippe here is a model patient on the whole. Stubborn, certainly, and impatient to be up and mobile again…"

"That's understandable."

"… but, he trusts his physician absolutely and the results are there for everyone to see. The prognosis is very favourable too. In addition, Doctor Armand is insistent that Phillippe remains here until *he* says his patient is ready to travel back to England. We've had a bit of a to-do with my C.O. on that score, I can tell you. But *le docteur français* was, and in my opinion still is, an expert in his field. Phillippe will make a better recovery if he remains here at present rather than going back to England to be treated. Besides which, he's not ready physically to make the journey yet."

"When I go home," said Phillippe emphatically, "I want to walk onto the ship that carries me back to my wife and walk into her arms on the other side. Until then, I shall stay here and make my recovery."

Bertie had to admire this man. Here was true courage and fortitude in the face of personal adversity. He wished him well and shook his hand. "If there's ever anything I can do…" he said as he turned to leave.

"There is one thing," replied Phillippe. "When you can spare him, please send Alastair over. I should like to see him very much. He writes every day and I appreciate this greatly. Please tell him I am sorry I cannot answer yet."

"He understands. And yes, as soon as he can be spared, I shall send him to see you." He smiled and said quietly, *"Au revoir, Phillippe."*

"Au revoir, Bertie."

Before he left the hospital, Admiral Ramsay spoke privately to Michael's C.O. and, diplomatically (while being aware that it was actually Michael's achievement), said that he had never seen a more efficiently run hospital and that he would pass on to the powers that be what excellent progress the eminent General du Laurier was making under the commanding officer's care. It was such a relief to know that he would be able to stay here until he was fully recovered and would not have to be uprooted to make the perilous journey across to England, especially with the unseasonal weather and the ever-present threat of E-boats and mines. He was concerned that to do so could jeopardize Phillippe's recovery. He trusted that the C.O. would prevent that from happening. The facilities here at Creully were second to none and, as a personal friend of General du Laurier, he was delighted to see him so well cared for.

Immensely flattered and having fallen under the persuasive spell of the Admiral's charm, the C.O. let drop the matter of his eminent patient's peremptory return to England, and with a total change from his previous obstructionist attitude, welcomed Dr Armand into the hospital and insisted that General du Laurier could remain as long as he wished so that his recovery was complete.

Thus informed a couple of hours later, Michael nearly passed out with shock. He and Phillippe never did find out why there was such a complete *volte-face* on the part of the previously reluctant and difficult C.O.

However, despite Bertie's willingness to send Alastair across, it would be a while before he could be spared. The weather, which had been very unsettled and unseasonal since the beginning of the month, finally erupted into a ferocious gale on D-Day plus thirteen, the like of which had not been seen for forty years. It vented its fury for three disastrous days, slowing the build-up of the invasion forces and supplies to such an extent that Eisenhower was to write after the war that such was the seriousness of the situation, it had endangered the Allies' foothold on the continent.

To make matters worse, the storm blew from a north-easterly direction, which meant that the whole of the Normandy beachhead area was on a dead lee shore, and both there and out to sea, it left such a trail of chaos and destruction as to cause much grief and heartache to many officers and men who had laboured so long and so hard to ensure the uninterrupted flow of *matériel* and reinforcements to their army.

At the height of the storm, the American Mulberry 'A', one of the precious artificial harbours upon which so many hopes were placed, began to disintegrate, partly because it was slightly more exposed to the north-easterly winds than the British Mulberry 'B', but mainly because, in their rush to save time and have their harbour completed before the British one, the Americans had planted their blockships from the outer ends of the breakwater, leaving a large gap in the middle through which the rough sea and abnormally high tides now surged. Thus exposed, the Phoenix caissons filled with water and broke up, and the blockships slewed round and settled so deeply into the mud that the waves broke over the top of them. Piers and roadways vanished, and hundreds of landing craft piled up on the beaches. It was an unmitigated disaster, especially so for the admiral in charge who, following Admiral Ramsay's critical visit, had finally managed to establish greater order and organization on Omaha beach.

Mulberry 'B' off Arromanches fared better as the position of each caisson and blockship had been carefully surveyed by the British before planting or sinking. As a result, they stood their ground and one hundred and fifty-five ships and craft were able to take shelter – even a small amount of stores could be landed. By the time the heavy seas had gone down, Mulberry 'A' was damaged beyond repair, but Mulberry 'B' had survived the onslaught. It was decided to focus all efforts there, especially as on land, the Americans had made good progress and were about to capture the port of Cherbourg at the northern edge of the Contentin Peninsula.

Overall, however, eight hundred vessels were damaged or beached as a result of the storm. The repair organization that had been created by Admiral Ramsay as part of Operation Neptune to deal with such an emergency situation sprang into action, and within two weeks, seven hundred of those vessels were temporarily repaired or refloated. The repairs to Mulberry 'B' were completed a week later and the army could once more be supplied. But it had cost the Allies dearly and planned offensives had to be postponed.

Alastair finally managed to visit Phillippe when he accompanied Bertie across to inspect the damage, on 23rd June. Mines thrown up by the storm had become a real menace, and until this threat could be eliminated, progress near the Assault Area was slow.

After lunch on board the headquarters ship, *H.M.S. Scylla*, they landed on Mulberry 'B' at Arromanches and drove along Gold beach. Craft still littered the sands, including a destroyer which had been mined and driven ashore.

Bertie was critical of the apparent lack of repair work going on, but Alastair made the observation that the storm had only just abated and everyone was possibly in what amounted to a mild state of shock. Bertie agreed, but said pointedly that it was his job to maintain the army whatever the circumstances, and he had to ensure this was carried out as efficiently as possible. Alastair nodded, understanding the concerns that underlay his commander's tetchy mood, knowing that the other British admiral whose direct responsibility it was, should have been working more quickly to see things were set straight.

Bertie continued his inspection while Alastair was driven to Creully to spend an hour with Phillippe. He found his friend relatively cheerful, still making good progress, but in a great deal of pain. After they had greeted each other and exchanged news, Phillippe, hungry for word of his wife, immediately said, "How is Lily? Have you seen her recently?"

"I'm afraid not. With the storm, things have been very hectic and we haven't had a moment."

"I haven't heard from her in days."

"I shouldn't worry. Nothing's been getting through because of the weather. Today's the first." He looked at his friend compassionately. "I spoke to her on the telephone last night to say I'd be seeing you today. She sends her all her love and asked me to say that she misses you terribly."

Phillippe's eyes filled with tears. Alastair saw that beneath the apparent cheerfulness, his friend's spirits were low.

"Will she not go to Mistley House as I have asked her?"

"Not at the moment, I'm afraid. My headstrong daughter and your headstrong wife is refusing to stay with Mary and Mrs Thringle. Says she prefers to be in the Kensington house on her own." He omitted to tell Phillippe that V-1 rocket attacks had started up a week after D-Day and since then had been causing a huge amount of indiscriminate damage and loss of life in London and the Home Counties, or that he was worried about Lily.

"How does she sound?"

"Subdued. Miserable."

Phillippe nodded. "I must go home quickly. We have much to discuss. But Michael tells me that I will do more harm than good if I try too much too soon. It could take months." He sounded despairing.

"What if we were to somehow arrange for Lily to come here?"

Phillippe's face lit up. "That would be too wonderful. The prospect of further separation is not pleasant. It is taking longer than I thought it would to be able to walk. So much for my great and glorious ambition to be able to walk into my wife's arms!"

Alastair smiled. "Bertie was most impressed when you told him that. Hang onto that thought Phillippe, keep it as your goal. In the meantime, I'll see what can be done to get Lily here." His time was almost up. Reluctantly, Alastair had to leave.

"Tell her that I long to see her with all my heart and soul."

"Of course."

"Alastair?"

"Yes?"

"How was she with you?"

"Difficult to tell."

Phillippe nodded with understanding. "Come again as soon as you can."

"I shall. Thank you for your letters. It's good that you're able to write now."

"Thank you for all of yours."

Briefly, Alastair placed his hand on Phillippe's uninjured shoulder before leaving the room. He called in to see Michael on his way out, as Michael had been elsewhere when Alastair arrived.

"It's good to see you," said the younger man, standing up to greet him.

"And you," replied Alastair, though his mood was serious. "What's Phillippe's prognosis?"

Michael took a deep breath. "Well, he has a fifty percent loss of range of motion both forwards and backwards and in rotation from side to side. Put simply, he can't bend over as yet nor twist round, although I'm hopeful these will happen, given the other improvements. Obviously he can't walk yet, but there seems to be no permanent paralysis below or above the lumbar region. He's continent, fortunately, and Lily should... er... have no cause for concern when they are together again!"

"He's lucky then."

"Very. It could have been much, much worse. The bullet lodged in the lumbar region near the pelvis. It missed the spine but was close enough for the trauma to impact on the spinal nerves and surrounding tissue. Our German sniper was having an off-day, fortunately. One bullet grazing the neck and shoulder and the other in the lower back."

"Will he walk again?"

"With rest and careful exercise, yes, Dr Armand believes he will."

Alastair nodded. "Thank you, Michael. Now, I must go, I'm afraid. I'll come again as soon as I can. Katherine sends her love."

"Thank you. Send mine back to her."

"I shall. You're doing wonderful work here."

Michael smiled. "Just doing what I have to do." He stood on the steps of the hotel and waved as Alastair left. He thought his friend looked very tired.

He was, but not as tired as Admiral Ramsay's Chief of Staff. They returned home to Portsmouth to find that he had collapsed during the day and had been rushed into hospital suffering from complete nervous exhaustion.

After Bertie had been to visit him in hospital the following day, and had been told that there was no chance that his C.O.S. would be fit for duty for some time, without hesitation he made Alastair temporarily Chief of Staff, with all the accompanying responsibilities and duties that this entailed.

"And you a mere R.N.V.R.!" Katherine quipped when he told her. She was immensely proud of him and he knew it.

"Less of that," he replied. "I shall give you extra work if you're not careful."

"Yes, sir," she said, batting her eyelashes at him then hastily lowering her eyes to the work in front of her, as someone came into her office with a document to be signed.

However, as Alastair descended the gentle curve of the staircase to his own room, he could not help smiling. Even if the post proved ultimately to be temporary, what a privilege this was. He felt sorry for the C.O.S, of course, but at the same time, he felt excited and energized by the prospect of taking on such responsibility as this.

CHAPTER 40

France (1)
September, 1944

Dear Mary,

So we've arrived at last! Our leave went by all too quickly, but it was lovely to be with you and the children for such a long time, and for all of us to be able go to Cairnmor for a couple of weeks. It was good to see everyone again and for Alastair, Anna, Rupert and I to be able to stay in my old cottage. It needed a deal of cleaning though, didn't it?! Still it didn't take too long with all of us pitching in.

The children loved the freedom and open spaces. And to be able to go onto the beach most days was a real bonus. It's so sweet the way that Rupert and Rose are inseparable, and how protective he is of her – and that Anna seems to take it all in her stride. Remarkably, the three of them get on so well, with very few disagreements. It's good that they are growing up together. Just as we did!

The children have grown so much and seem happy and settled in your care (not to forget Mr and Mrs T) while we're away. Thank you for being so wonderful with them. I feel reassured that you really do love looking after them and that you are content living at Mistley House while Michael is abroad.

After we left you, we went across to the Far Shore, as it's known in Navy parlance, on a destroyer – very exciting – and then transferred to a landing craft (climbing down a scrambling net to get onto one of those is an interesting experience!) before mooring next to one of the piers of the Mulberry Harbour at Arromanches. We were met by a staff car and driven down the floating roadway onto Gold beach – the very beach where Michael landed on D-Day.

I can't tell you what a thrill it was to do all that. I made them stop the car so I could get out and walk along the sand. Alastair came with me, of course, and we were given a guided tour of the harbour and beach. The facilities and organization are amazing and the amount of matériel being handled is just phenomenal, given that there are no wharves or cranes or any of the normal paraphernalia you see at dockyards. They handle about twelve thousand tons of stores a day, double the original estimate. Goodness knows how many hundreds of thousands of men and vehicles have passed through here since June, and are still doing so as we continue to supply the army.

I'm sorry to wax lyrical about this, but I've lived with, written and talked about D-Day, the assault areas and the Mulberry Harbours for so long, that to actually be here, even though it's three months after the event, is just amazing. Conditions outside the blockships and caissons were choppy, but inside the harbour, the water was as calm and serene as a mill pond!

We then drove along to Juno at Courselles, where Phillippe landed, and Alastair showed me the defunct German defence positions. Frightening. They were and are brave men who had to face and are still facing the enemy.

We called in at the hospital on our way – and I have the best news to tell you! Phillippe is now walking and is making such good progress that his doctor says he can return home. A new department for spinal injuries has just been set up at Stoke Mandeville Military Hospital in Aylesbury where arrangements have been made for Phillippe to continue his treatment. Apparently it's quite revolutionary and new, but follows on well from the rehabilitation programme that Dr Armand has been carrying out.

Phillippe is now busy making preparations as he is obviously anxious to go to England and be with Lily, especially as she wasn't able to come over here. Michael will be bringing him across within the next week or so, where he'll be settling him and overseeing his recovery for a while. He'll be in England for a month in order to do this, which is lovely news for the both of you (I understand he's already written to you about this).

Michael is looking well and sends all his love to you and Rose. We had an exclusive guided tour of his hospital. He's doing a fantastic job, Mary. You have every reason to feel proud of him, and he looks very distinguished in his new captain's uniform, proudly sporting the three pips on his shoulder straps!

I had to stop myself from shedding a few tears when I saw Phillippe as he walked across the room to greet us. He gave me such a wonderful hug. He looks very well, all things considered, though much older and thinner, with some greying around the temples. But his personality and his zest for life seem unchanged, and he and Michael have struck up such a friendship that in many ways, Phillippe seems to have filled something of the gap left by Alex – for Michael as well as Alastair. We had lunch with them, which was lovely.

Phillippe is a great favourite with the local people and the Hôtel is never short of eggs, cheese or butter. They seem to have adopted him and the hospital as the focus of the village. Michael told us afterwards that they are quite heartbroken by the prospect of their most famous resident leaving, and are arranging some sort of farewell party for him. I'd love to go to that. I said to Michael that they should be persuaded to invite Bertie (and us, of course!).

After that, we drove to our new headquarters. Because it's been such a wet summer, the countryside looks lovely and green and is very attractive, with hedgerows and views across to rolling hills. But the roads, since the drier weather's arrived! Clouds of white dust everywhere! We had to keep the windows firmly wound up, which was stifling as it was a hot day. And all along the roads are bombed out buildings and villages. Very sad. But the local people seem to be coping. They prefer freedom to oppression, and, après tout, buildings can always be rebuilt, they say! A real example of French pragmatism.

The place where we're staying and working is quite nice – an old château – but very dark and cold as it's surrounded by large trees, which give an enclosed feeling. I shall miss Southwick House very much. I loved the airiness of it and the way the sunlight streamed in through the windows. But especially my office and my little attic bedroom. It had such beautiful grounds where Bertie, Alastair and I would often go for long walks during the five months that we were there, sometimes with our C.O. not saying much, sometimes using the time to discuss and resolve problems – immense problems, as you can imagine – as well as little niggly ones. Or just generally escaping from the constant pressure.

It was sad for all of us to leave, but even worse for the officers who are leaving us, as we are to be a much smaller group. We've all worked together so well that we had become something of a family. Bertie has a gift for making everyone feel special. He has such a youthful outlook and creates a real sense of companionship with those around him. But watch out if you don't come up with the goods...! Fortunately, neither Alastair nor I have ever been in that position.

When they came to say goodbye to Bertie, a great many of our officers said, "Thank you for having me on your staff, I've enjoyed it so much," almost as though they'd been to a party. He was touched by their genuine expressions of gratitude, remarking to Alastair afterwards that he didn't really understand it as he'd pushed everyone extremely hard during the preceding months.

In the end, after his final press conference and farewell 'do', I think Bertie was quite glad to be gone as he always finds saying goodbye upsetting. He's in Paris at the moment attending a ceremony in which Gen. Eisenhower is presenting a plaque to the city to commemorate its liberation by the Allies. It seems only yesterday that it was D-Day. Look how far we've come in a few short months!

Oh, I must tell you. The Wrens' officer contingent have now arrived, and that makes our party complete. They're all terribly excited at being in France and we all feel very smart in our new uniform – a blue battle dress jacket with shoulder straps, a beret with a badge on the side and – (ta da) – trousers! No more skirts and stockings. Hurrah! It gives so much more freedom. I've always preferred wearing trousers, as you know.

Well, I must stop now. We begin in earnest tomorrow. My new job!

Tell the children I'll be writing soon.

Love from

Katherine xxx

Katherine's new appointment was Principal Administrative Officer with her own department and office. However, Bertie said that even though he had been assigned an R.N.V.R. secretary, he would still need her shorthand skills, provided she wasn't too grand now to do that for him. She'd narrowed her eyes at him and replied that if she was, then it was all his fault as he'd made the appointment. "I suppose you'll want me to act as interpreter as well," she added, her expression mischievous.

"Of course. I only brought you across because you speak fluent French."

"And there's me thinking I was coming to France for a holiday!"

"Now whatever gave you that idea?" Bertie pretended to be incredulous. "I shall work you as hard as ever, if not harder."

"And now that I've been promoted to commodore and appointed Chief of Staff, I shall, of course, do exactly the same," observed Alastair. He winked at her and she laughed.

"Huh!" she said.

"You're welcome."

Bertie smiled affectionately at both of them. "It's good to be here, though, isn't it? If I'm to be responsible for getting the Channel Ports in France up and running and then supplying the army through those ports, *this* is where we need to be. It's no good flying over from England all the time as I have been doing. Although I must admit, it does seem a little strange here at the moment," and he frowned briefly. "Things need to be made a little more homely," he added, before turning his attention to the pile of papers in front of him. "Now onto today's tasks..." and business-like, they set to work.

The army was making such rapid strides into France and Belgium that there was a danger they would outrun their supply line. Le Havre, Dieppe, Boulogne, Calais and Ostend were now in Allied hands, having been captured from the landward side rather than seaward, and with the fall of Dunkirk imminent – a significant moment – this went some way to easing the situation. However, the enemy had done a thorough job in demolishing most of the infrastructure of the ports and there was no equipment powerful enough to lift the fabricated bridges, locomotives and other heavy materials needed by the army on the front line. It would be many weeks or even months before all of them would be fully operational.

At the beginning of September, the port of Antwerp in Belgium was captured intact before the retreating Germans could destroy it, and shortly after moving to Granville, Bertie and Alastair flew there on an inspection visit before going on to a civic ceremony and reception in Brussels. They were impressed by the extent of the docks and the facilities.

"This is just what we need to get the supplies through to the army. Except for the one major problem, of course... Antwerp is seventy miles from the sea and the enemy still holds the entrance to the River Scheldt which leads up to it, as well as all the islands and surrounding mainland."

"And all of it is very heavily fortified," added Alastair.

"Absolutely. So, without capturing all of that, the port is useless to us. Being intact as well makes it doubly frustrating. It needs a quick offensive now to clear out the enemy, then the Allies would be laughing all the way to Germany."

"The war could be over by Christmas."

"I've got a five pound bet with Monty that it will be."

"Let's hope he listens to you."

Bertie's expression was grim. "No one seems to be listening to me at the moment, five pounds or not. Anyway, I couldn't mount an operation from the sea to support the infantry on land if I wanted to. We've lost much of our amphibious capability to other theatres. Even the Royal Marines have had most of their landing craft taken away. No one at Supreme Headquarters seems to have considered what sea power can do to help accelerate the advance towards the Rhine. They're so tied up with their own military strategy that they've forgotten to look at the broader picture."

"We shall have an uphill battle to persuade them."

"Unfortunately, we shall. But persuade them we must, however long it takes."

Phillippe found it much harder than he had anticipated. It was one thing to walk around the hospital, it was something completely different to go on a long sea voyage. Even by the time they had reached Arromanches, a twenty minute car journey from Creully, and embarked on the ship, he was exhausted. Beads of sweat poured down his face with the sheer physical effort and pain. He then found the constant uneven motion of the Liberty Ship difficult to contend with, as there was no regular pattern for him to gear himself to. Michael began to wonder if it was too soon.

"*Non, ce n'est pas trop tôt.*" Phillippe was adamant. "It is not too soon. *Je veux être avec ma femme.* I have been away from Lily long enough. It is time."

They had been given a wonderful send-off. Phillippe had stood on the steps of the *Hôtel* and given a speech to the gathered crowd, replying to that of the Mayor. He promised he would return when the war was over and bring his beautiful wife to see his friends. He thanked them all for their kindness and said that if he had had to spend a long time anywhere recovering, then he could think of no finer place than Creully, among his fellow countrymen. He would be filled with gratitude for as long as he lived, for the care and hope that Doctor Armand had given him, not forgetting Michael's life-saving contribution, without which he "would not be here, my friends, speaking to you today." Phillippe had added that he was overwhelmed by their thoughtful gifts, especially when they had so very little.

"*Vous allez nous manquer !* We are going to miss you," they said as they came to shake his hand.

Michael had helped him into the waiting car, sensing that his friend was about to become emotional, settling him into the front seat. Alastair, Katherine and Bertie stood on the steps and waved as the two men departed, before being invited, as distinguished guests of Creully, back to the Mayor's house for lunch. Here they ate a fine meal (which was probably black market – they didn't enquire too closely), with the Mayor proving to be something of a raconteur, and had a thoroughly enjoyable afternoon.

Some hours later, Phillippe and Michael were leaning against the railings of the ship, watching the outline of the Isle of Wight grow ever larger and more distinct. The Nab Tower cast its welcoming beams over the water and sometime after they had passed its beacon of light, the ship docked in Portsmouth Harbour. For Michael, it was England, his home; for Phillippe, a country that he had always loved, but above all, today, it was the place where he would find his precious Lily.

They showed their passes at the exit to the dock and there, waiting for them just outside the gates, were Mary and Lily. Unhesitatingly, Michael put down his suitcase and medical kit and he and Mary, smiles lighting their faces, ran into each other's arms.

Phillippe and Lily stood for a moment, looking at each other, their hearts beating fast in anticipation. She remained still, waiting, watching while, unaided, he walked slowly towards her and embraced her passionately, not caring that they were in a public place.

"*Ma chérie,*" he whispered into her ear. "*Je t'aime, je t'aime.*"

"Oh, my darling, you've come back to me, you've come back to me," was all she could say, clinging onto him with every ounce of strength that she possessed and giving herself up to the man whom she loved more than anything. If she had been shocked at first by his appearance, if she had been afraid he would not respond to her because of her stupidity, she kept these things to herself, and in any case, from that moment on, neither ceased to matter.

They were brought back to reality by a discreet cough from Michael who, after collecting Phillippe's suitcase and returning the discarded walking sticks to their owner, picked up his own luggage as the four of them made their way to the Grand Hotel, where they were to spend the night.

After breakfast the next morning, with time to spare before they were due to leave for Stoke Mandeville Hospital, Lily sought out Michael, who was sitting in the hotel lounge reading the newspaper.

"Hello," she said.

"Hi, honorary sis," he replied, looking up as she perched herself on the arm of his chair. "What's on your mind?" he asked, sensing her need to talk.

"How much more is Phillippe likely to improve?"

"That depends. Given the progress he's made in the last four months and is still making, I don't see why, with his exercise regime and this new treatment at Stoke Mandeville, he shouldn't reach about eighty, eighty-five or even ninety percent mobility. He'll always have to use a stick and probably experience considerable pain, but his long-term outlook is very good, I'd say. And his life expectancy."

"Life expectancy?" Lily was suddenly anxious.

"Very few patients survive spinal trauma like his beyond a year. The first half-hour is critical and he was lucky that he could be treated within that. The extent of the damage was minimized and we were fortunate to have such a knowledgeable surgeon to hand in Creully. Having survived the operation, and given the fact that he is now regaining his health and strength, his chances of living to a ripe old age have increased a thousand fold."

Lily was silent. Then she said, "I'm expecting a baby."

Michael looked at her in surprise, before his expression became one of great joy. He gave her a hug. "Congratulations! That's wonderful news!"

She promptly burst into tears. He frowned. A terrible thought occurred to him. Surely she hadn't been with anyone else? "It is Phillippe's, isn't it?"

Highly offended, she shot him an angry look. "Of course the baby is Phillippe's! I am not my mother!" she declared.

Michael apologized. "It's just that given your reaction, I wondered if you were hiding some deep, dark secret."

"I wouldn't tell you even if I was. And I'm not."

"I believe you. But why are you so upset? Are you worried in case it will all be too much for you to cope with?"

"Oh no, of course not. I'm anxious that it will be too much for Phillippe to cope with."

"You take it from Doctor Michael, this is the best thing that could have happened. He'll love being a father and it will take his mind away from his injuries – and the fact that he may have to give up his military career, which I don't think has occurred to him yet. I've sort of skirted round the issue so far. It's important that you don't say anything on that score, either. He has to realize it for himself. But as far as the baby is concerned, I think it's wonderful news!" Michael was struck by a sudden thought. "Haven't you told him yet?"

She shook her head.

"Lily!" He was shocked. "You go upstairs this instant, young lady, and tell your husband that he is about to become a father. When you tell Mary and me later, I shall pretend to be surprised."

Lily kissed him on the cheek. "Thank you, Michael." She was silent again, her lovely features creased into a frown.

"Okay, so what else is there, squirt?"

"Beast. It's just that, when I last saw you in January, I made a perfect fool of myself. I still do have difficulty with Daddy and Katherine being together, but I was very wrong to say what I did so publicly."

"I agree. But I'm glad to see you have realized the error of your ways. Have you told 'im upstairs yet?"

"No."

"Then you've got two things to say." Michael smiled at her. "So, go to it, sis! Tell me all the juicy details later."

Lily put her tongue out at Michael, just as she used to do when she was little, but this time she checked first to see that no one was looking, given the clientèle in the worn-out but still vaguely luxurious surroundings of the Grand Hotel.

Phillippe was overjoyed when she broke the news. She sat down beside him on the bed and he kissed her hand. "But this is wonderful, marvellous news! But when is our baby due? Why didn't you write it to me in a letter?"

"Because I wanted to tell you myself, in person. I wanted to see your reaction close up." She was not to be disappointed.

He pulled her down to him and kissed her deeply, caressing her as she lay beside him. He turned to her and grimaced with pain. "I want to make love to you, *ma chérie*, but I cannot as yet. But it will happen, I promise you." He looked at her reassuringly. "The only reason is my mobility, not any other."

Lily laughed, snuggling up to him, happy and content. "I can tell!" She blushed and looked at him impishly, her words tumbling out in a rush. "Perhaps we can explore other things. Experiment. Find different ways that will suit you until you have more movement." Having thus been very frank, she turned her face into his shoulder to hide its colour, which was now a bright shade of red.

Phillippe laughed, enjoying the prospect of her suggestion. With his hand, he gently lifted her chin and kissed her again, very tenderly. "*Je t'aime*," he said. "*Merci, ma femme*. I like this idea very much! And do not be embarrassed. We are husband and wife. There is nothing we cannot share. Now, let me feel our child."

Lily proudly showed him the smooth rounded shape of her body where the growing infant was beginning to show. "Our baby is due in February. Depending upon how long your treatment takes at Stoke Mandeville, he or she might be born

292

in the lovely little cottage that I've found for us just outside Aylesbury," (she was proud of herself for this) "or in London at Cornwallis Gardens. I've sort of adopted that for the time being as my home."

"Have you honestly managed well on your own?" He needed to know this from her, to see if what he had read in her letters was really true.

"Of course. But, I would much rather we had been together. I've missed you terribly and worried about you, and been very miserable and lonely, especially when Daddy wasn't able to find a way for me to come across to Creully because I'm a civilian. But I'm very independent-minded and kept myself busy by organizing things for our life together. Fortunately, I'm able to speak up for myself..."

Phillippe grimaced and put his arm over his eyes to hide his expression.

"What is it?" asked Lily, full of concern. "Are you in pain, darling?"

"No."

"What then?"

He looked at her. "I know this thing only too well!"

"What thing?" She looked puzzled for a moment, then: "Oh," she said quietly. "You mean my outspokenness."

"Oui."

Lily propped herself up onto one elbow, an expression of sadness and regret in her eyes. "I was so horrid to you before you left."

He looked up at her, the corner of his mouth raised in an ironic smile. *"Oui, ma chérie*, you were. I did not like you very much."

"I'm not surprised. I didn't like myself either for a long time afterwards." She stopped. He took her hand. "I shouldn't have said what I did to you then or before, at Mistley House in front of Admiral Ramsay."

"Non."

"I should have listened to you."

"Oui."

"I was very mean that day to my father and embarrassed him in public."

"Oui."

"I was unfair to Katherine."

"Oui. Very unfair." It was time to say more. "And she has not heard from her mother since you wrote to her."

Lily was horror-struck. "But Mhairi has written to me."

"Yes, but not to Katherine."

"What have I done, Phillippe?!"

"Something very thoughtless and cruel." He was totally honest with her.

"But I thought you put everything right when you wrote to Rupert?"

"With him, certainly. But Mhairi would not allow him to write to Katherine. And he is the kind of man that will do as his wife wishes, even if he thinks she is wrong. This I have told Katherine."

"I should have done as my husband wished."

"Oui."

"I realize that now. I am so, so sorry, Phillippe."

"Je comprends."

"Tell me if I ever become headstrong and stupid again and I promise I will listen to you."

"I hope so, *ma chérie*." He pushed her hair back from her beautiful face. "I do not wish to be as miserable as that again."

"No, Phillippe." She was very contrite. "But what do I do now?"

"You will have to find a way to make it right with Mhairi. And you will find that difficult."

"Yes."

"Because, somehow, you will have to overcome your disgust over Katherine and your father being together. Because until you can do that truthfully and honestly, then Mhairi will never understand. You have become another daughter to her, and she has listened to you and been influenced by what you feel. In many ways, she has become closer to you than Katherine. You have spent more time together."

"It's a huge responsibility to put things right."

"*Oui*, and it will not be easy." *This is what maturity means*, he thought. Wisely he kept it to himself. "If it is any help, *chérie*, Alastair and Katherine are truly in love."

"As much as us?"

"As much as us. They are right for each other and very happy together."

"Like us?"

Phillippe smiled. "Yes, like us. They need each other and cannot bear to be apart."

Lily was reflective. "I suppose I should be glad that my father has found real love after the dreadful way my mother treated him for so many years."

"That is a good place to start."

"Katherine always has been on my side. And Alex is gone forever."

"*Oui.*"

She was learning, growing. Just like their child inside her. Phillippe lay back onto the pillow and closed his eyes, allowing happiness to steal over him. Perhaps Lily was the woman of his dreams after all. If so, he thanked Alastair for the gift of such a daughter.

Pain shot through his back and down his legs. He winced at this reminder of his infirmity. He *had* to get well again. For his own sake. For his wife's. But above all, for that of his unborn child.

CHAPTER 41

France (2)
September-December, 1944

Admiral Ramsay and his staff were having difficulties keeping up with the strategies at Supreme Headquarters, despite Bertie's strenuous efforts and copious advice as to the most vital course of action that should be taken next: securing access from the sea to the Port of Antwerp, to keep the army supplied and facilitate progress into Germany itself.

Rather than making the capture of Walcheren and the other islands at the mouth of the River Scheldt his priority, however, Monty had other ideas as to the best way to cross the Rhine, and had persuaded Eisenhower to allow him to attack Arnhem. Unfortunately, for many reasons, including lack of supply and inaccurate intelligence, Operation Market Garden was a major defeat for the British Army and resulted in a heavy loss of life. Yet even after this débâcle, there was still no progress on 'Infatuate', as the operation to seize the estuary of the Scheldt had been codenamed.

Notwithstanding this, Bertie set about planning the offensive with the 1st Canadian Army, who, together with the Royal Marines, would be responsible for carrying out the operation once on land. The amphibious assault was to be mounted from Ostend and directed by Bertie in concert with the Canadian Army Commander. All he needed now were the requisite number of ships and landing craft.

While all this was going on, Bertie and his staff moved from Granville to St Germain-en-Laye in order to be nearer to Paris. This was a beautiful part of the Île-de-France with stunning open views over the River Seine and the French capital, which was only a half-hour's drive away. However, the officers' mess was at Château St-Léger, a terrible place: tawdry, threadbare and dirty, having suffered neglect and abuse during the years of occupation. Just to add to their misery, the senior officers' sleeping quarters were plagued by mosquitoes that proliferated in the large pond close to the château, and they had to beg, borrow or steal nets until the insects disappeared with the onset of colder weather.

The same fate of neglect and misuse had overtaken the Château d'Hennemont, five minutes' walk away, which was to be their headquarters. But, having been sweet-talked by Bertie's flag lieutenant, the elderly lady caretaker did her best to brighten things up when they first arrived by placing flowers in all the rooms. All the same, nothing could disguise the fact that the interior was in a dreadful condition. The once beautiful salons were filthy and littered with rubbish, and there was nowhere to sit or work. The furniture was gilt, and what hadn't been broken by the Nazis before they left was totally inadequate and impractical. It took the staff a couple of back-breaking weeks to arrange everything to their satisfaction and make the place more homely, something that Bertie felt to be essential wherever he was. In the meantime, business had to go on as usual.

Katherine was very taken by this grand building, despite its run-down state, and fascinated by its architecture – a haphazard combination of towers, turrets, and a redbrick and stone façade, that somehow managed to create a satisfying whole. As soon as she had the opportunity, a few days after their arrival, she spent some time wandering around their headquarters and exploring the grounds and terraces.

As she stood looking up at the Château d'Hennemont, she was soon joined by Alastair, who had been watching her from his office window.

"Penny for them," he said.

She smiled, briefly and discreetly touching his hand. "I was just admiring the view."

"So was I," he said, raising an eyebrow at her, "looking at you from up there," and he indicated his room with a nod of his head, "standing out here all alone and looking particularly beautiful."

Her heart beat a little faster and she blushed and touched his hand again.

"Why, thank you, *Monsieur*. You may take me to Paris if you wish, the most romantic city in the world, so I have heard."

"With pleasure, *Mademoiselle*." They laughed. "So, what were you thinking?"

"That in all the time I've been with the Royal Navy, I've lived and worked in some spectacular buildings. Most of them steeped in history and tradition, all of them different, but all very special. This is yet another one – apart from inside, I hasten to add, which at the moment is dreadful."

"Isn't it? We're going to have our work cut out to get it into a habitable state. But I know what you mean about the buildings in general. Being a senior staff member in the Royal Navy is a privileged existence in many ways, and I've always felt very proud to be a part of it."

"I'm trying to savour every moment. This opportunity won't come our way again after the war is over."

"No, it won't."

"And do you know, darling Alastair, the thing that makes it all so special is that we are sharing it, and in the years to come all this will add to the memories that bind us together."

"And keep it alive for both of us."

"Yes."

"You've really come to love the Royal Navy, haven't you?" he said, his voice full of appreciation.

"Yes. I think it's a very special Service and I wouldn't have missed all this for the world. But I love you more," she added sweetly.

Alastair chuckled. "I should hope so." He touched her hand minutely. "I love you more as well," he said, his eyes warm.

"Just as well," replied Katherine.

"Why?"

"Because you're stuck with me now."

"And I can't think of anything more wonderful." And together they walked up the steps, returning inside to resume their work.

In keeping with the naval tradition of giving shore establishments the name of a ship, their H.Q. was given the official title of *H.M.S. Royal Henry* by the Admiralty. Once they were settled, there was a cocktail party to christen the Royal Navy name of the château, and to celebrate having at last got everything shipshape and organized to Bertie's satisfaction.

By the beginning of October, he was flying here, there and everywhere inspecting ports, holding meetings on their condition and restoration at the Admiralty in London as well as on the continent, while still trying to obtain agreement for the attack on Walcheren and the Scheldt to go ahead.

Supreme Headquarters said it had first priority; Montgomery said it did not, and suggested that the Canadians (who came under his jurisdiction within the 21st Army Group) were acting unilaterally. He even protested about the use of landing craft for training.

In desperation, flying in thick fog, Bertie and Alastair travelled to London to the Admiralty in order to obtain the First Sea Lord's approval for Ramsay's policy. In this they were successful, and returned triumphantly to France.

The next day, at a high level meeting at Supreme Headquarters, Monty made the shock announcement that the Allies could take the Ruhr without Antwerp.

"You should have heard Bertie fly at him!" said Alastair to Katherine, after he had returned from this meeting. "I've never seen him so angry! He was eloquent, passionate and brutally frank. He finally let go of the frustration that has been building up ever since we took Antwerp. He kicked up a real stink in front of Ike, Tedder, Leigh-Mallory, Monty, Bradley, General Devers and, most notably, the Chief of the Imperial General Staff, Alan Brook – who was there on a visit – about the faulty strategy that had been allowed to develop, saying that if we had got the Scheldt instead of going for the Arnhem corridor, then the army would not now be virtually grounded for lack of supply, and we would be in a far better position to deliver the final blow to the enemy!"

"Good for Bertie! I wish I'd been there to hear him. How did everyone react?"

"Well, Ike's C.O.S and Tedder gave him very approving looks and after the meeting, both of them, together with Brook, told him that they agreed with him and that it was high time something was said, or words to that effect."

"What happened next?"

"We broke for lunch and held various meetings, at which the lines of operation for Infatuate were set in motion."

"Do you think Monty will be forced to make it a priority now?"

"We'll have to wait and see."

"He's going to be very sore about it."

"Especially after Arnhem, which was his brainchild."

"It wasn't entirely his fault it went wrong though, was it?"

"No. There were many factors, but as he was C.-in-C. of the operation he does have to bear the ultimate responsibility, especially as the original plan was his."

"Which is what would have happened to Bertie if Neptune had been a disaster. They won't replace Monty though, will they?"

"No." Alastair was sure about this. "He's masterminded too many successful campaigns and is acknowledged by everyone as a great military leader, which he is, of course."

Three days later they heard that the 21st Army Group had now '*modified its plan of campaign to give greater priority for the Canadian Army to concentrate on the entrances to Antwerp.*'

When he was told the news, all Bertie said to Alastair was, "Well, that must have been because of my address at the recent C.-in-C.'s meeting." After this modest understatement, he went off for a walk round the pond smiling to himself, his hands clasped behind his back in characteristic fashion.

"Some address!" remarked Alastair to Katherine as they stood at the window of the dining room and watched him. He chuckled. "I think we can definitely say that there goes a happy man!"

"I'm so pleased for him. He's always been convinced of the importance of Antwerp. He's stuck to his guns, whereas a lesser man might have given up."

"Absolutely. But this is going to be a difficult campaign to win. If the Germans have got any sense, they'll hang onto those fortifications to the bitter end. I don't see how they can fail to be aware of the significance of Antwerp as a means of supplying the Allies deep into the heart of Europe."

In the October gales, the Mulberry Harbour at Arromanches was badly damaged. Repairs were quickly in hand but Bertie again used this as a lever to impress upon everyone at headquarters the extreme urgency of opening up the Scheldt.

He and his staff continued to work hard at the joint plan. Only when there was complete Allied agreement would Bertie allow Infatuate to go ahead, as it had to be a team effort and he was very much a team player. It took another month before Monty finally added his approval.

Katherine sat back in her chair with relief. "At last I can get these operational orders out," she said. "How long has it taken us to get this far? Two months? I wonder how many mines the Germans have now planted along the whole length of the river, while certain top brass have been shilly-shallying around? If this had gone ahead in September when Bertie wanted, it would have saved time, energy and probably lives as well."

The battle for Walcheren and the Scheldt did indeed prove to be a hard-fought conflict. Many valuable lives and craft were lost, but the importance of defeating the enemy was instilled into the soldiers and sailors by their commanding officers and they carried out their orders with bravery and resourcefulness. Bertie directed the naval proceedings as planned, but true to his style in a combat situation such as this, he gave his Royal Navy Commanders the freedom to act as they saw fit right from the start. German resistance finally crumbled during the first week of November.

Katherine was quite right in her assessment of the condition of the Scheldt. In the two months since Antwerp had been taken, the river had been filled with mines. After the battle was won, it took more than a hundred and fifty minesweepers three weeks of hard slog to clear the seventy mile channel, until the first supplies were triumphantly unloaded in Antwerp on 28th November.

Soon afterwards, the December gales in turn played havoc with the Mulberry Harbour. But this time, no repairs were carried out. It had served its purpose and was eventually dismantled. This particularly ingenious piece of British design and engineering had proved a vital factor in enabling the Allies to make a success of the invasion, by keeping the armies supplied until a major port was fully operational.

Bertie's delight in the success of the latter was heartfelt but restrained. Now that he could continue to do his job properly, he immediately moved onto his next task.

In between military and naval concerns, the staff at Château St-Léger also found time to relax. On one of his walks Bertie discovered a golf course not ten minutes away, and whenever his duties would allow, he spent much time there. It was his way of keeping fit and unwinding, enabling him to keep his mind clear and alert.

He was made an honorary member, and after one memorable match against the President and Vice-President of the Club, there was a presentation at which he had to make a speech. Forewarned that this might be the case, he asked Katherine to help him prepare his reply *en français*. After this, he and Alastair, whose game had improved immensely during the past year, made an impressive team during pairs matches, usually winning against all comers.

Then there was bridge. Tournaments were organized, rubbers played, and the cold, dark evenings were occupied in friendly competition. But the one game that gave the greatest fun in the bitter weather that followed November into December was… table tennis (or 'Ping-Pong' as Bertie always called it). The matches were fiercely contested, but had everyone in stitches when shots were missed or balls ended up in the most obscure places. Anyone who came for meetings and stayed for supper or overnight found themselves cajoled into playing.

There was one occasion when Bertie held a formal dinner party for two admirals – one French and one American – three generals, one lord, two captains and one commodore (Alastair). Katherine organized the occasion with the help of selected Wren officers, and it was very successful. However, she was dismayed to find that after supper, the illustrious guests, mischievously inveigled by Bertie, had embarked upon multiple games of Ping-Pong.

"You should have stopped him!" she whispered to Alastair.

"Why?" he said. "Look, they're all enjoying themselves!" And he was quite right.

As well as attending official occasions in Paris, there were days free for sight-seeing. Alastair and Katherine made the most of these – visiting the Arc de Triomphe, the Champs-Elysées and Versailles among others, and taking the promised romantic strolls beside the River Seine.

"It's a beautiful city, isn't it?" she remarked late one Sunday afternoon as they travelled back to St Germain-en-Laye after visiting Notre Dame.

"Yes. After the war is over, we must come back for a proper holiday. Your French is excellent. How does it feel to be speaking it while being able to live in France?" asked Alastair.

Katherine laughed. "Amazing actually. I never imagined for one moment that I'd ever come here or be able to make use of the language officially."

"I'm glad Paris is undamaged," observed Alastair, after they had left the city centre. "Whenever I've accompanied Bertie these past couple of months as we've flown around the ports, it's been terrible to see places like Caen and Le Havre in total ruin."

"Cities can be rebuilt," replied Katherine, "but you can never replace the centuries of history and tradition contained in the original buildings. That's lost forever. However, the French seem to be philosophical. *C'est mieux comme ça que pas du tout.*"

"Meaning?"

"It is better this way than not at all. In other words, this is preferable to what they had before."

"Occupation."

"Yes." Then Katherine said, "It's going to take decades to rebuild Europe. The world really will be a very different place, won't it?"

"For everyone."

They smiled at each other meaningfully.

"Yes, my love," she said.

Once they had arrived back at St Germain and left the car, Katherine put her arm through Alastair's and, relaxed and philosophical, they walked up the steps of the Château St-Léger and indoors for the evening meal.

Unfortunately, on the war front, it wasn't all plain sailing for the Allies in their advance. In December, the Germans broke through the centre of the U.S. Army lines in what became known as the Battle of the Bulge. The enemy even threatened Antwerp.

Throughout the second half of the month, Bertie anxiously awaited news of progress. He attended many meetings with senior army commanders, including Monty, who had set up his H.Q. just outside Brussels. This all added to Ramsay's already heavy flying schedule, visiting the ports for which he was responsible.

Bertie was in a difficult position regarding suitable aircraft to carry out these trips, especially in the worsening wintry weather. All the other commanders-in-chief had their own specially fitted-out planes, while he had to rely on borrowing one, or using a small Beechcraft or very slow Dominie. It was a most unsatisfactory situation.

Eventually, he felt obliged to write a heartfelt plea to the Board of the Admiralty for his own aeroplane, given the considerable distances he had to travel, adding that if they expected him to come to meetings in England whenever they requested it (as they had been), without a suitable aircraft, this might prove impossible in the future.

The strategy worked and Bertie was at last given his own plane, a Hudson. At his request, he was also given exclusive use of his favourite pilot, in whose judgement he placed the utmost trust, having come safely through many difficult and dangerous journeys together, often in appalling conditions.

When Katherine questioned the wisdom of his embarking on some of these trips, Bertie replied that, "Lewis will get us there all right." It didn't help her anxiety that Alastair frequently accompanied the admiral and came home with some hair-raising tales of their journeys.

"Do you honestly like flying?" she asked him one day, after he had described a particularly terrifying expedition.

Alastair was silent for a moment before replying. "Let's just say that after the war, I shall only travel by car, train or ship but never by 'plane. Sometimes it's wonderful – like that day when we flew over the Channel ports and saw the sunlight glinting off the sea, and the wide green expanse of the French countryside, as well as the coast of England. You were with us then, remember?"

"I do remember and it's a sight I shall never forget."

"Likewise on my first ever trip, soon after D-Day, when Bertie and I had a fighter escort. That was exciting, I have to say. They were special flights."

"But now?"

"Now, I'm beginning to dread the journeys, especially as the weather has closed in and turned wintry. When it's bitterly cold on the ground, in the air it's excruciatingly so. And the fog. Fog makes flying most unpleasant."

"Do you have to go?"

"Yes, I'm afraid I do."

"I worry about you, and Bertie, every time you go up now."

"Well, it's nearly Christmas. There won't be any flying for a few days I shouldn't think."

"The war won't stop for Christmas though."

"No, but apart from a few meetings here, we shall. And there's the party to look forward to," said Alastair, trying to lift her spirits.

The post, which had been very erratic for a few weeks, arrived with perfect timing on Christmas Eve and meant that everyone was able to open their presents on Christmas morning. These were invariably of a simple nature, but much appreciated nonetheless, and Bertie was delighted with his. He had a scarf from Lewis, his pilot, a book from his secretary, two golf balls from his flag lieutenant, and books from his family. Katherine knitted him some fingerless gloves, as he had often complained of being unable to write properly because his fingers were so cold, and a thick pair of socks to wear with his Wellington boots. Alastair gave him *Sense and Sensibility*, as Bertie had taken to reading Jane Austen during their long flights.

At the morning staff meeting, the admiral wished everyone a "Happy Christmas" and kept it as short as possible so that they could all take a well-deserved day off. Many of the senior staff went with him to the service at the British Embassy Church.

On their return, having checked that all was in hand for the Gala Dinner that evening, to which all the officers on Ramsay's staff were invited (the ratings were having their own), and where formal dress uniform for the gentlemen and evening dress for the ladies were obligatory, Alastair and Katherine ate a quiet lunch together before joining the others in several games of ping-pong, from which Bertie emerged victorious as overall champion. After this, he went out to feed his ducks and geese, feeling sorry for them as the pond was frozen solid, before retiring to his room and putting his feet up for the rest of the afternoon in front of the fire.

The evening was a special occasion with a huge log fire burning in the hearth of the largest salon, and where for the first time, everyone was actually warm. Candles lit the smaller room, where a log fire also burned brightly, and both looked very festive, with a beautifully decorated Christmas tree, boughs of evergreen draped across the mantelpiece and other prominent places, while the crystal chandeliers had been polished until they sparkled. After an excellent supper, Santa Claus made a surprise appearance to distribute presents, and then there was dancing until the early hours of the morning. It was, as Bertie wrote in his diary afterwards, a 'very jolly party'.

Someone produced a sprig of mistletoe and held it above Katherine and Alastair as they returned to their table for a breather, unable to resist staying together for several dances despite their agreed intention that, for propriety's sake, they would limit how many they danced consecutively with each other.

They looked at one another, unsure what to do. "Kiss her!" came the chorus around them, hoping to encourage their highly regarded C.O.S. and P.A.O. to do what everyone had been wanting them to do for ages.

So Alastair obliged, and to everyone's great delight, stood up and brought Katherine into his arms and kissed her on the lips. The cheer that went up from those around them brought tears to her eyes, and she buried her head in his shoulder to hide her emotion at this unanticipated public gesture. Several people said afterwards they thought the two of them ought to get together, as they obviously got on so well and were such good friends. If only they knew, she thought to herself, and smiled at Alastair, who knew exactly what she was thinking.

But neither of them would be drawn, and they continued to follow their path of discretion, mindful of their positions of responsibility within the Service, keeping their relationship a very private one.

Later, when Bertie danced with Katherine, he congratulated her and Alastair on the way they had handled the mistletoe episode. "To have done nothing would have dampened everyone's spirits; to do what you did struck exactly the right note. Oh, and by the way, thank you for the gloves and the socks – they're just what I needed!"

"I'm so glad. Thank you for your presents too, and for what you've just said."

He nodded in reply and whirled her away expertly across the dance floor, before handing her back to Alastair at the end of the dance.

When the dancers were exhausted, they gradually filtered into the small salon, where Katherine took over from the resident pianist to give him a break. More and more people gravitated towards the room, some joining Alastair in leaning against the piano, others, like Bertie, sitting on a chair, or perching on the arms of a sofa. Together they sang Christmas carols and the many songs written since the outbreak of war, now so familiar and uplifting.

Bathed only in the magical, atmospheric glow of candlelight, the singers became absorbed in their own world, enchanted by an evening that was an oasis of warmth and joy in the cold desert of conflict.

It was an occasion upon which to look back and treasure, and a well from which to draw strength during the tragedy that was to come.

CHAPTER 42

France (3)
January, 1945

If the weather was bitterly cold before Christmas, it was even more so afterwards. Initially, on the war front, the news from the Americans was encouraging. However, by New Year's Eve, Bertie was once again concerned and wanted to go further into the situation regarding the defence of the islands north of the Scheldt and south of the Maas in Holland, where the enemy seemed to be concentrating troops, thus endangering Antwerp yet again.

To this end, he decided to postpone his leave and fly to Brussels in order to discuss the situation with Monty and present his plans for naval co-operation in defensive support of the 21st Army Group. He arranged that he, Alastair and Flags would fly out on 2nd January.

On New Year's Day, Alastair found that he had been awarded a C.B. (Commander of the Bath) in the New Year's Honours list, with Katherine discovering that she had an O.B.E. Bertie individually congratulated the several of his staff members who had received honours, each award being commensurate with their rank, and all of them on his recommendation.

When it came to Katherine's turn, she went into his office, ready to impart some news of her own as well.

"Thank you," she said, after he had congratulated her.

"You deserve it."

"I've loved every moment and still do. It's going to be quite hard to let go of all this when the war is over."

Bertie chuckled. "Well, I for one will find it easy to let go. I've held a position of great responsibility for the last five years or so with very little leave and all I want to do now is go home to my wife and family, and retire to my house in the country. I'm nearly sixty-two and I feel I've done my duty. But I have enjoyed the challenges and the creativeness of it. Most of what I've had to do has never been tried before, and things have had to be thought up from scratch, which is all the more exhausting, but at the same time, very rewarding."

Katherine smiled. "No one else could have done what you've done."

Modestly, Bertie acknowledged her praise by saying, "Well, maybe. Now, you said you had some news for me," he said pleasantly, changing the subject.

"Alastair is finally free! So, as soon as the war is over, we shall be married. Will you come to our wedding?"

"I shall dance at your wedding!" Bertie smiled, genuinely pleased for them. "And also, when the war is over, I should like to invite you both to stay with my wife and me in Scotland. The children can get to know each other."

Katherine was surprised and delighted. "Why, thank you. We'd like that very much." She paused before saying, slightly hesitantly, "I've always hoped that we would be able to keep our friendship."

"And we shall."

304

"I'm very glad. Thank you, Bertie," she said.

"What for?"

For a moment she couldn't speak, her eyes inexplicably filling with tears. She just shook her head and smiled.

He winked at her and said, "Now send that husband-to-be of yours in to see me, will you, Matty? There are some things I'd like to discuss with him before we go to Brussels tomorrow."

"Yes, sir. Oh, and Bertie?"

"Yes, Katherine?"

"Will you promise me that you really will take your leave as soon as you get back from Brussels?"

"Can't wait to be rid of me, eh?!"

"Oh no!"

Bertie laughed at her horrified expression.

"No! We'll all miss you dreadfully. It's just that your wife and family must be longing to see you."

"As I am them." He smiled. "Don't worry. I have every intention of going home *very* soon; probably at the weekend if the weather's good enough. The situation in Belgium should have stabilized by then."

That evening, the temperature plummeted several degrees below freezing and conditions underfoot became extremely treacherous. As she was walking down the steps of *H.M.S. Royal Henry* on her way back to the château for supper, Katherine slipped on the icy surface and fell, her left ankle crumpling underneath her with a pronounced 'crack'. Alastair was beside her in an instant but could do nothing to stop her falling.

After being helped inside and examined by the navy surgeon, she was taken to the American Hospital on the outskirts of Paris, where an X-ray showed she had broken a bone in her ankle and would need minor surgery to repair it. Alastair came with her, of course, and spent a few anxious hours pacing up and down the corridor while she had the operation. He was there at her bedside when she came round after the anaesthetic.

"Hello," he said gently, when she opened her eyes.

"I'm so sorry," she muttered groggily. "Stupid thing to do..."

"It couldn't be helped." He took her hand and held onto it. She curled her fingers through his.

"I should have been more careful."

A nurse approached and, having discreetly disregarded Alastair's rapid removal of his hand, said, "Good. You're back with us again." She felt Katherine's pulse and wrote something down on the chart at the end of her bed. Now you just lie still, honey, and I'll go fetch the doctor."

"As if I'm going anywhere," said Katherine, looking down at her leg raised up on some kind of small platform.

In her sleepy state, she chastised herself again. "If only I'd been more careful. What's Bertie going to say? I won't be able to work for a few days at least."

Alastair smiled. "He's more concerned about you and your ankle. He was very worried last night when it happened."

"I know. He was so upset." She closed her eyes again. "I'm thirsty…"

The doctor arrived and said that the operation had been successful but she was not to put any weight on her leg for the time being, otherwise she would undo all his handiwork. The hospital would supply her with a wheelchair and crutches. "However, I know you Brits by now," he said. "Won't be able to keep you away from your duties. You're with Admiral Ramsay, aren't you?"

Katherine nodded.

"Well, he's the worst. Been here several times for courses of heat treatment on his back. Won't rest it though. Carries on working and then goes and plays several rounds of golf. He says it'll be all right – he'll just come back for more treatment in the meanwhile."

Katherine and Alastair exchanged a smile.

"Now, you ought to stay in bed for a week at least, but I guess that's an impossible request; you'll just plague me to go back to work. So that I can get some peace and quiet, you can go home in a day or two. But keep off that leg!"

"Yes, Doctor." When he had gone, Katherine asked, "I've never met him before. How did he know I'd plague him?"

"I told him."

"Meanie."

She had a drink of water and lay back against the pillows. She closed her eyes again and very soon she had drifted off to sleep. Alastair kissed her gently on her forehead and reluctantly returned to the château.

He had a dreadful return journey as it was snowing very heavily. The car slipped and slithered all over the road, and the windscreen wipers were barely unable to keep pace with the rate of snowfall. His driver had to stop frequently to physically clear the screen himself, and by the time Alastair reached the château, it was not worth going to bed. So he sat in his easy chair and worked on some papers, watching the dawn creep over the horizon. Gradually, the snow began to ease until it had stopped falling completely. The clouds cleared away, leaving a fine, clear morning with sunshine and blue skies – perfect flying conditions for their trip to Brussels. The scenery looked magical with the snow sparkling in the sunshine but it was cold, bitterly cold.

After the morning staff meeting, Bertie spoke to Alastair and said that, along with Henderson as planned, he had decided to take Rowell with him to Brussels instead of Alastair. "I'd like you to stay behind and be with Katherine," he added, by way of explanation. "But I shall need you to brief Commander Rowell and take him through the way we planned to handle this meeting. If you come with us to the airfield, then we can do that in the car on the way."

"Are you sure you don't want me to come with you to Brussels?"

"Of course I'd prefer you to be there. We make an excellent team you and I – on and off the golf course! But it will be good experience for Rowell. As we have often remarked in the past, he's a brilliant staff officer with a great future ahead of him. Long after you and I have retired, he'll be the one to watch." Regarding his friend closely, Bertie put his hand on Alastair's shoulder. "I can see that you're

306

torn and I do understand. But Katherine needs you and I need her back at work as soon as possible. She'll recover more quickly if you help her. Hobbling around in this weather is not going to be easy."

"I understand. Well, it's a fine day for flying, anyway."

"Better than it has been!"

They drove to the airfield at Toussous-le-Noble, and by the time they had arrived, everything was clear and settled about the meeting. They got out of the car and Bertie and Alastair stayed behind for a few moments while the others went across to the plane. Admiral Ramsay spotted a camera at the edge of the tarmac, busily filming.

"Those Americans," he remarked, as he put on his flying jacket. "If it moves, they film it. If it doesn't move, they still film it!" He looked across to the camera. "Well, I suppose we'd better give each other a salute. They seem to like that sort of thing."

So with amusement, Alastair saluted his friend and Bertie returned the compliment. They smiled at each other. "See you in a few days," he said, and with that, he turned and walked to the plane.

The Hudson revved its engines and moved forward on the tarmac. It seemed to have great difficulty in taking off and Alastair became rather anxious. About a hundred yards from the end of the runway, it finally struggled into the air. The plane rose to about three hundred feet and banked sharply to the left.

Suddenly, without warning, it went into a nosedive and plummeted to the ground, where it burst into flames.

For Alastair, the world went into slow motion. For no more than a matter of seconds he stood there, stunned, unable to believe his eyes. Then all at once he and everyone else on the airfield started to run towards the wreckage. Fire extinguishers and hosepipes were rapidly brought to the scene and the fire eventually put out. Medical personnel arrived but it was hopeless, useless. Alastair fell to his knees and covered his face with his hands.

There were no survivors.

The Royal Navy surgeon was called from a conference in Versailles and arrived on the scene very quickly, but there was nothing he could do. Deeply distressed, Captain Miller and Alastair looked at each other in utter desolation.

The news spread like wildfire. There was shock and disbelief. No one could believe it; it just wasn't possible. How could it have happened? What could possibly have gone wrong?

As soon as he arrived back at *Royal Henry*, Alastair immediately sent a despatch rider to the American Hospital with an urgent message for Katherine telling her the awful news and letting her know that he was safe. He would be with her as soon as he could, he said.

This message had to be his first priority because Alastair knew that if she heard the news before he could tell her, she would assume he was on the plane, as she would not have known that the plans had been changed. He had to let her know he was all right.

Next, as Chief of Staff, the overall burden of responsibility for overseeing everything in the immediate aftermath fell to Alastair, but it was a terrible time for him. He couldn't think straight: his personal grief was overwhelming and profound, and his mind and body barely able to function. There was an investigation to set in motion, people to contact, funeral arrangements to be made, but Alastair couldn't think of how to begin or in which order things should be done. He responded to people as they spoke to him, but he took nothing in, nor afterwards remembered anything they had said or asked during the lost, grief-blurred hours immediately following the accident.

At lunchtime, Captain Miller returned from the hospital, where he had gone to deal with the sad, and for him emotionally difficult, assignment of liaising with the mortuary. The surgeon had seen some tragic days in his career but seldom one to match this. He knew that without exception, all the staff had been devoted to their C.-in-C. and that everyone, including him, would feel Bertie Ramsay's passing acutely.

His sorrowful duty done, he now returned to the château, and with him from the hospital came Katherine.

Alastair immediately took her into his office, kneeling down beside her wheelchair and resting his head on her lap. It was only then, in the complete privacy of his room with the woman he loved, that he could finally let go of the emotions he had had to keep under control. Katherine, her eyes red-rimmed from her own tears, stroked his hair and comforted him, in the process relieving a little of her own sorrow and heartache.

After this, Alastair somehow managed to find the strength to begin his painful duties, digging deeply into his emotional reserves in order to do so.

That afternoon, he held a meeting for the entire staff and gave them the news officially, haltingly describing the tragic events in the way that he had witnessed them, all the while trying to keep his own emotions in check. But no amount of careful phrasing could soften the blow, nothing could lessen the impact of his words on all those in the room.

He looked at the pale, shocked faces before him as the silent grief from nearly a hundred and fifty people reached him – palpable, tangible – as he spoke.

"This is a terrible tragedy. We have lost forever our beloved Admiral and four other dear friends and colleagues. Many of you have asked me what caused the accident. I'm afraid I cannot answer with any certainty as yet. The sky was clear, the weather good. It may have been the snow last night or the below-freezing temperatures this morning. It could have been a frozen fuel-line or frost on the main body of the plane. Nor can we rule out pilot error. There will be an inquiry, but my feeling is that we shall never know for certain. And in a way, not knowing makes it all the harder to bear. The accident seems so futile, so unnecessarily cruel. Even now, I find it hard to believe that Bertie Ramsay won't just walk in through that door and wonder why we're all still here and not at our desks busy with our assignments." The gathered Royal Navy and W.R.N.S. personnel smiled at this – the picture vivid, the observation real.

"The days ahead will be difficult for all of us," Alastair continued after a pause. "But somehow, we must find the strength to carry on with our tasks, just as the

Admiral would have wished us to do. We must continue with the important work that he initiated until a new C.-in-C. tells us otherwise."

Alastair paused again, taking a deep breath, his eyes filling with tears. "Each of us will remember Admiral Ramsay in his or her own way. He had a particular gift for making all of us feel that we were special, no matter what our position or rank might be. He created a feeling of companionship that was unique, and I shall remember him as both a great Commanding Officer and as a wonderful friend. We shall all of us miss him acutely and, even when the first phase of grief has passed, we shall none of us ever forget him or all that he achieved. It is a great privilege to have known and served with such a man."

In thick snow, a week after the accident, Admiral Ramsay's coffin and those of his companions were brought to the chapel of *H.M.S Royal Henry* where they lay bathed in candlelight and guarded throughout the night by four sentries: British, French and American, standing with their heads bowed and their rifles reversed.

In silence, the men and women of his staff came to pay their last respects, spending a few final private moments with their friends, but above all with their Commanding Officer who had meant so much to them.

Grieving, Katherine and Alastair stood close together and added their heartfelt contribution to the gathering bank of flowers that surrounded Bertie's coffin, saying their own final, reluctant farewells to a man who had become very dear to them.

The next day, Lady Ramsay and her two small sons, General Eisenhower, the Admiral of the Fleet Sir Andrew Cunningham, the British Ambassador, the French Military Governor of Paris, the Chief of the French Naval Staff, Allied Service Chiefs and French civil authorities, Senior Staff members of A.N.C.X.F. and W.R.N.S. officers all followed the gun carriage bearing Admiral Ramsay's coffin.

Katherine and the other mourners stood in the cemetery of St Germain-en-Laye waiting for the cortège to arrive. She found some small comfort from the fact that Bertie would be laid to rest in such a lovely setting, where the hills sloped gently down towards the River Seine, with open views of the countryside that he had loved wherever he found it.

Beside her and supporting her stood Michael, an expression of deep sadness etched on his face, who had come to say his personal farewell to a man who had inspired him and whom he felt privileged to have known.

They listened as the sound of Chopin's funeral march, played by a French naval band, gradually became louder and louder as the cortège drew near, winding its way along a route lined with British and American soldiers, until finally the procession reached the graveside and the burial service began.

Admiral Sir Bertram Ramsay, together with his four companions, was buried with full naval honours in the country where he had died while on active service, and whose liberation he had done so much to secure.

It was fitting that on the same day in England, at Westminster Abbey, a memorial service was held to which came members of the Cabinet, Allied Service

Chiefs and representatives of the nations who had joined together in the struggle for victory over a common enemy.

Lieutenant-General Phillippe du Laurier was there on behalf of the Free French and sat with tears in his eyes as he listened to the service which strove to honour the man whose work had encompassed both inspired improvisation and consummate planning and execution.

He knew that his friend had served the Royal Navy and the Allies well with his great achievements, and that he was owed an enormous debt of gratitude by everyone in the free world, for Admiral Sir Bertram Ramsay's work was a crucial component in the victory that surely was to come. He would miss him greatly, both as a friend and as a man of unassuming greatness.

As the final moving words of the service were spoken, Phillippe looked up in wonder when the Abbey was flooded with golden light as, outside, the sun suddenly broke through the clouds, illuminating the beautiful vaulted ceilings above, while the pure, poignant notes of the Last Post floated upwards, touching the hearts of all those present.

The Naval Reveille that followed became their awakening: calling them back to their own duty. Then, to the sound of a half-muffled peal of bells, the distinguished congregation left the Abbey, uplifted by the tribute to the inspirational man they had come to honour.

CHAPTER 43

France/England
January-August, 1945

Admiral Ramsay's replacement took over as Allied Naval Commander in the middle of January and met with each of the senior staff members in turn, informing them as to what their next posts would be. Inevitably, there were changes.

The interviews were brief and to the point.

"Good morning, Commodore Stewart," he said, as Alastair entered the room.

"Good morning, sir."

"Now, I'd like to begin by thanking you for the excellent work that you did while you were on Admiral Ramsay's staff."

Alastair wondered what was coming next.

The admiral looked down at the papers in front of him. "I'm sure that you would be willing to continue as C.O.S.," and he looked across at Alastair, who remained silent, "but, as you are probably aware, I shall be wanting to establish my own staff. So, after a period of leave, you are to become Naval Assistant to the Fourth Sea Lord at the Admiralty. In time you'll be sent to sea again, I have no doubt."

In other words, thought Alastair, *they don't quite know what to do with me. If I were R.N., I would have been given a knighthood and made a rear-admiral, but as I'm only R.N.V.R., I can't go above the rank of commodore.* It felt like a demotion, although it wasn't, as the post was traditionally held by a commodore. "I understand, sir."

"Very good. Well, then. That will be all. Good luck, Commodore Stewart." The admiral stood up and offered his hand, which Alastair took, before saluting.

Katherine was waiting outside the room. "Well, what did he say?"

"Naval Assistant to the Fourth Sea Lord at the Admiralty."

"At least you're home." She took a deep breath. "Now it's my turn," and she went into the office.

It seemed strange to see someone else sitting in Bertie's chair, at his desk. Putting aside her crutches, she held onto its corner while she saluted.

"Chief Officer Mathieson, do sit down. How is your knee?"

"My ankle is on the mend, thank you, sir."

"It can't be easy hobbling around." He seemed amused, rather than sympathetic.

"I manage, sir."

"Now, after a period of leave, you are to be transferred to Supreme Headquarters here in Paris. It's quite an honour."

Katherine's heart sank. For her, serving with A.N.C.X.F. had been the greater honour. Supreme Headquarters was a huge, unwieldy organization, as this man would quickly discover. It would be all too easy to become lost in its enormous staff. "What would be my position?"

"You're to be a staff assistant to Admiral Scott."

"*An* assistant, sir?"

"Yes. I believe he has several."

Probably. She would be a very small cog in a very large wheel, serving no useful purpose. Katherine took a deep breath and came to a decision. "Sir?"

"Yes?"

"I appreciate the… honour, but I'd like to request a transfer back to England. You see, sir, I have two young children and I haven't seen them much in the last nine months. I should like to go home for my next posting."

It was time. She needed to be with Rupert and Anna. Alastair would be in England. Above all else, she needed to be with him.

"Well, you are within the conditions of your service to make such a request. Put it to me in writing and I'll see what can be done."

"Thank you, sir." She stood up, saluted, collected her crutches and hobbled her way out of the room.

Letter from Mhairi to Katherine

10th April, 1945.

Dear Katherine,

I'm not sure how to begin this letter. It's not easy for me to put pen to paper after all this time. I've behaved stupidly and irrationally and allowed my moral judgement to overshadow my concern for your happiness.

Lily tells me that you and Alastair are very happy together. I'm glad for you, dearest, but I cannot yet get over the fact that he was once your father-in-law. It seems very odd to me. Perhaps I'm being old-fashioned.

Your father tells me that times have changed, that wartime creates situations that would otherwise not have arisen. He says that if Alex had not died, then you and Alastair would not be together in the way that you are. He also says that right from the beginning, you and Alastair have always had your own friendship, a relationship that was completely separate from the conventional one of father-in-law and daughter-in-law. I believe both these things to be true. I have to, otherwise I could not begin to accept the two of you being together.

I have no right to judge. You were conceived out of wedlock, but I loved your father dearly, therefore I would have gone anywhere and done anything to be with him. Which I did. Which he also did to be with me.

If that is how you and Alastair feel about each other, then please forgive me. Forgive me also for not allowing Rupert to write to you as he wanted. Because of his great love for me, he abided by my wishes.

I regret this period of silence on my part. We took so long to find each other that to risk losing you over my inability to see things in a different light is very foolish. You are a mature woman, capable of making your own decisions and I have to respect and abide by that.

Write to me soon.

Love,

Mhairi

312

Letter from Katherine to Mhairi.

1ˢᵗ May, 1945.

Dear Mhairi,

It was good to receive your letter concerning Alastair and me. If it helps in any way, I ceased to think of there ever having been a connection between us, other than the one we now have, a very long time ago. Alastair and I have been together as a couple for eighteen months, and three and a half years have passed since Alex died. The life we led all that time ago seems like a distant dream. The children are a tangible reminder, of course, but Alastair was always more of a father to them and a husband to me, even when Alex was alive. The bond between us has always been very deep and strong.

Of course, I can assure you there was never even the remotest suggestion of anything untoward between Alastair and me while Alex was alive. But I can look back now and honestly know that I've always loved Alastair, although I didn't realize it at the time as I was so besotted with Alex. Now there's a thought to conjure with.

Yes, we've flown in the face of convention. Yes, we've crossed invisible lines. But we've always been discreet, have never flaunted our relationship, and have told very few people. I am in truth more married to Alastair than I ever was to Alex and I really do not care that he was once my father-in-law. That means nothing to us now.

I hope you will understand when I say I have been upset and hurt by your silence. But I'm glad you feel that at last that you can accept us.

The war will be over soon and then Alastair and I will be married. It will be a quiet occasion in a Registry Office, but that will suit us very well.

Love from Katherine

Soon after Katherine received her mother's letter, Phillippe and Lily were invited by friends to Claridge's for a dinner dance. Their little baby daughter was now four months old, and Lily felt confident enough that she could be left with next door's nanny at their house in Chelsea.

Once Alastair and Katherine had returned from France, with both of them now working at the Admiralty, it was only natural that they should take up residence in Cornwallis Gardens. Although Lily had come to accept their situation, it was right that she and Phillippe should have their own place, even though the Kensington house had sufficient room to accommodate them all. She had found for herself and Phillippe a lovely three-storey house in Cheyne Walk.

Éloïse Lily du Laurier had been born, on time and without too much difficulty, in their little cottage in Aylesbury, where they still stayed whenever Phillippe went for treatment at Stoke Mandeville.

She was a beautiful child, smiley and sunny, and her parents doted on her. She was the perfect baby – except at night. She needed little sleep and even after she had been fed, would be wide awake and alert. This Lily found difficult but not so Phillippe, who, because of the continuing pain in his back, was unable to lie down for long periods. Glad of the distraction, he would lift Éloïse out of her cot and

313

keep his precious little daughter amused. Lily would come downstairs in the morning to find the two of them fast asleep in the large easy chair, with Éloïse cradled safely in her father's arms.

On the whole Phillippe's progress was good. His rehabilitation regime was one of exercise, special diet and massage, strengthening and restoring muscle tone while helping the nerves to heal. He still needed two sticks with which to walk, but he could now bend forwards and backwards, and even from side to side. He refused to resign from the army, but knew he was not yet well enough to accept the high-ranking position he had been offered by General de Gaulle in the French Military Government in Paris. Regretfully, he had had to decline, and therefore remained on indefinite sick leave.

It was on a fine May evening, sunny and warm, when they set out for Claridge's. It was good to go out for a meal. Everywhere in London there was a general air of excitement. The war was nearly over.

Phillippe and Lily took a taxi to Mayfair and joined their friends at a large table in the elegant surroundings of Claridge's restaurant. The dining room was crowded and the dance floor already full to capacity. Officers from every Service were there; everyone seemed to be celebrating, some a little too much.

Lieutenant-Commander Edward Stewart was without a ship. He had been called to task over running his destroyer aground after colliding with another vessel in the English Channel. He was to face a board of enquiry, and with his previous record of negligence, it would probably mean the end of his career. He was not a happy man.

It was all Lieutenant Jack Rutherford's fault. If he hadn't been transferred to the Admiralty way back in January, then this wouldn't have happened. Rutherford's replacement had not been as willing or as helpful. Clearly, it was all his fault. Edward considered the matter again. In fact, it wasn't Jack's fault, it was Alastair's. He'd requested that Rutherford be transferred in the first place. Silly old fool.

Edward had had too much to drink. Perhaps Claridge's was not the best place in which to drown his sorrows, but what the hell. At least old Rutherford had agreed to come out with him this evening for old times' sake. No one else had.

Edward sat at the bar, morosely drunk. *Come to think of it, where was Jack? Oh, yes, he'd gone home, hadn't he? Muttered something about needing an early night. Pathetic. Some drinking companion he turned out to be.*

He wandered unsteadily into the dining room, where he spotted… *Good Lord! Lily! Was it her?* He hadn't seen her since she was about fourteen. She'd certainly grown up into a stunning woman. He went over to her table and sat down.

"Lily!" he exclaimed, rather too loudly. "Lily! My little sister."

She was shocked. "Edward?"

"The same." He leaned forwards to give her a kiss but she recoiled from him. "Come on then, Sis, haven't you got a kiss for your big brother? I am your brother still, aren't I, even though Alastair isn't my father anymore?"

"Go away. You're drunk."

"Come on, Sis, just one… on here." He poked his cheek with his finger.

314

"No. Go away."

But he wasn't to be deterred. "Go on!"

"NO!"

He then spotted her wedding ring. "Married, eh?! My little sister married. Who'd have thought it! Who's the lucky bastard then?"

"Someone far greater than you'll ever be."

"Hoity-toity, young lady." Having got nowhere with this, he tried a different tack. "So how's your Daddy? Enjoying life shacked up with his fancy bit of stuff?"

"How did you know? I mean…"

Edward laughed harshly. "So you think of it like that too. Well, well."

Hastily, Lily sought to redefine her unthinking response. "I do not think of it like that."

"Aw, are they in *love* then…" he said, mocking both Lily and the emotion.

She glared at him. "How did you…?"

"How did I find out?" He went to tap the side of his nose but missed and almost fell of the chair. Recovering himself, he said, "Your letter to mother who then told me."

Lily was silent. Once more she had cause to regret her thoughtless and damaging communications of the previous year.

"So, how is the old man?" persisted Edward. "Run out of energy yet? Can he keep up with her?"

Lily was shocked. "Shut up Edward. You'll be overheard. And you're being very rude and insulting."

"Don't you tell me to shut up." Looking at her defiantly, he repeated what he had said, but very loudly and crudely this time. Conversation faded as he carried on. "Commodore Alastair Stewart is having it off with his…" but before he could finish the sentence, Edward found himself being hauled out of his chair, manhandled from the room into the foyer before being summarily ejected out of the front door of the hotel.

In great pain and breathing heavily from exertion, his strength fuelled by anger and adrenaline, Phillippe said, in a voice of unmistakable authority, "Do not ever speak any such words in public again."

Edward stared at him belligerently and overrode his instinct to obey a direct command. "And who the hell are you?"

"I am Lieutenant-General Phillippe d'Artennes du Laurier. Commodore Stewart is my friend, Lily is my wife and you insult them both with your words and bring your position as an officer in the Royal Navy into disrepute." Beads of sweat covered his forehead and he held onto the door frame for support.

Seeing this, Edward looked him up and down and sneered at him, saying: "But you're nothing but a cripple! And a Frog at that. I don't have to take anything from you."

No sooner had he uttered the words, than Phillippe punched him squarely on the jaw and Edward found himself flat on his back on the pavement.

"Bravo, sir," said the Commissionaire. "If you hadn't have done it, I would have. Even if I'd lost my job. Nasty piece of work he is. Been here before.

Disgrace to the Navy. Shall I get someone to call the Military Police, sir? I'll be a witness if you need one."

"Thank you, and yes, please," replied Phillippe, rubbing his knuckles.

He smiled to himself. It had been a long time since he'd done that to anyone. He looked at the foolish man, lying on the pavement, now exploring his jaw tentatively with his hand and struggling to reach a sitting position. Well, he deserved it.

Phillippe watched as two M.P.s took Edward away, bundling him into a van. He gave his statement to the accompanying sergeant, as did the Commissionaire, and once the formalities were completed, he and Lily returned inside to discreetly see what damage, if any, had been done to Alastair's reputation and to restore his good name. It was to prove unnecessary, as Phillippe's prompt action had prevented any embarrassment to his good friend.

In the process of removing Edward from the room, Phillippe rediscovered an inner confidence in his physical ability – a strength that would mark the turning point in his recovery.

By August 1945, the war was finally over. V.E. Day and V.J. Day had been celebrated, with crowds of people out on the streets of London and other major cities up and down the country, dancing and singing with relief and exuberance. Church bells were rung, lights went on in the streets and blackout curtains were jubilantly removed once and for all.

At the end of August, on a lovely summer's day, Katherine and Alastair were strolling down the Mall, her arm tucked into his, having just come away from their investiture ceremony for his C.B. and her O.B.E. at Buckingham Palace. They were enjoying the heady atmosphere that was still in the air, and felt a great sense of pride in all they had achieved.

They walked across Horse Guards Parade and stood in front of the Admiralty building.

Relaxed and happy, Katherine said, "Well, at least neither of us has to go into work today. Even after all these months, I still can't believe our good fortune. You, working for the Fourth Sea Lord, and me for the Director of W.R.N.S., with both of us at the Admiralty."

"It makes me think of Phillippe when he says there are things that are beyond our comprehension: eddies and currents drawing people together." He smiled at her. "We're incredibly lucky."

"Ssh," she said, touching her head and then his.

Alastair chuckled. "What would you like to do now?"

"I know it's out of our way and we'll have to double back on ourselves, but I'd like to have a look at Norfolk House again. Despite being in London, we haven't been back since before we went to Portsmouth."

"Then that is what we shall do."

The building, with its warm red bricks reflected in the sunlight, looked just the same to them as it always had done: very dear and familiar. There were so many memories here, so many people that they had met and worked with, so much they had learned. Including, of course, Bertie Ramsay.

"I'll always miss him," she said.

"So shall I. He was a very special man. I'm very glad we knew him."

"Oh, so am I."

Alastair kissed her lightly on the lips, publicly risking all, outside the very first building where they had protected their privacy and their reputations so assiduously, and yet had been absolutely free to be themselves.

He stood behind Katherine, his arms around her, as they continued to regard the building thoughtfully, remembering. Then he said, "When we're married, where are we going to live?"

She turned round, her face alight with wonder. "When we're married... goodness, it almost doesn't seem possible that it's about to become a reality, does it? I still can't quite believe it. Do you know, I don't mind where we live. It's strange. When I was married to Alex, all I wanted to do was to live on Cairnmor; I was almost *desperate* to live on Cairnmor. But now, it really doesn't matter."

"Do you think that's because you've been away from the island for so long, or because living in so many different places has changed the way you feel?"

Katherine considered. "Possibly both. But I think the real reason is because wherever you are, then that is home."

Alastair kissed her forehead. "I feel the same. But I should *like* to make our home on Cairnmor. Michael and Mary will be there, once he's demobbed from the army. It's a wonderful place for the children to grow up."

"Perhaps we can divide our time between Maybury and Cairnmor – say, spend term-time at Mistley House and our holidays on the island. The children are settled and doing well at their school, and there's so much music going on for them, which they need. We could let Cornwallis Gardens or Lily and Phillippe could live there, while Mr and Mrs Thringle could stay permanently at Maybury, if they wanted to."

"I think they'd be overjoyed. Neither of them is getting any younger and she loves that house."

"So do I. That's one reason why I would be reluctant to give it up permanently. Rupert and Mhairi might even come across from Canada. Oh, Alastair, wouldn't that be perfect? And we could also begin to make the changes on the island that we wanted to before the war. Actually put into practice the results of the survey."

He chuckled. "Yes, it would and we could. So that, my darling, is what we shall do."

"I love you so much."

"I love you, too."

Buoyant and optimistic, they walked to Piccadilly, to the Burlington Arcade. Alastair stopped outside a jewellery shop and Katherine looked at him in amazement, but he just smiled enigmatically and led her inside.

A picture of the Argyle Street Arcade in Glasgow sprang into her mind: the place where she and Alex had bought their wedding rings. Her heart skipped a beat and for an instant, the past intruded giving the present an air of unreality.

Could this really be happening to her? Was it possible that she and Alastair would one day be married? It seemed like a distant dream and yet it *was* real, very real, and she felt gladdened and warmed by its promise and prospect.

317

It felt right as Alastair slipped the chosen engagement ring onto her finger and held it there briefly before kissing it.

She held up her hand to admire the ruby and diamond ring. "Thank you," she said simply. "This is lovely."

Alastair nodded and smiled, unable quite to believe it himself.

"Had you planned this for today?" she asked, as they came out into the bustling, busy thoroughfare, having completed their transaction.

"Oh, yes. I thought it would be just the thing after the Palace."

Katherine laughed. "You are a wonderful man."

"No. It's you who's wonderful. Now, lunch at Claridge's would make this a perfect day. Shall we?"

"Oh, yes please."

Alastair hailed a taxi and off they went.

They arrived at Mistley House late that afternoon. Outside the house they were very surprised to see an R.A.F. staff car and driver. As soon as she heard the key in the Yale lock, Mrs Thringle was at the door to meet them.

"There's an Air Force gentleman in the sitting room. I said I didn't know when you'd be back, but he insisted on waiting and speaking to you personally. I gave him lunch. He's been here since twelve o'clock."

"Did he say what he wanted?"

"No, he wouldn't leave a message. Just said he would wait."

"Thank you, Mrs Thringle." Alastair opened the door and they went inside.

"Hello," said their guest, standing as they entered the room. "I'm Group Captain Robertson."

"I'm Commodore Stewart and this is Chief Officer Mathieson." They shook hands.

"Mathieson?" The Group Captain seemed confused.

"My maiden name."

"Ah, yes, of course. Please forgive the intrusion. Your housekeeper has been very kind, but I wanted to wait and speak to you personally." He paused, smiling broadly. "I have some wonderful news for you both. You see, Commodore Stewart – Chief Officer Mathieson – your son and your husband, Squadron Leader Alexander Stewart, is alive, safe and well, and currently here in England."

Alastair went pale with shock and had to sit down.

Katherine fainted.

CHAPTER 44

Maybury/Aylesbury
August, 1945

When Katherine awoke, she found herself in bed. The evening sun shone into the room, casting a rosy glow onto the floor. Sitting in a chair beside her was Alastair, with concern, care – and what else? – sadness, pain, written clearly in his expression.

"Hello," he said gently.

"Hello," she replied and held out her hand, which he took, kissing the palm, and then taking it in both of his. His eyes were full of tears and tears rolled down Katherine's cheeks in response. She wiped them away. This was not a bad dream, but a very difficult reality that would have to be faced and overcome.

"I'm sorry I fainted."

"It's all right. The Group Captain was somewhat taken aback by both our reactions. I think he had expected joy and delight."

"I feel sick."

"That's not surprising." Tenderly, he stroked her hair.

"How did I get here?"

"You walked." Alastair smiled at Katherine's surprised expression. "Mrs Thringle found some smelling salts and you came round just long enough for me to lead you upstairs and put you to bed. Then you fell asleep."

"I don't remember anything." Her head ached and she felt woozy. "What about the Group Captain?"

"He'd gone before then. He was most concerned."

"Oh, Alastair…"

"I know."

"Do we know what happened with Alex?"

"No, not yet. Apparently, Alex wants to tell us himself, or something like that. I couldn't take it in. I still can't."

"What are *we* going to do, Alastair?"

"I don't know." He shook his head and touched her cheek. "On a purely practical level, we're to meet Alex tomorrow, if you're well enough, at R.A.F. Halton."

"I don't feel very practical."

"Nor do I."

"But I'm glad Alex is alive. I'm so glad he's alive. But I don't want to see him."

Alastair nodded but remained silent. The emotional conflict within them both was indescribably painful: they did not need to express it in words. Both of them knew and understood the implications of the news that had been brought to them.

"I think we have to," he said eventually. "He wants to meet us on 'neutral ground' apparently."

"Why 'neutral ground'?"

"I have no idea."

"What are we going to do?"

"I don't know."

"Please hold me."

"I don't think I should."

Katherine looked up at him, horrified. "Oh no, oh no. You can't do this. You cannot take a unilateral decision about this. It has to be both of us."

"But your husband is alive. He is my son. I am once again your father-in-law. It really would be adultery and all the other things besides."

"Oh, and I suppose Roberta being alive was of no significance?! We neither of us worried about that."

"That was different. The marriage was over."

"But I have no marriage to Alex." Katherine was vehement in her assertion. "I haven't had for the past five years. We thought him dead. We made a new life. In any case, we have been together far longer than Alex and I ever were, before the war or during it. He was always so involved with his work that we were never able to truly establish any kind of lasting depth in our relationship. I wonder now whether he was even capable of that at all. But you were always *there*, in so many ways more of a husband to me than Alex. Even before we were told he was dead. Even before you and I slept together. Looking back, I see that now."

"Perhaps I shouldn't have been."

Katherine was astonished by Alastair's words. "That's a stupid, hurtful thing to say. That's how it *was*, and it made no difference to how I felt about Alex at the time. I saw you as a wonderful friend, whom I loved dearly. You know that."

"Yes, I'm sorry." Alastair chastised himself. "I shouldn't have said that."

"What happened with us after we were told that Alex had died was a natural progression, an inevitable consequence of two people who were very close, who cared for each other. I have never regarded you as some kind of father, even when we first met. To do so would have been abhorrent, unnatural. I love you, Alastair, I'm *in love* with you, and nothing can ever change that."

"I know. I love you too. But, within the law, Alex is your husband and he's still alive. Therefore, I am your father-in-law and you my daughter-in-law."

"Damn the law." She turned away from him, agony piercing every fibre of her being.

"We cannot change those facts. You have a duty as his wife. The children have to know their real father. Alex has to know them."

Katherine turned back to Alastair. "You have always been more of a father to Rupert and Anna than Alex ever was. They don't know him. They think of *you* as their father. They're settled and happy and I don't want to upset their lives and cause them distress and confusion by taking what they do know away from them..."

Katherine stopped speaking, realizing the significance of what she had just said, realizing it was almost history repeating itself – their new situation producing in her the same emotional response that had led Mhairi into deciding to leave Katherine on Cairnmor with her adoptive parents, rather than going to Canada with her and Rupert, whom she had never known.

Immediately, Alastair saw it too. They looked at each other.

320

"And would you deny him and them that chance?" he said quietly.

Sadly, resignedly, Katherine shook her head. She closed her eyes, as if by doing so, she could shut out and ward off the nightmare. "All right, I will meet with him tomorrow."

"We have to. There is no choice."

Bravely, she started to say the words they had not yet expressed: "He is your son, you have to see him. But oh, Alastair…"

"And do you think that I haven't thought about the ramifications of all of this? Of us? Of Alex and you? Of Alex and me?" Distress and guilt made his manner unusually sharp.

"No. Not for a moment." She reached up and stroked his hair. "But, whatever happens tomorrow, stay with me now, tonight. Please."

Alastair sighed, a deep shuddering sigh. He loved her so much. How could he give her up? And yet he knew that he would have to. Duty and, in this case, paternal loyalty and love were writ large in Alastair's make-up.

This was a very difficult, unprecedented situation that they were having to deal with, and he knew there could be no return to the uncomplicated pre-war companionship the three of them had once enjoyed. Alastair could not deny his desire for Katherine ever again, nor his need of her warmth and consolation, just as he knew she needed him. They had shared so much, shared so many experiences together, how could he possibly relinquish her? To do so would tear him apart, would tear them both apart.

Against his better judgement and newly-acquired resolve, he undressed and slipped into bed beside her. Disregarding the inevitable emotional consequences of guilt and remorse, and shutting out of his mind the uncomfortable reality of what they would have to face the next day, he took her into his arms and they made love with a deep-seated, passionate need for each other and a heightened sense of urgency that transcended all other considerations.

Eventually, Katherine fell asleep in his arms, but Alastair stayed awake, just looking at her, never wanting to let her go, holding the moment in his mind forever.

The next morning, Katherine still felt queasy and slightly shaky, but well enough after a morning resting in bed to be able to face what had to be done. To delay would be only to put off the inevitable.

Still on active service, they dressed in uniform and travelled by train to Wendover, where they were met by an R.A.F. car and driver, who took them to R.A.F. Halton. Group Captain Robertson was there to greet them as they drew up at the main entrance to the station building. He shook hands with them both.

"I'm very glad to see you looking a little better, Chief Officer Mathieson. You had me worried yesterday."

Katherine's smile was forced, but she acknowledged his concern. He was a kind man who meant well and seemed genuinely concerned for her welfare. They followed him as he led the way to his office.

A woman dressed in civilian clothes, with auburn hair swept back in a loose knot at the nape of her neck, was sitting by the desk in his office. She stood up as Bill Robertson introduced them.

"Commodore Stewart, Chief Officer Mathieson, this is Doctor Rachel Curtis."

"Mathieson?" Rachel's reaction was the same as the group captain's had been the previous day.

"Yes. When I joined the Women's Royal Naval Service, I decided to use my maiden name."

"Oh, I see." Her words were brief, but there was no mistaking her Australian accent.

The thought occurred to Katherine that Dr Curtis was finding this as much of an ordeal as they were. The silence in the room was tense. Where was Alex? Why was he not here? Why was she here instead?

Bill Robertson cleared his throat. "Please do sit down." He took a deep breath. "Alex has requested that Dr Curtis should speak to you first. Perhaps I should explain. We have been looking after him in the hospital here for the past month, since he returned to England..."

"Returned to England? From where?" Alastair was finally shocked into speaking. "If he's been here that long, why haven't you or he made contact with us?"

"We'll come to that. But, for the moment, I can tell you that I have been acting officially on his behalf. I was stationed for a while in Singapore and we became good friends, although I left before the Japanese invaded. It was me that he found and contacted when he and Dr Curtis arrived in England. Officially, he is still in the R.A.F. and has not yet received his discharge."

Katherine began to feel sick again and the room started to spin. She must have gone very pale, because Group Captain Robertson was immediately solicitous and asked if she was all right.

"I'll be fine," she replied, "but a glass of water would be good."

Dr Curtis eyed her professionally, but offered no advice or help. Alastair seemed rooted to the spot; he could neither speak nor move, but the briefest of glances revealed to Katherine his concern for her. She loosened her collar and tie and took off her hat and her jacket. Naval etiquette would have to be put aside for the moment.

"So, are we to hear what happened?" Katherine wanted to know, to have this over and done with, to know what she was going to do with the rest of her life.

How ironic it was, that just as she was going to live on Cairnmor once again, Alex comes back into her life, scuppering those plans with impeccable timing.

Immediately, she chided herself for being selfish and unfeeling, but at the same time she knew that was not so – her present physical state was testament to that.

Dr Curtis looked at both of them and in a detached, unemotional way, began to speak.

"Alex has been suffering from post-traumatic amnesia as a result of injuries to the head that he received in Malaya from the Japanese. He was very fortunate not to have had permanent brain damage. Many soldiers did. In his case, the post-traumatic amnesia also resulted in what is termed 'retrograde amnesia', which is where a person is unable to recall some or all of their life, and most crucially, their identity prior to the onset. However, new memories of events and present life are remembered and retained."

322

"So what you're telling us is that Alex is safe and has been since 1942, but that he has been suffering from memory loss as a result of his injuries and did not know who he was." Alastair was trying to make simple sense out of Dr Curtis's first words.

"That's correct."

Katherine sat there, stunned. Alex. Alive. All the time. But with no idea of his identity.

"But he can remember things that have happened to him since the injury caused him to lose his memory?" she asked hesitantly.

"Yes." Rachel Curtis was blunt, matter of fact. "There was also evidence of dissociative amnesia – a psychological condition wherein a person, because of stressful or traumatic events, represses the memory of those events. This was where we had to work carefully with Alex, coaxing him gently to release the memories of what had happened and not press him too far in case he suffered a relapse. Eventually he felt strong enough to be able to speak of what had happened.

"So, this is Alex's story. It's not pretty, and difficult as it's going to be, I shall tell it as he did, except that I am recounting it in one go. With him, we gradually, painstakingly, pieced it together over a series of months as he could only cope with small bits at a time."

Rachel shifted her position and took a sip of water. "As you know, Alex was stationed in Singapore during 1940 and 1941. His role during that time gradually evolved from merely being the 'legal eagle' for the British at C.O.H.Q. in Singapore into a Liaison Officer advising and dealing with legal matters for all the Allies present in Singapore and Malaya – the British, the Indians, but particularly the Australians, with whom he got on well.

"Then one day in January 1942, about a month after the Japanese invaded Malaya, he was sent there to investigate the case of a young, newly-arrived Australian recruit, a sapper, who had supposedly deserted his post while under fire. Some idiot of a high-ranking officer decided the case bore further investigation, making a knee-jerk reaction to the information he was given instead of weighing up all the odds and giving it careful consideration. He sent Alex into the jungle to sort it out, a decision which should never have been made. The young recruit in question should just have been held under close arrest and brought back to Singapore. It was not a time for legal 'niceties' in the field...

"The Japanese were advancing rapidly. They had total air supremacy. The *Prince of Wales* and *Repulse* had been sunk back in December at the beginning of the invasion, which meant that the Japs now had freedom of the seas around Malaya and could land anywhere ahead of the retreat and cut off the opposing armies without fear of attack from the sea. The Allied reinforcements were under-trained and under-equipped; morale was generally very low. They were in a fighting retreat and there was chaos and confusion. Very often the soldiers were surrounded and cut off faster than they could withdraw. Communications were in a parlous state. Command and cohesion were disrupted.

"The situation was daily becoming more dangerous. I can only think that Alex's C.O. in Singapore did not have a sufficient grasp of the reality of the combat situation, and that was the reason why he sent Alex into all this mayhem. But that is something we shall never know for certain.

"When Alex and his driver, who was called Dave, reached their destination, there was no sign of anyone. The brigade in question had cleared out. There were signs that the Japs had already been there and left. But there was nothing to indicate that any struggle or atrocity had taken place or that prisoners had been captured.

"Alex and Dave took a different route out of the area, hoping to avoid any possible detection, only to get lost in the narrow tracks and roads that criss-cross the many rubber plantations. Eventually, they found their way back to the main road, only to come across a brigade of Japanese troops nonchalantly making their advance southwards on bicycles.

"However, following them was a column of motorized transport, the front vehicles of which opened fire as soon as they spotted Alex and Dave in their car. Fortunately they missed. They detached themselves from the group and tried to give chase but were held up by the cyclists, who were slow at getting out of the way. Alex and Dave set off across country back among the rubber plantations, imagining the enemy to be in hot pursuit. They drove over some pretty rough terrain and the vehicle was badly damaged before coming to a stop on an isolated track. They had no idea where they were and night was beginning to fall.

"Dave was trying to fix the car and Alex had gone to wet some cloths to try and get a grip on a spanner to remove the sump covering. Suddenly, there was a terrific explosion which blew up the vehicle and Dave, and propelled Alex into the undergrowth, rendering him unconscious. The car had unfortunately stopped in the middle of a minefield – British, Australian or Japanese, no one will ever know." Rachel paused to have another drink of water.

Quietly, and with some difficulty, her mouth dry and her stomach churning, Katherine managed to say, "We were told that a platoon of British soldiers, who had been cut off and lost for days, and who were trying to make their way back to the British lines, found Alex's dog tags after witnessing the aftermath of the explosion. They assumed the owner of these was in the vehicle. That's why we were told it was so absolutely certain that he had died. They said no one could have survived the blast."

"And that's true. If Alex hadn't been going off into the jungle at that moment, then he would have suffered the same fate as Dave." Rachel shivered, the first sign of any emotion up to that point. "You see, Alex had taken off his dog tags and chucked them aside because they were getting in his way while he was helping Dave."

Alastair ran his hand over his face and over his mouth.

A terrible error.

He could hardly bear to think of these things happening to Alex. His Alex. His son. But worse was to come. Rachel spared them no details.

"When he came round, it was dark. He had no idea where he was. He was concussed and without any means of identification. He was thirsty, weak, disorientated. He wandered around aimlessly for hours without a clue as to what he was doing or where he was going.

"In this confused state, he came across a group of British soldiers being held captive by the Japs and unthinkingly, walked right in on them. The details of exactly what happened are still hazy in his mind, which is probably fortunate. We can only assume that, along with the other Brits, he was viciously beaten and left to die. The soldiers must have come back later and shot anyone who was still alive, because Alex saw dead bodies all around him when he came to.

"Alex survived because he was so deeply unconscious that he was hardly breathing, at least that's what he assumes. It could also have been that the soldiers were called away and never got to him." At which point, Rachel lit a cigarette, her hand shaking.

The silence in the room was palpable, broken only by Alastair's exclamation of "Dear God!" as each one of them tried to come to terms with what they had just heard. For Rachel, it was reliving the trauma of Malaya, because every time she spoke of it, it revived the horrors that she herself had witnessed. Time had not yet lessened the impact; it probably never would. For the others, it was the visualization of the unspeakable cruelty of war.

"Alex was the only survivor. Later that day, a Chinese plantation worker from land nearby, bravely came to see if he could help anyone. He found Alex still alive, took pity on him, helped him back to his shack and dressed his injuries as best he could, treating him with Chinese medicine. He also gave him food, water and shelter for a few days until Alex had recovered just enough to go on his way. This man undoubtedly saved his life. However, he couldn't let Alex stay any longer because the man was terrified of the Japanese.

"I stumbled across Alex in the jungle. I was trying to escape from the Japs myself. They had destroyed the field hospital where I had been working – I won't go into details, but suffice to say, it still gives me nightmares. By the time I found him, he was barely alive and hadn't managed to get far from the plantation before collapsing. He couldn't speak and I could find no means of identification. I tended to his needs the best I could and we shared my canister of water.

"The Japs were everywhere. In trying to avoid them, I'd hurt my shoulder and my leg, and couldn't go anywhere, so I stayed with him and we awaited our fate.

"We sat there for hours until eventually, a small party of Aussie soldiers came along, carrying one of their mates on a stretcher. Boy, was I glad to see them!"

Rachel smiled at the recollection of the cheerful, indomitable group that had been her and Alex's salvation, remembering their mutual shock and the surprise of discovery, and the unspeakable relief that neither party were the enemy. She stubbed out her cigarette and continued.

"Their mate died that night, so we covered him with large-leaved ferns and dressed Alex in his clothes, put this guy's dog tags on him in case we were captured and took him with us on the stretcher. I hobbled along as best I could, and miracle of miracles, after two days of hacking our way through the jungle, we came across a small convoy of British lorries that took us all the way onto Singapore Island and straight down to the harbour.

"We were lucky. We were one of the final groups to cross the Causeway. On the last day of January, they blew it up to try to stop the Japanese from getting across the narrow stretch of water that separates Malaya from Singapore. It didn't work of course. The Japs came anyway.

"The last guys across the Causeway were about two hundred and fifty Argyll and Sutherland Highlanders, whom we had seen sitting on a grassy bank when we drove past. We heard later that they were waiting so that they could be the last to cross, which they were, with their two remaining regimental pipers at the head of the soldiers playing 'Heilan' Laddie'. They went down in legend as the last unit to go across, piped all the way by their pipers. How ridiculously British is that?! The Causeway was blown up immediately afterwards."

Alastair sat there in shock. But Alex had survived. His son had survived.

"What happened next?" asked Katherine, her throat dry and her chest tight.

"As I said, our lorry took us down to the dock. There was a general evacuation going on, but there didn't seem to be any sense of urgency, which there should have been, given what was happening in Malaya. We all knew it would only be a matter of time before the enemy reached Singapore.

"There was a ship in the harbour called the *Empire Star* which we found out was headed for Batavia and then Australia. They were busy loading the wounded and some nurses and civilians on board. You couldn't get on without a boarding pass, so the whole group of us went to see the guy who was in charge. It turned out that I'd known him back in Aus when I first joined the army. So I sweet-talked him a bit and he gave Alex and me a pass. I asked for passes for the guys who'd saved us. He would have given us them too, but they said that they were going to stay. It had become personal now as so many of their mates had been killed. They were brave lads, and I never found out what happened to them."

Tears pricked her eyes. Resolutely, she carried on.

"Before we got on board, I promised them I'd let the parents of the boy whose clothes Alex was wearing know that he was dead. Then an air raid started and planes began bombing the harbour and the docks. My Aussie guys waved nonchalantly and headed off back into town. The *Empire Star* weighed anchor and set off for sea, half empty. We were lucky to be on board and for the ship to survive the raid."

Unseen by anyone except Rachel, someone slipped into the room and sat on a chair by the door. Her eyes never left him as she continued to speak.

"Eventually, we arrived back in Australia, where I could begin treating Alex. Not only was his memory impaired, but he had broken ribs and other internal injuries which have since healed.

"Gradually, his memory returned and we were able to piece together the threads of his story. We were brought back here to England by the R.A.F. a month ago. Unfortunately, the journey was too much for Alex and he became quite ill when we got here.

"You see, he is still mentally fragile, with a very low stress threshold, which is why he asked me to speak to you both first. To have to tell of these events again would have been too traumatic for him. Physically, he's not in bad shape now, but he is still taking medication to help him recover from recurrent bouts of the malaria he contracted in the jungle. This can affect his moods and it will take

326

many years before he is fully fit again. If ever." Tears pricked her eyes again, and something in her expression made Katherine turn round.

Alex.

Thin, gaunt, almost unrecognizable and... what was that? Wary.

Alastair was the first to move. He went over to his son, who stood up and allowed himself to be embraced but without seemingly being able to respond.

His father sensed something else in his manner. What was it? Guilt?

Katherine also stood up but she could not move. She was filled with so many conflicting emotions that in the end, with each one blocking out the others, she had no idea what she was feeling. All the time Rachel was watching her, her expression also wary but with a defiant edge.

Alex looked at Katherine and, without preamble, as though he had rehearsed the lines beforehand, said, "I know there are many things to sort out but I should like us to be together. To try to make a new start."

She didn't answer him immediately, but out of the corner of her eye, she saw Rachel wince and Alastair put a hand to his mouth.

Then Alex came over to his wife and took her into his arms and Katherine felt a rush of emotion over which she had no control. For that brief moment only she responded to him. He was her husband, the man she had fallen in love with and married. The man she had thought was dead and who had now, miraculously, been found to be alive.

But after the moment had passed, she felt nothing for him. No warmth. No desire. Nothing.

Unseen by anyone else, Katherine reached out to Alastair with her eyes and saw her pain reflected in his.

CHAPTER 45

Mistley House
September, 1945

My Darling Katherine,

This is the hardest letter I have ever had to write. It will be hard for both of us to bear, but there are things that have to be said and actions that we have to take.

It is very important you understand that I am not leaving you. I could never leave you. I love you with all my heart and soul and for either of us to leave the other would tear us both apart. We know how close we are, what we mean to each other, the wonderful life we have made together.

But, for the sake of all that you and Alex both felt and shared before war intervened and changed everything, you have to give your marriage a chance. I know that you have said to me that you have no marriage. In spirit, that may be so at the moment, but within the law, you are still recognized as husband and wife. That fact cannot be ignored. There is a legal duty and moral obligation here to try and make it work – for your sake, for Alex's sake, for you and me, but above all for the children.

Give it six months.

If, at the end of that time, the marriage is making both of you desperately unhappy, then at least we shall know everything possible has been done that can be done. Then it will be time to speak the truth and you and I can be together for always with a (relatively) clear conscience. We shall have to deal with the consequences, of course, but as a couple we have the strength to do that.

I suspect that Alex will find it all as difficult as you. I also think that he and Rachel are much closer than they have revealed; indeed, you and I both surmised as much when we talked about things after the meeting at R.A.F. Halton. And why should they say anything? It was and is their business, not ours (not yet, anyway). We have not revealed the extent of our relationship. And that is how it must stay for the time being, otherwise there is no chance of anything. You and I are all too aware of the horrendous complications that would arise if Alex found out about us and the whole thing became public knowledge. It doesn't bear thinking about. We are not being deceitful, just protective.

We know that Mrs Thringle is taking all this very hard. As for telling our family, I shall write to Lily and Phillippe, but impress upon them the need for secrecy. Phillippe will understand and I hope that Lily will think carefully before she speaks. Her reaction is likely to be the most unpredictable as she will want to see Alex, although fortunately, that may be difficult at the moment given that Phillippe cannot be left.

We'll wait to tell Mhairi and Rupert until we're certain of what will happen ultimately. I shall leave Mary and Michael for you to tell. These are the only people who know about us now, apart from our very loyal housekeeper and her husband. I am thankful that we remained discreet, even after my divorce.

Please don't worry about me, my darling, although I know you will. I'll be all right. I have no intention of doing anything stupid. I am here if ever you should need me. You know where to find me. If my situation changes, then of course I shall let you know. Don't write for the first month unless you have to. It will be easier (harder) that way.

Alex is my son, whom I love dearly. But I love you more deeply than I have ever loved anyone in my life. I have a duty of care to look after and protect both of you.

The conflict within me is very great (I can only imagine what is going through your mind at the moment) but this is the only way that I can think of for us to honourably resolve the dilemma in which we find ourselves. It isn't a unilateral decision; it is the only possible course of action. It is a very hard rock and an exceptionally hard place. It is somewhere neither of us considered that we would ever be.

Remember, I shall always be here waiting for you. We love each other and nothing can ever change that.

Your very own, Alastair

After Katherine had finished reading the letter, she didn't weep, because she believed and trusted every single word that Alastair had written. But she did compare it to the similar ending of a letter that she had had from Alex while she was living on Cairnmor, written before they were married, telling her who her real parents were and that she was not who she thought she was. Alex had declared then that his feelings for her would never change but they had, and within a very short space of time.

But this was different. This time she knew beyond any shadow of doubt that Alastair's feelings for her would never change, nor hers for him.

Six months. I have to hang on to that.

He was quite correct, of course, that for her to go back to Alex was the only possible course of action. However, for Katherine, it was not because of all that she and Alex had shared, either before or during the time they had been married, but for two different, yet interconnected, reasons.

Firstly, by the simple expedient of her husband's reappearance, Alastair was now once again her father-in-law. Secondly, he was still a high-ranking officer in the Royal Navy with a distinguished career, and until he was released from active service, there was no alternative. Katherine loved the Navy too much and had served too long herself in the W.R.N.S. not to understand the deep disgrace that such a scandal would cause if they ignored convention and went off together now; a scandal that would affect not just themselves but the Service itself. She did not wish for either of them to have to live with that sense of shame.

Alastair had not put any of this in his letter, but she knew him too well not to realize that he would have considered all the implications. She also knew that he would always put her first and not worry for himself or make the latter his *modus operandi.* Therefore, she had to worry on his behalf and be protective of him because of it.

Six months. I shall treat it as a posting.

She put the letter down in her lap. Katherine knew that the man with whom she was truly in love was a very brave man. His war record proved his physical courage and steadfastness. But, did she possess the same kind of emotional and moral courage that he also had in such abundance, knowing that, impossible as it might seem to deal with, Alastair's solution was indeed the only one.

For some time she sat very still and stared unseeing out of the window, thinking and planning until finally, she had decided upon her best approach to the situation in which she was about to find herself.

Carefully, she folded up the letter and put it in the deep pocket of her dress. Then she opened the door of the study and went to the kitchen where, being very thirsty, she drank several glasses of water. She had felt queasy again most of the day, but it had been an emotionally traumatic few days and was therefore hardly surprising.

The doorbell rang exactly at the appointed time.

When she opened the door, Alex was standing on the step. They stared at each other for what seemed to be a very long time.

"Hello," she said warily.

"Hello," he replied, his voice clipped and unfamiliar.

He didn't try to kiss her as he came inside the house and for this she was grateful. Hesitantly, he put his suitcase down in the hall and they went into the sitting room. They stood there awkwardly, neither sure what to do. Alex smiled at her, but there was a bleakness in his eyes.

He's finding this as difficult as I am, thought Katherine. "Do sit down." She sounded as though she was talking to a complete stranger. He *was* a complete stranger.

"Thank you." This was his home. Why was he thanking her?

Six months. Perhaps we can be friends, she thought, watching him.

They sat in silence, not knowing what to say. Then they both went to speak at the same time. It reminded Katherine of the time they were at the ceilidh when they first began to know each other.

Was there anything left of their chemistry, of their former feelings for each other? Did she want there to be?

She had thought Alex dead, had grieved for him for a long time. But eventually, the pain of loss had healed. After that, she had never entertained any hopes or dreams that he might yet return, nor had she ever felt her love for him to be still alive. She really had got over him and fallen in love with someone else. Alastair. His father. A man with whom she shared the deepest bond imaginable. A man with whom she wished she could be, now, at this moment.

Tears filled her eyes.

Seeing her emotion, Alex looked away. He could offer neither comfort nor consolation, nor did he have the inclination to do so. This whole thing was a mistake, a ghastly mistake. Why had he even thought that trying to rekindle their marriage was the right thing to do? And then he'd made matters worse by agreeing to his father's suggestion of a six month trial, causing both himself and Rachel unnecessary pain and uncertainty in the process.

Rachel. The woman who had saved his life, transforming him in the process. He truly had been reborn and he loved her for making that happen.

Katherine belonged to his old life, his old *persona*. To be with her now, at this moment, was a retrograde step. However, because she was legally his wife and because he had to salve his conscience for what had happened in Singapore, he had to try. But exactly how or why he should do so didn't seem very clear at this moment.

He had a headache.

Six months. An endurance test.

Katherine looked at the clock on the mantelpiece, its tick abnormally slow and loud. The children would be home from school soon. *This man is their natural father, but they don't know him. He doesn't know them. They know Alastair as their father. What do I tell them? How do I tell them? They're too little to understand.*

Right on cue, the front door banged. The twins came rushing into the sitting room and threw themselves at Katherine, bouncing on the sofa either side of her.

"Mummy, Mummy! We're home!"

"I can see!" she observed drily.

"I got a gold star for my spellings!" said Anna.

"I got a gold star for my sums!" said Rupert.

"Brilliant, you two. Well done!"

"There's a concert in the village hall next Tuesday. Mr Kalinowski wants both of us to play the piano. Can we, Mummy, can we?"

"Of course you can. What will you play?" She couldn't think at that moment.

"That duet we've been practising, of course. Silly Mummy. What else would we do?" said Anna.

They spotted Alex, sitting on the other settee, a pained expression on his face.

"Hello," said Anna.

"Who are you?" said Rupert.

Alex looked at Katherine, panic-stricken. He didn't know what to say, how to respond. Could these boisterous – how old were they? six, seven, eight? he couldn't remember – unruly children really be the babies he left behind?

Taking a deep breath, Katherine said quickly, "This is Alex, your... your... father. He's come to live with us."

"You mean like Mary and Rose do sometimes and then they go back to their home or live with Michael when he's on leave?" asked Anna, her head on one side, regarding Alex with an open gaze.

"Something like that." Katherine's heart started to pound. This was uncomfortable, difficult.

"Oh," said Anna, the whole concept of him being her father going over her head as she didn't understand it. "Well, whatever you are, I shall call you Alex."

"You're not any sort of father," declared Rupert decisively. "Daddad is though. He's in charge of lots of ships," he solemnly informed Alex. "But soon, he'll be back home with us forever because he's going to retire from the Royal Navy. He told me so. He's a Coomoodore, you know," he added proudly.

"Mummy?" asked Anna, who had continued to observe the strange man sitting on their sofa.

"Yes, darling?"

"Why's Alex so pale?"

"Because he's been very ill."

"Are we looking after him to make him better? Like we did with Mr Kalinowski?"

"Perhaps."

Six months. A journey into the unknown.

"Mummy, can we go and have our milk and biscuits with Mrs Thringle now?" asked Rupert.

"And then go out and play in the garden until teatime?" added Anna.

"Of course."

Happily, the children ran off into the kitchen.

"I suppose I'd better unpack," he said.

"Yes."

"Where shall I sleep?" Alex regarded her with speculative interest. He wondered what she was like in bed. He couldn't remember. All he could picture was Rachel.

"In your old room." There was no hesitation in Katherine's words.

"And you?"

"In the blue room." The one she and Alastair had always shared. "It's best that way."

"Is it?"

"Yes."

"To start with, maybe."

For always, thought Katherine. Out loud, to appease him, she said, "Let's take it a step at a time, shall we?"

"That's one way of looking at it."

"It's the only way."

"Is it?"

"Yes. I thought that perhaps we could start by being friends."

"Just friends? We're husband and wife."

"Are we? In name only."

"Isn't that enough for us to sleep together?" Although, thinking about it, did he actually want to do that?

"No."

"Don't you love me?"

Katherine was silent. How honest should she be?

"I still love you," he said.

She glanced at him. He felt uncomfortable within its penetrating power.

"Do you really, Alex?"

"Well..."

At last, some honesty. "As I said before, perhaps we can be friends."

332

She's changed, thought Alex. *She's stronger, firmer, less compliant. I rather like that. Perhaps this isn't going to be so bad after all.* "Perhaps we can," he said and smiled.

Katherine remembered that smile and the effect it always used to have on her. She would not let it do that to her now. She wondered if he would still be as work-absorbed as he had always been, wondered whether life for her, if by some remote possibility they were to be together, would once again become the compromise it was before he went to Singapore?

She felt the slight warning tremor of identity loss but immediately put the emotion out of her mind. It had no place here.

He had been through a horrendous experience beyond anything she could possibly imagine. And he had survived. He needed kindness and sympathy, not censure.

Together, they went upstairs to Alex's old room where she helped him put his belongings away. He looked exhausted, so she suggested that he rest. If he wished, he could have supper here in his room. Gratefully, Alex took off his shoes and lay on the bed where he fell instantly asleep. Katherine covered him with the eiderdown and sat for a moment in the easy chair, studying him.

Had this stranger once been her husband? The man she had once loved and cherished? This was going to be much, much harder than even she had imagined.

Six months. An eternity.

CHAPTER 46

London/Maybury
October, 1945 - March, 1946

On a beautifully sunny autumnal morning, Katherine left the Admiralty for the last time as a regular member of the W.R.N.S. She stood on Horse Guards Parade before the building where she had spent eight fulfilling months, and said goodbye to a Service she had come to love.

She had been on extended, compassionate leave ever since Alex had returned, hoping that she would be able to come back to her work. This had proved to be impossible given his needs. She had therefore sought, and been given, permission to end her wartime service early on compassionate grounds. Signing her release papers to that effect had been a huge wrench.

Not just a compromise, but a sacrifice.

With tears in her eyes, Katherine saluted. Viewed from the outside, it appeared to be directed at the building but in her heart it was her tribute and mark of respect to the Royal Navy. She then turned and walked slowly through Admiralty Arch and down Whitehall, past the Cenotaph to the Houses of Parliament and Westminster Bridge. Here, she stood for a long time looking at the River Thames, watching the water as it flowed swiftly downstream, staying as long as she could before moving on to her next appointment – a doctor in Harley Street, someone whom she had already seen and from whom she had kept her identity secret.

He confirmed what Katherine had suspected for a while – that she was expecting a baby. Her queasiness had had nothing to do with the emotional trauma of the past few months, but everything to do with pregnancy.

"Yes, Mrs MacDonald, there is no doubt," he said. "I'm sure your husband will be delighted. You can tell him that the baby will pop out at the beginning of April."

Katherine opened her eyes wide at this and quickly picked up her handbag ready for a hasty exit.

"Where is he at the moment?" continued the doctor conversationally.

"Er… he's abroad, with the Royal Navy." At least that part was truthful. She hated all this deception.

"Ah, keeping it in the Senior Service family, what?!" And he laughed at his own witticism, his shoulders lifting up and down, his double chin wobbling. "Good, good. Now do come and see me in a few weeks' time for a check-up. That's the thing. Have a word with my receptionist on the way out."

Katherine smiled enigmatically and left as quickly as she could without making a further appointment.

As the baby had not yet begun to show, Katherine decided that she would keep the news to herself for the time being and deal with the fallout when she could no longer conceal the fact that she was going to have a child.

It was just one more complication in a highly complicated situation.

Alastair had been away since September at the Royal Naval Base in Trincomalee, in Ceylon, having requested an immediate posting overseas (given their complex personal circumstances) and had it granted. It would be at least April before he could come home, and this would be his last position before the end of his active war service with the R.N.V.R.

Katherine had waited one month, as Alastair had suggested, before writing to him. His eagerly awaited reply had taken the form of a 'family' letter, written to both her and Alex. Upset, but reading between the lines as to why he had done this, Katherine had replied in kind. It was all very unsatisfactory but at least they had communication and this was vital to her.

With difficulty, her thoughts returned to the present. Alex had spent that morning at Lord Cameron's Chambers and they were meeting for lunch. She arrived at the appointed time to find him agitatedly walking around the gardens outside the adjacent Middle Temple building. His expression was thunderous.

"How did you get on?" she asked cautiously.

"They want me to do a period of retraining and then six months shadowing a colleague in court cases." He was deeply offended. "Me! Retrain! It's ridiculous. I was one of their top barristers before the war."

Katherine sighed. "Perhaps things have changed since you were away. Perhaps there are new procedures, changes in the law that you need to catch up with."

He gave her a stony look. "How can you know what's gone on?"

"I don't. I'm just speculating." She took a deep breath. "Look, why don't we find somewhere for lunch? I wonder if that little restaurant is still there – you know, the one we always used to go to when you'd finished your sessions at the Royal Courts of Justice?"

He looked at her blankly. "I don't remember."

He put his hand across his forehead in frustration. There were so many things he couldn't recall. It had been so much easier in Australia where everything was new and he could build up his life without having to worry about whether he remembered this or that.

He wondered what Rachel was doing at this moment.

They emerged onto the Strand and two Wrens passed by and saluted Katherine. Automatically, she returned the action, smiled and carried on walking as though it was the most natural thing in the world, which it was, of course, or rather had been, for a very long time.

For some reason, this simple action made an impression on Alex. It was the first time he had been out with her while she was in uniform. He wondered for a moment about her war service. She had said very little.

They reached the restaurant only to find it closed and derelict like so much of London, so they continued along the Strand, where they were lucky enough to find a table at the Savoy Grill. They selected their food from the menu and sat in silence, both of them observing the other diners, most of whom were in uniform and most of whom were American.

Katherine looked at Alex and wondered how she would feel about him had she not fallen in love with Alastair. Would there still have been this gulf between them? Even after two months of living in the same house, he still felt like a stranger.

"Why are we doing this, Alex?" she asked dispassionately.

"Because we're hungry?" His reply was evasive; vaguely teasing.

"That's not what I mean."

"You're much too serious." Once again, Alex avoided giving her a direct answer; he was unable to give her a direct answer. So he said, "Perhaps if we went to bed together it might help."

Katherine was silent. "I can't," she said at length.

"Why not?"

"I don't love you anymore, Alex."

"You did once."

She looked at him in surprise. "I thought you'd forgotten."

He knew he had, but he wasn't going to admit to it, gambling on the fact that originally, she must have loved him enough to marry him.

But why couldn't he remember?

"It might help you to love me again," he observed.

"No. It would just be sex."

Alex smiled. "And what's wrong with that?"

She eyed him sharply. Where was the man who had once so respected and cared about her?

"Everything. I'd feel cheap." *And unfaithful to the man I do love.*

"Thanks. I find that very insulting. I'm a good lover, you know."

"Yes." *But not as good as Alastair, who is wonderful.*

"Well then?"

She shook her head.

"I'm sure we'd be good together." A picture of Rachel came into his mind. But Katherine…?

"Ah, so you don't remember?"

Alex looked down at the water in his glass, embarrassed. She had caught him out. "No," he said.

He remembered Patricia in Singapore. He could recall the stunning contours of her body, his overwhelming physical desire for her, her audacity and complete abandon. Even now, his own body leapt spontaneously to life at the thought – recollections that came to him clearly and easily.

But with these memories there came feelings of guilt, shame and humiliation. Why? He couldn't remember. A fleeting recognition that he had been unfaithful to the woman sitting opposite him made him shudder with suppressed remorse.

Why had he been unfaithful? What had it been like with Katherine? Why was the memory of their marriage so blurred and indistinct yet his illicit affair so vivid? Why couldn't he remember what it was like to make love to his wife?

In fact, why was he even trying to be reconciled with her, when all he wanted to do was to be with Rachel?

Ah, yes.

He'd promised his father that he would give this sham of a marriage six months.

He thought of Rachel and how special she was, how she filled his mind and body with love, how he'd never known anyone like her, how he needed her in a way that he had never needed any other woman, even the one in Singapore, how much happiness and contentment she had brought him.

Perhaps he didn't want to take Katherine to bed after all.

Their lunch arrived and he dropped that particular topic, much to Katherine's relief.

"How much do you remember of Cairnmor?" she asked presently.

Alex became agitated. "Why do you keep asking me if I remember this or that? It's not going to bring my memory back any quicker."

"I'm sorry. I thought it might help you and me to get along better."

He glared at her. "And be friends?"

His tone stung her. "We were once."

Unexpectedly, her eyes filled with tears. Fond images came flooding back of their courtship. How she couldn't wait for him to arrive on the steamer. Of his attractiveness, his charisma. Of their long walks at sunset on the beach. The way he used to take her in his arms. The fun and the laughter. She recalled the idyllic week of their honeymoon and the poignant memory cut through her like a knife.

In the cold light of present reality, could it be that all of these memories were mere illusion without substance or foundation: romantic, idealized recollections enhanced over time?

Hastily, she excused herself from the table and headed for the ladies' room, where she locked herself in a cubicle and wept silently. The things she still treasured from their time together couldn't be shared with this new Alex. There was no love here, no friendship, no connection. This Alex was not the same man she had married and for a brief moment, she wanted the old one back – oh, how she wanted him back, the man she had loved with all the sweetness, joy and exquisite pain of first love.

But, in that moment, Katherine knew with absolute certainty that this man would never come to her again, that he was gone forever, and she mourned the loss of both him and her marriage just as surely as when she had first heard that he was dead.

And, in the midst of her tears, stronger than her present heartache, stronger than any residual attachment she might harbour from the past, more potent and life-enhancing than anything she had experienced with Alex, came her feelings for Alastair, who always had been and always would be the greatest love of her life.

When Katherine arrived back at the table, her moment of grieving done, her equilibrium restored, Alex had disappeared and, along with the bill, the waiter presented her with a note which said that he had someone to meet and that he would be back home later.

It was to be the first of many such increasingly lengthy absences, and Katherine began to find these something of a relief. She didn't enquire too closely where he went, but she had a suspicion it might have had something to do with Dr Curtis.

337

She experienced no jealousy or resentment. She was just glad for both of them. And herself. And, of course, for Alastair.

In December, Alex became seriously ill with another bout of malaria and was rushed to the Hospital for Tropical Diseases in London. Rachel, who had managed to procure a six-month secondment there, came to see Katherine after he had been admitted.

"How is he?" asked Katherine, who had been frightened by the sudden onset of the disease.

"Comfortable. He's on heavy medication but you got him here quickly. I'm so grateful to you for that."

Katherine perceived that Rachel's concern went beyond mere professional appraisal and took her to one side, away from prying ears.

"I'm going to be completely frank with you, Dr Curtis. Please don't be shocked or offended," she said.

Rachel looked wary. "Oh?"

"You care for Alex, don't you?"

Taken aback, Rachel looked for an accusatory tone in this woman's voice, but found none. "Yes," she replied cautiously, uncertainly.

"Are you in love with him?" asked Katherine, to the point but not unkindly.

Rachel wasn't sure how to respond. This was Alex's wife she was talking to. She, Rachel, was having an affair with this woman's husband. She ought to leave. But running away was not her style.

She decided to be honest.

"Yes," she said quietly.

"Is he in love with you?" The question was put simply, as though the enquiry was being made by a concerned friend.

Rachel hesitated for a moment then, with a hint of defiance and possessiveness in her voice, said, "Yes."

Katherine smiled enigmatically. "Aye, well then, be patient. All good things come to those who wait," and she walked away, leaving Rachel dumbfounded.

As she watched Katherine leave, Rachel decided not to tell Alex of this particular conversation, but it had given her reassurance and hope, real hope. She had been upset when Alex had said on that terrible day at R.A.F. Halton, without her prior knowledge, that he wanted to try for a reconciliation with Katherine. And then, as if that wasn't enough, Alex had compounded the situation by agreeing to undergo this ridiculous six-month trial to please his father.

However, despite having been through all sorts of emotional agony – her jealousy and concern refuelled each time Alex returned to Mistley House – he had made it very clear that the marriage wasn't working. Rachel, naturally, was glad and had made no bones about saying so.

She and Alex had been spending more and more time together at her flat in Hammersmith – an unanticipated bonus. Once the requisite six months was up and her secondment completed, Rachel felt certain that they would be able to go back to Australia and resume their life in complete freedom, confident that all had been done that could be done. She had a new post, a very good post waiting for

338

her as a consultant in Tropical Medicine at the hospital in Melbourne, and she couldn't wait to go home.

Rachel missed their little house on Adelaide Avenue and the life they had shared together. She wanted that back, oh, how she wanted it back. And to have Alex, who meant more to her than anything or anyone she had ever known, to herself again.

In January, Alex returned to Mistley House. He was very weak and all thoughts of resuming his legal career had to be put aside for the time being. Katherine kept him supplied with law journals and he read these with some gratitude and appreciation, thus making their life a little less strained.

However, he was extremely sensitive to noise and became agitated and irritated by the natural liveliness of Rupert and Anna. Practising the piano had, therefore, to be done at school, and Katherine would sit supervising their talented offspring every day. She found it exhausting, as this could take anything up to an hour with each of them.

Towards the beginning of February, Michael and Mary came to stay. Just before Alex had come to live at Mistley House, Mary had moved back to Cairnmor, knowing the war was over, to begin making preparations for their life together once Michael was demobbed. This had now become a reality, and Michael was anxious to spend time with Alex before heading up north.

He was shocked by his friend's appearance and changed manner, and upset by the complete absence of their old rapport. He tried to talk to him about their time at Oxford together – the high jinks they used to get up to, the Scottish country dancing classes they went to after Michael broke up with the one and only serious girlfriend he ever had before Mary, how Alex had helped him through finals, supporting him as he overcame his heartbreak, and how grateful Michael would always be to him. He tried to engage Alex in talking about some of the cases they had worked on together at Royal Court Chambers, or the Appeal at the House of Lords.

But it was all to no avail.

In the end, for Michael, it proved to be an unequal struggle. Either Alex would not, or could not respond. He seemed to have no memories of any of these things, nor any desire to try to recall them. Eventually, even Michael gave up in the face of stony silence or a shrug of the shoulders.

Professionally, he found it difficult; personally, he found it devastating.

One afternoon, while Alex was sleeping, Katherine, Michael and Mary went for a long walk. Michael was downcast, upset. Mary was anxious, protective. The only time she had seen him as despondent as this was when he had first heard the mistaken news that Alex was dead.

The three friends talked at length about Alex's lack of responsiveness, and the difficulties in coping and communicating with someone as unpredictable as he had become.

"How much do you know about post-traumatic amnesia?" Katherine asked Michael.

"Quite a lot. But even I wasn't prepared for the change in him. It's as though he's a totally different person. I feel as though I've lost him all over again."

"I know," she replied gently. "So do I. Is there any chance that the Alex we used to know is in there somewhere?"

Michael was silent. He looked at Katherine, so pale and wan. She was not happy, that was obvious. She had also put on weight. A lot. He and Mary exchanged a glance and Mary put her arm through Katherine's just as she used to do when they were growing up together on Cairnmor.

"Have you tried prompting him with small memories, that kind of thing?" asked Michael.

"Yes, but just as he's been doing with you for the past couple of days, he either blanks me out or gets upset and angry. He really cannot remember."

"What *does* he recall?" Michael's question was borne of his own frustration in not being able to reach Alex rather than a lack of expertise.

"Fragments of his childhood. Who I am, but not much else of our life together. The law. Certain court cases. Usually how to get from A to B in London. Being in Australia."

"Have the remembered details from his earlier life increased since September?"

"No."

Michael sighed. "Then I would hazard a guess and say that these will probably never come back. Just as Phillippe will never have his full physical mobility, so Alex has probably lost those memories forever." He put his arm round Katherine's shoulder. "I'm so sorry."

"No, no," she said, trying to reassure him. "I'd suspected as much. I'm sorry for you, too. He was your best friend." Katherine sighed. "As you know, his medication affects his moods too. He can be quite volatile sometimes, especially with the children."

Michael was concerned. "He's never been violent though?"

"Oh no, just impatient and flies off the handle easily."

"When he is calm, does he take much notice of Anna and Rupert?" asked Mary. She had been upset by his apparent indifference to these two lively, loving, intelligent children.

Katherine shook her head.

"Before we came?" She wondered if their presence in the house had changed anything.

"No. He can't seem to relate to them at all. I feel so sorry for him. He's missing out on so much. Part of this… charade… was to give Alex the chance to get to know his children."

Mary was sympathetic. "Well, you've done everything you can."

They walked on in silence. Then, unexpectedly, Michael said, "So, when's the baby due?"

Katherine gave a sharp intake of breath. "How did you guess?"

"A-ha!" Michael smiled at his wife, his mood lifting.

"I mean, I was huge with the twins, but I'm quite small with this one. My pregnancy hardly shows at all with all the baggy jumpers and fisherman's smock I've been wearing. I was so certain the baby was hidden from view!"

340

"From the uninitiated, maybe. But this is Doctor Michael and your best friend Mary that you're talking to." He saw her face light up for the first time since she had greeted them. "So, when is it due?"

"In April."

Mary smiled. "And Alastair's the father?"

"Of course! There's absolutely no possibility of anyone else."

"We'd noticed you and Alex have separate rooms," said Michael. "Very wise of you under the circumstances, if I may be so bold."

Katherine laughed. "You may."

"How are you in yourself? Any problems?"

"No, I'm fine. Touch wood. The baby is moving around well, especially at night and in the bath!"

"Have you seen a doctor?"

"Only for the initial confirmation of the pregnancy."

"Are you going to?"

"No. Too complicated."

"Does Alastair know?"

"No. I want to surprise him. But also, I'm keeping to the six month rule. This would only create confusion and cloud the issue while he's away in Ceylon. There's time. He'll be home before the baby's born."

"What are you going to do after the six months are up?" asked Mary.

"Be with Alastair, of course. That was always the arrangement if things didn't work out with Alex. And they haven't."

"That's patently obvious," said Michael.

Katherine smiled ruefully. "Even without my pregnancy, Alex and I have no marriage. I can see no future for us, and with his lack of memory, there's not much left of the past. I don't love him anymore, and apart from the children, we have nothing in common, no foundations upon which to build. We don't even have a friendship, which I regret more than anything else. But at least I can honestly say that I've tried and am fulfilling Alastair's six months. Though it's been very, very hard."

"It must have been," said Mary. "I can't even begin to imagine what it must be like for you. I couldn't do it."

"There are going to be stormy times ahead once the truth comes out," observed Michael. "Come to us if you need help. We'll always be here for you and Alastair, you know that."

"Thank you. We may need that support one day." She looked gratefully at both of them.

They arrived home to find that Alex was awake and reading one of his law books, but he seemed unwilling to discuss the topic with Michael, who tried one last time to engage him in conversation.

Alex stared at him as though he didn't know him or want to know him. Hurt, despite his medical training, Michael lapsed into silence. There was nothing he could do or say to rekindle the connection between them, a connection that had once been so vibrant and close. Inwardly, just as Katherine had already done, he once again mourned the loss of his friend and knew he had to let go forever.

A little later, Mrs Thringle came in with afternoon tea and a large package. "The postman brought this for you while you were out."

The writing on the front was unfamiliar and the postmark was smudged. But the stamps were...

"It's from Singapore!" exclaimed Katherine. "That's odd."

Alex looked up from his law journal in shocked surprise, every muscle tense.

Katherine opened the parcel and onto her lap fell a letter, some photographs – which had escaped from an envelope where the glue had failed – a bundle of Katherine's own letters, photographs of her and the children, various other personal items, and a diary with a very distinctive red, gold and black cover.

Alex immediately recognized the diary and a glimpse at one of the photographs from the envelope was enough to make him look at Katherine with a horrified, panicked expression, his mind unable to cope as his body was engulfed by the guilt and shame of discovery.

He jumped up from the settee and rushed out of the room. Moments later, they heard the front door slam.

Katherine was so taken aback by his abrupt departure that it was a while before she began to look at the photographs. However, when she did, she was even more astounded and sat there with her mouth open.

They were of Alex with a woman whom she did not recognize – at a party, on the beach, on the tennis court. Laughing, hugging, sharing drinks and meals with friends, or together in some romantic setting. There was even one of him openly kissing her at a table in some restaurant, with other people looking on and smiling indulgently. There was also a photograph of Alex with a different woman, standing by a car with the ocean and palm trees in the background, his arms enveloping her while she leaned back against him.

All of them implying intimacy, all of them unmistakable.

The final one Katherine looked at was a studio portrait of the first woman, on her own – glamorous in a low-cut, figure-hugging *haute-couture* dress, back-lit, looking provocatively over her shoulder. On the back he had written *My Darling Patricia, October, 1940.*

Her abdomen tightened. The baby kicked inside her. Instinctively, she put her hand to her stomach. Michael and Mary were beside her in an instant. Silently, she showed them the photographs.

Michael was livid. "How dare he! He may have been my best friend but how dare he do this to you! It's just as well he made such a cowardly exit, otherwise I would have been tempted to punch him, weakened state or not."

Katherine was silent, stunned, trying to make sense of what she had just learned.

Alex, *knowingly* unfaithful to her, not just once, but *twice* during their marriage, when all was to her exactly as it always had been – before she believed him to be dead, before he suffered the trauma of his memory loss.

It was almost beyond her comprehension.

She picked up the letter. "You read it," she said, giving it to Mary. "I can't bear to."

342

"Dear Mrs Stewart," she began, *"I Squadron Leader Stewart housekeeper. My English not good. I find you address in Squadron Leader things. I send them you.*

"When Japanese come, I bury his things in garden. We all bury our precious things in garden. Enemy soldiers bad. Very bad. Destroy everything.

"Now war end, I dig them up. I know Squadron Leader Stewart killed but I send you things I keep safe. So you have keepsake. I do not know what in them I not read. Private. I send you everything. I hope you well.

"She's signed her name, but it's not very clear. Mrs Mawar, I think."

Katherine picked up the diary and turned to October, 1940. There it was, in black and white: Alex's handwriting chronicling in intimate detail his love affair with Patricia – the passionate intensity of their relationship, how much he wanted her, how he couldn't give her up. She read on – his anger at Patricia's unfaithfulness to him *(that was rich!)*, his humiliation at her rejection of him, his grief at her departure. His guilt and remorse *(at least he felt that!)*. His frustration with his work. His need to come home. Then Miriam – who was a 'delight' in bed, a wonderful 'distraction'. The change in his feelings for Katherine.

Suddenly, she could read no more. It was enough. Everything had gone now. There was nothing left. It really was over.

"What do I do with this stuff?" she said, handling it with distaste as she put it back into the envelope.

"I'll look after it," said Michael, having briefly glanced through the contents. "You're going to need a good divorce lawyer. This is evidence."

"Yes, I suppose it is." Katherine stood up and took a deep breath.

Suddenly, she felt free, as though a great weight had been lifted from her shoulders. She and Alastair could be together now for always with a clear conscience.

Alex could say nothing.

Smiling at Michael and Mary, she briefly took their hands in hers and thanked them. She then went out of the room to write a very long letter to the man with whom she would be spending the rest of her life and whose child she carried within her.

EPILOGUE

Cairnmor
April, 1946

"I can see land! I can see land!" shouted Rupert, jumping up and down with excitement. "Look! Look! We're almost there!"

"Where is it? Where's the land?" Anna held on tightly to her mother's hand. She was still feeling sick. The ship had gone up and down too much for her liking and rolled around from side to side for far too long. She peered through the railings. "Oh, yes, there it is," she said, with as much enthusiasm as she could muster. "Will Daddad be there to meet us?"

"No. He's coming next weekend."

Anna was disappointed. "But he has left the Royal Navy now, hasn't he?"

"Oh yes, but only just. He still has things to sort out before we can see him." Katherine could hardly believe that Alastair's seven months abroad were finally over, and that very soon he would be home with them for good. "Michael and Mary will be at the quayside, though."

"I shall see Rose! How long are we staying for?" asked Rupert.

"A month, until school begins again."

"A whole month! Goody, goody."

"Ooh, Mummy!" exclaimed Anna. "Look at those clouds! They're so big and black. I've never seen clouds like that before."

"I have," replied her mother. "And I shall be relieved when we reach Lochaberdale. The wind is getting worse. There's going to be a storm before long."

"I don't like storms," said Anna, in a small voice.

"I do!" said Rupert.

"No you don't. You hide under the bed."

"Only sometimes." Rupert was downcast, but he brightened up when he saw two very familiar figures standing on the quayside, waving at them. "Look, there's Uncle Michael and Auntie Mary!"

The steamer docked at the pier and Katherine felt her spirits rise. With her children, she stepped onto her beloved island of Cairnmor and knew that she was home at last.

"Wow, you've grown!" Michael said to Katherine, and then to the children, "What *has* your Mummy been eating? Hm," he rubbed his chin in pretend contemplation. "Well you two look healthy enough. It's obviously not *your* rations!"

"Silly Uncle Michael. Mummy's going to have a baby! We're going to have a new brother or sister. I hope it's a girl." Anna wanted a little sister.

"I want a boy."

"Girl."

"Boy."

"Girl!"

Tired and hungry after the journey, there was imminent danger of a squabble developing between the children, so Michael said, "Now, now, both of you. Let's go and find the ponies and traps. As you can see, we've got two lined up. Special treat. Auntie Mary is going to take you two ragamuffins off to the Granger abode in ours, where a splendid feast awaits you."

Rupert looked at him quizzically. "What do you mean, a splendid feast?"

"In your language, as much food as you can eat, young man. Then you can play with Rose for as long as you like. She's sitting at home waiting for you with her grandma. I'm going to take your mummy up to see her old cottage, for which purpose I've borrowed John's pony and trap from the hotel."

"I thought we were staying there," observed Anna, who liked hotels. Not that she'd stayed in many.

"First things first," said Mary, exchanging a knowing look with her husband.

"This all sounds very nice, but wherever I'm to be taken, I do need to sit down as my back is aching rather badly," said Katherine.

Michael helped her into the trap. "You see, I have thought of everything. A special step for Your Ladyship so that in your advanced state of pregnancy you don't have to struggle or rely on Mary and me heaving you up into your carriage in a most undignified manner!"

"Thank you, kind sir. But why am I to be taken up to the cottage?"

"I have my reasons," he replied mysteriously.

Too tired to argue, after waving farewell to her offspring, Katherine allowed herself to be transported to her old croft.

As ever, it was a gentle journey to start with but soon, when the terrain became uneven as they tackled the steepest section of the ascent, the trap rocked precariously, making Katherine feel very uncomfortable. All the time, the wind continued to rise.

"I don't think we should stay too long," she remarked, the pain in her back becoming more pronounced. "There's a nasty storm brewing."

"Oh yes," said Michael gleefully. "It has all the signs of being a biggie." He drew up a little way from the cottage. "Here we are then," he added, before alighting from the trap and helping her down. He put her suitcase on the ground beside her. "It's very light, you'll be able to manage it fine. Mary's got the rest of your luggage."

Katherine was appalled. "What?! You're just going to abandon me here?!"

"You're quick, very quick!" He kissed her on her cheek and got back into the trap. "Have fun!" and with a chirrup to the pony, he set off back down the hill.

Feeling annoyed, Katherine stood for a while watching his departure. Then, before going to the cottage, she took the path leading down towards the beach, to her favourite place where she had so often come. She sat on a flat, rocky outcrop taking in deep breaths of the pure, clear air, closing her eyes, lifting up her head, trying to savour every moment of being home, trying to calm her displeasure at Michael's inexplicable, cavalier treatment of her.

Her back was still troublesome. The pain had not gone away, but had stayed there, unrelenting, and she could not escape from it. It began to occur to her that this was no ordinary backache. Her abdomen tightened.

The baby wasn't due for another two weeks. What if it was coming early? She was all alone. Michael was irresponsible to bring her here. She was foolish to have let him.

Leaving her suitcase behind, Katherine started to make the long walk down the hill back to Lochaberdale. She had gone no more than a quarter of the way, when suddenly, without warning, the storm broke directly overhead, streaks of lightening shearing across the bay below her, to be followed almost immediately by deafening thunder.

At the same time, a terrific, sickening pain in her back shook her, making her stumble, almost bringing her to her knees. It was closely followed by waves of discomfort in her abdomen. With a shock, she realized she was going into labour, that this must be the first real contraction.

What should she do? Continue on down to Lochaberdale or go back up to her cottage? Katherine stood still, hesitating, uncertain.

However, some strong maternal urge took over and she knew she would never reach Lochaberdale in time. She had to go back to the cottage, to her home. There, she would have to deliver the child herself, just as thousands of other women had done on the island over the centuries.

The last few yards were almost impossible for her. Rain began to fall, huge droplets that cut into her face like a knife. Another wave of pain coursed through her. She fell against the door hammering on it, even though she knew there could be no answer. She just didn't have the strength at that moment to push it open.

Miraculously, though, the door did open and suddenly, there was Alastair, with one supportive and reassuring arm round her shoulders, helping her inside, and with the other, pushing the door shut against the force of the wind, bolting it to keep it in place.

His greeting was a mixture of joy and concern. Katherine couldn't speak, but just held onto him tightly as though she was never, ever going to let him go again. He embraced her lovingly, tenderly, and she kissed him back, only to break away when another surge of pain took over. He held her through that, instinctively breathing with her.

After it had passed, he quickly removed her wet coat and carefully sat her down on the settee, taking off his jumper and putting it on her. Katherine snuggled gratefully into its comforting warmth.

"I can't believe it! You're here! But how?" she gasped, in between contractions.

Alastair smiled. "I managed to get away a couple of weeks early and came straight here to the island, where Michael and I hatched up this little plan of surprise for you. But I must have dozed off in the chair while I was waiting for you this afternoon. I'm so sorry I didn't hear you arrive!" He smiled at her ruefully, apologetically. "Though talking of surprises, I think it's you who've surprised us!"

He held her through the next contraction and the next. He rescued her suitcase from outside, using all his strength to shut the door once again. Then he put the kettle on for the hot water he knew they would need, and fetched some towels from the cupboard.

Katherine was impressed. "How do you know what to do?" she managed to say. The contractions were coming close together now. It would not be long. She needed to lie down.

"I grew up on a farm, remember? My mother helped deliver a few babies – the wives of farm hands, I think. I was always despatched to fetch clean towels and hot water, which I had to leave outside the door. Because I was very young at the time, I never did manage to work out what they were for! Also, I helped my father deliver lambs and calves. Under protest though, I have to say, as I was never particularly keen on it. I do realize you're not a sheep or a cow," he added, teasing her gently.

"I'm very glad to hear it," and she did her best to smile.

"So, although it's been a while, I'll be able to help you. I hope," he admitted honestly. "You'll have to guide me though."

"I'll try…" she gasped.

Not that it mattered. Nothing mattered, only that they were together and she was about to give birth to their child.

Another contraction. Then her waters broke. Another, then another. She could feel the baby's head.

"I need to… lie down. Ah… the baby's coming!"

Alastair took her through to the bedroom and helped her onto the bed, supporting her through each wave of pain and then, with his encouragement, Katherine began to push with each contraction.

Within half an hour their baby was born, a much quicker and simpler process than the agony of the twins' prolonged arrival, much to her relief.

It was a little girl.

Alastair put her onto Katherine's stomach and she told him how to tie the umbilical cord with string before cutting it. Gently, he wiped the small, wrinkled yet perfectly formed baby clean, wrapping her in a towel and soothing her cries before giving their child tenderly back to Katherine.

The bond between them really was unbreakable now.

After a while, having changed the sheets and made sure both mother and baby were warm and comfortable, he checked with Katherine that all was indeed well and sat on the bed beside her while she fed their baby. Outside the storm raged, but inside, all was happiness and joy. The little girl, innocent and content, fell asleep.

"You were amazing!" he said, full of admiration.

Katherine couldn't speak, but looked at him with such love that he could do nothing else but kiss her. They sat together, looking down at their sleeping child.

"What shall we call her?" he asked, gently stroking with his forefinger the little head with its few wisps of fair hair.

"Grace. I'd like to call her Grace," said Katherine.

"Then that is what she shall be." Alastair kissed her tiny perfect fingers. "Hello, Grace," he said quietly.

Then he looked at Katherine, leaning against him. Happy but exhausted, she was falling asleep. Alastair helped her down into a more comfortable position and with the baby between them, he lay down too, keeping watch, checking that little Grace had plenty of room.

For two precious days, the storm blew. For two precious days, they lived a secret life. No one visited them, no one disturbed them. Katherine rested and slept; Grace fed, slept well and thrived, while Alastair cared for his precious family.

He fashioned a cot for their baby using one of the drawers from the chest in the spare bedroom, and at night slept with Katherine by his side or in his arms, settling the baby in her makeshift cot. They allowed nothing to intrude on their mutual happiness, companionship and delight in the child they had created…

The day dawned quietly, just like any other day. The sun emerged over distant mountains, casting deep shadows across the valley below. Light filtered slowly into the bedroom of a thatched-roof stone cottage set high upon a hillside, gently awakening a woman as she lay beside the man she loved.

She turned to face the morning sun, revelling in its warmth through the uncurtained windows, and looked down at the baby girl sleeping peacefully in her cot. She did not stir, nor did the little boy and girl in the bedroom next door.

Quietly, Katherine dressed and went outside into the fresh, clear air. Presently, Alastair joined her and wordlessly, put his arms around her, kissing her tenderly. Enveloped in the beauty of Cairnmor, they held each other close, knowing they were home, deeply thankful that at last they could be together.

The distant horizon stretched before them, timeless as the future they would share.

ACKNOWLEDGEMENTS

I am, as ever, indebted to my family, Peter, Tim and Elizabeth, and my 'reading panel': Annette Vidler, Christine Lord and Katie Boughton for their unstinting support and encouragement; to Carol Dodd and Jackie Readwin at my local library for locating the sometimes obscure material that I needed during the course of my research; to Elsa Waghorn for her help in ensuring accuracy in the use of idiomatic French; and to Ben Jones of Ozaru Books for his eagle-eyed editing skills and continued publication of my books. Last, but not least, I should like to thank Major-General Charles Ramsay, whom I have met on two memorable occasions, for his generous support and for writing the Afterword below.

Changing Times, Changing Tides is a broad canvas and could not have been written without extensive research. I have used many resources in my quest for authenticity – historical accounts, biographies, diaries, films, the internet and my own experience in visiting many of the locations mentioned in the novel.

The era in which the story is set is close enough to my childhood for it to be within my consciousness. My late father, Ernest Quick, seeing that war was inevitable, volunteered for the R.A.M.C. as he did not wish to carry arms but wanted to play his part in the war effort. He chose not to train as an officer, remaining a private throughout the war. I grew up with stories of his experiences (including the football match in the snow – for 'Michael' read my dad) in Norway (where he rescued ammunition from a burning jetty during an air raid, for which action he was Mentioned in Despatches) and France (from where he was brought out two weeks before Dunkirk and to where he returned on D-Day+2, landing on Gold Beach) as well as in Belgium, Holland and Germany. My father retained a lifelong interest in the history of the conflict and I remember many Sunday afternoons spent watching the best of the old films and talking to him about his involvement. With hindsight, I wish I had asked him more.

My mother, Eva, was an officer in the Women's Junior Air Corps as well as under-manageress of a greengrocer's shop in Cheriton, Kent. She has often shared with me her recollections of life on the Home Front – rationing, air raids, fire-watching, lack of sleep, the pulling together and optimistic spirit that prevailed even during the darkest days of the conflict. In addition, my grandfather was a captain in the Home Guard, so reflections of the Second World War really were part of my upbringing.

For a while, my father was stationed at Dover Castle and as far as I can ascertain, was there at the same time as Admiral Sir Bertram Ramsay. The entrance to the R.A.M.C. dressing station and hospital was and still is situated next to the casemate tunnels' entrance for Vice Admiral Dover – perhaps, my father might even have seen Admiral Ramsay without realizing who he was. Given his later extensive knowledge of the conflict, Dad must have been familiar with the Admiral's contribution, but we never talked of it.

Therefore, when I began my research for this novel, I have to confess that I had not heard of Admiral Ramsay – a grievous oversight on my part given the importance of his achievements, but not entirely surprising as it is only recently that he has been receiving the wider recognition that he deserves, not least through the efforts of his son Charles, who is a true advocate for the crucial role his father played.

At first, in *Changing Times, Changing Tides*, Admiral Ramsay was going to be merely a distant authority figure but while I was writing, his character in the novel had other ideas, becoming an important part of the story.

I hope I have done justice to the real man.

Afterword

"I am delighted that my father, Admiral Sir Bertram Ramsay, should feature in this book. He was a wonderful man, who had a great career in the Royal Navy, and contributed enormously to the ultimate victory in World War II – mainly through commanding the Dunkirk evacuation, and as Naval Commander-in-Chief on D-Day."

Major-General Charles Ramsay

OTHER PUBLICATIONS FROM
ŌZARU BOOKS

The Call of Cairnmor
Sally Aviss

Book One of the Cairnmor Trilogy

The Scottish Isle of Cairnmor is a place of great beauty and undisturbed wilderness, a haven for wildlife, a land of white sandy beaches and inland fertile plains, a land where awe-inspiring mountains connect precipitously with the sea.

To this remote island comes a stranger, Alexander Stewart, on a quest to solve the mysterious disappearance of two people and their unborn child; a missing family who are now heirs to a vast fortune. He enlists the help of local schoolteacher, Katherine MacDonald, and together they seek the answers to this enigma: a deeply personal journey that takes them from Cairnmor to the historic splendour of London and the industrial heartland of Glasgow.

Covering the years 1936-1937 and infused with period colour and detail, The Call of Cairnmor is about unexpected discovery and profound attachment which, from its gentle opening, gradually gathers momentum and complexity until all the strands come together to give life-changing revelations.

"really enjoyed reading this – loved the plot... Read it in just two sittings as I couldn't stop reading." (P. Green – amazon.co.uk)

"exciting plot, not a book you want to put down, although I tried not to rush it so as to fully enjoy escaping to the world skilfully created by the author. A most enjoyable read." (Liz Green – amazon.co.uk)

"an excellent read. I cannot wait for the next part of the trilogy from this talented author. You will not want to put it down" (B. Burchell – amazon.co.uk)

ISBN: 978-0-9559219-9-5

Where Gloom and Brightness Meet
Sally Aviss

Book Three of the Cairnmor Trilogy

When Anna Stewart begins a relationship with journalist Marcus Kendrick, the ramifications are felt from New York all the way across the Atlantic to the remote and beautiful Scottish island of Cairnmor, where her family live. Yet even as she and Marcus draw closer, Anna cannot forget her estranged husband whom she has not seen for many years.

When tragedy strikes, for some, Cairnmor becomes a refuge, a place of solace to ease the troubled spirit and an escape from painful reality; for others, it becomes a place of enterprise and adventure – a place in which to dream of an unfettered future.

This third book in the *Cairnmor Trilogy*, takes the action forward into the late nineteen-sixties as well as recalling familiar characters' lives from the intervening years. *Where Gloom and Brightness Meet* is a story of heartbreak and redemptive love; of long-dead passion remembered and retained in isolation; of unfaltering loyalty and steadfast devotion. It is a story that juxtaposes the old and the new; a story that reflects the conflicting attitudes, problems and joys of a liberating era.

ISBN: 978-0-9931587-1-1

Reflections in an Oval Mirror
Memories of East Prussia, 1923-45
Anneli Jones

8th May 1945 – VE Day – was Anneliese Wiemer's twenty-second birthday. Although she did not know it then, it marked the end of her flight to the West, and the start of a new life in England.

These illustrated memoirs, based on a diary kept during the Third Reich and letters rediscovered many decades later, depict the momentous changes occurring in Europe against a backcloth of everyday farm life in East Prussia (now the north-western corner of Russia, sandwiched between Lithuania and Poland).

The political developments of the 1930s (including the Hitler Youth, 'Kristallnacht', political education, labour service, war service, and interrogation) are all the more poignant for being told from the viewpoint of a romantic young girl. In lighter moments she also describes student life in Vienna and Prague, and her friendship with Belgian and Soviet prisoners of war. Finally, however, the approach of the Red Army forces her to abandon her home and flee across the frozen countryside, encountering en route a cross-section of society ranging from a 'lady of the manor', worried about her family silver, to some concentration camp inmates

"couldn't put it down... delightful... very detailed descriptions of the farm and the arrival of war... interesting history and personal account" ('Rosie', amazon.com)

ISBN: 978-0-9559219-0-2

Carpe Diem
Moving on from East Prussia
Anneli Jones

This sequel to "Reflections in an Oval Mirror" details Anneli's post-war life. The scene changes from life in Northern 'West Germany' as a refugee, reporter and military interpreter, to parties with the Russian Authorities in Berlin, boating in the Lake District with the original 'Swallows and Amazons', weekends with the Astors at Cliveden, then the beginnings of a new family in the small Kentish village of St Nicholas-at-Wade. Finally, after the fall of the Iron Curtain, Anneli is able to revisit her first home once more.

ISBN: 978-0-9931587-3-5

Skating at the Edge of the Wood
Memories of East Prussia, 1931-1945... 1993
Marlene Yeo

In 1944, the twelve-year old East Prussian girl Marlene Wiemer embarked on a horrific trek to the West, to escape the advancing Red Army. Her cousin Jutta was left behind the Iron Curtain, which severed the family bonds that had made the two so close.

This book contains dramatic depictions of Marlene's flight, recreated from her letters to Jutta during the last year of the war, and contrasted with joyful memories of the innocence that preceded them.

Nearly fifty years later, the advent of perestroika meant that Marlene and Jutta were finally able to revisit their childhood home, after a lifetime of growing up under diametrically opposed societies, and the book closes with a final chapter revealing what they find.

Despite depicting the same time and circumstances as "Reflections in an Oval Mirror", an account written by Marlene's elder sister, Anneli, and its sequel "Carpe Diem", this work stands in stark contrast partly owing to the age gap between the two girls, but above all because of their dramatically different characters.

ISBN: 978-0-9931587-2-8

Travels in Taiwan
Exploring Ilha Formosa
Gary Heath

For many Westerners, Taiwan is either a source of cheap electronics or an ongoing political problem. It is seldom highlighted as a tourist destination, and even those that do visit rarely venture far beyond the well-trod paths of the major cities and resorts.

Yet true to its 16th century Portuguese name, the 'beautiful island' has some of the highest mountains in East Asia, many unique species of flora and fauna, and several distinct indigenous peoples (fourteen at the last count).

On six separate and arduous trips, Gary Heath deliberately headed for the areas neglected by other travel journalists, armed with several notebooks... and a copy of War and Peace for the days when typhoons confined him to his tent. The fascinating land he discovered is revealed here.

"offers a great deal of insight into Taiwanese society, history, culture, as well as its island's scenic geography... disturbing and revealing... a true, peripatetic, descriptive Odyssey undertaken by an adventurous and inquisitive Westerner on a very Oriental and remote island" (Charles Phillips, goodreads.com)

ISBN: 978-0-9559219-1-9 (Royal Octavo)

ISBN: 978-0-9559219-8-8 (Half Letter)

West of Arabia
A Journey Home
Gary Heath

Faced with the need to travel from Saudi Arabia to the UK, Gary Heath made the unusual decision to take the overland route. His three principles were to stay on the ground, avoid back-tracking, and do minimal sightseeing.

The ever-changing situation in the Middle East meant that the rules had to be bent on occasion, yet as he travelled across Eritrea, Sudan, Egypt, Libya, Tunisia and Morocco, he succeeded in beating his own path around the tourist traps, gaining unique insights into Arabic culture as he went.

Written just a few months before the Arab Spring of 2011, this book reveals many of the underlying tensions that were to explode onto the world stage just shortly afterwards, and has been updated to reflect the recent changes.

"just the right blend of historical background [and] personal experiences... this book is a must read" ('Denise', goodreads.com)

ISBN: 978-0-9559219-6-4

Ichigensan
– The Newcomer –
David Zoppetti

Translated from the Japanese by Takuma Sminkey

Ichigensan is a novel which can be enjoyed on many levels – as a delicate, sensual love story, as a depiction of the refined society in Japan's cultural capital Kyoto, and as an exploration of the themes of alienation and prejudice common to many environments, regardless of the boundaries of time and place.

Unusually, it shows Japan from the eyes of both an outsider and an 'internal' outcast, and even more unusually, it originally achieved this through sensuous prose carefully crafted by a non-native speaker of Japanese. The fact that this best-selling novella then won the Subaru Prize, one of Japan's top literary awards, and was also nominated for the Akutagawa Prize is a testament to its unique narrative power.

The story is by no means chained to Japan, however, and this new translation by Takuma Sminkey will allow readers world-wide to enjoy the multitude of sensations engendered by life and love in an alien culture.

"A beautiful love story" (Japan Times)

"Sophisticated... subtle... sensuous... delicate... memorable... vivid depictions" (Asahi Evening News)

"Striking... fascinating..." (Japan PEN Club)

"Refined and sensual" (Kyoto Shimbun)

"quiet, yet very compelling... subtle mixture of humour and sensuality...the insights that the novel gives about Japanese society are both intriguing and exotic" (Nicholas Greenman, amazon.com)

ISBN: 978-0-9559219-4-0

Sunflowers
– Le Soleil –
Shimako Murai

A play in one act
Translated from the Japanese by Ben Jones

Hiroshima is synonymous with the first hostile use of an atomic bomb. Many people think of this occurrence as one terrible event in the past, which is studied from history books.

Shimako Murai and other 'Women of Hiroshima' believe otherwise: for them, the bomb had after-effects which affected countless people for decades, effects that were all the more menacing for their unpredictability – and often, invisibility.

This is a tale of two such people: on the surface successful modern women, yet each bearing underneath hidden scars as horrific as the keloids that disfigured Hibakusha on the days following the bomb.

"a great story and a glimpse into the lives of the people who lived during the time of the war and how the bomb affected their lives, even after all these years" (Wendy Pierce, goodreads.com)

ISBN: 978-0-9559219-3-3

Turner's Margate Through Contemporary Eyes
The Viney Letters
Stephen Channing

Margate in the early 19th Century was an exciting town, where smugglers and 'preventive men' fought to outwit each other, while artists such as JMW Turner came to paint the glorious sunsets over the sea. One of the young men growing up in this environment decided to set out for Australia to make his fortune in the Bendigo gold rush.

Half a century later, having become a pillar of the community, he began writing a series of letters and articles for Keble's Gazette, a publication based in his home town. In these, he described Margate with great familiarity (and tremendous powers of recall), while at the same time introducing his English readers to the "latitudinarian democracy" of a new, "young Britain".

Viney's interests covered a huge range of topics, from Thanet folk customs such as Hoodening, through diatribes on the perils of assigning intelligence to dogs, to geological theories including suggestions for the removal of sandbanks off the English coast "in obedience to the sovereign will and intelligence of man".

His writing is clearly that of a well-educated man, albeit with certain Victorian prejudices about the colonies that may make those with modern sensibilities wince a little. Yet above all, it is interesting because of the light it throws on life in a British seaside town some 180 years ago.

This book also contains numerous contemporary illustrations.

"profusely illustrated... draws together a series of interesting articles and letters... recommended" (Margate Civic Society)

ISBN: 978-0-9559219-2-6

The Margate Tales
Stephen Channing

Chaucer's Canterbury Tales is without doubt one of the best ways of getting a feel for what the people of England in the Middle Ages were like. In the modern world, one might instead try to learn how different people behave and think from television or the internet.

However, to get a feel for what it was like to be in Margate as it gradually changed from a small fishing village into one of Britain's most popular holiday resorts, one needs to investigate contemporary sources such as newspaper reports and journals.

Stephen Channing has saved us this work, by trawling through thousands of such documents to select the most illuminating and entertaining accounts of Thanet in the 18th and early to mid 19th centuries. With content ranging from furious battles in the letters pages, to hilarious pastiches, witty poems and astonishing factual reports, illustrated with over 70 drawings from the time, The Margate Tales brings the society of the time to life, and as with Chaucer, demonstrates how in many areas, surprisingly little has changed.

"substantial and fascinating volume... meticulously researched... an absorbing read" (Margate Civic Society)

ISBN: 978-0-9559219-5-7

A Victorian Cyclist
Rambling through Kent in 1886
Stephen & Shirley Channing

Bicycles are so much a part of everyday life nowadays, it can be surprising to realize that for the late Victorians these "velocipedes" were a novelty disparaged as being unhealthy and unsafe – and that indeed tricycles were for a time seen as the format more likely to succeed.

Some people however adopted the newfangled devices with alacrity, embarking on adventurous tours throughout the countryside. One of them documented his 'rambles' around East Kent in such detail that it is still possible to follow his routes on modern cycles, and compare the fauna and flora (and pubs!) with those he vividly described.

In addition to providing today's cyclists with new historical routes to explore, and both naturalists and social historians with plenty of material for research, this fascinating book contains a special chapter on Lady Cyclists in the era before female emancipation, and an unintentionally humorous section instructing young gentlemen how to make their cycle and then ride it.

A Victorian Cyclist features over 200 illustrations, and is complemented by a fully updated website.

"Lovely... wonderfully written... terrific" (Everything Bicycles)

"Rare and insightful" (Kent on Sunday)

"Interesting... informative... detailed historical insights" (BikeBiz)

"Unique and fascinating book... quality is very good... of considerable interest" (Veteran-Cycle Club)

"Superb... illuminating... well detailed... The easy flowing prose, which has a cadence like cycling itself, carries the reader along as if freewheeling with a hind wind" (Forty Plus Cycling Club)

"a fascinating book with both vivid descriptions and a number of hitherto-unseen photos of the area" ('Pedalling Pensioner', amazon.co.uk)

ISBN: 978-0-9559219-7-1

Lightning Source UK Ltd.
Milton Keynes UK
UKOW02f2042130215

246256UK00002B/83/P